BLACK GOLD

Forge Books by Fred Bean

Lorena
Black Gold

BLACK GOLD

FRED BEAN

A TOM DOHERTY ASSOCIATES BOOK
NEW YORK

Fiction
Bea

BLACK GOLD

This book is printed on acid-free paper.

A Forge Book
Published by Tom Doherty Associates, Inc.
175 Fifth Avenue
New York, NY 10010

Forge® is a registered trademark of Tom Doherty Associates, Inc.

Library of Congress Cataloging-in-Publication Data

Bean, Fred.
    Black gold / Fred Bean. —1st ed.
       p.   cm.
    "A Tom Doherty Associates book."
    ISBN 0-312-86062-5 (acid-free paper)
    I. Title.
    PS3552.E152B57   1997
    813'.54—dc21   97-19361
                             CIP

First Edition: November 1997

Printed in the United States of America

0 9 8 7 6 5 4 3 2 1

In Memory of
David Lynn Cobbs
and
Sam Dunlap

BLACK GOLD

1

Outlines of wooden oil derricks rose into a night sky to the west, and the sour smell of raw crude hung heavy in the still, humid East Texas air. Some men found the sulfurous odor around oilfields unpleasant, too acrid. William Dodd thought it smelled delicious, despite its stickiness and the way it seemed to cling to everything, including his clothes. The petroleum smell was a fragrance of success to men like Dodd, H. L. Hunt, Sid Richardson, and Kenneth Davis. Bill Dodd only hoped that he could find success on the same grand scale as they and a handful of others had. Parts of Texas were turning dozens of men into millionaires literally overnight. Almost anywhere a drill went down came a black geyser so bountiful it made the earth shudder when spewing forth its dark riches.

No one could guess how extensive the subterranean pools were, nor did anyone seem to care as long as the wells kept coming in. Prime leases were being gobbled up at an astounding rate, and tonight William Dodd stood on his very own recently acquired oil-lease property, adjoining the latest bonanza held by Haroldson Lafayette Hunt. The so-called "Dad" Joiner lease, over four thousand acres, lay immediately west of the land leased by Dodd. Tonight, staring up at a star-filled sky, he allowed himself to dream of William Porter Dodd's name becoming as well known as Hunt's, Joiner's, and Richardson's. He was certain that his feet were planted on soil covering oil pools connected to Hunt's seemingly bottomless wells. Tomorrow his lease would be legally recorded and that would be the beginning of everything, and the end of years of poverty and fruitless wildcatting elsewhere. Coming to East Texas had been the smartest move of his life. Sara hadn't wanted to come, he remembered. Her reluctance to follow him up from Beaumont was the reason he'd started seeing Molly occasionally, to help ease his loneliness those first few weeks.

Walking away from the driller's tent, his hands shoved deep in his pockets, he thought about the times he'd asked Sara to pack up and move at a moment's notice, when the next promising wildcat spot had lured him away from his most recent failure. He had stopped counting dry holes long ago, and the money he'd lost, the years of living hand-to-mouth on beans and dreams. A wildcatter's life was always feast or famine—mostly famine, unless you struck it big, really big, like Hunt had. Sara would be glad she'd stuck with him through thick and thin. Beginning tomorrow, she could start planning shopping trips to Houston or Fort Worth to buy a new wardrobe, even some expensive furs if she wanted them. Mrs. William Dodd would soon be able to afford the best of everything. He might even buy Molly something special, as long as Sara didn't find out. Molly had been especially kind to him until Sara made up her mind to move to Longview.

This sudden turn in their fortune was due to clever moves on his part, not to the blind luck of a kind that seemed to follow men like Hunt and Joiner. He had simply outmaneuvered everyone else by doing his homework, tracking lost heirs to Galveston, San Saba County, and

Baton Rouge. Getting the right signatures on a lease worth millions had cost him almost everything he had, while Hunt was too busy drilling the Joiner lease to locate the owners of the adjoining property before Dodd found them. He liked the sound of it—William P. Dodd, Oilman. If luck was with him, he would soon be the youngest millionaire in the Oil Patch before 1932 came to a close.

Near a stand of young oak trees, he stopped to look west, in the direction of Hunt's property. Oil derricks stood like black skeletons atop distant hills. Even though it was well past midnight, men were still moving about near the drillers' shacks, while trucks continued to labor back and forth along rutted roads to Hunt's storage tanks—he could see weak headlights jittering over rough ground and hear engines straining in the distance. One of these days real soon, they'll be truckin' my crude out of here, he thought.

For a time, he simply watched the activity on the Dad Joiner lease, lost in pleasant daydreams of his own forthcoming wealth. He'd already plotted the first well to be dug, marked it with a stake, certain of its location along the same geological formation where Hunt's derricks sprouted from the earth spouting oil. He could almost feel the ground tremble beneath his boots today when he drove his stake in the ground, as if the marker itself might be enough to start black crude bubbling from the ridge he chose to drill. But tomorrow he must record his lease in county records, making everything legal, making the oil he coaxed from the earth the property of William P. and Sara Louise Dodd.

The signed lease had come in today's mail, after the last signature was affixed before a notary in San Saba. Just in the nick of time too, he learned today, following a phone call from a lawyer in Houston. A wildcatter named Buster Davis had contacted one of the heirs, offering more money but too late to undo a lease already signed. As soon as it was recorded with the Gregg county clerk, it would be legal. This was going to be his first order of business tomorrow morning. Then, with his lease as collateral, he'd sign the note with Molly's friend to pay the heirs the advance money they were entitled to. Molly was the one he should thank, for telling him about the guy who loaned money. And it helped that he already knew someone else who could arrange to get him the note.

A pair of dim headlights came shivering down the rough country road running past the gate where he'd parked his battered Ford. He watched the automobile approach, wondering about the hour, why anyone was out driving so late at night down a deserted roadway. He experienced more surprise when that same car wheeled through his gate, sputtering and coughing its way up a rutted lane toward the spot where he'd left his Model A. The car slowed, then stopped, its motor idling. Someone was looking for him, he surmised, more curious than ever how anyone knew where to find him, why they'd come out here so late. Hurrying away from the trees, he hoped it wasn't some sort of emergency, some accident involving Sara.

"Over here!" he cried, waving his hat, breaking into a trot down the grassy slope, his heart pounding. "Is anything wrong?"

He saw two men climb out of the car after its headlamps were extinguished. The larger of the pair was wearing a dark business suit and it appeared the other wore some kind of uniform. Now he was convinced that something had happened to Sara, some dreadful disaster. Running faster, he raced toward the pair of shadows as hard as he could, silently praying no ill had befallen his wife.

As he stumbled to a halt, the uniformed man asked, "Are you Bill Dodd?" He tried to make out their faces in the dark and for the moment, he couldn't recognize either one.

"Yes. Is something wrong?"

"Just a few questions." It was the big man wearing the suit who spoke now, a much taller and heavier fellow. "Somebody said you leased this property, only there isn't anything recorded at the county courthouse yet."

He glanced to the man in uniform, unable to see him clearly on the other side of the Dodge automobile. "I'm recording the lease in the morning," he gasped, out of breath from his breakneck run, at the same time bewildered by the question. "Why are you out here so late looking for me? I thought something dreadful might have happened to my wife, some kind of emergency . . ."

The gleam of metal reflecting starlight abruptly ended what he was saying as the driver took an object from inside his coat and strode forward quickly.

"You won't record nothing, Dodd. You figured you were smart, only you just outsmarted yourself."

He saw the gun and took a half step back. Then a flash of bright light accompanied a loud bang. Something struck his head, making his ears ring. In the momentary glimmer of light, he saw a face, then it suddenly dissolved in darkness. He thought he knew the face, a man he vaguely recognized, but just then he couldn't recall exactly from where or who he was—only a dim feeling that he'd met him through the guy who was loaning him the money.

He sank to his knees when a stabbing, white-hot pain began in his skull. The dark sky tilted crazily above him. He thought he heard an indistinct voice talking gibberish, words he couldn't quite understand. Now the ache inside his head was excruciating, spreading in waves while something wet and warm spilled down his face into his eyes. He reached for his forehead, trying to find some explanation for the pain. His fingertips touched a jagged hole above his right eye, a hole the size of his thumb.

He felt himself falling and now his pain was less. His last thought was of Sara before he fell facedown in a clump of blood-stained grass—he hadn't told her where he'd hidden the lease.

Gregg County Deputy Sheriff Sam Dunlap knelt beside the body for half a minute before he allowed two pale-faced attendants from the county coroner's office to load it into the hearse. "I reckon you can haul him to Longview now," he said. "It's easy to see a bullet killed him. Damn near blowed his head in half. I'd guess it happened sometime last night. He ain't been dead all that long, looks like. Whoever shot him wanted to make damn sure he was dead, judgin' by the size of that hole. The back of his skull is plumb gone . . ."

A worn leather wallet lay near the body in a patch of bloody grass. "Appears he was robbed," Dunlap said, thumbing the wallet open, finding no money. "Let's see who he was."

An inspection of the wallet gave him the dead man's name on a bill of goods from Longview Driller's Supply. "William P. Dodd is who he is. Gives an address on Baker Lane. That's where the woman called from, someplace on Baker. I believe she said her name was Sara. I reckon I'll have to be the one to tell her that she's a widow now."

He watched the attendants load the body on a stretcher. One of them gagged and spat a mouthful of bile when a plug of the dead man's brains fell on his shoe. Dunlap shook his head and turned to the east, facing a golden sunrise. There could be only one conclusion drawn from the killing—it was an execution. Dodd had made enemies somewhere. Since there was no gun within the dead man's grasp, it couldn't be called a suicide. Someone had killed him at very close range with a large-bore gun, probably a .45.

When the body was loaded into the back of the county's Nash hearse, Dunlap sauntered over to Dodd's Model A Ford to look for clues, waving to the driver when the coroner's men drove away in a cloud of blue smoke and dust. The Ford showed signs of heavy use, with dents here and there, worn tires, worn seat covers. If the car was any measurement, William P. Dodd didn't have much money. So why had he been robbed and executed? Since the oil boom came to Gregg County, there had been all manner of violence. Workers in the Oil Patch were violent men. And the peddlers who came to Longview selling the vices oilfield workers wanted were no better in most respects. Bootleggers and pimps worked the oil camps in growing number, and small gambling operations were springing up all over the county.

It was no secret that Sheriff Perry Bass turned a blind eye to it, and there were rumors Perry was on the take. Big oilmen wanted contented workers. Roughnecks and roustabouts demanded whores, whiskey, and other pleasant diversions. Big operators gave huge donations in political races to men who would ignore the whiskey and prostitution trades and, more recently, the dozens of roving gambling tents. Despite the hue and cry coming from the Longview church pastors and their faithful, the business of sin in Gregg County was growing by leaps and bounds as more oil was being found. Local businessmen were also enjoying a rush of new prosperity, making them unlikely to file any complaints against whiskey parlors or a few whorehouses when it could mean the loss of their oilfield business.

A brief search of the car provided nothing. Dunlap closed the door and took a last look around the murder scene. Tracks in the dust revealed that another car had driven up the lane. Footprints here and there. No evidence that would lead to a killer. But it was apparent that someone else had arrived last night by automobile. Whoever came had killed Dodd at close range with a gun. It was a crime unlikely to be solved, unless Dodd was important to someone who had clout in county politics.

Dunlap climbed into his Dodge sedan bearing the insignia of the Gregg County Sheriff's Department on its doors, dreading the moment when he informed the dead man's wife of her loss. It was a necessary part of the job, yet he always found it distasteful. Dealing with a sobbing woman, he supposed, was no worse than being called to break up a fight in an Oil Patch saloon tent.

He drove slowly down the lane and turned for Longview. In the distance, off to the west, men drilling holes in the earth swarmed like ants around derricks spread across the Joiner lease, and Dunlap was sure that the murder of William Dodd would quickly be forgotten. Oil was more important than anything else in this part of Texas. A killing every now and then had virtually become meaningless in a mad scramble to make millions in the oil business. The Dodd case would probably be closed without any further investigation, unless his widow raised a stink.

2

Lee Garrett found the address on Baker Lane and switched off the motor. He listened to the Packard's radiator hiss softly in the following silence, its engine overheated by a hard drive from the district office in Waco. Parked in the mottled shade below an oak tree next to the curb, he glanced down at the report to Texas Ranger Headquarters sent up from Austin. A twenty-six-year-old oil speculator by the name of William Dodd had been killed close to Longview on the twenty-third day of June, shot in the head, his pockets emptied. His wife, Sara, had requested a further investigation, stating in her letter that she believed Gregg

County Sheriff Perry Bass had done little or nothing to track down her husband's killer. A valuable oil lease was involved in Dodd's death, according to his wife, and now the lease document was missing, never having been recorded at the county clerk's office.

Lee examined the widow's tiny house. It was a box-shaped affair made of clapboard, bespeaking poverty, probably a rental similar to the kind sought by oilfield workers, who never bought a permanent home because the next boom would force them to move elsewhere. It was possible that Sara Dodd merely wanted compensation from someone for the loss of her late husband's income. Or maybe she wanted the Texas Rangers to find the lease so she could cash in on the royalty money it would earn. The last possibility was, on the surface, the most likely—a grieving widow wanted justice for her dead husband. But for nearly twelve years as a Texas Ranger, Lee Garrett had learned to look below the surface of things. Placid waters sometimes ran deep, and almost as often, they turned murky.

He climbed out of the car and put on his Stetson, glancing at his reflection in the Packard's rear window. He thought he looked a little thinner since last year, a bit older too, with deep lines he hadn't noticed before beside his mouth and around his eyes. It was the job, he told himself. Too many hours without sleep, too many investigations to handle alone. A Ranger's caseload had almost doubled since the big oil strike in Gregg and Rusk counties two years back.

Bootlegging and gambling were running rampant around the oil camps, with no letup in sight. If one bunch of operators was arrested, another soon showed up to take its place. It was like trying to put out a forest fire with a teacup when so many drillers' camps were springing up in every cattle pasture, full of men who had plenty of spending money. A sudden increase in crime was the reason Captain Ross gave for sending him all the way to Longview. The Ranger in charge at Tyler, Roy Woods, had been in Henderson County with his hands full, trying to find a moonshiner's still and end a major bootlegging operation believed to be supplying most of the Oil Patch saloons near Rusk.

Carrying the case file under his arm, Garrett walked to the steps and knocked on the battered screen door. Summer heat plastered his shirt to his back. Sweat trickled from his hatband. He could see an empty front room full of mismatched furniture and hear a radio playing somewhere in the back. Down the street, a dog barked. He knocked again, harder this time.

"Who's there?" A rather plain young woman wearing a faded cotton dress came from another room wiping her hands on a dish towel. Her brown hair was bobbed short, making her look a little boyish at first glance.

"Texas Ranger, ma'am," Lee replied, tipping his hat politely the way his mother had always insisted he greet a lady. "Name's Lee Garrett. I need to ask you a few questions concerning your late husband. I won't need but a few minutes of your time."

She came to the screen door and unhooked it. Her eyes were red as though she'd been crying. "Please do come in. I'm Sara Dodd." The door was pushed outward for him.

"Sorry to hear about your husband, Mrs. Dodd," he said. Stepping inside, he noticed the smell of boiled cabbage lingering in the front room, and another scent he recognized—whiskey—on the woman's breath.

"Please take a chair," she said, pointing to a rocker near an open window. Her voice had a nasal quality that would make it hard to listen to for more than a few minutes. "I hope you'll excuse the house and the way I look. I wasn't expectin' company an' I haven't been feeling well lately."

"I understand, ma'am. I've only got a couple of questions right now." He settled into the squeaky rocking chair, doing his best to ignore the cabbage odor, rested his hat on his knee, and opened his case file. A warm breeze came through the window. He noted that the woman was staring at his badge. She sat across from him on a lumpy blue sofa tilted to one side where a leg was broken, while fixing him with a slightly vacant stare. "I wanted to ask you about this oil lease you say your husband had. Your report says it hasn't turned up, that it's still missing."

"It was stolen," she said tonelessly. "He got it the day he was killed. It came in the mail, but it was too late for him to get it recorded at the courthouse. He was gonna do it the next mornin', only somebody saw to it that he couldn't." Tears began to form in her eyes and she looked away.

"Have you got any idea who would kill him over the mineral rights to a piece of property?"

"Bill said it was worth millions. He knew plenty about the geology of oilfields." She sniffled. "Whoever done it knows it was worth a ton of money, that lease was. I told Sheriff Bass it was real easy to find out who shot Bill. Wait an' see who shows up an' records a lease on that Hawkins place. That'll prove who done it."

"Maybe. Maybe not. A valuable oil lease is probably being sought after by plenty of people in this area." He took out his fountain pen and jotted down the name, Hawkins.

Sara turned her face to the floor. "I know he was killed on account of that piece of paper. He went to a lot of trouble to find out who the heirs were on that land. He tracked them all down an' got 'em to sign it. Then, soon as it comes in the mail, he gets shot the very same night."

"It does sound like more than a coincidence. I'll look into it after I talk to the county sheriff and the officer who found your husband's body."

"They claim he got robbed," she said, "that it didn't have nothin' to do with the lease. But I know different. Any fool would know Bill didn't get himself robbed out in the middle of a cow pasture. Somebody knew about the paper comin' in the mail and they set out to get it before he got it registered with the county clerk."

"Did your husband have any enemies that you know of? Any people he owed large sums of money to, or anyone who might have something against him?"

"No, sir. Bill never had an enemy in the world."

"Did he mention having any new friends? Had he met someone recently he might have told you about?"

A fleeting look of recognition crossed her face, then it was gone as though she meant to hide it. "Nobody who'd kill him. He did make a few friends."

"I'll need their names."

She looked askance. "I don't remember all of 'em. There was a guy named Charley who drank coffee with him of a mornin', and some feller he didn't name down at the pipe supply. We'd only lived here a couple of months. Bill came up ahead of me to see what things looked like. We were livin' in Gladys City, right close to Beaumont—that's where Spindletop is, in case you didn't know. There wasn't any good leases to be had down there, so we moved here, where the boom started. Bill was always dreamin' of drilling a big gusher like Spindletop . . ."

"Anyone around Beaumont who might have a grudge against your husband? Somebody who didn't like him, maybe?"

The woman was crying now. "Everybody liked Bill. He didn't have any enemies."

Lee made a note about Beaumont and Gladys City. "In most murder cases, it's someone who knew the victim beforehand. That's why I need as many names as you can give me. It could have been somebody he knew casually who heard him mention he had a promising lease he'd been working on. I'll try to find out who Charley is, and look for anyone who knew Bill at one of the supply companies. Can you remember anyone else he knew?" He was sure Sara was trying to conceal something.

She fingered tears from her eyes and then spoke very softly. "He knew a woman here, a hooker. He never knew I found out about it, about her. All I know is, her name is Molly. She worked at this place called Maude's. It's a whorehouse over on Dogwood Street, next to the railroad tracks."

Lee wrote down the information while the woman talked; he had the feeling that at last he might be onto something important. "I'll talk to her," he said.

"She didn't mean nothin' to him. Men get lonely for a woman now an' then. It's a man's nature, if you know what I mean. He didn't go down there anymore after I moved up to Longview. I'm nearly sure of it . . ."

"How did you find out about Molly?"

Sara toyed with the hem of her dress. "It was somethin' I found in his pocket while I was doin' laundry. A little piece of paper with 'Molly' written on it, an' the address on Dogwood Street. I walked down there one day while Bill was out of town workin' on that lease, tryin' to find all those heirs to the Hawkins place. That's how I know she's a whore. I saw it was a whorehouse. But she wouldn't have killed Bill for that lease. He wouldn't have told her about it. Wouldn't be no reason to."

Lee said nothing about his feelings to the contrary, sparing the woman any unnecessary agony until he talked to the prostitute himself. "Was Bill much of a heavy drinker?" he asked, capping his fountain pen. "It would help to know if your husband ever got drunk, drunk enough to talk too freely about his affairs."

"Everybody around the Oil Patch drinks whiskey," Sara said matter-of-factly. "He didn't drink no more than the rest of 'em, I don't suppose. He was hardly ever drunk, if that's what you mean."

The smell of whiskey on the woman's breath made her

a bad source on the subject—it was the middle of the afternoon. "I can't promise you anything, Mrs. Dodd, but I'll look into your husband's death." He closed the file and stood up with his hat in his hand. "I'll let you know what I find out after I make a few inquiries. I may have more questions for you."

"You find out who records a lease on the Hawkins place an' you'll know who killed him," she said, coming to her feet to show him to the door. "That paper was worth millions, accordin' to what Bill said."

"I suppose he put it in his pocket that day it came in the mail?"

"He left the house as soon as it got here. He said he was goin' out to the place to drive a stake where he aimed to drill the first well. The mail came too late for him to record it. He told me he was gonna set up his tent so the drillers would have someplace to sleep an' store their gear. Bill was real excited that day, tellin' me we were gonna be rich as kings." She dried her eyes again as Lee opened the screen.

"What time was that? What time did the letter come?" He wanted to know how much time Dodd had had, time that needed to be accounted for between the arrival of the letter and his death.

Sara turned thoughtful, holding the screen door open after Lee went down the front steps. "A little past four. Like I said, the mail was runnin' late that day."

"I'll keep in touch," he told her, replacing his hat before he started toward the car. "Good afternoon, ma'am."

A warm wind swept dust down Baker Lane, reminding him that it was late in July as he returned to the Packard for a drive to the sheriff's office.

He wondered about the feeling he'd had earlier, the sense that Sara Dodd could be hiding something. Was it only that her husband had been seeing a prostitute? Or was there more?

He started the car and drove off, grinding into second gear because his mind was elsewhere. Instinct told him that a hooker named Molly was the key to solving this murder. After he'd met with Sheriff Bass and seen the investigating officer who'd found Dodd's body, he would have a talk with Molly.

3

Gregg County Sheriff Perry Bass had an office in the basement of the courthouse, behind a glass-paned door with COUNTY SHERIFF painted on it in enormous black letters. When Lee came in, a deputy saw his Ranger badge almost immediately and took his feet off the desk in the middle of the cramped outer room lined with file cabinets. Beyond the desk was a door marked PRIVATE. Lee closed the front door behind him, taking note of a ceiling fan circling lazily above the young deputy's chair, stirring warm air without doing much to allay Longview's sweltering midsummer heat.

The deputy quickly came to his feet as a flush crept into his waxy cheeks, backgrounding a face full of darker freckles. "Howdy," he said, glancing at Lee's badge again. "You ain't Roy Woods, but I can see you're a Texas Ranger. Roy's usually the one who . . ." He let his voice trail off as though something made him cautious.

"I'm Lee Garrett. Headquarters assigned me the William Dodd case and I need to see Sheriff Bass." He walked over to the desk and offered his hand.

"Tim Carter," the deputy said, taking Lee's handshake,

his face still deeply colored. "Sorry 'bout havin' my feet up. I'll tell Perry you're here to see him." He released Lee's palm hurriedly and made a turn for the door behind him. Knocking softly once, he went in without an invitation. Muted voices came from the office, then Deputy Carter peered around the door frame and motioned Lee in. "The sheriff'll see you right now, Mr. Garrett."

Lee walked into a smaller office, nodding his thanks to Tim Carter. Seated behind a cluttered wooden desk, a thick-set man of about fifty watched him from hooded eyes, bald head glistening with sweat in the heat of the room despite the ceiling fan above him. Perry Bass reminded Lee of an English bulldog, with fleshy jowls hanging loosely over his shirt collar. Bass got up from a swivel chair with obvious effort to offer Lee a gnarled hand.

"Perry Bass," he said gruffly, almost grunting it, giving Lee a quick look of appraisal. "Have a seat. Tim tells me you're here to investigate that Dodd killing we had a few weeks ago."

After a perfunctory handshake, Lee took a chair opposite the desk, sensing that Bass wasn't altogether happy to see him. "We got a request from the widow of William P. Dodd to look into some of the circumstances surrounding his death," he began, thumbing his hat back on his forehead while the sheriff sat down heavily. "I talked to Sara Dodd a few minutes ago. A lease to some mineral rights on land known as the Hawkins place is missing, according to the woman. She told me it was worth a lot of money."

Bass shrugged, but his gaze remained fixed on Lee and there was a hint of concern behind his eyes. "We never found no lease paper. I looked into the matter personally. That woman keeps sayin' there was this big conspiracy against her husband, so he wouldn't get no legal claim to the oil out there. But we never found no lease on his person or in his personal effects, an' it wasn't recorded upstairs at the clerk's office, so I'm inclined to think the whole thing's a bunch of bullshit. If you ask me, I think his wife's a goddamn gold digger. I happen to know she drinks a helluva lot of corn whiskey durin' the daytime, so I wouldn't put much stock in what she says."

"Corn whiskey's illegal," Lee said, then grinned.

Sheriff Bass seemed concerned until he saw the grin. "It'd take the whole United States Army to flush every bootlegger out of these East Texas pine woods. Hell, I'd bet there's more corn squeeze 'round here than there is gasoline. It's too big to put a stop to it. About all the law can do is try to slow it down some. Which reminds me, how come Roy Woods ain't investigatin' this Dodd business?"

"He's busy down in Henderson County, so I got the job. I'd appreciate your cooperation, Sheriff. I'm gonna look into this matter and that missing lease for a few days, to see what I can turn up. If you don't mind, I'd like to look at your file on the case and talk to the investigating officer."

Bass slitted his eyes a fraction. "I'll have Tim fetch you the file. Sam Dunlap was the deputy who found the body, but I can tell you straight-out there wasn't anything at the murder scene . . . some tire tracks, I think, an' maybe some footprints. If I remember right, there was blood all over the place. The undertaker told me the back of Dodd's head was blown to bits."

"Was he killed from behind?" Lee asked, wondering why Bass seemed apprehensive about an investigation by the Rangers. If it happened the way Bass said it did, there was no reason to worry if the case were reopened.

The sheriff frowned thoughtfully, like he couldn't recall. "I believe he was shot in the forehead. Close range. Sam said it must have been a helluva big gun."

"Where was the body found?"

Bass was a little more certain of this answer. "Out at the

Hawkins farm, the place he claimed he had leased. We got a call from Dodd's wife early that mornin', sayin' her husband hadn't come home. She told us where to look, an' sure enough, that was where we found him. Dead as a fence post. Sam judged that he got killed sometime the night before."

"I'd like to talk to Sam Dunlap."

Bass leaned back in his chair, folding his hands across his ample stomach, apparently more comfortable now. "I'll tell him to hunt you up. He's out servin' a few civil papers right now. In the meantime, I'll have Tim fetch you the Dodd file. I can't quite figure why the Rangers would take the time to look into somethin' like this. Hell, it's just an unsolved murder in an oil boom town. We have 'em all the time, two gents get mad at each other over one thing or another an' somebody goes for a gun or a knife. Oilfield types are generally rough sons of bitches who don't scare easy. Takes a killin' now an' then to remind some of 'em they ain't bulletproof. Right now there's thousands of roughnecks camped all over Gregg County. They get hot under the collar an' wind up in fights damn near every night. We try to answer as many calls as we can, but I ain't got nearly enough men to do the job right. I'd need fifty deputies to keep the peace around here."

Lee merely nodded, thinking back to something Bass had said a moment earlier. Dodd was killed from the front at close range. Had he known his killer well enough to let him get close? Or had the killer only surprised him in the dark? And there was a more obvious conclusion coming from his talk with Perry Bass: the law in Gregg County wasn't all that interested in how or why William Dodd had died. Lee was sure there was something about the sheriff's manner that wasn't quite right. Did he know, or suspect, who it was that wanted Dodd out of the way, and did it have something to do with the oil lease? Lee was pretty certain he wasn't guessing when it appeared that

Sheriff Bass knew more than he was willing to say. It wouldn't be unusual for a county sheriff to be involved in friendships with powerful people who supported him at election time.

Bass leaned forward in his swivel chair. "Tim! Get me the file on William Dodd!" His booming shout rang off the office walls, eliciting a quick "Yes, sir" from the front room.

"I need to find a hotel," Lee said. "Any suggestions?"

"The Grand is okay. Two blocks south on Commerce Street."

"Can you tell me anything about a prostitute at a place called Maude's over on Dogwood Street? She goes by the name of Molly."

His question clearly surprised the sheriff. "Never heard that name, not one of 'em who calls herself Molly, but there is a place down by the tracks called Maude's. Look here, Garrett, we tolerate that sort of thing in Longview so long as it don't get out of hand. Nobody can keep some women from sellin' pussy in an oil boom town. We've got roughnecks runnin' all over the county with pockets full of money lookin' for whores an' whiskey soon as they get paid. You can't stop it. Me an' Howard Laster, Chief of Police, sorta turn the other way when it comes to whorehouses. Men are gonna find women who'll fuck 'em, one way or another. It keeps our local womenfolk safe from men with strong urges if we allow places like Maude's to operate quietly. Surely you didn't come all the way to Longview just to shut down a whorehouse?"

Although Lee didn't like Bass's implication, that a Ranger would overlook a house of prostitution if he found it, he shook his head. "That's not why I'm here. Sara Dodd told me she knew her husband was seeing a prostitute named Molly. William Dodd was a drinker, and I'm wondering if he said more than he should have about that oil lease to the wrong woman."

Deputy Carter came in just as the sheriff was about to say something. "Here's the file," Carter said, dropping a folder on the desktop.

Bass gave Carter a questioning look. "You ever hear of a whore down at Maude's who goes by the name of Molly?"

Carter wasn't sure how to answer, judging by the look he gave Sheriff Bass. Again, the deputy's cheeks grew pink behind his freckles. The ceiling fan made a soft whirring noise while Carter chose his words carefully. "I don't go in there, Sheriff. So I wouldn't know none of their names."

Bass looked across the desk at Lee. "It'll scare hell out of Maude if you show up all of a sudden." He glanced at a black telephone on the edge of his desk. "Let me give her a call, so she don't have a case of the rigors when she sees you at the door wearin' a badge." He reached for the phone.

"That might not be such a good idea," Lee protested. "If the girl is there and she knows I'm looking for her, she might go on the run."

The sheriff's hand froze on the receiver and he frowned. "But I'll tell her not to worry, that you only aim to talk to one of her girls. She's liable to think you're there to arrest her an' shut her down."

"I'd rather you didn't call, Sheriff. If there's a girl by the name of Molly at Maude's place, I don't want her taking off until I question her." Lee had the feeling Bass would call the woman anyway as soon as he left the office. Maude had some sort of arrangement with the sheriff keeping her doors open; however, this wasn't the reason for his visit to Longview. Shutting down whorehouses was usually a matter for local peace officers, unless a complaint reached Austin.

Bass made a face. "I hope Maude don't suffer a stroke over this," he complained, letting go of the phone. "She runs a quiet place an' we never have any problems down there. Seems proper to call her ahead of time." He shrugged and slumped in his chair, returning one hand to his stomach, the other to the butt of a .38 Colt revolver holstered around his waist. Perhaps it was only the light spilling through the office window, yet it appeared his bald spot was sweating more profusely.

Lee picked up the file folder and opened it. A report form contained scribbled entries that were hard to read. "Dunlap has lousy handwriting," he said, reading down the first page, past a few facts he already knew: the deceased man's full name, address, surviving relatives. The report was dated the twenty-fourth of June and the time was given as 9:15 A.M. Cause of death was listed as a gunshot to the head.

On the following page there was a note:

> Found empty wallet, so it looks like victim was robbed. Pockets turned inside out. Recent tire tracks beside victim's Ford. Several footprints. Time of death was probably midnight. Body wasn't stiff yet. Hole above right eye where he got shot. Back of skull ruptured. Weapon was probably a .45. Coroner picked up body at 9:30 A.M. Took it down to Watkins Funeral Home for burial. Informed deceased man's wife, Sara Louise Dodd, at 10:20 A.M. Woman asked about a paper. Was a mineral lease in his pockets? Told her there was nothing but an old wallet, no money, no paper like she described. Filed report at 12:30 P.M. Signed, Sam Dunlap, Deputy Sheriff, Gregg County.

"This report doesn't say much," Lee observed quietly. "I'd like to talk to Sam Dunlap as soon as possible. Tell him I'll be staying at the Grand."

"Take it easy on Maude," Bass said. "She'll cooperate

with you any way she can. She never gives us any problem. She's been a friend of Mayor Wilson's for years. Pays her taxes on time, a good citizen, 'cept for the fact she runs a whorehouse."

Lee closed the file and returned it to the desk. "I've got no orders having to do with prostitution in Gregg County. It's this murder Captain Ross wants me to investigate."

"I still don't believe there ever was no lease," Bass said flatly. "I think it's that widow's imagination."

A thought occurred to Lee when he stood up. "Has anyone checked the clerk's records to see if someone recently recorded a mineral lease on the Hawkins farm?"

For only a moment, the sheriff's eyes flickered to Carter. "I hadn't bothered. Don't see how it would prove anything. Hellfire, every acre of ground in Gregg County is probably leased by now. Anybody could have leased that land. It joins Hunt's big strike, you know. That's gotta be prime drillin', only I don't figure William Dodd ever owned the rights to it. Hunt wouldn't let some small-time operator get the jump on him like that. If there's one man who knows the oil business, it's H. L. Hunt."

"So I've heard. Still, I'd like to know if someone else has leased the Hawkins property. I'll stop at the clerk's office on my way out." He nodded to both men and headed for the door.

Upstairs at the county clerk's office, he was informed by Helen Robbins, after a thirty-minute wait while she searched record books, that mineral rights to the property in question had been leased by C. W. "Buster" Davis. A week later, they were transferred to Hunt Oil. Lee wrote the names and dates down in a notebook he kept in his shirt pocket, then left the courthouse to find Maude's, knowing he would be expected there by now.

4

Maude's had once been an old boardinghouse, now converted to more profitable ends when times had changed with the oil boom. A weathered frame house, it sat forlornly at the edge of a dirt road running beside the railroad tracks passing through Longview. Maude's needed a coat of paint and some work on the roof, where splitting wood shingles curled up like scales on a dead fish. A covered porch ran the length of the place, embraced by ivy vines and honeysuckle, providing some shade, and perhaps anonymity for those customers seeking entry without being seen.

Across the dusty road, strings of railroad tank cars sat on sidings awaiting locomotives to pull them to a refinery. Crude oil clung wetly to their sides — oil spilled during the wildcatters' haste to ferry cargos of "black gold" out of town. Small steam switch engines labored back and forth in the rail yard, hooking strings of tank cars together. Overlooking all this activity from a shady spot nestled among huge oaks on the far side of the tracks, Maude's seemed uncharacteristically serene, quiet for a place where young women sold themselves. It was simply too early in the day for Maude's customers.

Lee parked out front in a patch of shade below some leafy tree limbs and got out, leaving his gun and holster beneath the car seat the way he usually did when no trouble was expected. Some Rangers wore their guns everywhere they went. Most peace officers carried their sidearms all the time, but Lee found it was often more useful to appear less threatening, and he knew how to take care of himself without a gun in most instances. Fighting was something he was good at. His size helped—at six feet and three inches, packing better than two hundred solid pounds, he found few men his equal when fists decided the outcome. He'd been fighting with his older brothers for as far back as he could remember, and there was very little he didn't know about throwing or taking punches.

He climbed the sagging porch steps and knocked, knowing he was expected; he had no doubt Sheriff Bass had called to warn Maude of his arrival. For a time he heard nothing, then footsteps creaked on the other side of the door. A face peered out when the door was opened a crack, a face he couldn't see clearly in the darkness cloaking Maude's front room.

"I'd like to talk to Maude," he said. "I'm Lee Garret and I figure I'm expected." Something smelling like incense came from inside, a sweet odor that might have been perfume.

A woman spoke. "You're the law, ain't you? A Texas Ranger."

"I'm only here to ask a few questions. A girl named Molly works here and I need to talk to her. It won't take long."

"She's asleep upstairs," the woman told him as the door opened a little wider. An older woman, in her late fifties, looked out on the sunlit porch, shading her eyes with a hand. She was heavy, wearing a silk dressing gown that failed to cover the folds of loose skin and deep wrinkles around her neck and bosom. Her hair was dyed red, done up in tiny curls framing what appeared to be an overfed face covered with thick makeup. The sweet smell became stronger.

"It's important. Are you the owner of this place?"

A hesitation. "I'm Maude Sims. I reckon I can wake her up if it's as important as you say. She ain't in no kind of serious trouble, is she?"

"I only need to ask her a few questions about a customer she knew. It shouldn't take long."

Maude swung the door all the way open. "Come in. I'll wake her up. It's damn near too hot to sleep anyways. Wasn't for all them trees, this place would be like an oven. I'll switch on a lamp yonder by the divan. She'll be down in a minute or two."

She showed him across the dark living room. A lamp came on and he saw Maude clearly for the first time, in the light from a bulb behind a pink lampshade. Lee pulled off his hat, taking note of the fact that three sofas were arranged against the walls so that seated customers could have someone sitting beside them. A few bawdy paintings decorated the faded wallpaper around him. Coffee tables held china ashtrays on lace doilies. A dark blue rug covered the floor.

Maude disappeared into a back room and then he heard the creak of stairs. An electric fan purred softly on an end table. He sat on a sofa near the lamp and rested a booted foot on one knee, idly wondering how different Maude's place would seem late at night crowded with eager patrons. He had a legal responsibility to close down an operation like hers if the letter of the law were put to the test, but his orders did not include an investigation into prostitution in Gregg County. It was more or less an unwritten rule that until someone complained, whorehouses were to be tolerated, a matter for local jurisdictions. Waco had its share of whorehouses, and Captain Ross left them to McLennan County authorities.

Lee had no personal feelings regarding prostitution, regarding it as a victimless crime. If men wanted to spend their money on scarlet women, he had no quarrel with that. His own experience with women of any kind was somewhat limited, being a confirmed bachelor himself. A time or two he'd given some thought to conducting a thorough search for a wife, or even for a steady girlfriend. But things never seemed to work out in his favor and at the age of thirty-six, he had all but convinced himself to remain single forever. He was set in his bachelor ways to some degree, and as time passed, he gave his prospects of finding a woman less and less consideration. Being single wasn't so bad, and Rangering kept him on the move so frequently that there was little time to worry about his personal circumstances.

He tried to visualize the girl named Molly while waiting in the silence of Maude's front room. Would she be tall? Short and fat? Few prostitutes he'd seen could be called pretty. He meant to ask her if she'd seen William Dodd on the day he was killed, for one lingering unanswered question stood out: how had the killer known Dodd received his lease in the mail that day? Whoever murdered Dodd had had a motive, and the most obvious thing making Dodd a target was that piece of paper providing ownership in the oil reserves below the Hawkins land. The only other possibility was that some dark event in Dodd's past had given him enemies his wife didn't know about. Lee hoped Molly could give him some answers, some clue as to who might have wanted the man dead.

A few minutes later, stairs creaked again at the back of the house. Maude came into the room, followed by a slender, dark-haired girl. Lee got up when he saw them, directing most of his attention to Molly. The girl held back as though she meant to hide behind Maude—she was chewing her bottom lip, and her eyes were round with fear.

"This here's Molly Brown," Maude said quietly. "She's near 'bout scared to death of you, mister. She swears she ain't done no wrong to nobody."

Lee nodded politely to the girl. She was wearing a red robe and slippers—he was surprised to find she was truly beautiful in a way he hadn't expected. She looked like anything but a whore. Her smooth, oval face belonged to someone quite young, hardly more than twenty. She lacked the robust figure most prostitutes used to attract customers.

"I don't know that she has done anything wrong," he said, disregarding the obvious fact that she worked as a whore. "I want to ask her about one of her customers, as much as she can remember. Please sit down, Molly. As far as I know, you had nothing to do with the murder I'm investigating. I simply need to know everything you can tell me about William Dodd."

"He's dead," Molly whispered, still hanging back despite his invitation to sit on the sofa. Her deep brown eyes were fixed on Lee and her hands were clasped in front of her. "He got shot. That's all I know." She flipped a long strand of brown hair away from her face with a fingertip. By her accent, she was not a native Texan; there was no trace of southern speech in her small voice.

Lee pointed to the sofa behind him. "Have a seat. I want you to tell me about the first time you met him, and how often he came to visit you."

Molly looked at the divan, then at Maude.

"It's okay, Molly," Maude said gently. "Tell him what he wants to know. He said you wasn't in no trouble."

Molly approached the sofa cautiously, her eyes flickering back and forth from Lee to Maude. She sat down and crossed her legs, being careful to keep her gown closed so she was properly covered below her knees.

"I'll be in the kitchen," Maude said, making the remark to Molly. She padded into the hallway and left them alone.

"You have nothing to be afraid of, Molly," Lee said, sitting on a far corner of the divan. "I want to know how well you knew William Dodd, how many times you saw him. Try to remember what he talked about. I'm trying to find out who killed him, and in order to do that, I need to discover the reason behind it, why somebody would shoot him."

Molly continued to chew her lip in a nervous way, yet Lee did not believe that she did it because she knew Dodd's killer. Her anxiety was probably due to his Ranger badge and the nature of her profession.

"I knew him pretty well, I suppose. He was a nice guy. I know he was married. Her name is Sara. Lots of guys who come in here are married men. Bill used to come down to see me a couple of times a week. That was before his wife moved here. He told me he really loved his wife, only that she said she was tired of moving all the time. She told him she wasn't coming to Longview unless he got something steady, some steady work."

Lee watched her face while she was talking. Molly's voice was so soft he had to listen closely to keep from missing what she said. "He was found dead on the twenty-fourth of June. Did you see him the day before, on the twenty-third?"

She looked down at her hands quickly. "Yes. He came by to tell me he'd gotten this important document in the mail. It was a lease to some oil rights he'd been working on. He was real excited about it. He said it was gonna make him rich, like that guy H. L. Hunt. Half the men in this town work for Hunt. Bill said he'd be a millionaire just like Hunt pretty soon. He told me he was gonna buy me something nice, a present, as soon as he brought in his first oil well."

"Did he show you that document? The lease? Did he have it with him?"

"I never actually saw it," Molly replied quietly. "All he did was tell me about it, that it finally came. Some lawyer down in Houston was doing all the paperwork for him, getting the right people to sign things so it would be legal. I don't understand exactly how it works."

"What time was he here that day?"

She shrugged. "Maybe five or six o'clock in the evening.

It was before we opened up. I feel kinda strange talking to a lawman about . . ." Her voice fell to a whisper and she couldn't say the rest of it.

"Was it five, or closer to six? Try to remember, Molly. It may be very important what time it was when you saw him. I need to know how long he stayed, what time he left. If I can, I want to account for every minute of his time that last day."

"I can't say for sure, only that it was between five and six in the evening. He stayed for about half an hour. We talked out under those trees in the front yard. He told me he knew just the right place to drill on that land, the place where he was sure he'd strike a big oil well. He said he was going out there as soon as he left me to mark the spot with a stake. He told me he was some kind of geologist, I think, only maybe he didn't learn it in school."

"Was he going out there alone?"

"He didn't say, but I'm pretty sure he went by himself. He didn't have many friends and he didn't trust people very much."

"Did he ever take you out to the land?"

She nodded. "We went one time in his car. It was real hot that day and I thought a drive would be nice. I hardly ever get out. Maude doesn't like it when we leave here."

Lee thought for a moment. Listening to Molly, his first impression was that she was probably innocent of any wrongdoing in Bill Dodd's death. Her answers seemed straightforward, yet there was still a possibility she'd said something to someone else about the lease. "Did you ever tell anyone about his plans, or the lease he was working on? A big oil strike would be good news in a town full of oil-field workers."

"He made me promise to keep it a secret. I think the only people who knew were his wife and a guy named Charley Waller."

"Who's Charley Waller?"

"Bill's friend. They drank coffee down at the City Café in the mornings. I think they knew each other before."

Hearing about the City Café reminded Lee that he was hungry. He hadn't eaten since breakfast. "I'll find Charley and talk to him tomorrow. Before it gets dark, I'd like to see what the Hawkins farm looks like. Someone'll have to give me directions. I don't know my way around Gregg County."

"I could show you," Molly said, reading his face. "It's too hot upstairs to go back to sleep. I can ask Maude if she'd mind me going. Only you gotta promise me I'm not in trouble with the law."

"That would be a help, if you showed me where it is. And you might remember a few things while we're driving out there, things you forgot to mention."

For the first time since they met, Molly smiled. It was a pretty smile full of even, white teeth. "I'll have to ask Maude if it's okay, and I'll need a minute to get dressed."

Again he found he was stricken with how beautiful she was, not at all what he'd expected to find in a whorehouse. Under any other circumstances, he could not have guessed what she did for a living. "While we're out, we can grab a bite to eat, if you're hungry," he said, before he thought about how it might look for a Ranger to be seen in a public eating place with a prostitute. Then he told himself it wouldn't make any difference, not in the least. What did he care what others thought? He was simply doing his job. "Tell Maude I asked you to show me where Dodd took you. I don't think she'll mind." He was sure Maude would cooperate with his official request, not wanting any trouble with the law.

Molly got up quickly, forgetting to close the front of her gown when she hurried to the hallway. Lee got a brief glimpse of milky skin where her gown parted near the top of her thighs. He also noticed that the girl was still smiling.

5

Molly was wearing a white-and-blue-print summer dress when she came hurrying down Maude's porch steps to the front yard where he'd been waiting for her in the shade, watching switch engines ferry tank cars to and from empty sidings. It took her less than ten minutes to get changed and when he saw her for the first time in daylight, he was even more surprised at how pretty she was. He'd been thinking about several things Molly had told him: that Bill Dodd left Maude's no later than half past six the day he was killed after telling Molly he meant to drive out to his newly leased property to mark the spot where he intended to drill his first oil well. That left an unknown number of hours still unaccounted for until his death later that night.

And there was Molly's mention of a name, Charley Waller, someone who may have known about the oil lease, another party he needed to locate and question. But when Lee saw Molly bouncing down the steps with her hair freshly combed and tied in a ponytail, smiling at him as though she was looking forward to their drive to the Hawkins farm, he momentarily forgot about everything else and simply stared at her.

"Maude said I could go, as long as I get back before nine," she said. Her voice sounded different somehow.

"That won't be a problem," he told her, allowing his gaze to wander down her frame. He thought again of how Molly would have fooled him completely if he'd been forced to guess her occupation, for she looked much too young and girlish to be a prostitute, compared to other women of the same occupation he had seen. Her figure was too slim to fit his notion of the kind of body a woman needed to lure men to her bed. "We shouldn't be more than a couple of hours, if that land isn't too far."

"It won't take us fifteen minutes to get there," she said, still beaming.

He walked beside her across the shaded grass to the passenger door of the Packard and opened it, smelling her perfume, thankful it wasn't the same sickly, sweet scent Maude had been wearing, which would have been almost intolerable in the confines of a car.

"Thanks," she said, sliding onto the front seat, arranging her skirt so it covered her legs. In the bright sunlight, he saw that her face was lightly freckled.

He closed the door gently and walked around the rear of the car wondering why he found Molly Brown so attractive. It wasn't like him to be this interested in the physical characteristics of a woman he scarcely knew. What was it about her he found so appealing? What was worse, he felt the beginning of a strange attraction to a woman he knew was a prostitute.

He got in and started the engine. "Point the way," he said while engaging the gears.

She aimed a finger toward the end of the street. "Turn left at that railroad crossing. I'll show you the back roads because it's shortest. The road's a little bumpy, but it'll be nice and cool on account of all the big trees making shade."

He'd been listening to her unusual Eastern accent. He let out the clutch and drove away from Maude's. "Where are you from, Molly?" It wasn't an important question—he was merely curious.

"Brooklyn. I grew up in a mostly Italian neighborhood, but my mom and dad were Irish."

He wondered why she used the past tense. "I don't suppose they know you work at a place like Maude's."

She glanced at him and then looked away, like it was

something she didn't care to talk about. "My dad got killed in the war over in France. Mom died of tuberculosis when I was sixteen, and then I didn't have any family. I had to quit school. There was this Italian guy in the neighborhood who told me I could make a lot of money if I'd . . ." She hesitated for a moment. "You can figure the rest out for yourself, can't you?"

Lee turned left at the crossing, steering over the rough bumps between the tracks. "I can't figure how you wound up in Texas. You'll have to tell me that part."

"Gino sends girls down to Maude. He's got some kind of deal with her. Turn right at the next corner, then it's about half a mile through town before we turn again."

Lee was puzzled by the information that an Italian named Gino in New York had an arrangement for sending girls to a whorehouse in East Texas. "Looks to me like there'd be plenty of places closer to Brooklyn. Why would this Gino send you all the way to Longview?"

Again Molly gave him a sideways look. "Maybe I shouldn't tell you that part. Will you put me in jail if I don't tell you? I don't see what it has to do with Bill getting shot."

He chuckled. "No, I won't put you in jail. I'm just a bit curious over why he'd send you so far away."

She contemplated her answer while staring through the windshield as the Packard lurched over chugholes in the quiet dirt street lined with small frame houses. "I don't suppose it matters. Gino has some other businesses here. A guy named Carlos Santini runs Gino's trucking company. Carlos is from Brooklyn, my old neighborhood. Carlos takes care of things in Longview for Gino. All that oil money is the reason Gino got in business here."

"Nothing wrong with owning some trucks," Lee told her, but with a suspicion there might be more. It was unusual that a New York trucking firm set up an operation in Longview, and by Molly's own admission, Gino was in the business of supplying prostitutes to Maude. A good many New York Italians were deeply involved in criminal enterprises like gambling and bootlegging, but not in any parts of Texas anyone in law enforcement knew about. He wondered if some illegal whiskey in East Texas was being trucked down from New York. If he asked questions carefully, maybe the girl would tell him a little more. He pushed the gearshift lever into third and let out the clutch.

"You seem awful young, Molly, to be at a place like Maude's. It sounds like you had a rough time of it, losin' your parents so early. I reckon you did what you thought you had to do at the time."

She continued to stare out the windshield with her hands folded in her lap, swaying in her seat when the Packard struck a bump. "I didn't have hardly any money. No place to live after Mom died, when our landlord came to tell me I had to get out. I couldn't pay rent on our flat because I didn't have enough money. That's when Gino heard about what happened. He offered to help me. I didn't want to do the things he said I had to do. I tried to find a regular job, only nobody'd hire me. Everybody said I was too young, being I was only sixteen. I looked younger than that. It made things even worse."

Whoever Gino was, he didn't object to putting Molly to work in a whorehouse at sixteen. Lee couldn't help feeling sorry for her. "Didn't your father leave some kind of army pension to his wife and daughter?"

Molly looked down at her hands. "He wasn't my legal father. He never married Mom—that's what she told me after he got killed in the war. They were real poor. Getting married cost money."

Deciding he'd pried into her past enough for now, he asked, "So, why do you think Bill Dodd was killed? Do you think it was over his oil lease? I'm just asking for your opinion. Take a guess."

"That's about all he had. Bill never had much money. He owned an old car . . . and some furniture, I think. I didn't really get to know him all that good. Honest. He came to see me a few times, and he took me out once, like I said, for a Sunday-afternoon drive. He seemed like a real nice guy. He wasn't the tough type who gets in fights all the time. He was always kinda quiet . . . talked real soft, except when he got excited."

"He was excited the day his lease came, I suppose."

She smiled a little. "He was about to bust wide open that day. He told me he was gonna be rich."

"Do you think he told Charley Waller about it?" Charley had to be considered a suspect. Lee wondered if Charley was in any way tied to Buster Davis, the man who'd recorded a mineral lease on the Hawkins farm not long after Dodd was killed.

"I never met Charley, so I wouldn't know," Molly replied.

He drove on in silence for a moment, every now and then giving her a sideways look. Her profile was pretty. With her hair tied back in a ponytail, she looked even less like a hooker. She had small breasts and a tiny waist. He would guess she barely weighed more than a hundred pounds. Curiosity got the best of him. "How old are you, Molly?"

"Almost twenty-two. Some men tell me I'm older than I look. I get customers who like me because I do look so young. I'm told that sometimes."

"I wouldn't have guessed it." She had worked as a prostitute for more than five years.

"Turn left at the next corner. That's the road we'll take out to the country. Watch for bumps. Some of them are real deep a little farther on. It's a real pretty drive. Some of those pine trees look like they nearly touch the sky."

He turned and accelerated, changing to third gear. "I

went by and talked to Bill Dodd's widow," he said thoughtfully. "She says whoever records an oil lease on the Hawkins place is sure to be the one who had something to do with her husband's death. I looked in the county records. A man by the name of C. W. Davis recorded his lease on it, then it was transferred two weeks later to Hunt Oil Company. Did Bill ever mention anyone named Davis?"

"I don't remember that name," Molly said, gazing out the passenger window now as they left town along a twisting gravel road into deepening pine and oak forests, past widely scattered farm houses in a few clearings. "Ain't it pretty out here?"

"East Texas has a lot of pine trees," he agreed, working the steering wheel to avoid chugholes and dry ruts. "I like the way they smell."

A silence passed before Molly spoke again.

"What's it like to be a Texas Ranger? Maude acted like she was afraid of what you'd do to us, but you don't seem like you're all that mean-natured."

He laughed at that. "It's a dangerous job, some of the time anyway. We run into some pretty tough characters occasionally."

"Brooklyn is full of tough characters. Italians are some of the meanest. Irish and Italians are both real tough. They used to fight all the time in the neighborhood where I grew up. They killed each other most every night. Sometimes they did it during the daytime, too."

"It sounds to me like you lived in a bad part of town. I've never been to New York. To tell the truth, I've never wanted to see it. Never was comfortable in a big city like Houston. I like it better out in the country."

"I like the country too," Molly said wistfully. "One of these days, when I save enough money, I'm gonna buy me a little place of my very own out in the woods."

Lee wondered if the girl made enough to save any of her earnings. Prostitution was a very profitable enterprise, yet most of its income went to the madams who ran the big houses. "You're a very pretty girl," he told her, steering around a deep rut running through a patchwork of shade from drooping pine limbs at the edge of the road. "Maybe one of these days you'll find the right young man and he'll marry you, so the two of you can own your own place."

His remark brought a trace of color to her cheeks. "Nobody is ever gonna marry me," she said. "Men won't marry women who make a living the way I do. But I don't think I'll mind it all that much, being alone. I can't hardly remember a time when I wasn't by myself."

"Not all men necessarily feel that way about—" He stopped before he used the wrong word.

"It's okay," she said, grinning a bit self-consciously with a deeper flush backgrounding her light freckles. "You can tell me I'm a whore. I know what I am, what I'm called. I got used to hearing it a long time ago. It doesn't really bother me anymore."

"That wasn't exactly what I was going to say," he lied.

She looked through the windshield again. "It's about two more miles to the gate. I'll show you where to turn in."

Lee discovered he was gripping the steering wheel with more force than usual. Glancing in his rearview mirror, he saw dust rising into the sky from the Packard's tires. Then, farther back in the trail of dust, he thought he saw a car following them from a distance. For a while, he drove without saying anything as he kept an eye on the road behind them. Every now and then he saw a glimmer of sunlight reflected off the roof and hood of a black car making its way through the swirling dust clouds in their wake.

"There it is," Molly said, pointing to a gate where a small Ford truck was parked beside the road. Someone was seated in a patch of shade below a tree near the gate. "Somebody's there."

Lee slowed the Packard and braked to a halt where an opening in the fence led onto the property. A burly man with his shirtsleeves rolled up over bulging muscles left his stool beneath the tree to approach the car. An old scar ran down the side of his right cheek, making him appear somehow menacing. Scowling, he sauntered toward Lee's Packard. Behind him, on top of a ridge running across the Hawkins farm, a drilling rig sat unattended, awaiting a crew.

"What the hell do you want, mister?" he asked before he got to the driver's window.

"Just taking a look around. I was told this is the Hawkins place."

"You ain't gonna take no look around here unless you work for Mr. Hunt," the big man growled, failing to notice the badge on Lee's shirt. He came over to the car, peering in at Molly. "An' this ain't no goddamn lover's lane," he added. "Now back that car out of here an' keep goin' wherever you was headed before."

Lee didn't like his gruff manner, yet he put a bridle on his temper and opened the car door, switching off the motor. "I'm a Texas Ranger," he said, getting out. "This is the scene of a murder I'm investigating."

"Ain't nobody supposed to come in here 'cept the drillers." The man said it angrily. "If you want on this here piece of land, you'll have to get permission from Mr. Hunt."

Lee closed the car door behind him. "I don't need anybody's permission," he said quietly, glancing back to the road as he heard the sound of an engine. He watched a black automobile approach. A Dodge sedan navigated the chugholes and ruts at low speed. It might be someone who lives farther down the road, he thought. Was he being too cautious?

The Dodge drove slowly past the gate and continued on. One man occupied the car, sitting behind the steering wheel wearing a snap-brim straw hat. The driver wasn't looking at Lee. Maybe the black car meant nothing, he told himself.

As he was turning back to emphasize his demand to be allowed onto the property, he happened to look at Molly. She was staring at the black sedan with a strange expression on her face. "What's wrong?" he asked, ignoring the gate guard standing behind him.

"That was Carlos," she said, and he was sure he detected a trace of fear in her voice. "I told you about him, that he works for Gino. I wonder if he was following us."

Lee frowned. "He's the man who runs the trucking company?"

"That was him," Molly replied. "I sure hope he isn't mad because he saw me riding with you. Maybe Gino wouldn't like it if he knew I talked to you."

He was about to reassure her when he felt a hand seize his upper arm in a viselike grip.

"I don't give a damn who you are, mister, you ain't gonna come on this land without—"

It was simply a reflex when Lee swung a punch at the man's jaw. His fist struck bone before he could think about what he was doing. He heard his knuckles pop and felt the shock of the blow all the way to his shoulder. The guard stumbled backward, windmilling his arms until he slumped to the grass on his rump, blinking furiously.

"Don't ever grab me again," Lee warned, working his sore knuckles, wishing he'd controlled himself before he took that swing. Captain Ross would raise hell if he learned about it.

The man rubbed his aching chin. He grunted once and didn't say anything, averting his eyes.

Lee climbed back in the car after a cursory examination of the hilltop, where a sagging canvas tent stood near a drilling tower. "I reckon I've seen enough for today," he said, starting the engine, grinding into reverse before the clutch was fully engaged, thinking about his burning knuckles—they'd be swollen before it got dark. "Let's find the City Café and get something to eat, if you're hungry."

Molly was watching him closely while he backed the car out. "You sure hit that guy quick," she said. "Hard, too."

"He shouldn't have grabbed my arm like that. Maybe it'll teach him a lesson."

The guard stood up and dusted off the seat of his pants as Lee shifted into low gear.

They drove off toward Longview into a setting sun. Lee was slightly embarrassed over the way he'd lost his temper in front of Molly, yet he said nothing about it, changing gears until the Packard got up to speed. His disposition had gotten him into trouble before. More than once his mother had reminded him that he'd inherited his father's bad temper.

On the drive back to town, he puzzled over the black sedan. Why had Carlos Santini followed them out to the Hawkins land? Was he, or someone else, worried about what Molly might say to a Texas Ranger? What could this girl know that might cause problems for a trucking company?

6

By the time they arrived at the City Café, it was almost dark enough to require the Packard's headlamps. He parked in front at the curb and switched off the engine. Molly had said hardly a word as they drove back to town and he wondered what was keeping her so quiet.

"Something bothering you?" he asked, opening the car door as soon as he set the parking brake.

"Maybe I hadn't oughta go in there with you. If Carlos sees us together . . ." She looked over her shoulder like she expected to see the black Dodge following them again.

Lee pondered it. "Why would he care, Molly? Is he afraid you'll tell me about something illegal he's involved in?"

His question struck a nerve. She couldn't look at him when she replied, "I never said he was doing anything illegal. I only told you he works for Gino. That isn't against the law, is it?"

"I reckon it depends on what he does for Gino. You told me he runs a trucking company."

Molly reached for the door handle. "I'd better get back. I can walk. It isn't all that far. I've told you everything about Bill and what happened that day, all I can remember."

"You're afraid of something, aren't you? Is it Carlos?"

She looked at him now. "Are you gonna arrest me if I don't answer? Look, all I know is that Carlos runs a trucking company down here for Gino. If they're doing something illegal, I wouldn't know about it."

"I think you know more than you're willing to say. I can find out myself if Carlos and Gino are breaking the law. For now, I'm only interested in finding out who killed Bill Dodd. If you think Carlos may have had something to do with it, I want you to tell me."

"Carlos isn't in the oil business. He has trucks." Molly gave the street a quick backward glance. "Every now and then he loans out money. I need to get going. Maude said she wanted me back early."

"She told you to be back before nine."

"I'm not hungry. Honest."

"I think you're worried about Carlos seeing you talking to me. Is that it?"

She fidgeted. "He might not like it, because you're a cop. Gino warned all of us not to talk to the cops if we get arrested while we're working for Maude. Gino has this lawyer who'll bail us out if the place gets raided. We're supposed to keep quiet and not say anything. If Carlos tells Gino I was talking to you, Gino might get real mad about it."

"But I'm not asking you anything about Maude or what goes on at her place. I'm investigating the death of William Dodd. Tell them the truth if they ask you why you drove out there with me."

Molly was still uncomfortable. "Carlos might not believe it. He's real mean, and so is Gino. I don't want any trouble, mister. I told you everything I know about Bill, so please let me go back now."

He studied her face in the light spilling over the sidewalk from the café windows. "I wouldn't let them hurt you, Molly, and if they've got good sense, they won't want any trouble with the Texas Rangers. I could close down Maude's operation and start looking into Gino's trucking company for violations. They don't want any problems with me. Tell Maude, and Carlos if he asks, that I'm only looking into what happened to Dodd and that's the reason I took you out to the place where Dodd was killed. I'll be staying at the Grand Hotel. If Carlos or anybody else bothers you, all you've got to do is call me or leave word for me there." As he said it, he flexed his swollen knuckles. "You've got nothing to worry about, and you're not in any kind of trouble. I may need your help in finding out who shot Dodd that night. Anything you can remember about him, the people he knew, the places he used to go, might give me the lead I'm looking for."

"There was just that one guy, Charley Waller. They drank coffee here nearly every morning, but he never told me much about him. I really oughta get back now. I swear I told you everything I know."

He reached for the ignition switch. "I'll drive you."

Molly opened the car door. "It'll be better if I walk, just in case Carlos happens to drive by."

"Why are you so afraid of him?" he asked. "If you tell him the truth about why you rode out there with me today . . ."

She closed the door and stood outside the car, looking both ways before she answered him. "Sometimes guys like Carlos and Gino don't believe anything you tell 'em." She gave him a weak grin. "Nice meeting you, Mr. Garrett. I hope you find the man you're looking for real soon." At that, she hurried across the road to the sidewalk in front of a row of stores and disappeared around a darkening corner.

Lee got out of the car, puzzling over Molly's fear of Carlos Santini. Did she have knowledge of some illegal activity Carlos was in, or was she simply afraid of him? It was clear that Santini had followed them out to the Hawkins farm, but for what reason? Was Carlos keeping an eye on the girl, or was he concerned about the arrival of a Texas Ranger in town?

Answering a rumbling in his stomach, Lee crossed the sidewalk and entered the café. Men in dirty overalls and work shirts gave him passing notice when he walked among the tables to an empty booth at the back.

A stocky waitress snapping chewing gum brought him a menu and plunked down a smudgy glass of water. "What'll it be?" she asked indifferently, as if she'd had a particularly long day. Her hair was tied in a bun and her face was perspiring heavily, despite half a dozen ceiling fans strategically placed above the customers' tables.

"Bring me a chicken-fried steak and whatever comes with it. Coffee." He handed back the menu, noting that the woman saw his badge. "By the way, can you tell me if Charley Waller is in here tonight?"

"That's him over yonder," she replied, aiming the end of her pencil toward a corner table.

A man in baggy khaki trousers and suspenders over a wrinkled starched white shirt was watching Lee above the rim of his iced-tea glass. When he felt Lee's gaze, he looked down at his empty plate.

"I'm obliged," Lee told the woman, sliding out of the booth, deciding that now was as good a time as any to ask Waller a few questions. He made his way to Waller's table, ignoring curious stares from the other patrons. He stopped when he stood at Waller's left elbow. The man looked to be in his middle thirties, slightly paunchy at the waist, with a rounded nose and close-set blue eyes. "You're Charley Waller," Lee said. "I'm Texas Ranger Lee Garrett and I've got some questions for you concerning Bill Dodd. We can talk now, or first thing in the morning."

Waller gave him a shrug. "Don't make no difference to me," he said, rattling ice at the bottom of his glass. "I knew Bill. We met down around Beaumont a few years back, but I wouldn't say I knew him all that well. Got no idea who shot him, if that's what you're after."

Waller wasn't inclined to offer Lee a chair. "Did you know about a lease he secured on some property around here? It's the Hawkins farm, west of town."

Waller seemed to grow edgy—it might have been Lee's imagination. "He told me about it. He spent damn near every dime he had tryin' to get all the heirs to sign it. Only he never got it recorded. Somebody killed him first."

Conversation at tables around them dropped to a hush as the patrons noticed Lee's badge. "Did you ever see the lease after it came in the mail?"

Waller wagged his head side to side. He, too, became aware of a silence in the café and apparently preferred to say nothing aloud.

Lee decided this was the wrong time and place for any more questions. "I'll need to talk to you again. Tomorrow morning, or right after lunch."

"I'm busy tomorrow," Waller said tonelessly.

At the end of what had been a very long day, it was the wrong thing for Waller to say. "I can haul you down to the county jail for questioning right now if that'd be more convenient. If it's necessary, I can keep you there all night asking questions."

Now the silence in the City Café was absolute. All eyes were on Waller's corner table. Someone coughed at the back and then a spoon rattled in an empty cup.

"I barely knew him," Waller complained, holding his voice down.

Hunger and fatigue kept Lee from pressing it. "Meet me here at eight tomorrow morning. We'll find a quiet place where we can talk. Don't miss our appointment, Mr. Waller. I'd hate like hell to have to come looking for you."

"You got no call to threaten me, Ranger. I got no idea who killed Dodd."

Lee let out an impatient sigh, growing exceedingly weary of Waller's attitude. "Right now I've just got a few questions for you. Be here at eight."

He sauntered back to his table, acutely aware of the attention the patrons were giving him, and of the quiet. When he sat down, he found dozens of faces staring at him. The hum of the ceiling fans and the soft flutter of paper napkins, held in place on scattered tabletops by tin knives and forks, seemed to grow louder.

Charley Waller got up and paid his bill at the cash register without looking at Lee. He took a toothpick and walked outside, trying to seem casual about it, moving slowly past the City Café front windows until he was out of sight.

A grizzled roughneck at a nearby table spoke to Lee, ending a long, uncomfortable silence. "You ain't the reg'lar Ranger who tends to affairs 'round here, mister. You here for some special reason?"

Everyone in the café awaited his answer, or so it seemed as they craned their necks toward Lee. He passed a glance across suspicious looks and the few blank expressions nearest him. "I'm only here to investigate a murder. A man got his head damn near blown off because of an oil lease."

"Nothin' else?" the roughneck asked pointedly, like he did not quite believe it.

"Nothing else. Bootlegging is for local police and federal marshals. Gambling and whorehouses are a local matter, unless the Texas Rangers get called in to provide assistance. I'm sure that Sheriff Bass would have asked for my help if he needed it. I'm only here to find out who killed a wildcatter by the name of Bill Dodd."

Whispered conversations commenced at several tables and now some of the patrons' attention was elsewhere. Two men in dirty khakis and grease-stained shirts got up to pay at the register.

"I knowed Bill," the roughneck said, keeping his voice low. "He had the worst luck of any man I ever seen. He went bust down 'round Houston. Sunk his money in dry holes an' worthless leases damn near every time. Word 'round here was, he got a prime lease next to the Joiner. Only he never got it recorded. Some son of a bitch killed him aforehand, making' that paper worthless."

"How well did you know him?" Lee asked, cautiously, so as not to seem too interested.

"Not all that good. He stayed off to hisself, mostly. He was flat busted most of the time an' nobody wants a friend who's broke. He drove this ol' beat-up Model A. Always havin' flats an' radiator trouble."

"His widow thinks he was killed on account of the lease, so it couldn't be recorded. Someone real close to him had to know it came in the mail that day."

At that, the roughneck shrugged and drank the last of his coffee. "It's mighty goddamn hard to keep a secret in the

Oil Patch, mister. Rumors fly all the time 'bout this or that spot havin' oil underground. Coulda been ol' Bill was just unlucky again. It ain't none of my affair anyhow." He got up slowly to take his money to the front counter, then he hesitated. "I seen you talkin' to Charley Waller just now. He knows Bill better'n anybody, I reckon, 'cept maybe his wife or one of them whores at Maude's. Bill was bad about spendin' time over at Maude's until his wife got here, but hell . . . that's just human nature. Sure as hell ain't no crime to need a woman once in a while."

Lee held up a hand to keep the man from walking off. "There was one girl at Maude's, a girl named Molly Brown. She said she was from New York. Hard to figure why a New York whore would be down in Texas, isn't it?"

"One of Santini's women." The man looked around to see who might be listening and quieted his voice. "Them goddamn Italians have got a nose for money. Soon as somebody struck oil 'round here, them goddamn Eastern gangsters started showin' up with gamblin' tents an' fancy city whores who know how to get every damn dime of a man's pay. They's like buzzards, feedin' off a hard-workin' man's pay envelope. I hate the greasy-haired bastards. We'd be better off without 'em."

Lee couldn't resist a final question before the rough-neck walked away. "What makes you say they're Eastern gangsters?"

Again the man hesitated to see who was listening. After a moment, making sure no one could overhear him, he said, "Everybody knows who they are, mister. This ain't no Sunday School picnic 'round Longview. There's big money to be made here, an' that's what draws them no-good crooks from back East. We don't grow no god-damn Italians in East Texas. They show up wherever there's dishonest money to be made. They run crooked dice an' roulette wheels, an' shave them cards so they can read 'em plain as day. Workin' men hadn't oughta tolerate

it, 'cept 'bout half the men workin' this oilfield is scared
of 'em."

"Why are they scared?" Lee asked.

The roughneck gave Lee an impatient look. "You hang
'round here long enough, mister, an' you'll find out soon
enough." He hurried away from Lee's table like he wished
he'd kept his mouth shut.

7

The Grand was anything but grand, a somber, red-brick
affair with oversized windows looking out on Commerce
Street from second- and third-floor rooms. The lobby was
quiet. A shoeshine stand near the door held a sleeping form,
an old Negro with twists of silver hair encircling his bald
spot. His head was thrown back and his mouth was open,
revealing smooth gums and only two upper teeth. His lips
fluttered almost soundlessly when he snored. A Tyler newspaper lay open on his lap. Tins of shoe polish beneath his
shine chair gave off a mild, waxy smell.

No one was behind the registration desk. Lee walked
across the tile floor, past a lumpy sofa and mismatched
chairs, to see if a service bell on the countertop would summon a clerk. The lobby was poorly lit, with only two naked
bulbs hanging from a ceiling stained by previous water
leaks from somewhere upstairs.

He rang the bell and waited. The old Negro stirred and
sat up, scattering his newspaper on the floor when he
rubbed his eyes.

"Miz Williams stepped out fer a few minutes," he said
in a thick, phlegmy voice. "Room's two dollars a night. I

kin fetch you a key . . ." He noticed the badge on Lee's shirt reflecting light from the electric bulbs. "You be the law, mister?"

Lee put down his battered cardboard suitcase. "Texas Ranger out of Waco. I'll be needing a room for a few days. I'd be obliged if you'd give me a key. A room with some breeze sounds mighty nice on a night like this."

"Rooms has got fans," the old man said, climbing down from his shine stand. "Southwest corner gits the best breeze when it takes a notion to blow." He limped toward the desk, wearing an apron darkened by shoe polish. He grinned and said, "Name's Cal Waters," as he went behind the counter, scowling at the rows of keys on hooks along the wall.

"Where's the nearest telephone?" Lee asked, reaching in his pocket for a money clip containing almost a hundred dollars he'd drawn from the bank before leaving town, to cover his expenses.

"In that hall yonder," Cal replied, taking a dull brass key from a hook. "Ain't got no pay phone yet. They's got 'em over in Tyler. Operator'll call back th' charges if'n you call long-distance. Mos' folks have to pay in advance, only I don't reckon Miz Williams be wantin' me to ask no Texas Ranger fer money up front."

Lee took the key. His captain, Bob Ross, would be at home by now and he might know something about New York gangsters being in East Texas, Longview in particular. On a hunch, he decided to ask Cal about Carlos Santini and the trucking company.

"Who's this guy Santini running a trucking outfit here?"

Cal shook his head. "Big troubles, that's who he be. Bad folks from way off. New York City, they say. He ain't nobody to fool 'round with, that's fer sure. Anybody who messes with them folks is liable to wind up being' fish bait."

"Are you saying Santini killed someone?"

Cal looked askance, like the question made him uncomfortable. "I couldn't say fer sure, mister. Never saw him do it my ownself. Mos'ly it's jest what folks say . . ."

"But they say he's a killer?"

The old man nodded reluctantly. "Hadn't oughta be talking' 'bout it, don't reckon. Might not be healthy. You ask around in town. Don't say Calvin Waters said nothin'. I got to make me a livin' here. Nine grandkids to help feed an' I'm too old an' bad crippled up to work in the Patch. Some outfits won't hire Nigras anyways. I shine plenty o' shoes an' boots an' I keep this ol' mouth shut real tight."

"I'd never repeat anything you told me, Cal. I'm curious as to why the sheriff doesn't do anything about Santini if it can be proved he killed anyone."

"Maybe that's it," Cal said through a weak, toothless grin. "Maybe Sheriff Bass can't prove nothin' on him." He glanced to the front door. "Or maybe he's scared of him, same as everybody else."

Lee was sure the old man knew more than he was saying. "It don't figure, how one man can run his bluff on the sheriff's department and city police."

Cal smiled again, but now there was genuine fear in his eyes when he spoke. "Never said he was bluffin', mister. Only that I ain't never seen him kill nobody. There's been folks who up an' disappeared after they had troubles with Carlos. An' he ain't just one man. There's a bunch of truckers who works fer him an' they's mean types too, from back East. Folks claim they's all Italians. They sure as hell stick together when they's in town. Don't hardly never see jus' one off to hisself."

"What sort of trucking are they involved in?"

The question relaxed Cal a bit. "Haulin' crude. They's got so much crude comin' to the railroad can't nobody haul all of it, so some goes down the highway, too. Trucks is big business now, if a man's connected-up right."

"You mean if he knows the right people?"

"Big operators, like that Hunt feller. Man's gotta be in with one of them big wheels or he'll starve plumb to death ownin' a truck."

Lee rested his elbows on the counter. Cal was giving him more than he expected. "I've heard Santini is into bootlegging and gambling, that he's behind some of it. I'm wondering if he cut a deal with some of the bigger oilmen to provide whiskey and game tables. I already know he furnishes women for a whorehouse called Maude's over by the tracks. What's got me puzzled is why he bothers with trucks. Looks like there'd be enough money in running whiskey and gambling."

"You gonna try an' arrest him, mister?"

"That's not the reason I'm here. A wildcatter by the name of Bill Dodd was killed. Executed, it looks like, over a lease on some land called the Hawkins farm. It happened a few weeks ago . . ."

Cal looked down at his feet. "Somebody made mention of it, seems like. He got shot in the head, if'n I remember right."

"Did you know Bill Dodd?"

Cal was almost too quick to deny it. "No, sir. If I shined his shoes, I never knowed his name. I got reg'lar customers, only some ain't never tol' me who they was. Never did know nobody by the name Bill Dodd, an' that's the gospel truth."

"Do you know Charley Waller?"

"I knows Mister Charley, all right. He gits a shine once a week on Fridays."

"What sort of guy is he?"

Cal shrugged. "Wears good shoes an' he keeps 'em nice fer a man works in the Patch. That's nearly all I kin tell you 'bout Mister Charley."

"What sort of work does he do around an oilfield?"

"Spec'lator, they calls it. Buys up good leases an' sells 'em fer more money to somebody else."

A warning bell started ringing in Lee's head. Waller was in the lease-peddling business, making him knowledgeable as to what a prime lease like Dodd's was worth. Had Waller known about the lease? And could he have peddled that information to someone who was willing to kill Dodd to prevent him from recording it? Or was it possible that Waller himself was Dodd's killer? Waller's involvement with Dodd was starting to look like the best place to begin the investigation.

"You've been mighty helpful, Cal," Lee said, taking a one-dollar note from his money clip. "Don't worry about me repeating anything you said." He handed the old man the money. "I'll need to use that phone and put my suitcase in my room."

"Room's number two-twelve," Cal said, pocketing the currency quickly before giving Lee his key. "I'll tell Miz Williams that a Texas Ranger rented this here room. You kin register in the mornin' an' pay fer them telephone calls. Like I done tol' you, the operator's gonna call back with them charges. I write 'em down, is all. If'n you want, I'll give them boots the best shine they ever did have, come tomorrow mornin'. Won't be no charge, seein' as you's so generous."

Lee picked up his suitcase and started for a set of stairs across the lobby, glancing into a dark hallway to a telephone on a wall badly in need of paint. He climbed the stairs to a hall lit by a single lightbulb. At room 212 he unlocked the door and flipped on a light switch. The room smelled musty, unused for a considerable amount of time. He crossed the hardwood floor and put his suitcase on the sagging, metal-frame bed with a discolored blue bedspread.

When he opened the room's only window, a humid

breath of air came across the sill, smelling faintly of oil. Lights from a number of buildings in the center of town winked at him from the darkness.

"Hell of a city to live in," he muttered, removing his gun and holster from his bag and hiding them under the mattress. "Place stinks worse'n a slaughter house . . ." He switched on an electric fan beside the window, its blades making an irritating clatter on the safety cage around them until they picked up speed.

A nightstand sat beside the bed. An ancient dresser with a cracked mirror stood against the wall across the room. A bath was at the end of the hallway, he remembered.

After locking the door, he went downstairs to call Captain Ross. His pocket watch read a quarter past eight.

"Roy Woods is the only one who'll know, Lee," Ross said in his typical monotone. "I can make a few calls tonight, if it's that important. By an' large, we've got no organized crime in Texas like in most Eastern states. If there's an Italian gangster operatin' over in Longview, I'm not aware of it. Maybe Major Elliot will have something on it. Tell me why you think it's related to this dead wildcatter whose widow is making all the fuss."

"Call it a hunch, Cap'n. Every time I ask about Bill Dodd, I keep hearing about how much he would have been worth if he hadn't gotten his head blown off, and about this Italian guy with a mean reputation who runs crude-oil trucks, maybe even killed a few people who got in his way. The local sheriff is tied to a whorehouse using girls from back East. This Carlos Santini brings 'em down from New York. He runs the trucking company hauling crude oil to the railroads. I've also heard that Santini is involved in gambling operations and bootlegging here. Some guy named Gino up in New York is supposed to be behind it. It's getting real complicated. From the sheriff's report, it sounds like Dodd was executed by a professional. I may be here longer than we figured."

"I can't spare you for very long, Lee. We've got cases that are bigger, stackin' up like cordwood on my desk. Governor Sterling is raisin' holy hell with headquarters because he's afraid Miriam Ferguson will defeat him in the next election over this Ku Klux Klan thing. He wants us to bust up this Klan business before Ma Ferguson makes it a big campaign issue. Major Elliot is runnin' scared. We need to solve some high-profile cases that'll keep Sterling happy. This Dodd business can't win a vote, no matter how it turns out."

"But if there is gangster activity in Longview, it would look good if we exposed it," Lee explained. It was becoming painfully clear that Captain Ross didn't want him wasting time on a case with no political value.

Ross sighed. The crackle of telephone lines filled a long, meaningful silence. "I'll make a few calls. Give me the number at your hotel. But don't plan on stayin' too long, Lee. We've got bigger fish to fry." Another silence. "I guess it would be a feather in our cap if we broke up a ring of New York gangsters operatin' out of Longview. It'd make good headlines an' Sterling would like that. Poke around and see what you can find out. It may be nothing. It ain't a crime to be a wop from New York. If there is a connection to gangsters back East, it'd sure look good to shut their Texas operations down . . . let 'em know we won't put up with that shit here. Make some inquiries. I'll make a few calls. If I was you, I wouldn't waste much time on that killing, the Dodd business, unless you think it's connected some way or another."

"It's just a hunch, Cap'n, but I've got a feeling there's a connection. Santini followed me and the whore who knew Dodd out to the murder scene. The girl's scared of him for some reason and I think she knows more about Dodd and his dealings with the Italian than she's saying."

"I didn't send you out there to take whores for a Sunday drive." Ross chuckled. "Give me the number at your hotel, an' I'll see what I can dig up. I'll leave word at Tyler for Roy to give you a call. If anybody knows what's goin' on there, it'll be Roy."

After he gave Ross the number and hung up, Lee felt tired, too tired to wait by the phone. He walked into the lobby and spoke to Cal. "Let me know if anybody calls for me, Calvin. I'll be up in my room getting some shut-eye."

Climbing the stairs, he felt frustrated, angry. The Texas Rangers weren't what they used to be when he got his appointment back in the twenties. They were becoming a political machine instead of a law-enforcement agency. A proud tradition was fading into obscurity.

"Gino Tatangelo," Ross said, his voice barely audible over a bad connection. "New York and New Jersey connections to one of the biggest crime organizations on the East Coast. Sicilians and Italians. Tough bastards, so they say. Texas doesn't have much to offer them without labor unions. They control businesses through labor union bosses, only we don't have unions, so we miss most of it. I'll check on a few more matters first thing in the mornin'. I can't reach Roy Woods tonight . . . they said he wasn't at home or in the office, but I left word for him to call you.

"This Carlos Santini works for Tatangelo. I made a call to the FBI an hour ago an' some asshole wanted to know why it couldn't wait 'til morning. But he read me the stuff in the guy's file. Hoover's boys are keepin' an eye on Santini to see what he's up to in Texas, only they say right now it's nothing but operatin' a fleet of trucks. But remember, you can't trust those feds. They don't always give us everything they've got. If it's a federal case, they've got jurisdiction, but the guy insisted they don't have anything on

Santini yet. Just suspicion, because of his connections to the Tatangelo crime family."

"I smell shit," Lee said sleepily, glancing at his watch. Cal had knocked on his door at eleven to say he had a telephone call. "I'll poke around some. G'night, Cap'n. I'll call soon as I find out anything."

He hung up the receiver, having the distinct impression that he was about to find out a great deal more than he or Captain Ross imagined. If he had a talent that made him a good peace officer, he supposed it was his nose for bullshit. He would bet a month's pay there was more going on in Longview than either he or Ross guessed right now.

8

Ranger Roy Woods was mad, mad over having to fight off one swarm of mosquitoes after another, mad at the two Treasury agents who insisted the still at Brownsboro was a major source of moonshine whiskey reaching oilfield saloons, mad at being out in the dark when he should have been in bed with his wife, mad at two Henderson County sheriff's deputies who didn't seem to know where they were just now. It was a bitter end to what had been a very long day. "We're lost," he said to County Deputy Frank Miller. "These goddamn pine woods are so deep I can't see a thing. Why don't we come back tomorrow when we can see what the hell we're doin'?"

"It's right over yonder," Miller replied. "Over the next hill. They don't make no shine in the daytime 'cause somebody might see the smoke. We're nearly there."

"You've been sayin' that for the last two hours," Roy said under his breath, swatting a mosquito feeding on his neck.

"It's unbearably hot out here," Treasury Agent Tom Simmons said, mopping his brow with a sodden handkerchief. Simmons was the senior Treasury agent in charge of halting the Texas moonshine operations, reporting directly to Washington. He carried a Fox double-barrel shotgun in the crook of his arm, a twelve-gauge. His shoes were covered with clay-loam mud after crossing a creek in the dark, and his trousers were wet to the knees.

Miller crept ahead of the others to the crest of a low hill, where he crouched down suddenly. "Yonder it is," he whispered.

Roy could see a distant fire flickering in a stand of tall pines, and the shape of a large still above the flames. "It's a big son of a bitch, all right," he said, watching the outlines of men standing near the copper coils of the evaporation tubes with glass jars and clay jugs in each hand. He raised binoculars to his eyes and adjusted the focus until the images were clear. "Let's spread out an' yell for 'em to throw up their hands."

"Them's the Jeffrey boys," Miller warned. "They ain't gonna come quiet. They been sellin' shine to that Italian feller over in Longview an' he's promised 'em protection. Those two Jeffrey brothers are mighty damn tough themselves. They'll start shootin' soon as they hear somebody holler."

Roy drew his Colt .45. He preferred an automatic to the standard revolver called for by Ranger guidelines, a holdover from earlier days when Texas Rangers rode horses and carried single-action pistols. If firepower was needed, he wanted the best. "Let the bastards shoot if they take the notion." He frowned. "What do you mean, Santini can give 'em protection? Protection from what? A damn bullet?"

"Them Italians has got big-time lawyers, so they claim. It was Rufus Jeffrey who told us that the last time we arrested him. A lawyer from Dallas paid his bond an' got him out the same day. It was like he hadn't done nothin' but spit on the sidewalk. Ol' Judge Barnes set him free quick as a wink."

Agent Simmons spoke. "This time we'll have a talk with the judge who set his bond. As a repeat offender, his previous bond has to be revoked. I'll call Washington. We'll get a district judge to deny bail."

"We ain't got 'em arrested yet," Deputy Dave Cobb whispered, working his fingers around the butt of his .38 Colt revolver. "I bet they start shootin' the minute they know we're here. Rufus an' Clyde are damn good shots with a rifle. We'd better be ready to duck some lead."

Roy was growing tired of the banter, of the mosquitoes, and of nights without sleep. "We ain't getting no place talkin' about it. Spread out, an' we'll give 'em a chance to come peaceful."

Deputy Miller's attention was on a shadowy form standing back from the fire. "There's somebody else over yonder. Don't know who the hell he could be. It ain't Rufe or Clyde—I can tell by his shape. He's a whole lot smaller'n either one of them Jeffrey boys . . ."

"Spread out," Agent Simmons said quietly. "I'll call for them to surrender their firearms. Give me about five minutes."

The men began moving through the brush. Roy crept forward until he had a good view of the still. Crouching down, he aimed his .45 and waited, brushing mosquitoes away from his face and arms.

"Treasury agents!" Simmons cried a few moments later. "Put down your guns and raise your hands!"

For a fleeting second, nothing moved and there was no sound. Suddenly the thundering staccato of automatic weapons fire erupted from a spot north of the still. A Thompson submachine gun exploded in rapid bursts, a .45-caliber, Roy judged by the heaviness of the blasts. Speeding lead whistled through the tree limbs above his head and all around him, snapping off branches, shattering dry pine cones, striking bark with a resounding whack.

"Big artillery," he muttered, staying low, watching men on the run trying to hide behind the trees near the still. He'd seen flashes of light from the submachine gun, yet he couldn't be sure of its location now. A typical East Texas moonshiner didn't own a tommy gun.

A rifle cracked in concert with a stabbing finger of flame winking briefly near a pine trunk. Then someone screamed, and Roy knew that one deputy or a treasury agent had been hit. The screaming became a series of groans, and he could hear thrashing noises in the forest.

"I'm hit, Dave!" a frantic voice cried—Frank Miller's, if Roy could judge by the tone of it.

A dog began to bark repeatedly and he wondered why the animal had not warned the Jeffrey brothers of their approach. Both Treasury agents made enough noise pushing through brush to alert any dog with good hearing. Gripping his pistol, he waited for a target, unwilling to give away his hiding place to whoever had the tommy gun.

"You boys better back off!" someone shouted from a dark spot near the still, "or we'll kill every one of you sumbitches!"

Deputy Miller continued to groan, whimpering with the pain of a mortal wound.

Roy thought he saw a shadow near the blacker outline of an older-model pickup truck. He aimed for the shape and carefully drew a bead, thumbing back the pistol's hammer while mosquitoes swarmed around his face. When his gun sights were steady on the figure, he gently squeezed the trigger.

The .45 exploded in his fist, slamming into his palm like a mule's kick. The roar of the gunshot echoed through the inky forest.

A man yelled, his cry beginning before the blast from Roy's pistol faded to silence.

"Shit! I'm shot!"

Noise made by scrambling feet came from beyond the fire, and then the sound of a softer thump when someone fell.

"Got the bastard!" Roy whispered to himself.

A rifle cracked, flame spitting from a spot behind another tree. Roy turned his pistol toward the flash of light and got ready to aim again.

The earsplitting roar of the tommy gun resumed its deadly rhythm. A stream of bullets sprayed across Roy's hiding place, blasting tree limbs to kindling, shredding pine needles above his head, showering the ground with debris.

Roy hunkered down. "Your aim ain't too goddamn good," he said quietly, unruffled by the nearness of so much hot lead. He had been in worse situations, a lone peace officer against larger numbers of wanted men. This was a federal operation, he thought idly. Let these Treasury boys take all the chances. He'd only been called in at the last minute to serve as backup because the Jeffrey brothers were notorious for playing rough and being good shots with a rifle.

"Holy shit, I'm hurtin'!" the same voice yelled from a black shadow behind the still. "The sumbitch got me in the leg . . ."

Off to the left, Deputy Miller moaned again. "Help me. I'm hurt bad. I'm bleedin'. Got blood all over me. Call somebody so's I won't die. I got kids to raise. Call the hospital. Tell Doc Green I'm gunshot . . ."

Another burst of tommy-gun fire blasted from a dense

thicket of pines, this one farther away than before and to the right of the still. The machine-gun shooter was moving through the night to keep from revealing his position by muzzle flashes.

"He's smart, but he damn sure can't shoot straight," Roy said. He aimed for the thicket and fired, a shot he knew had no chance of hitting anyone in the total darkness. He moved quickly to the other side of the tree as a spent cartridge casing tinkled to the ground near his feet when the Colt's mechanism spit out an empty round. "He's pullin' back so we can't find him. He ain't nobody's fool."

Roy tried to recall how many shells fit into a Thompson's drum, and he couldn't. They were U.S. Army contract weapons and hard to find, even on the black market. Whoever had been able to acquire the machine gun had good connections somewhere.

"Throw down your weapons!" Agent Simmons shouted. "We have you surrounded . . ." His demand was silenced by hammering gunfire from the tommy gun, bullets whining through the pines like a swarm of angry bees. Roy remembered hearing complaints that a Thompson wasn't accurate and that it frequently jammed, but he'd never fired one himself. Whoever was doing the shooting wasn't having much luck hitting what he fired at—perhaps it was the darkness ruining his aim.

Something moved near the still. Agent Simmons let loose a blast from his shotgun before Roy could identify what he'd seen. A dog yelped and the shadow tumbled to the ground, followed by a series of pitiful cries, the rattle of a heavy chain. Simmons, in his haste to end a standoff, had wounded the Jeffreys' guard dog while it was chained to a tree behind the old pickup truck.

A rifle blasted somewhere in the forest, among tree trunks so thick Roy couldn't see where the shot came from.

He heard a slug strike something soft and a man shrieked with pain. "My leg! He shot me in the leg!" Simmons howled. The much brighter muzzle flash of his shotgun had given his position away and he hadn't moved in time.

"Amateurs," Roy muttered. "Desk jockeys from Washington in fancy suits an' neckties."

Simmons began thrashing through the thick brush and pine limbs, trying to escape another deadly rifle shot. Sounds of his limp were easy to distinguish in the following brief silence until a stream of lead pounded from the tommy gun, filling the night with its deafening rattle.

Roy heard Simmons fall and the howling stopped. The Treasury agent was either dead or wise enough now to be quiet despite the hole in his leg.

Roy aimed for the spot where the Thompson had fired, slitting his eyelids, seeking the slightest movement, anything to shoot at in the sea of black ink. Frozen, resting his gun hand against the tree trunk, he watched for the glint of metal, unable to hear a sound beyond the still due to cries from the wounded dog and the much softer groans made by Deputy Miller. Deputy Cobb had been right: the men with rifles were excellent marksmen.

And then he caught a glimpse of someone creeping away from the still, hunkered down, moving cautiously. Roy steadied his front sight and nudged the trigger.

His .45 jumped, spitting forth its deadly lead slug, accompanied by a single gun blast. For a moment, he could not hear anything besides the ringing in his ears.

Before his hearing fully returned, he saw flashing lights and heard distant popping sounds from where his target had been. A man holding a submachine gun sank to his knees, his finger closed around its trigger while he fired blindly into the ground, light from the muzzle of the exploding weapon in his hands revealing his exact location. Seriously wounded, he apparently could not control the muscles tightening in his trigger finger. He went down shooting at the beds of pine needles around him, outlined by flashes of yellow flame erupting from his gun barrel.

Deputy Cobb fired his .38 from a secluded spot west of the still. The man holding the Thompson fell forward on his face, and his machine gun stopped firing.

"I got the son of a bitch!" Cobb cried.

Roy sighed. It was pointless to explain to Cobb that he had been the one to hit the shooter first. Who the hell wanted credit for this anyway? he wondered.

The dying dog's yelps became more heartrending. Treasury Agent Simmons was down and possibly even dead, or dying. Deputy Miller had a leg wound. One of the Jeffrey brothers was hit and perhaps still dangerous. One rifleman remained, one of the two proven marksmen.

"Everybody stay put!" Roy shouted, pulling back behind the tree. "There's at least one more of 'em out yonder someplace."

Deputy Miller's voice was filled with anguish when he said, "Get me to the hospital. I'm bleedin' like a stuck hog an' I'm gonna die 'less I see a doctor real soon."

Roy shook his head. Making midnight raids like this with a group of inexperienced lawmen was stupid, costing lives needlessly. He didn't care all that much that a Treasury agent from some Washington office proved to be a casualty—maybe it would teach those starched shirts a lesson. But local deputies were, for the most part, simple men who needed jobs and as a rule, did the the best they knew how when it came to law enforcement.

"Stay down!" Roy warned again. "One more bastard with a gun is out there someplace. We gotta make damn sure he lit out of here before we show ourselves."

"I'm dyin'," Miller whimpered. "There's blood all over the place an' I'm hurtin' somethin' awful."

Roy dismissed the notion to tell Miller he should be thankful to be alive with nothing more than a bullet hole in him.

9

"**Don't leave me,** Clyde," a gravelly voice pleaded from some distance away, from behind the truck, it seemed. Sounds were tricky to locate in the dense forest. "My leg's broke. Bone's stickin' out 'bove my knee an' it hurts worse'n shit . . ."

"Shut up, Rufe!" another voice demanded, an attempt to speak quietly to keep from pinpointing a position. "Jus' shut the fuck up an' stay down."

Both voices were too hard for Roy to find in the total darkness and he remained still, waiting. The dog's softer whimpering was less a distraction now. Miller was groaning. Deputy Cobb had fired from Roy's right. The other Treasury agent, Brad Whitaker, a bookish man who wore thick glasses, hadn't been heard from yet or fired a shot. If Roy remembered right, Whitaker was carrying a shotgun and a .38 Smith & Wesson pistol, and he was headquartered in Houston.

"Maybe Mr. Whitaker's got the good sense to stay put," Roy whispered. Both Jeffrey brothers were still dangerous, for even a man with a broken leg could shoot straight.

"Help me, Dave!" Deputy Miller yelled, as if suddenly his pains had grown worse.

Roy wagged his head, understanding Miller's mistake a split second before the bark of the heavy-bore rifle had come from the woods. The bullet had whined through the thick forest and struck something hard off to Roy's left, a tree trunk, perhaps. Frank Miller's cry when he was hit had told one of the Jeffrey boys exactly where to shoot.

Miller was silent now. Roy guessed that Agent Simmons

had to be dead or unconscious. Cobb was to the right, south of the still, and Agent Whitaker appeared to have vanished or decided to keep his head down and his guns quiet. Miller was too badly wounded to be of any help, leaving Roy and Deputy Cobb to finish the job they'd started.

At least Cobb can shoot, Roy thought. Cobb had hit the man behind the tommy gun, albeit a stationary target by that time. Roy knew it was unwise to move closer, and yet he was tired of fighting off mosquitoes and this sweltering summer heat, hiding behind a tree with his shirt plastered to his back.

"To hell with 'em," he said under his breath. "I ain't gonna stay behind this goddamn tree all night."

He inched backward without taking his eyes from the still or the circle of firelight around it. Staying low, he crept from tree trunk to tree trunk toward the spot where Agent Simmons went down, praying that Deputy Cobb wouldn't see movement and take a shot at him.

It's so damn dark under all these trees, he thought, careful with the placement of each boot so as not to make noise while crossing the dry pine needles and fallen twigs. It was too dark, the stars blocked out by thick limbs, to see where he was putting his feet.

Roy traveled roughly forty yards before he found the body of Tom Simmons sprawled between a pair of huge pines. He knelt when he came to it and peered closely at the bullet-riddled corpse. The right side of Simmons' face was a pulpy mass of bloody bone fragments and tissue. His shirtfront was puckered in at least half a dozen places where .45-caliber slugs had ripped through him, leaving dark red craters an inch in diameter across his chest and abdomen. This volley of machine-gun fire had been deadly accurate despite the Thompson's poor reputation.

"You shoulda stayed where you were," Roy said, as if the man could still hear him.

Deputy Miller was farther ahead someplace, judging by the direction his cries had come from. Roy left the Treasury agent's body, mincing forward on the balls of his feet with one eye on the still and the trees close by, covering his progress with the .45. One of the brothers was unharmed and also probably moving about in the dark to keep from being cornered—Roy didn't want to run headlong into a sharpshooting moonshiner unawares. And there was another risk factor out there someplace: a Treasury agent armed with a pistol and a shotgun who might shoot at anyone he dimly saw moving through the night . . . Whitaker wore heavy, thick glasses, Roy recalled.

A soft moan came from behind a massive pine trunk twenty or thirty yards away. He crept closer to the sound, batting swarms of mosquitoes from his face with his free hand. The moans could be a trick, to lure him out in the open upon hearing what might be a wounded fellow officer. Piney-woods hunters sometimes used wild-game calls to lure wolves and foxes into rifle range, and it was evident that the Jeffreys were skilled when it came to guns and hunting, especially when their prey turned out to be lawmen.

Cautiously, pausing often, Roy approached the tree and then he smelled blood. Relaxing a little, he inched around the trunk, covering the spot with his automatic.

He found Frank Miller curled in a fetal position on a pile of pine needles, holding his belly. Roy loosened his grip on the Colt's frame and trigger. When he bent down, Miller looked up at him, and even with an almost total absence of light, Roy could see tears in the deputy's eyes.

"Help me, please," Miller croaked. "I'm gonna die 'less you get me to the hospital."

"There's another gunman out there someplace," Roy whispered as he dropped to one knee. "No way to carry you back to one of the automobiles without runnin' the risk of gettin' killed while we're at it."

"I'm gonna die anyway," Miller said, clenching his teeth in a wave of renewed pain. "Send for Dave. Tell Dave he's gotta help me. Let them Jeffrey boys make all the shine they want. I gotta see a doctor right away."

"I ain't exactly sure where Dave is right now. Besides, he could get shot tryin' to help us. Nothin' we can do right now 'til we find that other brother."

"It's Clyde," Miller said softly, wincing. "Rufe's the one hollerin' about his leg bein' broke. Clyde's the oldest an' he's the worst. Mean bastard. Big, too. Ain't scared of nothin' on this earth . . ." The deputy coughed and Roy could see blood coming from his mouth and nose. "He'd as soon kill you as breathe air, Ranger. Tell them Treasury boys we oughta pull out now. I tried to tell 'em this mornin' how bad them Jeffrey brothers was, only they wouldn't listen."

"One Treasury agent is already dead, an' I ain't heard a peep from the other one. I figure he got scared an' ran off. The guy with the submachine gun is out of it now. It's down to Clyde an' his wounded brother. Deputy Cobb's still okay. I'm goin' after Clyde, only it's gonna take some time to slip around behind him. We've come this far, so I aim to finish it."

"He'll kill you," Miller sobbed quietly, gripping his belly with bloodstained hands. "We're all gonna die 'less you can get me to the hospital quick an' leave Clyde alone to tend to his brother."

Roy glanced through the forest. It was completely silent now — the dog was dead and only an occasional pop of wood sap from the still's fire interrupted the quiet. "I'll take care of Clyde quick as I can," he said. "Then we'll get you to that hospital."

He got up slowly, fighting back an angry urge to charge in a mad rush toward the still, counting on surprise and presenting a moving target to keep him alive. But Miller and Cobb had insisted that Clyde Jeffrey and his brother were deadly shots, and they'd done enough tonight to prove it. Better, he thought, to close in as quietly as he could and hope for a bit of luck.

He stepped away from the tree, keeping to the darkest places beneath the pine limbs, beginning his slow stalk toward the still and his adversary, his growing rage only made worse by mosquitoes on his exposed skin raising itchy welts everywhere they bit him. He ignored them for now, intent upon his objective, keening all his senses. He was no newcomer to taking on dangerous men, and unless Clyde Jeffrey was really good, Roy was sure he'd find a way to be the one to bring him down.

Employing less caution than was his regular habit, he moved from tree to tree rapidly, eyes roaming the darkness. Clenching his gun in a clammy fist, he found he was almost looking forward to the moment when he encountered Clyde.

"He can't be all that tough," Roy whispered, the words so quiet they scarcely made any noise crossing his lips.

A pine knot cracked in the fire, spraying sparks. Roy heard the sound and knew it too well to be fooled by it. He continued through the forest, his automatic leveled in front of him.

He reached a spot that gave him a clear view of the still. A Ford truck with battered fenders sat a few yards from the fire, its bed loaded. Masonry jugs and glass jars glistening with moonshine reflected light from the dying flames below the still.

That's a hell of a lot of shine, Roy thought. This wasn't a small-time operation.

Again he wondered about Agent Brad Whitaker. Had he taken off through the pines the minute the shooting started?

And where was Clyde? Was the moonshiner smart enough to merely wait for someone else to make the first move? There was logic behind lying low, but the night was unbearably hot and the mosquitoes were so thick they appeared as a cloud at times. Miller was mortally wounded. Simmons was dead. Deputy Cobb was somewhere to the south, and Whitaker's whereabouts were only a guess. This left him few options. Rufus Jeffrey might still be dangerous if he could use a gun, meaning that possibly two experienced riflemen were waiting for a chance to kill him.

"This lousy job don't pay enough," Roy complained, biting down around soft-spoken words. He had enough mosquito bites to keep him scratching for a week.

He moved to another pine tree and waited, listening, scanning every dark spot before he moved again. He could feel his heart racing now. If Clyde was watching the still, his gun sights could easily be on Roy's chest this very minute.

Roy paused behind a particularly large tree trunk to peer around it. The silence was absolute. He saw a dead dog wearing a collar and chain lying in a pool of blood beside the truck. A few jugs and jars lay broken near the end of a collection tube at the end of a copper condensation coil. And beyond the still was a body resting against the base of a tree, facedown, the man who'd fired at them with the tommy gun. The Thompson lay beside him.

There was no sign of Rufus or Clyde. Rufus had been shooting from a spot near the burlap bags of shelled corn used to make the mash for whiskey. Roy thought he detected a faint trail of blood leading from the bags into the woods, but with almost no firelight remaining, he couldn't be sure.

Then he heard it, the soft metallic click of a gun being cocked somewhere beyond the circle of light. He pulled back to the protection of the pine trunk awaiting a rifle shot. For one lingering moment, nothing happened—the explosion he expected did not come.

"Step away from that tree or I'll blow you in half," a thin voice said, coming from beyond the still. "With a shotgun, I can assure you I won't miss at this range. Drop that gun."

Roy immediately recognized Agent Whitaker's voice. He cupped one hand around his mouth and shouted, "I got 'em covered from over here, Whitaker. It's Texas Ranger Roy Woods."

Another silence, lasting much too long.

"Keep 'em covered!" Roy cried. "I'll be there in a minute to help you!"

Before Roy could move away from the tree, a thundering blast exploded west of the truck. Shotgun pellets sizzled through pine branches everywhere, pattering against the sides of the still. And then a growling voice bellowed, "You sneaky son of a bitch!"

Roy jumped and took off running toward the explosion with his Colt cocked and ready. As he ran past the fire, he saw a huge, red-bearded man in overalls staggering toward him. His jaw was hanging open—he was trying to speak around mouthfuls of blood dribbling down his chest. He carried a rifle loosely in his thick-fingered hands, although it was plain he was too badly injured to use it.

He stumbled a few steps more and then stopped, letting go of his rifle. The gun fell in front of him as his knees gave way in an odd fashion so that he collapsed on his rump, sitting down as quickly and quietly as worshipers do in a front pew at church.

Roy skidded to a halt and held his .45 on the bearded giant. A slender figure in mud-caked trousers carrying a shotgun came out of the shadows: Treasury Agent Brad Whitaker, his eyeglasses reflecting the glow from the still's embers.

"This one is Clyde Jeffrey," Whitaker said, calmly reloading his shotgun tubes. "The other one is lying back there unconscious with a fairly serious wound. I had no choice but to shoot Clyde in the back, Mr. Woods. He was turning around and bringing his rifle up, ignoring my warning to surrender his arms and give up peacefully."

Roy was all but speechless. "I didn't know where you were or what had happened to you," he finally said.

Clyde Jeffrey groaned and slumped over on his back in a pool of blood, and when he did, Agent Whitaker shook his head.

"I don't know how he walked at all," Whitaker said, closing his scattergun's breech. "I fired both barrels, and one shell had a slug in it. I heard it break his back, the cracking noise, but he walked fifteen or twenty paces anyway. I could not believe my own eyes."

Roy sighed, remembering Simmons. "Your partner is dead an' one of the deputies may be dyin'. He's gutshot. Cobb should be runnin' up any minute an' then we'll load Deputy Miller into my car." He could hear Deputy Cobb moving toward them now.

Whitaker frowned, pausing near the body of the man who had the tommy gun. "I'd almost wager my life savings, which isn't much, that this is one of Carlos Santini's men. They all work for a gangster in New York by the name of Gino Tatangelo. This may be the proof I need that organized crime is moving into East Texas to sell liquor. Until now, my superiors have ignored my reports to that effect. I'll look for his identification later, after we get the injured deputy to a doctor."

Roy allowed himself a weak grin. "You sure had me fooled, Whitaker. I thought you took off runnin' when the first shot was fired."

"I simply waited for the right opportunity, Mr. Woods. I can assure you I'm not a coward, even though it will be clear that I shot this big fellow in the back. He left me no choice."

"I'll tell your bosses how it happened," Roy said, suddenly feeling tired. He waved to Deputy Cobb. "Frank Miller is hurt bad over yonder an' we'll need to carry him to a car. It may be too late to save him."

10

The scene at Tyler Memorial Hospital attracted considerable attention from staff members and those ambulatory patients who could hear Rufus Jeffrey bellowing in the emergency room about the pain in his leg or threatening to kill whoever had shot him and his brother. Clyde Jeffrey's spine had indeed been shattered by Agent Whitaker's shotgun blast, and the harried doctors gave Clyde little hope of recovery. Deputy Frank Miller lay comatose in an adjoining room while receiving blood transfusions. The doctors also indicated that Miller would not survive the internal-organ damage from his stomach wound. Treasury Agent Tom Simmons' body lay on a slab in the hospital basement awaiting embalming as soon as Agent Whitaker notified the man's family in Maryland of his death and informed his superiors in Washington.

Roy Woods surveyed events in the emergency room with a bit of detachment, keeping an eye on Rufus even though he was cuffed to the frame of the hospital bed. Roy had seen plenty of grisly death during his career as a Ranger—it wasn't a job for men with queasy stomachs like young Deputy Cobb, who continued to vomit just outside the emergency-room doors after helping to carry his friend Frank Miller to the hospital. Woods and Whitaker had been left with the task of loading Rufus and Clyde and the bodies of Tom Simmons and the unidentified owner of the tommy gun into the back of the Jeffreys' truck. Almost as an afterthought, Roy put the carcass of the dog in the truck bed too, while Whitaker smashed jars and jugs of moonshine and shot bullet holes in the still with his .38. Now, as Roy sat beside Whitaker, each of them covered with dried blood, they were talking quietly about events at Brownsboro as dawn grayed the skies beyond the east windows. Roy held a message in one hand, given to him by Smith County Sheriff Wayne Crider a moment ago when he'd arrived at the hospital to see what the ruckus was about.

"Cap'n Ross sent a Ranger to investigate a murder, so this note says, an' he found more'n he bargained for, a connection to the gangsters you talked about. Ranger Garrett thinks he's onto somethin' tied to that Santini feller. To tell the truth, I don't know much of anything about Santini or his truckin' outfit. We got our hands full in my district with killin's right an' left, and stolen oilfield equipment. There's more thieves an' murderers around Longview than you can shake a stick at, an' I ain't quite convinced Sheriff Bass or the chief of police give much of a damn about some of it."

Whitaker waited until Deputy Cobb quieted another attack of dry heaves outside before he spoke. He wiped his glasses on his shirtsleeve, frowning a little. "Do you think Bass and the local police are taking bribes to look the other way?"

Roy sighed. "Maybe. They wouldn't be the first crooked cops I met. Right now I'm only guessing. Lee Garrett will get to the bottom of it if Cap'n Ross lets him stay. I don't know Lee personally all that well, but he's one tough hombre, I hear. He's got a tall reputation with the Rangers as a good investigator, an' I've heard he's meaner'n hell in a fight. I'll call his hotel shortly. Maybe drive over an' see what he's found out. If you think this Santini is bootleggin' in Texas, maybe you oughta have a talk with Lee before you drive back to Houston."

Whitaker nodded. "I suppose that will be up to my superiors in Washington. Perhaps they'll listen to me now, when they find out Tom is dead. I've been asking for the authority to launch a full-scale investigation in Gregg and Harrison counties, but my requests were always denied. Tom believed the heart of moonshine production around here was Henderson County. The Jeffreys' still was discovered only recently and Tom believed there were several more close by. But now, with the Italian's corpse we brought in tonight as possible proof of a New York connection, I may get a bit more consideration for my request to investigate Santini's operations out of Longview."

Roy thought about Whitaker's suspicions. He had to admit that Whitaker was a hell of a lot smarter and tougher than he looked. "Just because you say the guy's Italian, it don't mean he's in with New York gangsters, does it? Ownin' a tommy gun don't make him one of Santini's boys necessarily. There's Italians in Houston an' Dallas who ain't connected to organized crime."

"It's a beginning," Whitaker replied, adjusting his glasses on his nose, glancing down at the bloodstains and dried mud all over his shirt and trousers. "The other Ranger you mentioned, Lee Garrett, must have some basis for taking a closer look at Carlos Santini's trucking operations. It would have been a help if the Italian had some identification on him; however, these gangsters are smart— they leave a hard trail to follow sometimes. But if you examine closely what we have, the dead man was wearing an expensive, custom-tailored suit and thirty-dollar shoes. He had a Thompson submachine gun and a forty-five automatic under his coat. He isn't some ordinary watchdog hired by the Jeffreys to stand guard over a moonshine still with enough automatic weapons to stop an army. The

Cadillac we found parked on that dirt road can be traced by its vehicle number and I have no doubts it will lead us to New York, or to Santini. The car belonged to the guy with the machine gun, or to someone he works for. We'll find that connection. I'm quite certain of it."

Roy looked over at Rufus. "That one knows, only he ain't gonna tell us a damn thing. I know his type pretty well. He's as tough as he sounds, I'll bet, an' his brother would have shot you dead if you hadn't shot him first. I'll question Rufe when the doctors get done with his leg before I take him to the Smith County jail." He paused for a moment, deciding against telling Brad Whitaker about how a few Rangers got their information. "Why don't you drive to your hotel an' get some rest, make your telephone calls to Washington an' such. I'll stay here so I can ask Rufe about the Italian, and the Cadillac."

"I need a bath," Whitaker said, examining his clothing again before he pushed out of the chair. "I'll contact your office this afternoon, after I grab a few hours of sleep." He looked at Rufus. "I don't expect him to tell you anything, but I suppose it's worth a try. The car may be our best lead. Good morning, Mr. Woods. It has been a long night for all of us."

Roy watched the Treasury agent saunter through the swinging door leading to the parking lot. He waited a few minutes more, then got up and walked into a narrow room where Rufus had been taken, still handcuffed to the bed. Two nurses were applying a plaster cast to his leg over gauze bandages. Roy spoke softly to one nurse.

"Leave me alone with him for a spell. I won't take long an' then you can finish what you're doin'."

Rufus studied Roy's face as the women were leaving.

"Close that door," Roy added over his shoulder, moving closer to the bed, listening for the door to shut behind him. He heard the click of the latchplate, then soft footsteps moving down the hallway.

"Who was that Italian with the submachine gun?" he asked, taking note of deep red marks on both of Rufus' wrists where he'd put the cuffs on a bit tighter than necessary.

"Fuck you, lawman," Rufus growled. "He was Irish. Blond hair an' blue eyes, or is you blind?"

"Where'd he get the tommy gun?"

"He got it for Christmas. Santa Claus brung it to him."

"He's Italian, Rufe. He *was* Italian. What he is now is real dead, deader'n pig shit, which is what you're liable to be if you don't tell me who he was."

"Fuck you, lawman. You ain't got the balls to shoot a man tied up. But I'll goddamn sure kill you if'n I get loose. I'll be out of jail before you can git home."

"Don't count on it," Roy said quietly, edging closer to the bed. He drew his .45 and cocked it. Very slowly, to give Rufus plenty of time to realize what he was doing, he turned the muzzle of his pistol downward and held it a few inches from Rufe's nose. "I'm gonna say you were tryin' to escape," he whispered, knowing the walls were very thin between examining rooms. "I'm gonna say you lunged at me, an' that one of your handcuffs wasn't locked shut. I'll tell 'em I didn't have no choice but to blow your goddamn brains all over that wall yonder, an' how sorry I am for makin' such a mess. You ever see a man's skull pop when a forty-five slug comes out the back of his head at real close range?" He waited for a moment. "It ain't a pretty sight, Rufe. There's blood, an' pieces of skullbone, an' hunks of hair all over the place. It makes this crackin' noise, like when you split a hunk of kindlin' wood for a fireplace."

Rufe's eyelids slitted, not with fear, but with hate. "I know you're bluffin', lawman. All you lawman are the same. You talk big, but you won't shoot no unarmed man."

Roy waited. Time and opportunity were on his side. "I'm different, Rufe," he said, moving the barrel of his

Colt until it touched Rufus' lips. "I never bluffed a man in my life. When I play poker, if I ain't got the cards, I toss 'em in. But when I got four aces, I bet 'em all the way to the hilt. An' what I've got right now is four aces. I can't lose. You see, I've done this before. There was this Meskin feller one time who said he wouldn't tell me what I wanted to know. I had him handcuffed to this big mesquite tree an' nobody was around. So I asked him one more time to tell me an' when he wouldn't, I blew his head off with this same gun I'm holdin' now. Made a hell of a mess. But I told my cap'n he was tryin' to escape. You know what the cap'n did? He gave me a commendation. Wrote it out on fancy parchment paper an' put a gold seal on it. I've got it on the wall of my office. Folks ask me about it all the time. It says I showed bravery in the line of duty, Rufe. An' I'm about to get myself another commendation right here unless you tell me who that guy with the tommy gun was." Pushing gently, Roy worked the muzzle of his .45 between Rufe's lips until the barrel touched his front teeth.

Rufus tried to wag his head away from the gun until Roy seized a fistful of his matted, shoulder-length hair.

"You can't go anyplace, Rufe," Roy whispered, "except all the way to hell when I pull this trigger. This is the last time I'm gonna ask you . . . who was the Italian, an' what was he doin' at your still last night? I promise not to ask no more questions. If you don't tell me what I want to hear, the next sound you're gonna hear is a click when this hammer falls. You won't hear a goddamn thing after that, an' that's a promise."

Rufe's arms trembled slightly and his eyes rounded. For a moment, he stared into Roy's face. "His name's Tony Bruno," he said, working his lips away from the Colt's barrel in order to speak. "He comes to count the shine. Takes us to a warehouse where me an' Clyde git paid."

"Who pays you?"

Rufe wagged his head despite Roy's grip on his hair. "Don't know his name. I swear."

"Where's this warehouse?"

"Longview."

"Where in Longview?"

"Down by the railroad tracks. Ain't no sign on it."

Roy thought for a moment. "This guy who pays you, is his name Carlos?"

"I swear I don't know."

"Is he Italian, like Bruno?"

"He's real dark. Curly black hair. How the hell should I know what Italians look like?"

Roy was about to ask more about the warehouse when he heard footsteps in the hall. He took his gun away from Rufe's mouth and gently lowered the hammer. "I may have more questions," he said quietly, holstering the pistol. "Later, an' you'd better not be lyin' to me."

The door opened. A doctor wearing a bloodstained apron gave Roy a questioning look when he saw him standing over Rufe's bed.

"One of my nurses told me you stopped them from putting on his cast," he said to Roy. "Why did you do that?"

"Questionin' a witness," Roy replied, turning so the doctor could see his badge. "Official business. It couldn't wait."

"He had his goddamn gun in my mouth, Doc!" Rufe shouted. "I didn't wanna answer no questions, only he swore he'd kill me if'n I didn't." He glared at Roy defiantly.

Roy gave the doctor a smile. "This man is under arrest for attempted murder and violation of the Prohibition Act. He may have killed a peace officer. He'd say anything to get rid of his handcuffs. As soon as that cast is on his leg, I'm takin' him to jail. He's a dangerous criminal who has to be watched closely."

"He's lyin'!" Rufus cried. "He had his gun right against my mouth . . . said he'd kill me."

Roy pointed to the plaster cast. "Have your nurses finish as quick as they can. If he keeps makin' too much noise like this so he disturbs the other patients, I'll put a gag over his mouth."

The doctor nodded solemnly. "The young sheriff's deputy, Mr. Miller, died from his wound a moment ago. The other patient you brought in will most certainly die as well. It is only a matter of time, in my opinion. His spine is broken and what is left of his spleen will not function. He's a very strong individual, but there is no hope of recovery, I'm afraid."

"You mean Clyde's gonna die?" Rufus asked, lifting his head off the pillow. He scowled. "The yellow sumbitch shot him in the back. Clyde never had no chance . . ."

Roy turned to Rufus and gave him a hard stare. "Two peace officers were killed last night by you and your brother. I aim to make sure you stand trial for murder." He gave the doctor a sideways glance. "Finish puttin' that cast on him. Don't worry too much about gettin' the bones set right, 'cause this man is headed for a death sentence anyway. A crooked leg bone won't be his biggest worry after he stands trial."

11

The next morning, Lee Garrett sat in a back booth at the City Café, watching the eatery's front windows for the arrival of Charley Waller at eight o'clock. He knew much more now, after talking to Cal, than he had when he first questioned Waller, even though Cal had been a bit evasive when he was pressed about Carlos. Scared was a better word for it; Cal didn't want to be known as a snitch or a stoolie.

Lee wondered if Waller was somehow tied to Santini. Or was Dodd's killing completely unrelated to Santini and his questionable operations? Running whores down from New York did not make Santini a murder suspect in the Dodd affair, yet several things were nagging some part of Lee's brain—why, for instance, he continued to feel that Dodd's murder had been a professional execution and not a simple robbery. A man by the name of C. W. Davis had recorded a lease on the same property as Dodd claimed, then a week later subleased it to Hunt Oil, making Davis, whoever he was, a prime suspect. And there was more: someone had to know that Dodd had the lease, someone had to order his execution, and the timing had to be perfect—before Dodd got his lease filed. It also seemed strange that Santini had followed him when he'd driven out to the Hawkins farm with Molly, although that may have been merely curiosity on Santini's part, to see what a Texas Ranger was doing in Longview nosing around at Maude's Place.

One thing was evident—Waller was the most likely person, other than Sara Dodd, to know the exact timing of the arrival of Dodd's lease on the day he was killed. Waller could easily have contacted the killer, or done the killing himself. Finding out if Waller was tied in any way to C. W. Davis was the first order of business, or if he had any connection with Hunt Oil, the ultimate winner if there was oil under the Hawkins land.

A clock behind the café's counter read five minutes to eight and Lee started to wonder if Charley Waller had skipped town when he learned he faced questions about Dodd's murder from a Ranger. Or was he only guessing when he suspected Waller was involved? There were too many loose ends at this point to make an educated guess, he decided. Sipping coffee, he watched the front windows, remembering Molly's pretty face. He was quite taken with her, he had to admit, despite knowing about her profession.

The café was almost empty. Oilfield workers started early and stayed late. It was demanding, backbreaking work, but the pay was high. In what was being called the "Great Depression," a record number of people were jobless and on relief. Should any oilfield worker refuse long hours, he would quickly be replaced by someone who needed money. It was rumored that Governor Sterling would impose martial law in the East Texas oilfields as a way of limiting production so as to keep crude oil prices high. If the governor restricted the number of barrels of oil a well could produce, it would eliminate more jobs. Texas banks continued to fail at an alarming rate, and Miriam Ferguson promised she would remedy a huge state deficit by allowing Texas oilmen to pump and sell as much oil as they could. It was a political war of words and promises no one fully understood, but in the Oil Patch, "Ma" Ferguson would be elected by a landslide. Until the election, martial law loomed as a real possibility in East Texas, and that would double the workload of the Rangers in the district.

Charley Waller walked up to the City Café's front door and peered through the glass before he came in. Dressed in khaki pants, suspenders, and a white shortsleeved shirt, he looked worried; nervous, Lee thought. He approached Lee's table with his hands shoved in his pants pockets, glancing around to see who might notice him there.

"I came like you wanted," he said, sliding into the booth. "But I already told you everything I know 'bout Bill. We was just friends, me an' him." Waller hadn't offered a handshake before he sat down. Beads of sweat glistened on his forehead, and his eyes flickered back and forth from Lee to the other patrons.

"I want to know what happened the day he was killed. All you remember . . . when you saw him, what he said, everything. I'd advise you not to hold anything back. This is an official investigation by the Texas Rangers and you'd better tell me the truth."

"I already told you. We knew each other from Beaumont an' was friendly. That's all. We drank coffee together. The day he got killed, I saw him an' he was all excited, like he'd struck the mother lode. Said he got his lease on the Hawkins place next to Hunt's big field. He said he'd never see another poor day an' he told me he'd arranged for drillers on a percentage. Bill didn't have no money left after he paid all the Hawkins heirs to sign for a piece of the action. That's the way it's done, in case you didn't know. The landowners take a piece of royalty income after you pay 'em a few dollars an acre for drillin' rights. Bill got everybody to sign an' got the lease back that afternoon, only the mail ran late that day an' he couldn't get to the courthouse to have it recorded until the next mornin'. He told me he was goin' out there to stake his first well an' put up his old driller's tent. That's the last I saw of him. Next morning I learned he was dead, shot through the head."

"Who is C. W. Davis?" Lee asked as Waller glanced over his shoulder to see if anyone was listening.

"That's Buster Davis. He's a lease peddler, like me, only he has close ties to H. L. Hunt. I heard he followed up on Bill's lease an' got signatures, paid the money, an' recorded a lease on the Hawkins farm after Bill got killed. Buster leased the place to Hunt."

"It took Davis only a few weeks to get his own lease on the Hawkins land. A week after that, it was subleased to

Hunt. Don't that strike you as being mighty quick to cash in on Dodd's work to track down the Hawkins heirs?"

"Not in this business," Waller said, perhaps too quickly if Lee was any judge. "Movin' fast in a hot oil patch is what makes a feller successful. You wait too long an' somebody else gets a shot at the land you want. There's a sayin', 'He who hesitates in the oil business is out of business.' "

Lee was certain Waller knew more. "Bill told you what time it was when the lease came in the mail?"

An involuntary twitch began in Waller's right eyelid. "I don't remember. Late that afternoon. Too late to get it to the courthouse. Said he was goin' in the mornin', first thing. He told me he wasn't gonna tell nobody about it until it was legal."

"But he told you."

"Me an' him was friends. I reckon he was about to bust a gut wantin' to tell somebody. He said he told his wife."

Lee recalled that Dodd had also told Molly. "Did you ever hear him mention a young prostitute by the name of Molly Brown?"

Waller swallowed. His eyelid continued to twitch. "He did talk about her some, before Sara came. He told me the whore was real pretty. Hell, a man gets natural urges now an' then."

"Have you ever had any business dealings with Buster Davis over an oil lease?"

The question made Waller visibly flinch, although he tried to control it quickly by rubbing his palms across his cheeks as a waitress arrived to take his order.

"Coffee, Charley?" she asked.

"Just coffee."

"You're out an' around kinda late this mornin', ain't you?" she asked, passing a glance across Lee's badge as she turned for the kitchen at the back.

He glared at her. "I ain't in no trouble, if that's what you're thinkin', Mildred. This Texas Ranger is askin' questions about Bill Dodd."

Mildred paused, gave Lee a frown, her freckled face etched by deep lines from too many hours in the sun. "Rumor is Bill got his hands on a valuable piece of oil property," she said, "but somebody killed him for the papers before he got it official. Nearly everybody liked Bill. Him an' Charley was in here together most every day for coffee. A speculator was what Bill called himself, only he never did have much luck. He drilled a bunch of dry holes—"

"Nobody asked you, Mildred," Charley snapped. "Go fetch my coffee so this Ranger can finish askin' me questions. I got lots of places I need to be this mornin'."

She wheeled for the kitchen and walked off, leaving Lee with the distinct impression that she knew more about Dodd. He made a mental note to talk to her later.

"Have you ever done business with Hunt Oil?" he asked.

Waller shrugged. "Some. Not enough to do me any good. Ol' H.L. is a tough trader. Won't pay a dime more than he thinks somethin's worth. He robbed Dad Joiner outa that big field on account of Dad was broke an' couldn't drill no more holes until he got his hands on some money. H.L. struck oil on the first hole he drilled out there. Dad was unlucky. I reckon the same can be said for Bill Dodd."

"Who would want him dead if he was so unlucky?"

Waller gave it a moment's thought. "It had to be somebody who knew he got that lease, I s'pose, unless he made some enemies over somethin' else. Maybe he owed somebody money. Money, or another man's woman, is usually the reason a man gets killed."

"Did he ever mention owing any money?"

Waller chuckled. "Bill couldn't get no credit. He didn't

own much of anything, some old furniture an' that beat-up Ford. He'd been down on his luck for quite a spell. A lease on that Hawkins land would have put him on Easy Street if there's oil under it, like Bill thought. Hunt's already got three drillin' rigs out there, so he must figure the same as Bill did. Oil's a hell of a lot like gold—it's where you find it. It's mostly luck an' Bill didn't have any. Those so-called geologists are wrong about half the time when they tell you where it's supposed to be. I'd rather be lucky. Some men are born with a knack for findin' it."

"Sounds like Bill Dodd's luck was about to change."

Waller wagged his head. "A man can't be called lucky if he gets killed before he can spend any of the money."

"I intend to find out who killed him, Mr. Waller."

Something about Lee's statement made Waller uncomfortable. He drummed his fingers on the tabletop as Mildred came with his coffee. She put it in front of him and left without a word.

"I've got no idea who might have done it," he said quietly. "Buster Davis was already a few steps behind Bill tryin' to get the Hawkins place. When the heirs got word Bill was dead, they done the natural thing—they signed with Buster. A dead man can't drill no wells or pay no royalties. Hellfire, that's the oil business."

"I suppose this Buster Davis told the heirs Bill was dead, so they'd sign his lease."

Waller's face developed a slight flush. "You'd have to ask Buster how he done it." He pushed his coffee aside, untouched. "Now, if you're done askin' me questions, I've got business out in the Patch. I've got to make a livin'."

"I guess that's all for now," Lee replied, knowing the time would come when he had more questions. He needed to learn more about Carlos Santini and Bill Dodd's personal affairs, including his financial status, before he went any further. He was hoping Ranger Roy Woods might shed some light on Santini's activities in Longview, and Buster

Davis needed to explain in detail how he got the lease on land Dodd had already leased but had not recorded.

Waller got out of the booth, obviously relieved. "You're wastin' your time," he said. "Bill coulda got killed for half a dozen reasons. Coulda been that whore he was so crazy about. I wouldn't put it past his wife to find herself a boyfriend who'd kill him for money. Sara ain't no white dove. She was a whore down around Beaumont when Bill married her. She's got some rough edges, so to speak. She might have found some ol' boy to shoot Bill for the mineral-rights paper he got. Don't never put it past a woman to do whatever it takes to get her hands on some money."

It was an angle Lee hadn't considered. "She's living in an old house over on Baker Lane. She doesn't show signs of having made any money off her husband's death."

Waller looked around again, worried that someone might hear what he was saying. "She might be smart enough to lay low for a while. Wait, until things die down. I never said she'd do it, mind you."

"But you think she could be capable of it?"

Waller adjusted his suspenders, licking his lips before he said any more. "A woman's liable to do most anything when big money is involved. But remember, I never said she'd do it. It was only an idea. She drinks a helluva lot an' spends time with some different characters."

"What do you mean by 'different characters'?"

"Men who stopped by from time to time when Bill was out of town. Now, I ain't sayin' she was up to nothin', but there was times when a Cadillac car was parked in front of the house when Bill was in West Texas talkin' to the heirs."

"Do you know whose it was?" Lee asked.

Waller shrugged again. "I'd see a strange car parked there every now an' then. Don't know whose it was."

"I think you know whose car it was. You've got some idea of who it belonged to."

"I'd be guessin', an' guessin' wrong can cause a man to go broke in the oil business. That's your job, to find out who owns the car I saw parked at Bill's."

"I'll look into it," Lee promised, forced to consider a new possibility, that Sara Dodd might have had her husband killed so she could own outright the fortune he was about to make. But if that were the case, why was she asking the Texas Rangers to look into her husband's death? There was another possibility—that she'd said something to the wrong person the day the lease came. "I'll probably have more questions for you later, Mr. Waller. Don't leave Longview unless you've talked to me."

"You mean you suspect me of killin' him? That's crazy." Waller turned on his heel and made for the front door in a fast walk. Lee watched him leave, wondering if the Cadillac that Waller saw might belong to someone connected to Carlos Santini.

12

He entered Sheriff Perry Bass's office shortly after nine in hopes of talking to Deputy Sam Dunlap and to ask the sheriff what he knew about Carlos Santini. Lee thought it might be revealing to see the sheriff's reaction to questions about Santini. There was a suggestion in what Cal told him that Bass was looking the other way when it came to Santini's illegal operations, and this usually meant that a peace officer was taking bribes or receiving a few special favors.

Deputy Tim Carter looked up when he came in. "Howdy, Ranger Garrett," he said. "I reckon you've come to talk to the sheriff about somethin'. I'll tell him you're here."

Lee tipped back his Stetson with a thumb and closed the door behind him. "I'd also like to talk to Sam Dunlap, if he's here."

"He ain't. He worked last night. He's on nights for the rest of the week." Carter got up and opened the sheriff's door without knocking. "Ranger Garrett here to see you," he said in a voice that could have hinted alarm.

There was a silence while Carter stood frozen peering around the door frame.

"Send him in."

Carter swung the door wide. When Lee entered the office, he noticed that Bass was hanging up his telephone.

"Have a seat," Bass said, inclining his head toward the wooden chairs across from his desk. "You find anything important havin' to do with the Dodd case?"

"A few things," Lee replied, settling into a seat. "I keep running across a name. Carlos Santini. He owns some trucking company here. Tell me what you know about him."

Bass's face did not register anything. He spread his palms and leaned back in his swivel chair. "He's from back East. New York or New Jersey. He runs a fleet of tank trucks haulin' crude to the railroad. Got big money behind him. Drives nice cars an' has more'n a dozen trucks. He wrangled contracts with Hunt an' a few others. He's got all the licenses required. That's about all I know."

"I keep hearing he may be involved in some crooked dealings. Gambling. Running whiskey, arranging for whores from the East Coast. The big money behind him is Gino Tatangelo, a gangster who's tied in with the labor unions. My boss, Captain Ross, called the FBI about Santini, but they say they don't have anything on him or his operations here. But when I ask around, I get the impression he's into more than hauling crude oil."

Bass frowned. "I never heard of no connection he's got with gangsters. What the hell does he have to do with Dodd's murder?"

"I'm not sure yet. It may be nothing. He's tied to a young prostitute who knew Dodd. Santini brought her down here to work at Maude's, along with several others."

The sheriff's frown deepened. "You ain't gonna crack down on Maude, are you? She runs a quiet place . . ."

Lee shook his head. "I'm not interested in the prostitution houses, Sheriff. But I intend to find out who killed Bill Dodd, and I keep coming up with ties to Santini between this girl Dodd was seeing at Maude's, and Dodd. I just wanted to know what you knew about him."

"He ain't broken any laws in Gregg County that I know of," Bass said. "He's only been here a year or two, but as far as I know, he runs a truckin' company. We've got our share of troubles with gamblin' and bootleggin', but moonshine is the sort of thing that can't be stopped. Men workin' around oil rigs are gonna be drinkin' an' lookin' for women. It's human nature. We ain't got enough jail cells to hold 'em all if we tried to arrest everybody who had a pint of shine or visited a whorehouse. You may not think I'm enforcin' the law to suit you, but we've got our hands full with fights an' theft of oilfield equipment an' civil papers to serve. Bein' a sheriff in an oil boom town ain't the easiest job. You gotta establish priorities."

"I understand," Lee said. "My only priority right now is to solve the Dodd killing, if I can. If gangsters are involved, I'll get to the bottom of it. As soon as Roy Woods gets back to Tyler, I'll ask him what he knows about Santini. In the meantime, I'd like to talk to your deputy, Sam Dunlap, about what he found when he went out to the Hawkins place that night."

"Sam's probably asleep. He's workin' nights."

"If you'll give me his address I'll stop by this afternoon, after he's had some sleep. I need to talk to another man by the name of C. W. Davis. Can you tell me where I might find him this mornin'?"

"That's Buster," Bass replied, glancing up at the blades of his ceiling fan whirring softly above his desk. "He rents one of them shoebox offices out on Judson Road. What's Buster got to do with this?"

Lee thought a moment, wondering why Bass hadn't checked to see who recorded a lease on the same land Dodd was after. "He's the one who got a mineral rights agreement on the Hawkins farm a few weeks after Dodd was killed. If somebody wanted Dodd out of the way, it's a logical place to start, to question the man who got what Dodd was after."

"Buster ain't no killer," Bass protested. "He's a speculator, like a bunch of men in this town. He buys leases and then subleases them to drillin' companies. I'd nearly take an oath he wouldn't shoot nobody to get what he wanted. A real likable guy who don't cause no trouble."

"He may have told someone else about Dodd's lease," Lee said matter-of-factly. "I aim to ask him a few questions."

Bass made a face. "Out Judson Road, on the left. I think you're wastin' your time, but it's on the left, a little wooden buildin' sittin' up on blocks for when it rains. The road ain't been graveled yet, so when it rains it's damn near a swamp."

"I'll find it. Tell me where Dunlap lives, and where Carlos Santini's trucking company is." He got out of his chair slowly. "There's a speculator by the name of Charley Waller who knew Dodd pretty well. Do you know him?"

It was only a guess, but Lee thought he saw something touch a nerve when he asked about Waller. The sheriff rocked forward in his chair. "I've heard of him, seems like. Can't remember why the name sounds so familiar just now." He stared into Lee's eyes a bit too long. "You suspect him of murderin' Dodd?"

"I haven't got a suspect yet. All I'm doin' is asking a few questions. I'd be obliged if you have those addresses for Dunlap and Santini."

"Ask Tim at the front desk. He'll call Sam's wife an' tell him you're comin' over. Santini's office is down by the rail yard beside the tracks. You'll see the sign. It ain't all that far from Maude's." Bass toyed with a fountain pen on his desktop and seemed preoccupied. "I never knowed of the Rangers gettin' so caught up in one murder investigation. Dodd wasn't nobody. He was flat broke, a drifter, movin' from one oil patch to the next without a dime to his name. What's so all-fired important about findin' who put a bullet through his head?"

The question was a surprise, coming from a man elected by Gregg County citizens and sworn to uphold the law. Could a peace officer become so callous he ignored a murder? "I guess it's still important to me to find out who's responsible for a killing, Sheriff. If I ever get to the point where that sort of thing doesn't matter to me, I'll quit and take up another line of work."

"But Dodd wasn't no ordinary citizen. Oilfields are full of his kind. They're like vultures, waitin' on a limb for some way to feed off somebody else's money. They don't pay no local taxes, an' they can't vote on account of they don't live in one place long enough to be a registered voter payin' poll taxes. They come an' go, and nobody misses 'em after they're gone. They clutter up a decent town. Hell, we've got hundreds of 'em here in Longview right now, livin' off profits from oil under Gregg County land. It don't seem fair to our taxpayers to spend our time lookin' for the bastard who killed somebody like Dodd. Decent citizens make their homes here. We gotta protect 'em from the riff-raff who follow these oil rigs from town to town. Bill Dodd was a nobody who made a profit off somebody else's oil. I never figured the Texas Rangers would spend so much time tryin' to find out who killed him. And now you tell me you intend to investigate the Santini Truckin' Company, a legitimate business that pays taxes an' license fees, because you think Carlos Santini may have known a whore Dodd associated with before his wife moved to town. It just don't make any sense . . ."

Lee was beginning to feel a strong dislike for Perry Bass. "I have reason to believe Santini may be looking for a foothold in Texas for a crime organization back East. My captain said Santini works for it. The two may not be tied together, Dodd's murder and Santini, but while I'm here, I aim to find out what Santini is really up to. It may be nothing. Call it a hunch, when things appear to point in the same direction."

"Roy Woods don't go off on wild-goose chases," Bass said in a flat voice. "Me an' Roy are pretty good friends. When you get a chance to talk to Roy, he'll set you straight on a few things. We work together when there's somethin' important to investigate. I ain't sayin' we won't cooperate with you, Mr. Garrett, but we damn sure won't waste any of our time lookin' for whoever killed Dodd. Truth is, I don't much care."

Lee's temper flared, then he caught himself. "I'd planned all along to handle it without any help, Sheriff. You've made it real plain you aren't interested in finding the killer. Like you said, Dodd wasn't anybody important and there may be nothing to the fact that Santini knew the same girl at Maude's. I'll poke around a bit. I s'pose I'm just doing a little guesswork. After I talk to Sam Dunlap and Davis, there may be nothing but dead ends and no solid leads to follow." He walked out without saying any more, halting at Deputy Carter's desk. "Give me Sam Dunlap's address and some general directions to his house. I'll drop by there this afternoon."

Carter gave him what he wanted while Lee's mind was elsewhere, on his growing suspicion that Perry Bass wanted the Dodd affair put to rest for private reasons. Bass had been too quick to dismiss the possibility that Carlos Santini was involved in business other than trucking. Bass wanted the Texas Rangers out of Longview.

He walked out and climbed in his Packard. He was already sweating in the muggy heat. "The smell of shit's gettin' stronger," he said to himself as he backed out of a parking space in front of the courthouse.

A sign read DAVIS OIL COMPANY above a clapboard office on Judson Street. Rows of similar offices lined the deeply rutted dirt road. Cars — many of them newer luxury models, Cadillacs and Oldsmobiles and the like — were parked in front of most buildings. It was readily apparent that money was being made on Judson Street.

He stopped in front of Davis's office and got out, taking note of a dark blue Cadillac parked beside the building. Davis is doing well enough to afford an expensive car, he thought. A tiny front porch below a slanted tin roof creaked under his feet when he went to the door. A few cars navigated the chugholes and ruts on Judson, sending up clouds of dust as he let himself in.

A balding man with a ruddy complexion looked up from a desk beside an open window. Stacks of papers fluttered on his desktop in the gentle breezes flowing through the window. Paperweights kept the piles from blowing away.

"Are you C. W. Davis?" Lee asked, noting that the man's eyes lingered on his Ranger badge.

"I'm Buster. I see you're a lawman an' if this has anything to do with those stolen drill stems, I already told the deputy who came out yesterday I can't find the goddamn receipt. I ordered 'em from Hughes Tool down in Houston. Sold 'em to Wilson on the very same day . . ." He quieted when Lee held up a hand.

"I'm not investigating a theft, Mr. Davis. I'm Lee Garrett and I'm with the Texas Rangers. I've got some questions for you concerning the Hawkins land and the murder of William Dodd." He closed the door behind him.

Davis's red complexion got darker. He had loose, sagging cheeks and thick lips, and appeared to be about forty years of age, Lee judged. At the mention of Dodd's name, his eyes flickered. "I barely knew Dodd, just enough to say howdy. Folks said he was jinxed, that he always dug dry holes. How come you're askin' me about him?"

Davis hadn't offered Lee a chair, and the little office was hot and stuffy. "I know you leased the Hawkins place a few weeks after Dodd was shot. Dodd supposedly had a mineral-rights agreement signed by all the heirs, but he didn't live long enough to record it. Seems odd that somebody came up with another lease so soon after Dodd was killed."

"I was after that property myself at nearly the same time," Davis said. "I followed up on all the heirs from deed records a week or so after Dodd started chasin' them down. It's the oil business, a coincidence, that we happened to be after the same property. Every speculator in Longview is lookin' for a lease with promise . . ." He was interrupted when a telephone on his desk began ringing. Davis glanced at it and took the earphone off its cradle hook, shouting "Hello!" into the mouthpiece as though he knew whoever was at the other end would have trouble hearing him.

Lee's gaze wandered around the office. Modest furniture, a few dusty photographs of oil derricks on the walls. Overflowing ashtrays on a rickety table between two wooden chairs and on the desktop. The scent of old cigar smoke lingering in the hot, humid air.

"I'm busy right now!" Davis cried. "I'll call you back in a few minutes!" He hung up the phone and looked at Lee.

"Like I was sayin', it's a coincidence I was after the Hawkins place. It was Dodd's misfortune to have a lease he never recorded. I read in the newspaper that he was killed at night out on the property. Don't it sound kinda strange he was out there at night before he ever got the document in the county record books?"

"I haven't talked to the deputy who found him. Maybe he was killed somewhere else and his body was dumped there. I'm getting all the facts right now, everything I can find out. I wanted to know if you knew him, and how it happened you acquired the same mineral rights so soon after he died."

"I already told you I hardly knew him at all, an' that it's pure coincidence we were after the same property. It adjoins the biggest oilfield in this county an' it's only natural speculators went after it. It's the business."

"And now Hunt Oil has it. You subleased it to Hunt."

"That's correct. H. L. Hunt is the biggest operator in this part of the state. Dad Joiner's lease is pumpin' more oil than anybody ever dreamed. It's the same as findin' gold, only this is black gold. I contacted Hunt as soon as I got my lease recorded. He made me a generous offer. I didn't commit no crime by makin' a profit."

Lee wondered if Davis's crime was murder, enabling him to make his profit. "Can you prove your whereabouts on the night Dodd was killed?"

Davis's eyelids fluttered. "You mean I'm a suspect?"

"Right now everybody connected in any way to Bill Dodd or that piece of property is a suspect, Mr. Davis. I'll ask you again . . . can you establish where you were that night?"

"I don't remember exactly what night it was. That was weeks ago. You can't really be thinkin' I'd kill a man over a damn oil lease, do you?"

"It was the night of June twenty-third. His body was

found the next morning. I need to know where you were that night."

Davis was clearly frightened now—his face paled despite his ruddy coloring. "I'd have to think back, only I'm sure I was at home with my wife. She'll vouch for me. I'd nearly swear I was home in bed that night, unless I happened to be out of town."

Lee was sure Davis was hiding something. He might not have been the killer himself, but he knew more than he was willing to say.

13

"Message for you at the desk," Cal said as Lee walked into the hotel lobby. "Miz Williams took the call."

He nodded his thanks, watching Cal pop a shoeshine rag on a pair of brown shoes belonging to an elderly man in a suit and necktie reading the *Tyler Herald*. The smell of polish mingled with the lobby's musty odor. Behind the registration desk, Ruth Williams smiled at him.

"A telephone call came for you a little over an hour ago, Mr. Garrett," she said, handing him a note. "It was a terrible connection. I wrote it down the best I could."

He read what was on the paper, that Ranger Roy Woods would be arriving in Longview this afternoon and leave word at the hotel where Lee could find him. A man by the name of Whitaker would be joining them. Lee frowned when he read the unfamiliar name, wondering who Whitaker was and if he had information about Santini, or Bill Dodd.

"Thanks," he said, folding the note into his shirt pocket as he turned for the front doors again. He'd been hoping for word from Captain Ross, more information concerning Santini and his connection to the New York gangster, Tatangelo. Bob Ross was good at worming information out of his sources. He wasn't above applying pressure or implying that a favor would be returned at some future date. But New York was a world apart from the kind of law enforcement handled by the Texas Rangers and Lee wondered if Bob would get anything from the New York police or a federal agency like the FBI. There had been newspaper stories of gang killings among rival gangs in the East. Federal agents were trying to break up bootlegging operations in the bigger East Coast cities and according to the papers, it was turning into a war where the gangsters outnumbered the police. Lee wondered if Carlos Santini had been sent down to Texas where pickings were easier, where there was less likelihood of having trouble with the law.

He climbed in his Packard and drove toward the City Café for lunch. He had Sam Dunlap's address in a notepad he carried in the glove compartment. It was unlikely that the deputy could give him anything useful, but at this point, with his investigation going nowhere, Lee was willing to chase down almost any scrap of information, any kind of lead.

Sam Dunlap wore a pair of faded denims and a T-shirt. He sat in his living room on an overstuffed easy chair while his wife, Edith, brought them glasses of lemonade. An oscillating fan hummed on a nearby table, making brief passes across the sofa where Lee sat, and Dunlap's chair.

"Thank you, ma'am," Lee said, taking a glass full of

lemonade with ice cubes in it. "This humidity sure melts a man in a hurry."

She smiled and gave her husband a glass. "It's been a dry year," she said. "Hardly any rain this spring, although the air is still wet enough to wilt a woman's hairdo soon as she steps outside."

"Leave us be, honey," Dunlap said. "Mr. Garrett needs to ask me about a murder." He ran fingers through his tousled, curly brown hair and rubbed sleep from his eyes. He spoke to Lee when Edith left the room. "It's so hot a feller can't hardly get no sleep durin' the daytime. That's the trouble with workin' nights in summer. Can't nobody sleep in this heat."

Lee took a sip of lemonade. Dunlap looked to be thirty-five or so. He seemed typical of the rural county deputies Lee had known, honest men for the most part who sought the security of a government job. They were given little training in investigative methods or Texas law. They kept the peace by breaking up fights and tracking down thieves, serving civil summonses or divorce papers, and were rarely ever asked to solve any serious crimes lacking eye-witness testimony or ironclad evidence of guilt.

"Tell me what you remember about finding William Dodd's body on the morning of June twenty-fourth," Lee began. "Try to recall every detail . . . what you saw. I read your report, but I wanted to talk to you personally to see if there might be anything else."

Dunlap rubbed the dark stubble on his chin. "The office got a call early in the mornin' from his wife, sayin' he hadn't come home, that he went out to the Hawkins place, where he was gonna be drillin' for oil. When I got there, I found him lyin' on his back right close to his old Ford. I seen he was dead right away. He had a bullet hole in the middle of his forehead. The back of his skull got blowed away. Whoever shot him was at real close range. Maybe it was somebody he knew, to let 'em get that close, or it could be it was so dark he couldn't see who it was until he got too close to run off. There was another set of tire tracks on the dirt lane runnin' into the place. Ain't nobody lived there in twenty years. House burned down, somebody told me, an' the family moved off. It ain't much of a farm.

"But there was that set of tire tracks. Real fresh too, so I figure the guy came in a car an' parked right beside Dodd's before he killed him. His wallet was empty of money so it could have been a robbery, only Dodd was broke an' the killer couldn't've got much. There was a bill of goods from a supply company with his name on it an' that's how I knew it was Dodd. Not much else I can tell you. I called for the meat wagon an' let the county boys haul him off about daybreak."

"Did you talk to Dodd's widow?"

"Sure did. Part of the job. I told her we found him dead an' that I was real sorry. She took it pretty good."

"How's that?"

"She didn't cry or nothin'. She shook her head an' closed the door, like she wanted to be alone."

"She didn't ask any questions?"

Dunlap thought for a moment. "I told her he got shot, an' the best I remember, she didn't ask me anything after that. Some of the women cry an' yell an' carry on when they lose a husband. If I remember right, she didn't say another word, just shut the door in my face."

"Did Sheriff Bass order an investigation?"

"He said to ask around to see if Dodd had any enemies or if he owed anybody money. I talked to a few folks an' hardly a soul knew Dodd. He was from Beaumont or Gladys City, I think. Hadn't been here long."

"He was seeing a prostitute over at Maude's. Did you ask her any questions?"

"Never knew about that. Nobody told me."

Lee phrased his next question carefully. "Was William

Dodd ever involved with a man by the name of Carlos Santini?"

"Not that I know of," Dunlap replied. "Santini hauls crude to the railroad. Dodd never had any oil to haul. Dodd was what some folks call 'a player'. He hung around the oilfields tryin' to make big deals, only he didn't have any money. The big boys like Hunt laughed him off, but when he got his hands on the Hawkins place, he was right next to the hottest oilfield in this part of the state. His widow claims he was killed on account of it, that he was shot to keep him from recordin' his lease."

"Is that what you think?"

Dunlap hesitated. "I was gonna look into it, only Sheriff Bass said to let it drop, that we had more important business to tend to. We've got unsolved cases all over Gregg County. Perry said it was just another Oil Patch killin' an' not to spend time on it."

"Do you know C. W. Davis?"

"You mean Buster Davis?"

"He's the one who got a recorded lease on that property only a few weeks after Dodd was killed. He subleased it to Hunt Oil."

"I didn't know. I wrote up my report an' gave it to Perry. He said to forget about it after I couldn't find anybody Dodd owed money to or learn if he had any enemies. It was like Dodd bein' killed didn't matter all that much."

Curious, Lee thought, that Sheriff Bass was so quick to let it drop. "Are Sheriff Bass and Buster Davis friends?"

For the first time, Dunlap seemed a bit uncomfortable. "I wouldn't call 'em friends. They know each other."

"How about Charley Waller? Is Waller a friend of Sheriff Bass?"

"I ain't really all that well acquainted with him. Charley is another player, a small-time hustler who gets a lease every now an' then. Him an' Dodd were friends, but Charley said Dodd didn't owe him any money."

"Were they close friends? Close enough so that Dodd would tell Waller about the Hawkins lease?"

"Hard to say. I didn't know Dodd an' I only know Charley by sight. We never had any trouble from either one of 'em."

Lee wondered why Dunlap was reluctant to talk about Buster Davis and the sheriff freely, but he decided to let it drop for now. "I hear rumors that Santini may be involved in gambling or bootlegging. I've already established that he has ties to prostitutes at Maude's and that the big money behind him is a New York gangster named Gino Tatangelo. Have you ever suspected Santini might be in something other than trucking crude oil?"

Again a hesitation, and Dunlap's gaze wandered to a window. "I may have wondered about it a time or two. He showed up here in Longview about two years ago with a fleet of big Autocar tank trucks. Leased an office an' a yard down by the tracks. He had big cars an' plenty of money to spread around. All his drivers are from back East someplace, Italians, just like him. They don't associate with local folks much. Stay off to themselves, the drivers do, but they don't get in any trouble an' Santini is a loner. You hardly ever see him outside his office."

"Has Sheriff Bass ever mentioned that he suspected Santini of anything?"

Dunlap wagged his head. "Hardly ever talks about him at all around me. We've got a heavy backlog of cases an' we stay pretty busy most of the time. Stealin' oilfield equipment is mighty big business these days. Drillin' companies hire their own guards to watch valuable stuff. So it don't seem out of the ordinary that Perry wouldn't talk about Santini. Him an' his men don't cause us no trouble at all."

Lee glanced at his knuckles, recalling a meeting with one of Hunt Oil Company's private guards. "The only lead I've got is a tie between a young prostitute and Dodd, a girl

Santini brought down from New York. Then there's Buster Davis, who got a lease on the Hawkins place right after Dodd was killed. It's not much to go on."

Dunlap thought for a minute, sipping his lemonade. "One thing I didn't tell you. Dodd's ol' car was torn up inside like somebody was lookin' for somethin'. Maybe it was that lease. Dodd's wife said she never saw it again after it came in the mail the day he was killed. That was when she came down to complain that Sheriff Bass wasn't doin' a damn thing to find out who killed her husband."

"The lease was worthless if it wasn't recorded. But it's interesting that Dodd's car looked like it was searched. Maybe the killer wanted to be sure the lease never turned up. Could be he found it in Dodd's car and destroyed it. Dodd might have hidden it someplace in his Ford."

"Or you figure the guy was lookin' for money or anything he could sell, if it was just a robbery."

Lee watched the fan sweep toward him and awaited a breath of moving air in the stifling-hot room. "I'm pretty sure it wasn't an ordinary robbery for what Dodd had in his pockets. He was killed to prevent him from recording those mineral rights. I'll keep on digging. Thanks for your time, Deputy. I may have another question or two later on." He put down his glass and got up with his hat in his hands. His mother never allowed menfolk in the Garrett family to wear a hat in a proper house.

Dunlap stood up and offered his hand. "Best of luck, Mr. Garrett. Let me know if I can help." He walked with Lee to the front door and went out on the porch, closing the door behind him carefully. "I didn't want to say nothin' in front of my wife," he added, speaking softly, "but you may be onto somethin' if you look close at Santini. I've got no idea how he'd be connected to killin' Dodd, but there's some strange things goin' on down at his place. Every now an' then a couple of big black Cadillacs show up with New

Jersey license plates, an' right after that, a truck comes to his warehouse. We don't ask no questions because as far as we know, there ain't a thing illegal about havin' a truck show up at a warehouse. But it happens late at night, like they don't want nobody to see 'em, an' they close the doors with that truck inside. When I asked Perry about it one time, he said to forget it, that Mr. Santini wasn't breakin' no laws. I'd sure appreciate it if you didn't say a word to Perry about what I just told you. I need my job, an' I got kids to raise."

"I won't say anything," Lee promised, thinking how right he was to sense that something was wrong with Santini's operations in Longview. A truck coming late at night, unloading behind closed doors, was worth looking into. "I appreciate you telling me about it." He put on his Stetson and went down the sagging steps to the brick sidewalk, feeling the July heat sweep past his face on a gust of westerly wind.

14

A message at the hotel desk informed Lee that Roy Woods was having a late lunch at the Longhorn Steak House on Marshall Avenue. He got directions from Ruth Williams and drove through the center of town slowly, finding the restaurant after a lengthy delay while he waited at a railroad crossing for a steam locomotive to pull a string of oil tank cars away from the city. Lee parked in a vacant space in front of the Longhorn and got out. He could see that the place was almost empty. It was past two-thirty and the lunch crowds were gone.

He recognized Woods from company meetings in Austin, where on occasion, all six Ranger companies from Houston, Dallas, Lubbock, Corpus Christi, Midland, and Waco assembled for briefings on new official policies and dire warnings that the legislature planned to have them incorporated into the structure of the Department of Public Safety, meaning the Highway Patrol, where their Ranger autonomy would be taken away. There had been plenty of complaining during the last meeting, Lee recalled vividly, and almost every Texas Ranger feared what would happen if Miriam Ferguson became governor again.

A slender man wearing glasses sat across from Woods in a rear booth. Woods was stocky, thick-muscled, and short at about five feet and six inches, weighing two hundred pounds. But he was said to be fearless, short-tempered, and a dead shot with a pistol. Some Rangers claimed he was growing more irritable as he neared fifty. He was widely known to hate the paperwork involved in arrests and investigations. His Dallas-based commander, Captain James MacDonald, was frequently in trouble at headquarters for Woods' inadequate, or missing, reports.

Woods stood up when he saw Lee. He offered his hand and said, "Good to see you again, Lee. This here's Brad Whitaker. He's with the Treasury Department. We've been down in Henderson County havin' a little disagreement with some moonshiners. I got the message from Cap'n Ross an' came over quick as I could. We didn't get much sleep last night."

Lee shook hands with Whitaker and slid into the booth beside him. A waitress came with a menu and he waved it away, saying "Nothing, ma'am." He looked at Woods. "Glad you could make it, Roy," he said. "Cap'n Ross looked into a few things for me regarding a murder investigation here in Longview. I keep running into a name—Carlos Santini. He runs a trucking outfit. He may not be involved in the murder at all, but there's something funny going on and I wondered what you knew about him."

"Didn't know much until yesterday," Woods replied, "but the Treasury Department believes he's involved in bootleggin' an' a few other pastimes. I'll let Agent Whitaker tell you what they know."

Whitaker spoke in a soft, controlled voice. "We can't prove a thing yet, but we know Santini is a front man for the Tatangelo crime family in New York and New Jersey. They're into everything—a big moonshine operation, prostitution, and bookmaking. They are usually in business in strong labor-union areas. They control most of the labor-union funds along the East Coast through rigged elections that put their men in powerful union offices. Texas is not a union state and thus it was strange that Carlos Santini set up operations here. Big money was the key, so much oil money in East Texas and so many men wanting liquor and women and gambling.

"As you must know, at the Treasury Department we are charged with enforcing the Prohibition Act, thus our efforts have been limited to breaking up bootlegging organizations. I reported my suspicions concerning Santini to my superiors in Washington, saying that I felt Santini was running liquor down here from somewhere on the East Coast and that he may be involved in other things. But my reports were ignored, until this morning. We learned a few more things about Santini, although at a terrible cost. A Treasury agent was killed, and a deputy sheriff. Two moonshiners are dead and one of them turned out to be some sort of armed escort for loads of moonshine headed for a warehouse in Longview, a man by the name of Tony Bruno, an Italian like Santini. We now believe the warehouse is Santini's. Ranger Woods extracted a confession from one of the moonshiners. He told Mr. Woods they trucked the liquor here to Longview, to a warehouse beside the railroad tracks."

Woods said, "Tony Bruno had a tommy gun. We found a black Cadillac parked on a dirt road not far from the still and Agent Whitaker believes the registration will lead to Santini, or to Gino Tatangelo."

Lee digested everything quickly. "It all fits with what I found out. Santini furnishes prostitutes for a whorehouse here and at least some of the women come from New York. I heard rumors that he runs gambling tents floating around the oilfields here, and that he also deals in liquor. A Gregg County deputy told me that late at night a truck comes to Santini's warehouse, pulling inside. They shut the doors. He said something about seeing Cadillac cars on the same nights, with New Jersey license plates. Cap'n Ross told me the FBI knows Santini is linked to Gino Tatangelo, but they told him they've got nothing on Santini running illegal booze or gambling tents or anything else. The cap'n doesn't believe it. He says the feds are likely to feed us bullshit when they're onto something."

"Your information sounds accurate," Whitaker said, toying with a fork across his empty plate. A slice of pecan pie sat untouched near his elbow.

"There hasn't been time to look into everything," Woods said in a weary manner. "I've got so many cases that I can't investigate 'em all. These goddamn roughnecks are either killin' each other or stealin' somethin' every night." He stared across the table at Lee for a moment. "What's the big deal about one lousy murder in Gregg County that they'd send you all the way from Waco?"

"The Dallas office is swamped, Cap'n Ross told me. I got the job because he said I needed a rest. We busted up an automobile-theft ring last month in McLennan County an' I logged too many hours. He sent me out here for a vacation, he said." Lee thought about something Woods said. "You mentioned trouble in Gregg County. What's your opinion of the sheriff, Perry Bass?"

Woods let his gaze roam to a window, watching the cars

pass on Marshall Avenue. "He's not much different from any other elected official. Tryin' to please important folks here, not wantin' to step on any toes. He turns a blind eye to prostitution so long as it don't make headlines in the newspapers. He's a politician, not a peace officer. He don't make waves in the wrong circles."

"I think he knows what Santini is up to," Lee said. "He may be taking money under the table to look the other way. He didn't investigate the murder of William Dodd, and that worries me. It's like he wanted it to go away without any fuss. He gave me a weak excuse, that Dodd was oilfield trash who didn't pay local taxes or register to vote. But I've got a feeling there's more behind what happened to Dodd. It's just a hunch. A young prostitute is involved. She came to Longview through Santini. She works at Maude's, beside the railroad tracks, and she told me she was sent down here by Gino Tatangelo. She knew Dodd and knew about a big oil lease he'd secured. The day Dodd got it, he was killed, before he could record it in the county records. A speculator named C. W. Davis recorded a lease on the same property a few weeks later, and the whole thing stinks. Sheriff Bass doesn't seem the slightest bit interested. He told the investigating deputy not to spend much time on it, to forget about it, that Dodd was nobody important."

Woods drummed his fingers beside his plate. "Perry Bass has always cooperated with me when I asked him for anythin'. But it does sound like he knows somethin' he ain't talkin' about. The chief of city police is Howard Laster. We can talk to him. He may know more about Santini an' what happened to this Dodd feller the night he got killed. It's worth a try. Laster is appointed by the City Council, so he ain't as worried about losin' his job as Perry Bass is. Maybe Laster will talk." He gave Lee a questioning look. "You figure this C. W. Davis is behind it somehow?"

Lee could only shrug. "I've got no idea. I talked to him, but he didn't give me much. He got nervous when I started asking questions about Santini."

"A number of local people fear Santini," Whitaker added. "When I tried to ask about him a few months ago, everyone was evasive or claimed not to know him at all. It seemed out of the ordinary for so many citizens to be unwilling to discuss him."

Woods sighed, looking impatient. "Let's go have a talk with Mr. Santini. I didn't drive thirty-five miles from Tyler to be pussyfootin' around. We'll search his warehouse an' see if he's got any shine."

"We'll need a search warrant," Whitaker said. "That may take some time."

"Like hell we will," Woods snapped. "We just walk in there an' start lookin' around. If he gives us any trouble, we'll put him under arrest. I'll take him for a ride in the country . . ."

Whitaker blinked, as though he couldn't quite believe what Woods said. "There are laws, Mr. Woods. You can't arrest him unless he's broken the law, and we can't legally search his place without a warrant."

Woods glared at Whitaker. "This is Texas. We do things a little different here. A Texas Ranger can go wherever he damn well pleases, an' if some son of a bitch don't cooperate, we put him in jail. I'll say he took a swing at me, or tried to pull a gun, assaultin' an officer of the law."

"But what if there are witnesses?" Whitaker asked, "and what if he doesn't have a gun?"

Woods smiled crookedly. "I carry a revolver in the glove compartment with the numbers filed off just in case somethin' like that happens. As to there bein' witnesses, I'll arrest 'em too, as accomplices. Leave the details to me."

"I don't believe I want any part of an illegal search like

this," Whitaker said. "I'll find a judge and ask him to give us a warrant."

"By the time you get one, me an' Lee will have already made a thorough search of the place," Woods promised, anger in his voice growing. "Right, Lee?"

When Lee felt Woods staring at him, he became uncomfortable. "We can question him while Agent Whitaker is getting a warrant, if that's what it takes to satisfy him. We don't need any official reason to question Santini other than suspicion."

"What we don't need is a goddamn warrant," Woods said hotly, and now his cheeks held a trace of color. "Let's drive to that warehouse. If Agent Whitaker here thinks he needs a piece of paper to make things proper, then let him go get it." He slid out of the booth and picked up his check, resting one callused hand on the butt of a Colt .45 automatic.

Woods scowled when he read the cost of their lunch. "You can damn sure tell this is oil country," he said, still sounding mad. "A goddamn steak costs twice as much here. You'd never be able to convince folks we're in the middle of a depression by the price of beef." He started for the cash register when Lee and Whitaker got up, still muttering under his breath. "A farmer gets fifteen cents a pound for a steer an' this joint charges me a fortune for one burnt slice of it."

Lee knew Woods was still angry over the suggestion they needed a warrant to search Santini's warehouse. Roy Woods was from the old school of lawmen, from a time when you did whatever it took to stop a crook, even if you bent the law a little. Lee had known some old-timers like him, men who rode horses and slept on the ground when pursuing criminals in the days before automobiles. They were hard-bitten types with a single purpose—arresting the men they were after. Most of their breed were retired now. Woods was caught in the middle, where an old generation gave way to newer methods.

"We'll take my car," Lee said when he glanced at the Ford coupe with state license plates parked out front, a car with dents and scratches marring its dark green paint. "Cap'n Ross got me a Packard this time an' it sure as hell has a soft ride."

Woods nodded assent as Agent Whitaker headed for a shiny new Studebaker. Whitaker spoke over his shoulder. "I'll locate a judge and bring a search warrant," he said, climbing quickly into his car.

"It won't be because we need one," Woods spat, wheeling for the passenger door of Lee's Packard, although Whitaker couldn't hear him above the roar of his engine as he backed away from the curb.

Woods slammed the door after he got in. "Goddamn feds have to do everythin' by the fuckin' book," he said. "It's no wonder the crooks are takin' over back East."

Lee started the car. "Times are beginning to change, Roy. I keep hearing that the legislature wants to put us under the Department of Public Safety. That happens, we'll have more regulations to follow than a man can shake a stick at."

Woods' face reflected his gloom as they drove away from the curb. "I've already got so goddamn much paperwork to do as it is, an' this job don't pay enough for me to do a damn bit more. I'll quit if they dump any more shit on my desk."

Lee said nothing, even though he felt much the same way when it came to reports. "All right, show me where Santini's warehouse is. I'm barely able to find my way around this town."

"Turn left at the next stop sign, then go straight 'til we come to the railroad tracks. It's down a ways on the right." As Woods spoke, he drew his .45 and worked a cartridge into the firing chamber, letting the hammer down gently before he holstered the weapon. He cast a curious glance across the car. "Where the hell's your gun, Lee?"

"I keep it under the seat most times."

"Strap it on," Woods said, like it was an order. "I want this Italian to know we mean business."

15

A rambling wooden warehouse bearing a sign, SANTINI TRUCKING, above the office door, sat close to a railroad siding. Two trucks coupled to tank trailers stood in a yard west of the warehouse, each with a similar sign painted on its doors. A gasoline pump was being cranked by a heavy-shouldered man in greasy khaki pants and shirt as he filled one of the truck's saddle tanks. Santini's warehouse was among rows of similar buildings along the tracks, some bearing signs, others nameless, looking vacant.

Lee stopped in front of the office and got out, noticing a black Dodge sedan and a blue Oldsmobile parked near the entrance. He knew the Dodge . . . it was the one Santini had used when he'd followed them to the Hawkins farm. To satisfy Woods, he removed his holster from under the car seat and buckled his gun on.

Woods swung his feet to the ground and stood up, giving the place a careful appraisal. "This buildin' could be plumb full of whiskey," he said. He shut the door and added, "No tellin' what else."

Lee came around the Packard, noting how closely the worker who was pumping gasoline was watching them. "That guy over there sees our guns and badges, Roy. He doesn't look happy we're here."

"Makes two of us. I don't like the looks of him either. If he heads for the office, I'll order him to mind his own goddamn business. I ain't in the mood to be pushed today." As an afterthought, he asked, "You got a shotgun in your trunk?"

"We won't need it," Lee assured him. "Santini isn't gonna be crazy enough to start any trouble in broad daylight, even if he is a gangster type. Let's go inside and see what he has to say about the bootlegger's confession you got last night. If he squirms, we'll know for sure we're onto something."

"I'll tell him we're gonna have a look around," Woods said. He reached the door first and started inside.

A man seated behind a mahogany desk looked up with a telephone held to his ear. He had dark curly hair and a hawk-beak nose, big hands, and a powerful chest straining the fabric of a white dress shirt open at the neck. Another man sat on a sofa across the tiny office, where an electric fan blew on his pockmarked face. The man on the telephone was big, but the other was even larger, with a protruding belly hanging over the waistband of brown dress slacks. He got up quickly when Lee and Woods walked in, an angry expression hooding his eyes as he drew his lips wide across clenched teeth.

"Don't you boys got any manners?" he demanded, taking a few steps toward them. "You ever hear of knocking on somebody's door before you bust in?" His gaze dropped to the guns Lee and Woods were wearing, then to their badges.

Woods squared himself and jutted his jaw, one hand resting on the butt of his gun. "We ain't gotta knock on nobody's damn door, mister," he growled, raising a warning finger in the big man's face, halting him in mid stride halfway across the office floor. "Sit back down an' shut your goddamn mouth or I'll put you under arrest for interferin' with an officer of the law. I ain't gonna warn you but once. Sit down an' shut your fuckin' mouth or you'll spend a few days in jail."

"It's okay, Paulie," the man holding the telephone said quietly. "Do as the gentleman asks. I assume these men are Texas Rangers."

Lee saw the bulge of a pistol under Paulie's shirt, hidden behind his back. "He's got a gun, Roy. It's behind him, stuck in his pants." Lee moved his right palm until it sat atop his pistol grips, but he kept his eyes on the man he knew to be Carlos Santini, sitting behind the desk. He could see both of Santini's hands and no weapon was in sight.

"I'll take his gun," Woods said evenly, drawing his .45 in a slow, deliberate motion. "Turn around. I'm gonna disarm you for now, while we're askin' questions." He aimed his Colt at Paulie and demanded again, "Turn around."

"Is all this really necessary?" Santini asked. "This is my private office. I'm a legitimate businessman."

While Lee was keeping an eye on Santini, Woods moved to one side and jerked an automatic pistol from Paulie's waistband, his .45 aimed at Paulie's head.

"That's better," Woods said. "Now sit down like I told you so we can get on with this."

Paulie sat down on the sofa, anger smoldering in his dark brown eyes.

Woods looked to the man behind the desk. "Are you Carlos Santini?" he asked, holstering his Colt, tucking Paulie's pistol in the front of his pants.

"I am," Santini replied coolly, unruffled by drawn guns or the tone of Woods' question. He hung up his telephone without a word to whoever was on the other end of the line. "What sort of official business do you have with me?"

Lee wondered how Woods would begin. His methods thus far lacked even a suggestion of subtlety. The old-time Ranger came out in him when he got mad.

"I got a confession last night from a bootlegger named Rufus Jeffrey over at Brownsboro. He said he sold you moonshine. One of your boys got killed durin' the raid—name of Tony Bruno—an' we found his Cadillac. I'm bettin' the car can be traced to you, or to your boss, Gino Tatangelo." The antagonism in Woods' manner was clear—he was prodding Santini as hard as he could.

"You must be mistaken," Santini replied, his voice as calm as ever. "No one by that name has ever worked for me, and I am not in the liquor business. I haul crude oil, as you can plainly see. Buying or selling liquor is illegal, as you know."

"We were sure you'd deny it, Santini. Me an' Ranger Garrett will take a look in your warehouse, just to be sure you ain't had a memory loss."

"Do you have a warrant to search my place?"

"Don't need one," Woods said. "I never said we was gonna search it. Just have a look around."

"It's the same thing, and it's illegal without a warrant," Santini remarked, reaching for the telephone. "I'll have my lawyer here in a few minutes to stop you."

Color rose in Woods' cheeks. "There ain't a lawyer in the whole state of Texas who can stop us from havin' a look in that warehouse. Call your goddamn lawyer. In the meantime, me an' Mr. Garrett are gonna look inside. If you or this fat boy over on the sofa try to stop us, I'll arrest you. I'll handcuff both of you to the fender of that car outside 'til we're done."

"You won't find anything," Santini promised, still without showing any signs of anger or distress.

Woods forced a smile. "If that's the case, then what's all this fuss about callin' a lawyer?"

"What you are threatening to do is illegal. It's as simple as that. I know my rights under the law."

"A man who buys moonshine ain't got any rights," Woods said.

"You have to prove it," Santini replied. "That is why we have a court system. Someone must prove I've broken the law."

Lee decided it was time to intervene, and to stall for time while Agent Whitaker was getting a search warrant. "I also want to know about your dealings with William Dodd, the speculator who was killed last month." He didn't want to mention Molly Brown's name, fearing Santini might harm her. "I have reason to believe you knew Dodd and had dealings with him."

"I never heard of him," Santini answered flatly. "I read about it in the newspaper."

"An' you never bought any corn whiskey from Rufus or Clyde Jeffrey," Woods snapped sarcastically. "Tony Bruno was just some Italian guy wanderin' around in the woods with a tommy gun. You never heard of Gino Tatangelo either, an' all you're doin' in Longview is haulin' crude oil."

"That's correct," Santini said, relaxing his grip on the telephone, "except that I am acquainted with Mr. Tatangelo. We are from the same neighborhood in New York. He was an investor in my trucking firm until recently. I purchased his shares of stock in the company. I moved to Texas seeking a warmer climate and a smaller city where things are less stressful. You can try if you wish, but you will never be able to prove otherwise in a court of law."

"We're still gonna look in this warehouse," Woods declared.

"I also intend to call the county sheriff."

"Suits the hell outa me. You tell Perry Bass that Ranger Roy Woods is down here lookin' around, an' if he's got the balls to try an' stop me, invite him over. I'll arrest him too, an' handcuff him too. A Texas Ranger has got jurisdiction in every county in the state. So just call Perry an' tell him Texas Rangers Roy Woods an' Lee Garrett are here."

Santini gave what might pass for a smile. "You sound

like you believe a Texas Ranger is above the law, Mr. Woods."

Woods wagged his head. "We ain't above it, Santini. We're just makin' damn sure nobody is breakin' it here. As I said, by the time you get your fancy-pants lawyer down here, we'll be through with lookin' around. It'll be your word against ours, unless we find some evidence you're in the bootleggin' profession. I suggest you let go of that telephone. You don't want me comin' back here every day, makin' your life miserable, searchin' your office an' your cars an' your warehouse. Followin' you everywhere you go. Watchin' your house at night, havin' lunch every day at a table next to yours so I can hear what you're sayin'. I'll go with you to the bathroom every time you take a shit, countin' the number of times you fart. You don't want me on your trail, Santini, because when I get on a man's trail, I stay there 'til hell is froze over, or until I put him in jail."

Santini, still unmoved, said, "You've made your position very clear, Mr. Woods. I'll speak with my lawyer. If he recommends that I grant you free access to my warehouse, I will be happy to accommodate you. Otherwise, I'm asking you to leave."

"We ain't leavin'," Woods snarled. "Call the President if you want, but you ain't gonna stop us from lookin'."

"You are a stubborn man," Santini said, lifting the earphone off its cradle. "However, despite your threats, I'll consult my lawyer and take his advice."

Woods gave Lee a nod. "Let's see what we can find in yonder while he's makin' his telephone call."

Lee had misgivings about a search—Woods called it "looking around." Woods strode over to a side door and twisted the knob. When he opened it, the scent of oil grew stronger.

Lee followed Woods into a cavernous room. It appeared to be an old cotton warehouse. Sunlight from cracks in the roof showed little detail at first; however, it was clear that the building was not used often. A few oil drums rested near one of the doors. Heat inside the place was oppressive, worsening its oil smell, and for a moment Lee felt nauseous, unable to breathe.

"It's empty," he said after a silence.

Woods said nothing, peering into the half dark.

"That moonshiner told you they brought the stuff here."

"He said they brought it to a warehouse by the railroad in Longview," Woods replied. "He didn't say which one. He told me there wasn't a sign on it, but he coulda been lyin'. Maybe it's another warehouse close by belongin' to Santini. You can bet your ass Santini is the one they sold it to. Maybe they move it somewheres else right after the Jeffrey boys deliver."

Lee recalled what Dunlap said. "That deputy told me a truck came late at night, pulling inside. They kept the doors closed. The truck could be hauling the shine someplace as soon as it got delivered."

Woods pointed to something against the rear wall. "Let's see what this is . . ." He walked slowly across the concrete floor to a canvas tarp covering a pile of objects Lee couldn't identify at first glance. Woods pulled a corner of the tarp aside. "Tables. What the hell . . . ?"

"No moonshine," Lee said, sweeping the building with another glance. "Just an empty warehouse, a few barrels, and some wood tables under a piece of canvas."

"We got the wrong warehouse," Woods said quietly.

"We'll have to search the others," Lee offered, "but it's gonna take time."

"We've got the right man, the wrong warehouse," Woods whispered, dropping the tarp. "They'll move the shine tonight some way or another. It won't be there by the time we get all these warehouses searched."

"We can say it was all a mistake and then keep an eye

on things tonight," Lee suggested, keeping his voice down. "If a truck shows up, we'll have 'em cold."

Woods made a grunting sound. "I never did like admittin' to a mistake. I can feel it in my gut we've got the right guy. Santini's cool as a cucumber. He's felt heat before an' it don't rattle him. He's our man, only he's too smart to keep a bunch of shine where he offices." He sighed. "Let's get outa here. We're wastin' time. It's up to the feds to break up a moonshine operation anyways. I've got a shitload of cases to work. Let Brad Whitaker handle it."

Lee followed Woods toward the office, breathing through his mouth to avoid the oil smells.

Carlos Santini was on the telephone when they walked in, and he abruptly ended his conversation. Paulie stood a few feet away with his hands in his pants pockets.

"Here's the fat boy's gun," Woods said, tossing a Remington .380-caliber automatic on Santini's desk. "Like I said, all we wanted was to look around. I'll ask that bootlegger for a better description of the warehouse. By the way, that's a nice collection of tables you've got. I'm sure nobody ever played any poker or rolled any dice on 'em."

"That would be against the law," Santini said, still holding the phone to his ear, expressionless.

"We appreciate your cooperation," Woods said, starting for the front door.

They walked out in brilliant sunshine just as a new Studebaker came roaring across the chugholes in a cloud of dust in their direction.

"Just in time," Woods mumbled, seeing Agent Whitaker's car pull up, braking to a halt beside Lee's Packard. "Now we've got a warrant to search an empty warehouse. No wonder the federal budget is screwed up. The government hires men like Whitaker, who can't find their ass with either hand, but they damn sure go by the book lookin' for it."

Lee had a feeling that Roy Woods' bullheaded methods would be just as ineffective as Whitaker's insistence upon following the letter of the law in trying to prove anything on Carlos Santini. It promised to be a chore, linking Santini to William Dodd's murder. The only tie-in between the two men was Molly Brown, and she professed to know nothing about the killing, or the lease.

Santini would prove to be a worthy adversary.

16

Brad Whitaker sipped coffee from a paper cup with a doughnut resting in his lap on a napkin. A gravel road running in front of the warehouses was empty, quiet. A few lights burned in small houses near the warehouse district even though the hour was late, close to midnight. Roy Woods was asleep in the back seat of the Studebaker, snoring softly. His shotgun lay in the floorboard. They'd been watching the warehouses for hours from a secluded alleyway two blocks from Maude's. No trucks had driven by since eight o'clock, although Maude's was busy with cars arriving, then leaving. Fourteen big tanker trucks were parked in rows next to Santini's office in an open yard between the buildings. A night watchman came outside every now and then, walking slowly between the trucks for a few minutes. Lee caught glimpses of him through binoculars once in a while.

Several buildings along the rail siding appeared to be empty. With idle time on their hands, the men speculated as to which one might hold moonshine. It had been too late in the day to see any official records at the courthouse to find out who owned a particular piece of property. Dozens of old cotton warehouses had been built beside the tracks, with loading platforms made for handling heavy cotton bales. But as cotton prices fell and oil consumption grew, the district had become a storage area for oilfield equipment, sections of pipe and drill stem, drilling rigs and tank trucks, the machinery needed to pull black gold from the ground.

"Two more agents are on their way up from Houston," Whitaker said. "We'll watch in shifts. I appreciate the two of you being with me tonight. I know this isn't ordinarily a matter for the Rangers."

"I've got my own reasons for seeing what Santini is up to," Lee said, indigestion causing his stomach to roil incessantly, a fact he'd neglected to tell Whitaker when he went for coffee and doughnuts. "I'm convinced he's involved in the murder I was sent here to investigate, but I've got nothing to go on besides what a prostitute told me. She knew about the dead man's mineral lease, and she came here because of Santini. It's a damn weak connection, but it's about all I have. Another oil speculator came up with the same lease a few weeks after Bill Dodd was killed. He got edgy when I mentioned Santini. The dead man's wife had some kind of visitor in a black Cadillac a few times, and a sheriff's deputy told me he saw black Cadillacs at Santini's warehouse on nights when a truck was driven inside. The guy with the tommy gun down in Henderson County drove a black Cadillac. Roy says he's sure he worked for Santini. It's all loose ends and a guess on my part, but I've learned to follow my nose during an investigation when there isn't anything else to follow. It's a stretch, but it's possible Dodd's wife was seeing one of Santini's men on the side. But then why is she still broke, wanting us to investigate her husband's murder? None of it adds up."

"Intuition can be a useful tool," Whitaker agreed, his eyeglasses fogging slightly when he held the coffee cup to his lips. "However, it's more than intuition that led me to Santini. We know about his involvement with the Tatangelo family in New York. His arrest record there is a yard long. Santini started out as a collector for horse-betting parlors run by Tatangelo. He moved up in the ranks rapidly. He's tough, and smart. He has had no convictions despite numerous arrests. I was puzzled when he came to Longview. This isn't typical of a crime family's way of doing business. I concluded there must be big money involved. It may be Tatangelo's way of expanding operations away from New York and New Jersey. Gangsters are fighting each other over territory on the East Coast. I think Gino Tatangelo decided to try running some of his operation in parts of Texas, where competition is not as strong."

"Oil money," Lee suggested, feeling his stomach burn.

"Precisely. Where there is sufficient cash flow and men who are willing to spend it, someone will show up to make dollars off the vices. In all honesty, I'm convinced Prohibition won't work in the long run. The government can't tell people whether or not to drink liquor. It's unenforceable. People are making their own beer in bathtubs. Drinking can't be stopped by legislation, and these are particularly hard times, when unemployed men are more likely to seek a drink to drown their sorrows. My father is a good accountant back in Boston and yet he cannot find a job. He ends up standing in line at soup kitchens for something to eat when the little bit of money I can send runs out. My mother worked at a bakery until it closed down. They are proud people, but now they are forced to accept charity."

Lee thought about his own family. Times were hard in Texas, but not as difficult as what Whitaker described.

"My folks live on a farm, so they can raise most of what they need. My brothers and I help out when we can. This Depression isn't as bad here as it is in other places, I reckon." He looked at Maude's, seeing another car drive up. "I suppose it's damn near impossible to stop men from drinking. Same might be said about prostitution. If a woman is willing to sell herself, I don't see no real harm in it. Hard times have forced a lot of women into the trade. The girl, Molly Brown, told me her parents were dead and she'd had no way to make a living in New York. That's how she wound up here, when Gino Tatangelo showed her a way out."

Whitaker fingered his cup. "But that's the way racketeers prosper these days, preying on people who have few choices, offering them escape from harsh reality with liquor or prostitution or gambling. You know, the trade in opium and heroin is rising rapidly. More of it is coming in through Houston ports, keeping the customs agents busy. These drugs may be our biggest enemy. We seem to know very little about why people become addicted to them in the first place."

"There're a few opium parlors run by Chinese on the east side of Dallas," Lee said, "and we're hearing more and more about heroin down in San Antone, but it's not that big a problem yet. Our biggest worry lately has been bank robberies and stickups. Most of the guys we've caught recently are first-timers who were flat busted. They get their hands on a gun and go after what they want. They're easy to catch because they aren't hard criminals with experience, just ordinary men who got desperate. They leave a trail a blind man could follow and when you corner 'em, they give up pretty easy. We've got our share of hard cases roaming the state, but most robberies are done by beginners, who aren't looking to kill anybody."

"Oilfield workers are different," Whitaker said. "They are, for the most part, very violent men. During investigations down in Gladys City and the Beaumont area, I've run across countless killings—stabbings and shootings over a crap game, or in many cases, nothing more than an insult while men were drinking. Too many times it's because of a woman." He glanced over to Lee. "Are you married, Mr. Garrett?"

"Nope. Never was, and probably won't be. I can't find the kind of woman who'll tolerate me being gone so much of the time. This job takes me all over the place and most women want a husband who stays home. Maybe there're exceptions, but I haven't had much luck finding one."

"I have a wife and two children. Mary doesn't say much when I have to travel. I miss her and my kids, but I need this job."

"These days, everybody needs a job."

"Tom Simmons lost his job last night. A tommy gun took away his job and everything he had. His wife was hysterical when I called her in Maryland this morning. They have a baby daughter. The sound of her voice has been haunting me all day . . ."

"That part's never easy," Lee agreed, remembering some of the families he'd notified of a death when local peace officers weren't available. Whitaker was younger, new to the darker side of police work. Lee wondered if Whitaker had ever killed a man in the line of duty. That first time, no matter how it happened or who it was, you never forgot the name or the face of the man whose life you took. A cattle thief named Bobby Sanchez had been Lee's first, before his second year as a Ranger was out. Sanchez had fired first, too hurriedly. Lee's aim had been better.

As if Whitaker could read Lee's thoughts, he said, "I may have killed a man last night. He isn't expected to live. I shot him in the back as he was turning around to shoot at me. I gave him ample warning to drop his gun. A doctor in Tyler said his back was broken and there was damage to his spleen . . ." His voice trailed off and for a moment, only the sound of Roy Woods snoring in the back seat invaded the meaningful silence.

"Will he be your first?" Lee asked, idly watching a car drive away from Maude's.

"If he dies, yes. But it sounds like a weak excuse if I say he deserved to die."

"That's all the reason you need. You'll always remember the first one. It never goes away. After a spell, you get detached from it, some way or another. It doesn't eat at you like it did the first time."

"I hope I never have to shoot anyone else."

The night watchman came out of Santini's office, walking slowly among parked trucks again. Lee raised his binoculars to adjust focus. "It don't appear anything's gonna happen tonight down here. Santini probably figures we'd watch the place. If nobody shows up, it means one of several things. The bootlegger was lyin' to Roy about where he took the booze, or there isn't any more of it here now, or maybe that Santini's too smart to lead us to it right away. He may be waitin' to see if you can find it, wherever it is. It damn sure ain't in his warehouse. That place was empty."

"There's nothing to do but wait," Whitaker said, taking a bite of his doughnut, dropping crumbs on his pants. He chewed thoughtfully. "Now that we have a warrant we can go in, if we have to. The judge squirmed a little when I asked for it. He wanted to know what I thought Mr. Santini was guilty of. When I told him, he seemed a bit flustered. It was also strange, when he appeared to be in a hurry making a telephone call as I was leaving his office. It would be pushing imagination to its limits to think that Judge Warren might be calling Santini to warn him, or perhaps someone else who would."

"We've had crooked judges before," Lee remembered. "Down in Starr County we caught a judge takin' a bribe to let a wealthy rancher's son off on a manslaughter charge. The District Attorney called headquarters when he smelled somethin' fishy, after the judge dismissed the case for lack of evidence. Hell, there was even a witness. Me an' another Ranger, an oldtimer named Clarence Webb, broke down the rancher who paid the judge. Webb took him off in another room an' got a confession that he'd paid a bribe to Judge Weeks." Lee shook his head. "That rancher had some knots on his head after Clarence questioned him. That was back in twenty-five, when things were a little different."

"You mean he beat a confession out of him?"

"Clarence said he fell down a few times, complainin' he was dizzy."

Whitaker tossed the rest of his doughnut out the driver's window. "Such harsh methods wouldn't be tolerated at the Treasury Department. We follow strict guidelines."

Lee thought about a number of questionable methods he'd seen used by other Rangers over the years. "Things are changin'. A few old-time Rangers are still around, but not many. Most of 'em like Clarence have retired. Major Elliot still gives us plenty of free rein an' he backs us up when there's a stir, but most of us follow procedures pretty much to the letter. I reckon there's been a few exceptions."

Whitaker looked over his shoulder. Woods continued to snore in a deep sleep. "Mr. Woods can be a volatile man at times. He conducted a search without a warrant as though he didn't need one at all and he became angry over my suggestion that we wait for a judge to issue one."

"Roy might bend the law at times, but he's got a good record with the Rangers. He's stationed in a rough part of the state, now that more oilfields are opening up here. Sometimes a man has to fight fire with fire."

"I know," Whitaker replied softly.

17

He'd been dozing, slumped against the car door, when he was awakened by Whitaker's voice.

"Someone's coming, a bobtail truck with a tarp over it. It's turning at one of the warehouses without its headlamps on. I see another vehicle behind it, an automobile also running without lights."

Lee came wide awake in an instant, blinking furiously to rid his brain of sleep fog. He peered through the dusty, bug-splattered windshield and saw a truck and a car drive slowly between two dark buildings. "This is it," he said, reaching over the seat to awaken Roy Woods. He shook the Ranger's shoulder. "Wake up, Roy. We've got company."

Woods grunted and sat up sleepily, rubbing his eyes. "Where are they?" he asked, scratching angry red insect bites on his face and neck.

"Behind those two buildings down the street. I'll get my shotgun out of the trunk and follow you. We can close off that opening with two cars so we'll have 'em blocked in." Lee got out quickly as Woods scrambled from the back seat cradling his shotgun, jumping in front beside Whitaker.

Lee ran back to the Packard and opened the trunk, reaching in the dark for his Savage 720 shotgun, a recoil-operated 12-gauge autoloader holding five shells. Fumbling for extra loads, he pocketed as much spare ammunition as he could and slammed the trunk closed. Whitaker drove off before he could get the Packard started. Grinding gears, he swung out of the alley with gravel spitting from his tires.

"They'll be armed," he told himself, wheeling around the chugholes without headlamps on, blinded by dust from the Studebaker. He wondered how useful Whitaker would be if any shooting started. The Treasury agent didn't seem like the type to remain steady under fire.

Whitaker turned sharply and drove to the opening between the two warehouses, sliding to a halt at an angle to block as much space as he could. Lee braked to a stop in a cloud of choking dust, his Packard further closing off any escape.

He jumped out with his shotgun as Woods and Whitaker ran for the back of both buildings. Whitaker had a shotgun, and he had told Lee he carried a Smith & Wesson .38. Being in slightly better physical shape than the others, Lee caught up to them before they reached the back.

Around the corner of the building to the west, a truck with bows covered by canvas was backed up to a loading dock. A dark automobile sat beside it. A man with a carbide lamp stood near the rear of the truck.

"Fan out, boys," Woods whispered, "so we'll make a tougher target if any shootin' starts."

"We must make sure they are moving liquor," Whitaker warned, a quiet plea in his voice.

A shadow moved in a doorway of the building. The man who held the light turned around.

"It's the law!" someone yelled.

The wink of a muzzle flash accompanied an explosion. A piece of lead sizzled above Lee's head. Crouching, he ran toward the truck along one side of the building, keeping to the shadows from an eave.

Woods growled, "There's your answer, Whitaker," hurrying to stay up with Lee.

Another gunshot banged from the loading platform, its echo reverberating off the wooden walls. Somewhere behind them a bullet struck earth, making a thumping noise.

Then a far deadlier sound began at the rear of the truck, a rhythmic pounding made by an automatic rifle. Bullets flew past Lee's face, splintering wood in the wall beside him. The gun was a large-bore, a .45, he thought, recalling Woods' story of their encounter with a Thompson subma-chine gun last night.

He dove for the ground, landing on his belly in rough gravel and chalky dirt, scraping his elbows when he held up the shotgun to keep it from being damaged, losing his hat somewhere in the darkness beside him. The tommy gun continued to roar and he saw flashes of light come from the truck bed, when suddenly there was a faint click and the gun stopped.

"The sumbitch's gun jammed," Woods said, struggling to his feet. "Let's rush 'em now." He took off in a stumbling run in the direction of the truck, bringing his shotgun to his shoulder.

Lee was a few feet behind him, running as hard as he could to catch up, gasping for breath while feeling blood trickle from his elbows. Thirty yards from the platform, Woods came to a halt and fired.

The concussion from a 12-gauge shell was magnified by Woods' closeness to the building. Above the roar some-one screamed as lead pellets blasted into a dark square where a pair of warehouse doors stood open.

A faint glow from the carbide light beamed at the rear of the truck. Before Lee could get a shotgun shell into the firing chamber, using the autoloader lever, Woods swung his gun toward the truck and fired again.

Pellets shredded the canvas tarp, puckering it inward as a huge hole appeared between the back bows. A strangled cry, muffled somewhat by the tarp and the explosion, ended when a man staggered from the truck bed holding his face with both hands. He took just two steps before Woods cut him down with another hail of shotgun pellets.

Lee fired when something moved behind the warehouse door frame. The Savage slammed into his shoulder, spitting flame and lead, filling his ears with its mighty roar. A shriek, like a woman's voice, told him he'd hit someone despite his hurried aim and poor view of his target. He caught a glimpse of a figure as a man slumped forward on his face across the loading platform, and now he could hear pain-ridden cries coming from the same spot. A full charge of 12-gauge shotgun pellets at close range pulverized human flesh and he could imagine the damage he'd done to whoever lay there, thrashing back and forth in agony.

Frozen against the warehouse wall, he waited for something to shoot at again, swinging his gun muzzle back and forth. Off to his right he saw Whitaker dash around the front of the truck, using the black sedan for cover. Roy Woods stood brazenly in a shadow near the platform, his shotgun trained on the opening.

A pistol cracked inside. Almost in unison, Lee and Woods fired at the flash of orange light. The roar of the two shotguns was deafening. Something fell. Seconds later Lee heard a groan and irregular footsteps, then a soft thump like a body falling on a concrete floor.

In the distance, he could hear a car engine racing, and the pop of gravel under tires.

"Somebody's coming in a hell of a hurry," he whispered to himself, unwilling to take his eyes from the doorway. It was likely that someone was being drawn to the warehouse district by the gunshots. He hoped it would be Longview policemen, not reinforcements for whoever was inside.

An eerie silence followed. One of the wounded men lying on the platform moaned and coughed wetly. The roar of the automobile engine grew louder, coming from the road in front of the rows of warehouses.

"Come out with your goddamn hands up!" Woods bellowed. "We got the place surrounded!"

No one answered his demand.

"Maybe we got 'em all, Roy," Lee said quietly.

After a silence, Woods said, "It's gonna take balls to walk up there an' see. They could be waitin' for us to do somethin' stupid. I say we give 'em a little . . ." Hearing the car arrive out front, he let his voice drop off. "Maybe you oughta see who that is," he added. "We sure as hell don't wanna be in no cross fire out in the open like this."

"I'll take a quick look," Lee replied, backing away carefully in the eave's shadow until he felt he was a safe distance from the platform.

He wheeled and broke into a trot, keeping his shotgun aimed in front of him. He could hear voices above the sounds his boots made on the loose gravel. He reached the corner of the building and peered cautiously around it, finding two uniformed men walking toward him through the dark, badges glittering in the faint starlight shining from a cloudless sky. He could see they carried drawn pistols.

"Texas Rangers!" he yelled, startling them when they heard his voice. "We've got some bootleggers holed up in one of these buildings!"

Both men stopped in their tracks.

One of the policemen spoke as he aimed his gun toward Lee. "You're gonna have to show us some identification, mister. Ain't no Texas Rangers stationed in Longview."

"I'm with Ranger Roy Woods from Tyler. My name's Garrett. I'm from the Waco office. Keep walking this way and I'll show you my badge and ID card. Make it quick, 'cause there's just three of us and we don't know how many of them are left inside."

They started forward again, still wary. Lee lowered his shotgun and stepped out in plain sight. "Are you Longview city police?" he asked, speaking softly now.

"Yeah," one officer replied when he was close enough

to see Lee's badge. "Nobody told us Rangers was in town. Roy usually tells Chief Laster what he's up to when he's around." He let his pistol drop beside his leg.

"There wasn't time. We're backing up Treasury Agent Brad Whitaker on this one."

"We heard all the shootin'," the other policeman said as Lee led them around the warehouse. "Sounded like the World War was bein' fought down here."

"One of them has a tommy gun," Lee said over his shoulder, striking a trot again. "We think the gun jammed. We shot three or four of 'em. Can't tell because it's so dark."

The policemen broke into a run behind him, their shoes crunching over stones.

Lee reached the place where Woods was hiding in a shadow a short distance from the platform. He spoke while trying to catch his breath. "A couple of Longview police officers, Roy. Came when they heard the shooting."

Woods looked over his shoulder. "We could use some help to flush the rest of 'em out," he said quickly. "Spread out behind that car an' truck. Stay down. I've ordered 'em to come out an' nobody's made a move. Maybe we got 'em all. Maybe not."

"Nobody told us you was in town, Mr. Woods. The chief never said a word."

"Spread out," Woods snapped, his patience obviously evaporating. "We ain't got time to socialize right now."

"Yessir," the officer replied, leading his partner away to hide behind the automobile.

Lee stepped up quietly beside Woods. "I figure we must have got 'em all or there'd be shooting. I'll work my way up to that door."

"Watch your ass," Woods warned. "These sumbitches can be sneaky as hell."

"I always do," Lee answered, inching forward with his

back pressed against the wall, covering his progress with the Savage.

He came to a set of wooden steps where he paused, listening. No sound came from the warehouse or the rear of the truck. A gaping hole in the canvas cover emitted light from the gas lamp in back. The light would outline him when he got to the doorway. He felt his heartbeat quicken. Two men lay on the platform and neither one appeared to be breathing. Dark bloodstains encircled both.

Gripping his shotgun, he crept slowly up the steps with his finger curled around the trigger. Keeping to the wall, he moved as soundlessly as he knew how to the opening and took a breath.

When he leaned around the door frame, he saw a body on the floor, lying in a pool of blood. Past the body, crates full of glass jars were stacked in neat rows.

Corn whiskey, he thought, . . . now all we gotta do is prove it belongs to Carlos Santini.

18

Using the lamp, they moved cautiously into the interior of the building, shining the light's dim beam toward dark corners, listening to a faint noise coming from somewhere near the back.

"Sounds like a little kid cryin'," Woods whispered. "Comin' from over yonder, behind those barrels."

A few oil drums stood in a corner. Lee looked down when he noticed dark circles on the floor near his feet. "There's blood on the cement here. One of 'em's wounded, hiding behind those drums. He's probably still armed." He turned to the police officer with the lamp. "Shine the light over there. Stand behind that door in case somebody starts shooting."

When the miner's lamp brightened the collection of barrels, a trail of wet bloodstains could be seen marking someone's route to the only place inside the warehouse offering concealment.

"Looks like a pistol lyin' there on the floor," Woods said. "Maybe he ain't armed after all. Could be he's hurt bad an' let his gun drop. Spread out an' we'll close in on him. Keep your guns ready." He started forward in a low crouch.

Lee moved to the left and crept silently toward the barrels with his Savage aimed. Whitaker widened their circle by going to the right, walking slowly along an interior wall, his shotgun against his shoulder. Lee could hear soft whimpering clearly now as they neared the drums.

Woods was first to reach the corner. He lowered his gun at once and shook his head. "It's a woman," he said. "She's shot all to pieces, bleedin' like hell. Tell 'em to bring that light over here. She ain't armed."

Both Longview policemen hurried over until a beam of light was shining on the floor behind a pair of oil drums. A girl in denims and a man's shirt lay on her back in a pool of blood, her arms folded over her chest. Bloody pellet wounds on her face and neck and arms bespoke the accuracy of someone's aim. She had close-cropped brown hair cut in a man's hairstyle. Her eyes were closed. A soft murmur of pain whispered from her lips every time she took a breath.

"Jesus," Whitaker sighed. "What a mess. We need to send for an ambulance."

"I'll go," one of the police officers said, handing the lamp to his partner. "The closest telephone is at O'Leary's

Service Station out on the highway. It's open all night. One of those guys out on the loadin' dock is breathin'. I'll ask for two ambulances. We ain't got any of them radios in our cars. The City Council said they was too expensive."

"Tell 'em to hurry," Woods said, resting his shotgun against a barrel. "This girl's gonna bleed to death pretty quick if she doesn't get some medical attention soon."

Lee walked around the drums and knelt beside her. "She's real young, Roy, hardly more'n a kid. I reckon I'm the one who shot her. I heard a high-pitched voice right after I fired at something moving in here. Damn the luck. She had a pistol and took a shot at us, so there was no way to tell who it was."

"Don't fret over it, Lee," Woods said. "She was with this bunch of bootleggers. Makes her the same as a man when she runs shine an' carries a gun."

Lee examined her face, her clothing. She had on a pair of run-over lace boots. Denim patches covered holes in the knees of her pants. "She could be as young as fifteen, maybe sixteen," he said sadly, wishing he could have known who he was shooting at in time. "She isn't what I expected, running moonshine for Santini. Hell."

Woods wiped his sweating forehead with his shirtsleeve. "I know how you feel, but it can't be undone. Forget about it. We can try to get her to the hospital in time an' that's about all we can do. She'd have killed you if you gave her the chance. It ain't your fault she's a kid. She's old enough to know how to use a gun."

Lee touched her cheek and when he did, the girl opened her eyes.

"It hurts," she whimpered, tears streaming down her face.

"Sorry you got shot," Lee said, his throat feeling tight, the words sounding strained. "We've sent for an ambulance."

Her eyes focused on him for a moment. "You're the law, ain't you?"

"Texas Ranger. We had these buildings under surveillance. Who sent you to pick up those crates of moonshine?"

She swallowed, glancing up at the lamp. "Pa said we had to move 'em tonight, to wait until late because the law was nosin' around askin' questions. The big man sent word to us to be real careful."

Lee strained to hear what she was saying. "Who's the big man who notified your pa?"

She shook her head slightly. "Never knowed his name. We'd bring the corn squeezin's down here an' a big feller pays us for it. He never told us who he was."

"Was your pa with you tonight?" Lee asked, feeling sure he already knew the answer.

"He got shot. He's layin' out there, bleedin' real bad."

"Who was the guy with the machine gun?"

The girl sniffled back tears. "He works for the big man. Drove his car out to meet us 'round midnight. He's some kind of foreigner. Don't hardly speak no English. He was supposed to watch out for the law, an' protect us if you showed up."

Lee kept pressing her for answers. "Did you ever hear of Carlos Santini?"

She shook her head again. "Never did. I'm hurtin' so bad I wish you wouldn't ask me no more questions, mister. I'm real dizzy, like I'm gonna faint. Lordy. I can't hardly see you no more . . ." Her eyelids batted shut and her arms relaxed, falling to her sides.

"She's dying," Whitaker said solemnly. "She'll bleed to death before an ambulance arrives. There is nothing we can do. She has too many pellet wounds."

Lee took a deep breath and stood up, hooking his thumbs in his gun belt. While the shooting had been unavoidable, it began to weigh heavily on his conscience. "One of you stay with her until the ambulance comes," he said softly. "I can't do it." He picked up his shotgun and walked around the drums, heading for the warehouse doors, balancing the Savage in his palm.

He heard footsteps when he got to the loading dock. Roy Woods put a hand on his shoulder. "Don't take it so damn hard, Lee," he said, looking around at the bodies. "One of these here bastards is her pappy. He's the one responsible for lettin' a kid like her come along to haul moonshine." He walked over to one of the still forms, kicking it with the toe of his boot. "I know how you feel, but you couldn't see who you was shootin' at in the dark." He frowned. "This one's the Italian who didn't speak English — you can tell by his greasy mop of curly hair. He had the tommy gun, an' he's dead." He stepped over to another body and bent down. "This sumbitch is still breathin'," he added with a noticeable change in his voice. He gave Lee a look. "Walk back inside for a minute or two. I've got a feelin' this bastard is gonna try to escape." He placed his shotgun on the loading platform and drew his Colt .45 automatic.

"Turn around, Lee."

Lee's stomach was churning. "Hardly seems any need for that now," he said, scarcely believing what Woods intended.

"Turn around," Woods said again, aiming his pistol, placing the muzzle near the prone form's skull. "That way, you didn't see it when this asshole tried to run off. Worst thing in the world a man could do is let a sorry bastard like him keep on breathin' after what he done to his daughter tonight. Look the other way."

Lee finally turned his back on the loading platform, disbelief crowding every other thought from his brain as he heard the click of a hammer being cocked. He closed his eyes and tried to close his mind to what Woods was doing. Senior Rangers like Roy Woods would never be questioned about their methods or casualties by anyone at headquarters.

The heavy thud of a .45 shell broke the moment of quiet. Lee winced. A gurgling noise followed the blast. The hollow rattle of an empty cartridge casing came a second later when it fell on the planks beneath Woods' feet.

"What was that?" someone shouted from inside.

Woods stood up and holstered his Colt. "One of 'em got up an' tried to escape!" he yelled, a curious hint of satisfaction in the way he said it. He lowered his voice. "He ain't goin' no place now." He turned to Garrett. "Any man who'd put a gun in a little girl's hands an' take her on a bootleggin' run don't deserve no more fresh air in my book. You forget what you saw just now, Lee. You didn't see a thing."

Lee knew he would never mention it to anyone. There was an unwritten code among Rangers to back up a fellow officer's words and actions no matter what the circumstances. He'd learned this early in his career, serving as Clarence Webb's partner down on the Mexican border. Clarence had made it clear that sometimes it was necessary to use a little force when no one was looking. It got results, he said, and over the years, he'd been proven right more often than not. But there was a difference in what Roy Woods had done tonight that was unsettling. Woods had become an executioner moments ago, deciding for himself that the girl's father did not deserve to live. There was a trace of madness in him, a belief he had the power of life or death in his hands because of his badge.

"I heard a shot," Lee told Woods quietly. "It was too dark to see what was going on."

At Longview Municipal Hospital, three men were pronounced dead by Justice of the Peace Millard Rountree. In the predawn dark, Justice Rountree's face looked milky when he came out of the room where the bodies lay on blood-soaked stretchers on the floor.

"I recognize two of them," Rountree said, the suggestion of liquor on his breath. "Boyd Jones and Francis Ward. They lived close to the little community of White Oak, a few miles from town. The one between them is a stranger. His face is so badly damaged it may be difficult for anyone to identify him."

One of the police officers spoke up. "Francis was in jail a number of times. I thought I knew who he was. He hauled loads of moonshine into Gregg County from Louisiana just lately. We arrested him last year, if I remember right. He was runnin' a crap game over at Beecher's Mound this spring. We had some old warrants, so the county brought him over to the city jail when they found him. Judge Warren let him go without postin' bond because the family didn't have no money for a lawyer."

"What about the girl?" Lee asked, in a black mood over the shooting that would not leave him no matter how he tried to put it in perspective. In the dark, he couldn't have known who was firing at them. He'd done the only thing he could when he shot back.

Rountree spread his hands. "Doctor Collins says she's lost so much blood that he doesn't think she'll make it. She's the daughter of Boyd Jones. A nurse who saw her said she dropped out of school last year to help her father on the farm. The family is very poor."

"She was helpin' make moonshine," Woods said, seated in a chair near the hospital entrance. "They was farmin' corn if it was a cash crop they planted. We caught 'em red-handed tonight an' the girl had a gun. She was old enough to know how to shoot it."

"The child isn't expected to live," Rountree said gravely. "Her wounds are extensive."

Lee shut his eyes, in part from fatigue, in part from

guilt feelings over shooting the girl. What had begun as a murder investigation was becoming far more complicated. He remembered something Molly Brown had told him, although it had seemed only a disconnected recollection at the time. She'd said Carlos Santini sometimes loaned out money. A possibility he'd overlooked might have been that Bill Dodd needed money to pay the Hawkins heirs the advance money he owed them. Could that have been the reason he was killed? Lee wondered. Was that a possible explanation for someone else knowing precisely when the lease arrived in the mail? Had Dodd been murdered by the man he asked for an advance against future oil royalties? Had Dodd called Santini on the afternoon he got the lease, asking for a loan? It might make Santini and Buster Davis partners in a scheme to rob Dodd of his mineral rights.

It was a puzzle with too many pieces; none of them quite fit. There were loose connections, but no direct ties, between a cast of characters as mismatched as any he could imagine. There was Bill Dodd's wife, who drank liquor during the day and had visitors in Cadillacs, although she evidenced no profit from having her late husband killed and she'd been the one to ask for an investigation into his death. There was Charley Waller, a speculator who knew Dodd but claimed to know nothing about his murder. There was Buster Davis, another oil profiteer who seemed nervous about certain questions. He'd made a profit when Dodd was out of the way, but he insisted he was already after the same lease before Dodd was killed. There was a tie between Dodd and a prostitute, a girl who was brought to Texas by a shady character from New York who had close ties to an East Coast crime syndicate.

And now there was bootlegging involved, which could most likely be tied to Santini and his New York bosses. Had Santini ordered Dodd's execution? If so, there had to be a tie between Santini and Buster Davis, perhaps with Molly Brown serving as a go-between, making the telephone call after Dodd informed her his lease had come in the mail.

Lee slumped down in his chair in the waiting room, tilting his hat over his eyes. Setting out to prove any of this was sure to be a lengthy process. Captain Ross would quickly lose patience with the whole investigation unless he could come up with something in a few days. Ross and Major Elliot wanted proof of a link between Santini and the Tatangelo family, hoping for political benefits to hand over to Governor Sterling if and when the Rangers made headlines. Dodd's death would quickly be forgotten if the eyes of Texas voters were on the breakup of an organized crime ring from New York operating in Texas.

He dozed fitfully, remembering the girl and how she'd looked when they found her, covered with so many pellet wounds it was like she had a bad case of measles. Then the sound of voices awakened him. Dawn had brightened the hospital windows when he opened his eyes.

A man in uniform slacks and a short-sleeved shirt with a star pinned to it was speaking with Roy Woods near the emergency-room door.

"I'll show you which warehouse it is, Howard," Woods said, looking tired after their bloody ordeal. "I want the records checked at the courthouse as soon as it opens. Find out who owns or has a lease on that buildin', because whoever it is, he's goin' to jail for bootleggin'. We think maybe it's Carlos Santini behind this. Treasury Agent Brad Whitaker has been investigatin' a connection between Santini an' some New York gangsters. We'll expect full cooperation from your police department."

Whitaker got out of a chair beside Lee's and walked over to the police chief. He held out his hand. "I'm Brad Whitaker. We have reason to believe Santini may be involved in various crimes, including gambling operations."

Lee pushed out of his chair for introductions. He might be needing cooperation from the chief of police, since little help appeared to be forthcoming from Perry Bass. He arrived at the door as Whitaker was shaking hands.

Woods said, "This is Ranger Lee Garrett from the Waco office an' he's lookin' into a murder here. Lee, meet Howard Laster of the Longview Police Department. He's chief."

Lee shook hands with Laster perfunctorily. "Morning," he said, only half awake.

"What murder are you investigatin'?" Laster asked, knitting his brow, searching Lee's face. Laster was tall and gangly, with a slow drawl coloring his speech. He looked to be in his early fifties.

"William Dodd's. It happened last month. A bullet through his skull, so the sheriff's deputy told me. There was an oil lease involved. It never turned up."

"I remember Perry mentionin' it, but that sort of thing goes on here pretty often these days. Roughnecks are just what their name implies, a bunch of rough characters who ain't afraid to put a bullet or a blade in damn near anybody. I've hardly got enough jail space for all of 'em we pick up at times. Our court docket is scheduled for months. Lawyers are gettin' as rich as oilmen around Longview. My men have to work in pairs because it's too dangerous to send one officer to break up a disturbance sometimes, an' I won't let them get hurt if I can help it. What's important about William Dodd bein' killed?"

Again Lee wondered why any murder did not seem important to a peace officer. "His widow requested help from headquarters. I think she believes Sheriff Bass wanted the murder swept under the rug for one reason or another."

Laster's gaze wavered for a moment like he might know, or could guess, the reason.

"Perry's men are as overworked as mine, Mr. Garrett. I'd be surprised if Perry did anythin' less than his best. He ain't got enough officers an' neither do I. This town is bustin' at the seams with seedy types an' tough guys. There's crooks workin' the Oil Patch day an' night. I don't believe Perry would try to sweep anythin' under the rug, like the widow claims."

"I'm just getting started with my investigation," Lee said. "As you know by now, we got sidetracked by this bootlegging thing, and I haven't had much time to chase down leads. I may have a few questions for you as things develop."

"Be glad to help any way I can. Roy'll tell you we co-operate with the Rangers whenever he asks."

Woods spoke to Whitaker and Lee. "I'm goin' home to Tyler for some sleep. Haven't hardly spoken to my wife in three days. Call my office when you find out who has that warehouse. If you need backup, I'll be right over. It's less than an hour's drive."

"Be seeing you, Roy," Lee said. "I'm headed to my hotel so I can grab a couple hours of sleep." He glanced at Whitaker as he started for the door. "Call me at the Grand when you get what you need for the arrest. Leave word where you'll be. They'll bring a message to my room."

Whitaker nodded. Lee shook hands with Chief Laster again and ambled out to the parking lot, wondering if the girl would be dead by the time he woke up. He wasn't going to think about it, if he could help it. Mistakes like this came with the job, he decided, although he knew now he'd been wrong to tell Whitaker that it was only the first killing a peace office remembered. This was one he was sure he'd remember for the balance of his career.

He climbed woodenly into the Packard and drove off as a ball of bright yellow sun rose above Longview. Within an hour or two, it would be hot enough to fry eggs on the hood of the car.

19

Soft tapping on his door woke him up. Sunlight poured into the room from open windows. The electric fan made its whirring noise on the nightstand, and for a moment he thought he might have been dreaming about the knock, until he heard it again. He was drenched in sweat, his boxer shorts clinging to him like a second skin as he swung his legs off the bed to answer the door. Out of habit, he asked, "Who is it?" before he released the lock.

"Brad Whitaker. I have some rather complicated news about the warehouse. Sorry if I woke you up."

Lee opened the door. "Pardon the shorts," he said, stepping back to admit Whitaker. "It's too damn hot in here to sleep any other way."

"I understand," Whitaker replied, entering the room while he mopped his face with a handkerchief. "It's unmercifully hot out there." He carried a notepad over to the dresser as Lee closed the door behind him. "I've run into a stone wall; however, I have people checking further. The warehouse in question belongs to a Marvin Young in Longview. He leased it to a firm out of Newark, New Jersey. It's a corporation called Ace Supply Company. Corporate records in New Jersey list three officers, and none of them is Gino Tatangelo or Carlos Santini. All three have Italian names, but as of now, we have no direct link to Tatangelo or the Santini Trucking Company. The department is looking into any possible connection, but these things take time. I called my boss in Washington and he has someone digging through the corporate files in Jersey. We can't arrest Santini until we have solid proof of his affiliation with Ace Supply. Longview police have impounded the moonshine as evidence. Until we get a break, our hands are tied. But it sure seems odd that a supply-company warehouse contained no oilfield supplies, no valves or pipe or anything of the kind. I think it's quite clear that the building is being used for some other purpose."

Lee sank to the edge of his mattress, sorting through what Whitaker told him. "They've covered their asses with names on corporate documents. Santini's as free as a bird unless we can find out who the guy with the machine gun was. If we can prove he worked for Santini, we've got grounds to make an arrest."

"He carried no identification on his person," Whitaker went on. "I'm tracing the black Oldsmobile now. It has Texas license plates. However, it was registered in Tarrant County, Fort Worth. I should know in a little while who owns it. They promised to call me back here at the hotel—I rented a room down the hall. I suspect I'll be here for a few days. My superiors in Washington are paying closer attention now, after Tom's unfortunate death. By this afternoon, I should know who registered the car."

"Don't be surprised if it's another dead end," Lee said as he wiped sweat off his forehead and chest with a thin towel from the nightstand. "If these guys are as smart as I think, we won't be able to trace the Oldsmobile directly to Santini or Tatangelo. It'll be hidden behind another name. It's a paper trail we'll be following, finding out who owns what and who's behind them. It's all a front to disguise the actual owners."

Whitaker leaned against the dresser. "I'm afraid I've got a bit more bad news. The girl died a short while ago. Her name was Miriam Jones. She was fourteen."

Lee stared vacantly at the floor. "She had a gun, Brad.

I saw a muzzle flash and I fired at it. How the hell was I to know it was a kid, a girl?"

"You couldn't. Don't blame yourself. It was an accident."

"I know," Lee whispered, trying to put the memory of her face from his thoughts, "but that doesn't change the fact that I killed a child. I reckon I'll have to live with it. Roy was right when he said her father was mostly to blame. Her old man shouldn't have put a kid in that kind of situation or given her a gun."

Whitaker cleared his throat, looking out the window. "I know what Mr. Woods did to her father. I was standing where I could see him put a bullet in that man's brain. I won't mention it when I send my report to Washington. Texas Rangers have an outstanding reputation in law-enforcement circles, and I wouldn't do anything to cast shadows of doubt, though I find it unconscionable that a man sworn to uphold the law would kill a defenseless person in such a gruesome manner. It was utterly senseless."

"I didn't see it," Lee said quickly, hoping to persuade Whitaker there were no actual witnesses.

"Your back was turned. I watched you turn around before the fatal shot was fired. I'm not questioning your ethics. I'm sure you were asked to look the other way."

"Let's talk about something else," Lee said. "I intend to ask the prostitute over at Maude's about the chances Bill Dodd meant to borrow money from Santini. I'm gonna talk to Buster Davis again. Leave word here at the hotel if you find out anything concerning the car, or Ace Supply Company. If we can, I'd like to put some pressure on Santini. He made a dumb move, asking those folks to haul the moonshine last night. Maybe if he feels more heat, he'll make another mistake."

"He's a block of ice under questioning," Whitaker recalled. "Mr. Woods said he wouldn't crack. He's used to a few brushes with the law. I don't expect him to make a stupid error unless we get very close to the truth."

Lee glanced at his suitcase, thinking it was time to get dressed in clean clothing and talk to Molly Brown and Buster Davis. He hadn't asked Davis about any previous associations with Carlos Santini. He couldn't sleep in this heat anyway. "Every instinct I've got tells me Davis and Santini are tied together. I'd nearly bet a month's pay they've got their hands in the same cookie jar."

"It may be hard to prove."

Lee shook his head. "I've never had many cases that were easy to solve, Brad. You keep on looking 'til you find a weak spot in somebody's story. Davis isn't all that smart, and the girl at Maude's is nervous. She might admit something she doesn't intend to tell me if I'm careful how I ask."

Whitaker folded his notepad and walked to the door, pausing with his hand on the knob. "You sound like a very thorough man, Mr. Garrett. I confess I'm not all that impressed with Mr. Woods or his methods. Working together, perhaps you and I can get to the bottom of this . . . without any more unnecessary bloodshed." He let himself out, his footsteps fading down the hall.

Lee wished the Treasury agent hadn't mentioned bloodshed as he was leaving. The memory of Miriam Jones' face floated before his eyes and he couldn't make it go away.

Buster Davis had a visitor. A green Ford truck was parked in front of his office. Lee got out of the Packard after the dust settled around it, feeling the heat blister his arms and worsen the sting in his raw elbows where he'd fallen in the gravel the previous night.

He let himself in without knocking. A man in a dog-eared cap smudged by oil stains sat in a chair opposite Davis. Davis gave Lee an impatient look, ending his conversation with his visitor.

"You'll have to excuse me, Barney. It's the law, an' they think I had somethin' to do with Bill Dodd gettin' his head shot off. Come back later an' we'll talk about fixin' that rig."

Barney got up, glancing sideways at Lee, saying nothing as he walked out the door. His khaki clothing reeked of oil and sulfur.

Lee went over to Davis's desk, taking a wrinkled notebook and fountain pen from his shirt pocket. "I told you there might be a few more questions. Let's start with how well you know Mr. Carlos Santini."

"Everybody in the oil business here knows him," Davis said, his fingers curling unconsciously on his desktop. "He trucks crude out of the Patch. No crime in that, is there?"

"Not if that's all he's doing," Lee replied, "but I keep on hearing that he may be involved in other things, like gambling tents in some of the workers' camps and bootlegging whiskey. I've got proof he's tied in with a gangster in New York named Tatangelo, who was an investor in his trucking company. Do you ever do any business with Santini?"

Davis shook his head quickly, maybe a bit too quickly. "I already told you, I'm a speculator in mineral rights. I'm not in the drillin' business."

"I just overheard you tell Barney you'd talk to him about fixing his drilling rig. Sounds to me like you're in the business."

Davis's sunburned cheeks appeared to turn a deeper red. "Sometimes I loan some drillers money when they get busted. It's a way of keepin' in touch with who's findin' oil an' where they're strikin' it. I call it buyin' information. It's good business."

"Did you ever loan, or offer to loan, Bill Dodd any money?"

"Didn't know him that well, just enough to say howdy when we passed on the street. I already told you that. You're askin' me the same damn questions."

"I asked you if you ever had any business deals with Santini and I didn't hear your answer," Lee continued.

"No dealin's. I know him, but that's all. I never heard of him bein' involved in no gamblin' or bootleggin'. He owns trucks an' as far as I know, that's the only business he's in. If he's in with some gangster from New York, it's news to me."

"Does he loan money?"

Davis shrugged. "How should I know? You're barkin' up the wrong tree, askin' me about Mr. Santini. We've got no dealin's together. Satisfied?"

"Not quite," Lee said, getting a little hot under the collar over Davis's attitude. "You still haven't told me if you can prove where you were on the night of June twenty-third. I need to talk to a witness who can vouch for you that night."

"My wife," Davis replied in a monotone. "She'll swear I was in bed with her."

Lee put his notebook and pen away. Davis wasn't giving him anything. "I'll talk to your wife later on," he promised, "just to be sure her story matches yours."

Davis let his impatience show. "You still think I'm holdin' somethin' back, don't you? Well, you're wrong. I didn't kill Dodd. I hardly knew him. It was his rotten luck that he got the lease ahead of me an' never lived to record it. It was purely a coincidence. Bad timin' on his part."

"That piece of land is a rich strike, isn't it?" Lee asked.

Davis nodded slightly. "One of the richest. Hunt's geologists say it's over the same pool of oil underneath the Joiner. If I was in the drillin' business, I'd have kept it myself, only I ain't in that business. I sell the rights an' make a profit."

"You made a handsome profit subleasing it to Hunt."

Davis's expression went blank. "That's between me an' him."

"Santini hauls crude oil for Hunt. If Hunt's gotten so rich, why doesn't he buy his own trucks?"

"You'll have to ask H.L. about that. Are you done askin' me questions? I've got work to do."

"For now," Lee answered, giving Davis a hard stare. "But if I find out you've lied to me about any of this, I'll be back, and the next time I won't go so easy on you. One more question. Do you know a man by the name of Charley Waller?"

"Never heard of him," Davis replied flatly. "Who's he?"

At the City Café the other morning, Waller had admitted knowing Buster Davis. Now Lee had proof that Davis was lying, most likely about everything. Was this the first bit of evidence that Davis and Waller had been parties to the murder of Bill Dodd? It was raw speculation, but Waller could have told Davis about the lease having arrived that afternoon. Davis might have called someone, making sure Dodd didn't live long enough to record it. Lee's nose for a warm trail alerted him. "Are you sure about that?" he asked.

"Pos'tive. I don't know nobody named Charley Waller. Not that I recall."

Lee made a half turn for the door. "I've got a feeling I'll be talking to you again," he said.

He walked out, blasted by hot wind from the southwest when he went to his car. The odor of bullshit was getting stronger.

20

Maude's looked vacant, unlike its resemblance to a beehive the night before. Lee parked under the same shade tree and switched off the engine. A number of things were beginning to add up and today he felt closer to putting them together. Buster Davis had lied to him about not knowing Charley Waller. Santini was in bootlegging up to his neck, despite all the corporations hiding his relationship with Gino Tatangelo. Two Italian gunmen had been killed carrying tommy guns while guarding shipments of moonshine sent from a still over in Henderson County to a warehouse leased to some New Jersey company. A pair of expensive automobiles, a Cadillac and an Oldsmobile, would be discovered registered, Lee was certain, to corporations shielding Santini and Tatangelo. But the link between William Dodd and Santini was still missing. He wondered if the young prostitute might unintentionally provide him with an answer.

He got out and slammed the car door, checking his watch. It was two o'clock, early, and he hadn't announced his arrival ahead of time. Maude would be unnerved by his sudden presence, this time without a warning phone call from Perry Bass.

He walked up the porch steps and knocked, listening to the chugging sounds made by laboring switch locomotives moving tank cars in Longview's rail yard on the far side of Dogwood Street. A few blocks down the road, he could see the warehouse where he'd killed Miriam Jones with a shotgun blast at close range. He didn't want to think about it, and yet the memory was there, the sight of her face and the blood, her soft cries of pain.

The door opened a crack. "We's closed," a Negro woman said. "Come back after nine. Maude don't do business durin' the day."

"I'm Texas Ranger Lee Garrett. I need to see a girl by the name of Molly Brown. I can't wait 'til nine o'clock."

"I'll have to ask Maude."

"Ask her. And tell her it's important."

The door closed in his face. He could hear footsteps beyond it, then silence. Wind brushed through the pine and elm limbs around the house, bending branches, making a gentle rustling noise.

Minutes later, a voice he recognized spoke when the door was opened again. "Molly ain't here. She went shoppin' downtown an' I don't know when she'll be back."

Something about the way Maude said it made him doubtful. "I need to talk to her right away." The smell of bad perfume wafted from the opening, making him feel queasy. "Where did she go?"

"She didn't say. Sometimes the girls go off shoppin' during their free time. How come you need to talk to her again?"

"Just a few more questions. What time will she be back?"

"Around nine, only she's real busy then. Can it wait? I'll be sure an' tell her you asked about her."

"It can't wait," he said, sensing something was wrong. "Tell me where she's likely to go. I'll look for her."

A hesitation, too long to be natural. "Down on Commerce, I think. The dress shops, maybe. She didn't say."

"I'd like to look in her room," Lee said. "You told me it was upstairs."

"She ain't here, Mr. Garrett. I can't let you in her room without her permission."

"I can come back with a warrant. You don't want any trouble from me. This is an illegal house of prostitution. I can make things rough on business if you don't cooperate."

Another pause. "How come Perry didn't call to tell me you was comin'?"

"He doesn't know. Now, let me in so I can see Molly's room or I'll be forced to go to the judge for a warrant."

"She ain't here," Maude said again, but now she opened the door to admit him. "Follow me upstairs, but you're wastin' my time an' yours."

Lee followed Maude across the parlor to a dimly lit hallway and a set of narrow, carpeted stairs showing plenty of wear. Boards creaked under their weight until they reached the second floor. Another hall lined with doors on each side ran the length of the house. It was so hot Lee found he was having trouble breathing.

At a door marked number 7, Maude took out a key. A tumbler clicked and she opened the door, flipping on a light switch.

What Lee saw when he entered the room brought him up short. The nightstand was overturned. A small electric lamp lay on its side, the lampshade crumpled. The wardrobe closet was open, clothing scattered all over the floor. A red-velvet drape over the room's only window hung crookedly from a curtain rod half pulled from the wall. The mattress on the cast-iron bed frame was tossed sideways as though someone had been looking underneath it.

"There was trouble here," he said, squaring himself in front of Maude. "Tell me exactly what happened. If you lie to me, I'll put you in jail and close this place down."

Maude ran a trembling hand through her dyed red hair as if to rearrange her curls. "She had a visitor. I heard a noise, but I didn't come up to look," she said. Fear made her voice tremble. "He . . . took her with him early this mornin'."

"Who was he?"

"I don't know. I swear on a stack of Bibles I don't know his name. He had a gun, an' he told me if I said a word or used the telephone to call the cops, he'd kill me. I never saw him before in my life an' I swear that's the truth."

Lee's mind raced, putting things together. Someone had come for Molly right after the moonshine raid before dawn. "What did he look like?" he asked, glancing around the room again, looking for signs of blood where a struggle might have taken place.

"He was huge, with this big potbelly. Six an' a half feet tall, if he was an inch. Taller'n you. He had black hair, an' there was somethin' strange about his face—there were pits all over it, like he'd had the chicken pox real bad when he was just a kid."

"Paulie," Lee said quietly, recalling the giant they'd had to disarm at Santini's office. He looked down at Maude and gave her an icy warning. "Don't call anybody. The girl's life may be in real danger. Lock this room and don't let anybody in. Don't touch anything."

"You know who's got her, don't you?" Maude asked, saying it very softly, her fingers working nervously around the room keys.

"And so do you," he replied. "Don't call anyone. I think I know where to look for her."

"But they'll know I told you about it. They'll come lookin' for me . . ."

He hurried out of the room, speaking over his shoulder while trotting for the stairs. "I'll say somebody saw him take her out of here this morning, somebody over at the rail yard. Right now I've got to get there before they decide to kill her to keep her mouth shut."

He took the stairs two at a time, wondering if he might be too late to save her.

Lee buckled on his gun belt as soon as he jumped out of the car, removing a hammer thong holding his Colt .38 Special in its holster. Two cars were parked beside the office: Santini's black Dodge and the dark blue Oldsmobile sedan. The yard where trucks were kept at night was empty now.

Lee knew it would have been wiser to ask for police backup, but a louder voice inside his head warned that he had run out of time.

He strode to the door and opened it with his left hand while his right hand stayed near his gun.

Carlos Santini sat behind his desk holding a telephone, just as he had upon their first meeting. To Lee's right, Paulie sat in the same corner in front of a fan. Santini said nothing, his eyes locked on Lee's face. As before, Paulie climbed to his feet.

"Stay where you are," Lee demanded, addressing Paulie first, making sure he could see both men's hands. "The first one to go for a gun is gonna get shot. Keep your hands were I can see 'em, and I'll take that Remington from behind your back. Anybody who moves is guaranteed to have a hole in him."

"What's this all about?" Santini asked, speaking in his usual cool manner.

Lee moved cautiously around behind Paulie and took the .380 automatic from his belt. "It's about a missing girl named Molly Brown. A guy at the railroad yard said he saw this chubby gent drag her out of Maude's this morning." He stuck Paulie's gun in his waistband and drew his .38, placing the muzzle gently against Paulie's spine. "He's gonna tell me where she is."

"Fuck you, cowboy cop," Paulie said. "I don't know nothing about no girl."

Lee's gaze flickered to Santini. Santini's face registered nothing. "Then I'm placing you under arrest," he said, giving Paulie's back a nudge with the barrel of the Colt. "Bring your hands behind your back so I can cuff you, and do it real slow or I might get nervous and pull this trigger. Somebody'll be busy all day digging pieces of your backbone outa that wall yonder. A thirty-eight Special makes a nasty hole. Now, put your hands behind you."

Paulie hesitated.

"Do as he asks," Santini said without emotion. He looked at Lee. "I've had my lawyers report your unorthodox procedures to your superiors in Austin, Mr. Garrett. You and Mr. Woods seem to believe you have unlimited authority to disregard my rights as a citizen. A complaint against both of you is being filed with the commander of the Texas Rangers."

"Gimme those hands, Paulie," Lee demanded, adding another nudge with the .38.

Paulie held his hands behind his back. Lee took a pair of manacles from his gun belt and closed them around the thick wrists corded with muscle. Then he spoke to Santini: "You'll be giving me just what I want, a full-scale investigation into what's going on here in Longview. There'll be Texas Rangers all over, asking questions, poking around, while me and Roy Woods and Treasury Agent Brad Whitaker show 'em that moonshine we got last night a few doors down the street from a warehouse leased by a company up in New Jersey. Or the registration on two automobiles we found while we were looking for moonshine. You'll be doing me a favor if you report what's going on here to headquarters. We'll have four or five more Rangers taking a close look at everything you have, what you're involved in, where you come from, and any ties you have to Gino Tatangelo. It'll be perfect."

Santini's face did not change. "I'm not involved in anything illegal."

"We'll see," Lee replied. "But right now I want to know where that girl is. If I don't get some straight answers fast, Paulie and I are going for a little ride in the country. It may help refresh his memory, the way I ask him questions when there aren't any witnesses. It'll be his word against mine, and I'm betting Paulie here has a criminal record somewhere a mile long."

"You're bluffing," Santini said.

Lee gave him a one-sided, humorless grin. "Sometimes a

gun goes off accidentally." He pressed his pistol a little harder against Paulie's spine, then pulled the hammer back until it cocked behind the ream pin. "Tell me where she is," he added in a hoarse snarl, "or you and I are going for a ride."

The muscles in Paulie's back tightened. He turned his head and watched Santini's face. For a moment, the two men stared at each other, until Santini spoke.

"The girl tried to rob him. She took his wallet and when he asked her about it, she lied. It happened last night. He went over to Maude's this morning to demand she return his money."

"That's right," Paulie said. "The bitch stole my money and I want it back. It was a couple hundred dollars she took."

"Where is she now?" Lee asked, certain the story was pure invention.

Santini blinked. "Show him, Paulie. It's this little house over on the east side of town. He's keeping her there until she tells him where she hid the money. A friend of Paulie's is keeping an eye on her."

"Let's go," Lee commanded, pushing Paulie toward the door by prodding him with the gun.

Santini watched them go out, then reached for the telephone.

21

Paulie's huge frame barely fit in Lee's front seat. He sat hunched over with his hands behind his back, his face only inches from the windshield. He easily weighed three hundred pounds.

"You're gonna regret this, cowboy cop," he growled, his lips drawn back in anger. "You've got no idea who you're fucking with."

The Packard jolted over bumps in the gravel road winding back and forth near the eastern city limits, a poor section of town given over to cheap rentals. "Tell me who I'm about to fuck with, so I'll know why I'm supposed to be scared of 'im," Lee replied, following Paulie's reluctant directions to Gorman Street.

"You'll find out soon enough, lawman, if you're lucky enough to know it before something bad happens to you."

"What's gonna happen, Paulie? Is my mailbox gonna explode? Is somebody gonna slip up behind me with a gun and shoot me when I'm not looking?"

"You'll see. You country hicks don't understand how serious this is, fucking with Mr. Santini. He's got powerful friends."

"Like Gino Tatangelo . . ."

"Maybe. I'll tell you this much . . . they aren't hillbilly cowboys who talk big. They mean business. You're gonna regret what you're doing. If you're smart, you'll let me go and forget the whole thing."

It was pointless to answer Paulie's threats with a warning of his own. Paulie was hired muscle, a bodyguard, and probably a collector if Santini was into loan-sharking. "Who's at the house where the girl's being kept?"

"Find out for yourself. I'm only taking you there because Mr. Santini told me to."

Lee wondered if he might be walking into a trap. Santini had reached for the telephone as they were leaving and it was a good guess he was warning whoever watched the girl to be ready. "If anything has happened to her, anything at all, I'm taking you for that ride in the country I promised you. And if somebody's got a surprise waiting for me at the house, the first bullet I fire is gonna be at the back of your skull. You're going in first, and I'll be right behind you, ready to blow your brains out if I see any sign there's trouble."

"You talk real big, cowboy, when I got my hands cuffed like this. Turn me loose and I'll rearrange your face."

Slow anger started to boil inside Lee's head. "If that girl is hurt, if anything's wrong with her, I'll do just that, Paulie. I'll take off those cuffs and we'll see how tough you really are with your fists."

"You won't do it. You're nothing but wind, cowboy."

He let it go for now, turning down Gorman Street. He wasn't going to let Paulie push him into a fight, he promised himself.

"That's the house," Paulie said, inclining his head toward the right-hand side of the road. "The one with the green roof."

A run-down cabin with peeling white paint sat on cement blocks at the end of the street. No cars were parked out front or in the gravel driveway. Had Santini's telephone call warned whoever was with Molly to take her elsewhere? Lee silently cursed his lack of foresight—he'd been in too much of a hurry. The girl could be anywhere now.

He stopped the car in front and switched off the motor, his practiced eye taking in every detail, every window, even the roof, in case a sharpshooter was waiting for him there. He got out and drew his pistol, moving around the Packard cautiously to open the door for Paulie. "Get out," he snapped, watching the house and Paulie. "Walk in front of me. I'm keeping this gun behind your head. If one thing goes wrong—if you trip over a rock, or if I see anybody moving around inside who might have a gun—I'm gonna feed your brains to the sparrows. You won't hardly feel a thing, Paulie, just a little cracking noise and then you'll be free of every worry you've got."

"You won't shoot a man wearing handcuffs," Paulie said as he got out of the car, sounding sure of it. "That would get your cowboy lawman's ass in deep trouble."

"I'll remember to take 'em off before I call the coroner," Lee promised, moving around behind Paulie, placing the muzzle of his Colt at the base of Paulie's skull. He cocked the gun, glancing left and right. "Now walk real slow to the front door. Be sure you tell whoever's inside that I'll blow a tunnel through your head if I see anybody with a gun." He pushed Paulie forward with his free hand. "If Santini called to warn 'em ahead of time, I'd advise you to set them straight on what I'll do to you if there's a shot fired."

"There's no telephone at this dump," Paulie said. "It don't even have electric fans."

They crossed a grassless yard, the dirt hardened by summer heat and lack of rain, to a pair of steps. Paulie climbed the first step, then the second, halting before a screen door covering a painted wooden door without windows.

"Tell whoever's inside to come out with his hands in the air," Lee demanded, tensed for the moment when something went wrong.

"Hey, Roberto!" Paulie bellowed. "There's a lawman out here with a gun pointed at my head! Don't shoot! Mr. Santini said to let him have the woman!"

No sound came from inside.

"Try again," Lee said, letting Paulie feel more pressure from the gun barrel, puckering his skin where the muzzle went deeper into the flesh.

"Open up, Roberto! Don't bring no gun to the door!"

Again no noises came from the house.

"Maybe Santini called somebody else and had 'em pick up your friend and clear out before we got here," Lee said. "The girl better be in there, and she'd better not have even one hair out of place. If somebody did something to her, you aren't gonna like what happens next."

"Open the goddamn door, Roberto!" Paulie shouted. "The boss said to give the whore to this cop!"

More silence.

Lee decided that enough time had been wasted. "Step

aside. I'll open it. You're going in first. You've got two choices. I'm gonna shoot you, or you walk in and tell Roberto to lay down his weapon." He moved Paulie aside and pulled the screen door open just enough to get his hand around the doorknob. Then he shoved Paulie directly in front of him and pushed the door open with his free hand, keeping his revolver against the back of Paulie's head as rusty hinges squeaked.

The front room, with water-stained hardwood floors, was empty. The lone upholstered chair was placed near a window where someone could sit and keep an eye on the street. Though the windows were open, the heat trapped inside was like an oven.

"Don't shoot, Roberto," Paulie cried without any urging from Lee. "This cop's got a gun to my head. Mr. Santini said to let her go."

Paulie's voice echoed through what appeared to be an empty house.

"Roberto took her somewhere," Lee said under his breath. "I figure Santini called somebody."

"She was in the back room," Paulie said, looking at a closed door opposite them.

Lee pushed Paulie across the floor with pressure from his gun. He opened the narrow door and peered around Paulie's wide body, blocking the door frame. A cot sat in the middle of the room and on it, her hands and feet bound with coils of rope, Molly Brown lay motionless, a cloth gag over her mouth.

"Step over against that wall," Lee ordered, jaws clenched in fury when he noticed dark bruises on her face. Her eyes appeared swollen shut, with purple circles around them where she'd been hit hard enough to draw blood.

Paulie went over to the wall, watching the girl's face. Lee crossed to the bed and bent over the prone figure.

"She's breathing," he said quietly. He gave Paulie a look before he put his gun on the mattress. "You try to run and I give you my word, I'll kill you," he warned hoarsely, untying the rag covering Molly's mouth.

He untied her wrists, then her ankles. She did not awaken when he touched her. The left side of her face was badly swollen and her lips were covered with dried blood. Angry red marks on her neck showed where she'd been choked. Lee nudged her gently and patted her unblemished cheek to wake her up, all the while keeping one eye on Paulie.

Molly's eyelids fluttered open. She stared at the ceiling for a moment, then murmured, "Please don't hit me anymore."

"Nobody's gonna hurt you again," Lee whispered. "I'll make sure nobody does . . ."

She looked at him, and for a time it appeared she did not recognize his face. "Are you that Ranger?" she asked, her words muffled by swollen lips and a puffy cheek.

"I'm Ranger Lee Garrett. You're safe now. Who did this to you? And why?"

She needed time to clear her head. "Carlos said I told you things I hadn't oughta, showing you where Bill Dodd got killed. This big guy brought me here and beat me up. He said he was going to teach me a lesson about who not to talk to. Carlos wanted me to give him that paper of Bill's but I told him I never saw it."

Lee turned slitted eyes toward Paulie. "Is that the man who beat you up, Molly?"

She could barely raise her head and when she did, he saw a look of fear cross her face before she fell back on the mattress. "Carlos said I can't talk to you anymore. He'll kill me if I tell who did it."

Lee stood up with his Colt in one hand. "I'll take you to the hospital so a doctor can see to your wounds." He looked at Paulie again, his temper suddenly completely beyond his control. "But first I'll take Paulie in the other room, so we can talk about what happened. Just lie still. We won't be gone but a minute."

He crossed over to Paulie and stuck his gun under the big man's chin. "Walk through that door. You and I are gonna have a little discussion about manners in the presence of a lady. It won't take long."

Paulie glared at him. "Take these cuffs off and I'll give you a lesson or two, if you've got balls enough to put down that pistol."

Lee shoved Paulie toward the door, and as he did, he tossed his revolver on the bed beside Molly. "Be real happy to oblige you," he said savagely, feeling his arms tremble with anticipation, the muscles tensing all over his body.

He closed the door behind them and took keys from his shirt pocket to unlock Paulie's handcuffs. When Paulie's wrists were free, Lee stood back, tossing the iron manacles to the floor with a clatter, waiting for Paulie to turn around.

"You gotta be a dumb son of a bitch," Paulie snarled, making a half turn toward Lee.

Lee's right fist struck Paulie's jaw with a suddenness and power shaped by years of practice, beginning with the fights he'd had with his older, larger brothers. Blind rage overwhelmed him as he swung a roundhouse left into Paulie's nose. The snap of cartilage dislodged by heavy knuckles cracked as Paulie went backward, staggering, blood squirting from both nostrils while he tried to keep his balance, doubling his fists for a looping right and left thrown almost in unison.

Lee ducked both punches easily, for big men were usually too slow. His knuckles stinging with pain, he sent a straight right for Paulie's temple with every ounce of strength he had, feeling a rewarding jolt move up his arm when his fist landed flush.

Paulie's eyes rolled and he tumbled to the floor on his rump with his back to the wall, blood pouring from his nose to the front of his white shirt. But Lee's uncontrolled rage was far from spent. He aimed a kick toward Paulie's face, and when the heavy cowboy boot landed square against the point of his chin, Paulie made a sound, a grunt, in the same instant his head smacked against the wall behind him.

"I'll teach you to hit a woman," Lee hissed between teeth gritted so hard they hurt his jaw.

Paulie fell over on his side, blinking furiously to remain conscious despite the heavy blows. He groaned and tried to push his body off the floor with trembling arms.

In a final moment of blind anger, Lee lifted his right foot and smashed the heel of his boot into Paulie's cheek, slamming his head to the floorboards, making a sound like a kettledrum. Gasping for breath, Lee stared down at Paulie, clenching his fists. Paulie was out cold, yet Lee spoke to him as if he were awake. "You said you were gonna rearrange my face," he said, knowing he'd let his temper get the best of him in spite of promising himself it wouldn't. "When you wake up, look at yourself in the mirror, fat man. This cowboy cop just gave you a lesson in manners."

He turned around when he heard a noise. Molly was standing in the doorway looking down at Paulie, leaning against the door frame to steady herself. She glanced up at Lee through eyelids that were purpled and badly swollen. "You sure are tougher than you look, Mr. Garrett," she said in a tiny voice. "But when Carlos finds out what you did, he'll kill me for sure."

Lee bent down to retrieve the handcuffs. "I won't let them hurt you again, Molly," he promised. "For a while, it'll be best if you stayed away from Maude's until this business with Santini is finished."

She studied his face for a time. "It doesn't appear I've got any choice but to trust you, Mr. Garrett."

He went over to her and put his hands on her slender shoulders. "You can trust me," he said softly, and now every trace of his anger was gone.

As he was helping Molly to the door, he stopped and replaced the handcuffs, binding Paulie's wrists behind his back. After he got the girl to a doctor, he'd stop by Longview police headquarters and have officers pick him up and arrest him. There would be plenty of charges to file — kidnapping, assault and battery, and resisting arrest, although the latter charge was simply necessary to explain the damage done to Paulie's face.

He assisted Molly out to the steps, looking both ways before he guided her to his car.

22

Molly's injuries were more extensive than he'd first thought. A Dr. Thompson at Longview Municipal examined her while Lee made a telephone call to the Longview police, giving them the address on Gorman Street, explaining the charges he would bring against Paulie. After the girl's ribs were taped where Paulie had kicked her a number of times, and her facial wounds treated with ointment, Lee helped her to his car and drove her to the Grand Hotel, noting Whitaker's Studebaker in the parking lot.

He took her upstairs to his room, perspiring heavily in the late-day heat. She'd said only a few words until he unlocked his door and showed her in. There was a message for him at the desk from Brad Whitaker, in room 206. The hotel clerk had given Molly a guarded look when he saw the marks and bandages on her face before they went upstairs. Cal had merely nodded when they came through the lobby, giving the girl a passing glance.

"They'll be looking for me," she said, her voice small and frightened as he locked the door behind them. "I've gotta get out of this town before they find me here," she added, walking over to the bed.

"Nobody's gonna bother you," he promised. "Do you have someplace you can go? Some relatives somewhere?"

She shook her head while sitting down on the mattress, in obvious pain due to her cracked ribs. Her arms were badly bruised and swollen. "I've got nobody. No place to go, but I can't stay here. Gino will tell Carlos to kill me when he hears about this."

Lee turned on the fan and aimed it at the bed, opening the window to let in air. "You've got my word that nobody will harm you again." He looked at her and felt something more than sorrow. A few more blows of the kind she'd taken might have killed her. As he gazed at her now, she seemed much too innocent to be in the profession she was in. She reminded him of a little girl, a child. "Lie down and rest. I'll be down the hall talking to a man from the Treasury Department. I won't be gone but a minute. I'll lock the door."

"I wish you wouldn't leave. I'm scared to be by myself right now."

"I won't be far away. I'll ask Brad to come to my room."

Tears formed in her eyes. "How come you're being so nice to me, Mr. Garrett?"

For a moment, he wondered himself. Why he had taken such an interest in this girl? "I suppose it has to do with the way I was brought up, to help a lady when she needs it. Besides that, I'm really only doing my job."

She looked down at the floor. She was crying but no sounds came from her lips. "I'm not a real lady and you know it. You know who I am . . . what I am."

"That part doesn't matter to me, Molly. I figure you did the only thing you could under the circumstances. I don't judge you by what you do for a living."

She cried harder now, gingerly fingering away tears from her swollen, purple cheeks. "Hardly anybody's ever been nice to me unless it was when they wanted something. I think you know what I mean. I don't exactly know what to say." She tried to stifle a sob and pressed her lips together, still staring at the floor.

"You don't have to say anything. And stop worrying that any of them will hurt you again. I won't let it happen." He spoke softly, trying to reassure her as best he could. "I'm not afraid of Carlos or Gino or damn near anybody. I'm not claiming to be all that tough, but I'm pretty good at doing my job, an' when it comes to handling tough guys, I've had a little experience."

"I saw what you did to Pauline Gambino," she said with a note of surprise. "He's supposed to be as mean as they come. Carlos hired him to beat people up because he was so tough nobody could whip him, not ever. He grew up in the Bronx . . . that's about the worst place in the whole world."

"I never heard of the Bronx, but I don't suppose it matters. I shouldn't have lost my temper like that, but I did, and nothing can change it. When I saw what he did to you, I lost my head, I reckon. I'd appreciate it if you didn't say anything about what you saw. You weren't supposed to see it."

"I won't," she replied, glancing up, tears threatening to spill over. "He had it coming after what he did, only Carlos has other guys working for him who'll be looking for me. He thinks I've got Bill's paper proving he owned that land. I swore I never saw it, but Carlos doesn't believe me.

Paulie searched my room. Carlos thinks I told you he was running moonshine and gambling in the oilfield camps. He saw us together that time. Paulie said I was lying about the lease paper. He tore my room all to pieces before he made me go with him."

"I know. I saw it." Lee wondered why Santini wanted Dodd's lease document now, since Buster Davis already had a lease on the land. Was there something in the lease, or with it, that could tie Santini to the murder? That document seemed to be more important than he'd guessed. In the beginning of his investigation, it seemed to be only a meaningless piece of paper. "Paulie's on his way to jail, and I won't let anyone else who works for Santini get near you. We'll talk again in a little while. Right now I've got to see what the Treasury agent found out about some New Jersey corporations and a couple of cars. I'll lock the door."

Molly stood up, doing her best not to cry. "I don't hardly know how to thank you." She gave him a half-hearted smile. "It sounds silly, but it made me feel safe when you held onto me back at that house. All you did was put your hands on my shoulders."

It was nothing more than an impulse when he suddenly reached for her and gently put his arms around her waist, being careful to avoid touching her bandaged ribs. He stared into her eyes, discovering they were a deep emerald green. "You'll be safe with me," he said softly, feeling something stir inside him while he held her. "Stop worrying. I can take care of anybody who comes along."

He let go of her somewhat reluctantly when it seemed there was nothing more to say. As he headed for the door, he wondered what had come over him that made him put his arms around a woman he scarcely knew.

Whitaker answered his knock. Wearing an undershirt and no shoes or socks, he peered out at Lee through thick eyeglass lenses. His room was even hotter than Lee's, despite an electric fan and open windows.

"I found out a few things," he said, stepping back so Lee could come in. "Not as much as I'd hoped, I'm afraid, but it's something to go on."

Lee remained in the doorway, glancing back down the hall to his room. "I've got some news too," he said. "The girl, Molly, is in my room. She was beaten half to death. Santini's bodyguard kidnapped her at Maude's and took her to a house on the east side. Santini wants to get his hands on Bill Dodd's lease for some reason, and he was willing to risk grabbing the girl in order to find it. I need to keep an eye on her in case Santini tries to get at her again. There's more . . . a speculator named Buster Davis lied to me about not knowing Dodd's best friend, so I figure he's lying about his involvement with Santini too. Santini is in the loan-sharking business. Dodd may have tried to borrow money from him to pay the landowners for the oil rights. It's still all tangled up, with no direct ties to Santini and the murder just yet, but I've got a feeling I'm getting a hell of a lot closer."

"Santini sent one of his goons to kidnap this girl?" Whitaker asked.

"The big guy named Paulie. I cuffed him and called the police to have him arrested. There was a little bit of a scuffle."

Whitaker went over to the bed, sitting down to put on his shoes and socks. His shirt hung on a bedpost over a shoulder holster holding his .38. "No word yet on the New Jersey corporation that leased the warehouse. The Oldsmobile is registered to a company in Fort Worth owned by another New Jersey corporation. The head man, president of the corporation, is a guy named Luciano. We're checking on him and all of his partners. The black Cadillac we found in Henderson County is a much better lead. It had a set of

New York license plates. The registered owner is a woman by the name of Marianna Tortelli. It turns out she's a married niece of Gino Tatangelo, according to my Washington office. The guy we shot at Brownsboro was Tony Bruno. He was Marianna Tortelli's brother-in-law, married to her sister. He had a criminal record, including extortion and bookmaking. His address is in Brooklyn and that puts him in Gino Tatangelo's neighborhood. It's a fair supposition that Tatangelo sent him down here to help with expanding the operations in East Texas. At last we're onto something we can prove."

"The girl may know a lot more," Lee suggested. "Right now she's scared to death they'll kill her. I won't be able to hand solid proof to the district attorney that Santini sent his bodyguard to grab her, but by now, Santini knows I've got Paulie in custody and that'll worry him some."

"He's beginning to make mistakes," Whitaker said, tying his shoelaces quickly. "You have one of his men in jail. He'll be worried that this Paulie fellow will sing to save his own ass. If we can establish that the warehouse we raided last night is leased by someone connected to Gino Tatangelo, Santini's house of cards will begin to crumble."

"We have to prove it first, and if I can, I have to find out who killed Dodd. It's just a hunch that Santini was behind it."

Whitaker slipped into his shirt and shoulder holster. "We can question the girl. Perhaps she knows something we overlooked, something that didn't seem important at the time."

"She's not in shape to answer many questions," Lee said. "I need to go down to the police station and file charges against Paulie Gambino. I'd appreciate it if you'd keep an eye on her in my room while I'm gone. I'll pick up some sandwiches for supper on my way back. Don't let anybody in, and keep your gun handy."

Whitaker nodded and came into the hallway, locking his room. "Do you really think Santini would be brazen enough to send one of his men here, knowing you're a Texas Ranger?"

Lee didn't have to think about it long. "He's got nerve and I don't figure he scares easy. If he comes after her, he'll send somebody we can't link directly to him. He wants that lease, and that convinces me more than ever he's behind Dodd's murder."

They walked side by side to Lee's door. As he unlocked it, he said quietly, "Don't question her too long today, Brad. She's had just about enough for one afternoon."

Lee found her lying on the bed, watching them through puffy eyelids as they came in. He noticed for the first time that her pale blue cotton dress was torn and bloodstained where she'd wiped her face on her sleeves. He closed the door and locked it.

"Molly, this is Treasury Agent Brad Whitaker. He's gonna help me keep an eye on you. He's investigating Carlos Santini's operations for the federal government. You'll be safe with him while I'm down at police headquarters filing charges against Paulie."

Molly's face showed doubt.

"Pleased to meet you, Molly," Whitaker said, nodding politely before walking to a window overlooking Commerce Street. "I see there is no fire escape. No one can come in except through the door."

Molly's eyes were on Lee. "I wish you didn't have to go," she said, sounding frightened.

He smiled. "I have to, so Paulie can't get out of jail to hurt you again."

Whitaker walked back and examined Molly's injuries. "He gave you a terrible beating, miss. He should be prosecuted to the full extent of the law."

Lee peered into the hallway before he went out, making

sure it was empty. He locked the door securely and pocketed the key.

Standing before a booking desk at the city jail, Lee asked a police sergeant named Tolliver to repeat what he'd just said. "How the hell can a judge set bond before charges are filed?"

Tolliver was older, close to sixty, and when he spoke, it was with a note of indifference. "Ask the judge. His office is up on the second floor, only he's probably gone home by now. I got a call from him an' he said he'd set bond at five hundred dollars on Paulie Gambino, an' that Gambino's lawyer would be down in a minute with an order for his release. I let him go, just like Judge Warren tol' me to. He's the county judge an' what he says goes in Gregg County."

Lee's hands balled into fists. Fury jumbled every thought in his brain momentarily. "Gambino was to have been arrested on state charges. I called the Longview police and told whoever was on the phone to pick him up, after I identified myself as a Texas Ranger. A goddamn county judge has no authority to release one of my prisoners."

Tolliver merely shrugged. "You'll have to take that up with Judge Warren. He tells me to let somebody go, I let 'im go."

Lee bent over the desk, his jaw jutted. "Where the hell do I find this Judge Warren if he isn't in his office? I'm gonna arrest that son of a bitch again, but first I'm gonna straighten out a county judge on matters of jurisdiction. And when I bring Paulie Gambino back to jail, anybody who lets him out without an order from a district judge will answer to me!"

"I was followin' procedures," Tolliver said, unmoved by Lee's obvious rage.

"Where do I find the judge's house?"

"His name is Judge Eldon Warren an' he lives on Surrey Lane, west of the sawmill. He's prob'ly at home now, like I said."

"I'll find him," Lee promised, wheeling away from the desk to hurry up a set of concrete stairs out of the basement at City Hall.

23

Sunset turned the skies west of Longview a brilliant pink as Lee spun the steering wheel toward the Grand Hotel's parking lot, a bag of grilled-cheese sandwiches and pickles on the seat beside him. Rather than driving out to Judge Warren's house now, he'd decided to follow procedures and ask a district judge in Tyler for a state bench warrant for Paulie Gambino, without bond until a hearing could be set. One thing was suddenly all too clear: the county judge, Eldon Warren, was in someone's pocket, possibly Santini's, or even Gino Tatangelo's. An arresting officer had to be involved for having allowed Paulie to make a phone call to his lawyer in order to arrange bail at almost the same time he should have been booked. The whole thing smelled of shit, of crooked cops and judges and sleazy payoffs. Now a dangerous man was on the loose because of it. Lee needed to warn Whitaker, and he felt it was too risky to make a phone call like that to the hotel.

He parked the Packard and jumped out, hurrying down the sidewalk in front of the Grand. He found Cal reading a newspaper as he walked in. No one was behind the hotel desk.

"Has anybody gone upstairs lately?" Lee asked, heading across the lobby without pausing for an answer.

"No, sir," Cal replied, "but some feller did call askin' if Texas Rangers was stayin' here. 'Nother feller called a while later sayin' he was a Texas Ranger hisself, askin' to speak to you. I tol' him you was gone. I seen you leave. He said you'd know him. Said his name was Bob Ross."

Lee stopped in his tracks. "Who was it called the first time?"

"Didn't say. He jus' asked if any Rangers was here. Mr. Williams was gone home an' Miz Williams ain't showed up yet, so I answered the phone like I always do. He didn't give me no name."

"But you told him I was here?"

"Yessir. I tol' the truth 'bout it. Didn't see no reason to lie to him. I tol' him what room you was in. By the by, I see a story in today's paper 'bout a big shootin' over in that warehouse district. Says here four folks got killed by lawmen an' federal agents over some whiskey. I reckon you know somethin' 'bout it, seein' as you was askin' 'bout bootleg whiskey when you got here."

"Thanks Cal," Lee said, ignoring the remarks about the gunfight, taking the stairs at a trot with his bag of sandwiches clenched in an angry fist. Someone, likely one of Santini's men, knew he was staying here, and now knew his room number. He had to move Molly to Whitaker's room immediately in case Santini made another try at getting to her. Cal couldn't have known he was giving Santini just what he needed to make a second attempt.

Lee ran down the hall and knocked before putting his key in the lock. "It's me," he said so Whitaker would recognize his voice, then entered as quickly as he could.

Whitaker sat on a windowsill watching the street. Molly lay with her head on two pillows, watching Lee lock the door. He did not want to frighten her unnecessarily, yet she had to be told the truth.

He spoke to Whitaker. "A county judge set Paulie free on a five-hundred-dollar bond before I could get there. This whole thing stinks. The cop who picked him up obviously let him make a call to a lawyer before he was booked. They didn't wait for charges to be filed. This Judge Eldon Warren has to be on the take from Santini, and there's at least one dishonest cop on the Longview police force. I brought sandwiches but to tell the truth, I'm not hungry right now. We've got to move the girl to your room."

Molly bolted upright when she heard about Paulie, wincing, clasping her damaged ribs. "He's coming to kill me tonight. He isn't scared of anybody . . ." She started to cry.

"He isn't gonna kill you," Lee promised, placing the bag of oily sandwiches on the bed beside her. "Nobody's gonna hurt you again. I give you my word."

Molly covered her eyes with her hands. "I know I'm supposed to believe you, Mr. Garrett, but you don't know Paulie. You got the best of him today, but he'll keep coming back until he gets me. He's crazy mean. Nobody ever whipped him in a fight until you did, and he won't forget about it. He's coming back tonight for sure."

"Let him come, then," Lee said, remembering their fight at the shack and getting mad all over again. He wished she hadn't made mention of the fistfight in front of Whitaker, but any damage to his reputation as a peace officer was already done. "We're gonna move you to Agent Whitaker's room. I'll be right here, waiting for Paulie to show up. I'll have a little surprise for him if he does . . ." He became acutely aware of Whitaker's stare just then and ended what he was about to say.

"You said there was a scuffle," Whitaker remarked casually. "Santini's bodyguard is huge. I'm sure that physical force could be required to subdue him if he resisted arrest."

"He's big, but kinda on the slow side. Let's get Molly down to your room. Keep your door locked and fetch your scattergun. If anybody shows, they'll come armed to the teeth, maybe with a tommy gun. I'll get my twelve-gauge out of the trunk and wait for 'em here. They'll come to my room. I'll tell the woman at the desk downstairs not to mention a Treasury agent being registered. I've got to call my company captain. Take the food and lock yourselves in. I'll be back upstairs when I'm done making telephone calls. I need to call Roy Woods so we can get the warrant for Paulie from a district judge. It's getting dark and if anybody's coming, they'll wait for the sun to go down."

"I can't believe Santini would be so bold," Whitaker said, leaving his perch on the windowsill, sweat glistening on his face and forearms. "He runs the risk of having federal agents swarm all over him if he tries shooting up a room at this hotel. I'm of the opinion he'll be more subtle. I don't see him taking a chance like that."

"It pays to be careful," Lee said. "No harm in being ready for anything."

"He'll send someone," Molly whispered, drying her eyes on a bloodstained dress sleeve. "You don't know Carlos. He won't let anything stop him from getting what he wants." She swung her legs off the bed and stood up slowly, her face twisting in agony when she moved.

Lee spoke to Whitaker as he was unlocking the door. "Go down and get your shotgun. See if there's a back way into the hotel. Give me the key to your room and we'll wait there until you get back. Then I'll call Roy Woods and Cap'n Ross."

Whitaker glanced down the hall and walked out when he saw it was empty, handing over his room key on his way toward the stairs with twilight darkening a lone window at the end of the hallway.

Lee felt the girl touch his arm. She held the paper bag in a trembling hand.

"How come you're doing all this for me?" she asked, speaking so softly he had difficulty hearing her. "It's because you think I haven't told you the truth, isn't it?"

"I'm doing my best to do my job, and that includes keeping you safe while I'm trying to find out who killed Bill Dodd."

She followed him into the hall, past the stairway to room 206, while he kept his hand near the butt of his pistol. When they went inside, he closed the door quietly and crossed to a pair of windows, standing behind the window frame to examine the street for any suspicious-looking cars parked along the curb, anyone who might be watching the hotel. Darkness crept across Longview with the coming of night.

"All's quiet," he told her. "Eat something and get as much rest as you can." He watched her sit down on the edge of the bed. "I know you're scared, but there's nothing to be afraid of anymore. Nobody'll know you're here."

She took a sandwich from the bag and opened the waxed paper around it. "You're the nicest man I ever met, Mr. Garrett. You talk so gentle when you talk to me. I like the sound of your voice. I know you've got a mean side, like when you went to kicking Paulie after he was down already. But you can be real gentle too, and that's unusual, how a man can be both."

"I lost my temper. It doesn't happen very often." He said it with a touch of embarrassment.

She got off the bed and came over to him, looking into his eyes. "I hope you don't mind if I kiss you," she whispered as she stood on her tiptoes. "It's about the only way I can think of to say thanks."

She kissed him so quickly that he wasn't fully prepared for it, a light peck on the cheek, and he couldn't think of a thing to say for a moment. "You don't owe me anything," he said, listening now to footsteps in the hallway.

Whitaker knocked and said, "It's Brad," before he came in, his suit coat draped over his shotgun to hide it from anyone in the lobby. "There's a back door coming off an alley. The Negro shoeshine man said they keep it bolted at night. I showed an elderly woman behind the desk my badge and instructed her not to tell anyone I was staying here. Of course she became worried when she saw my shotgun. I told her I was only cleaning it."

Lee started for the door. "I'll make those calls," he said without looking at Molly, wondering about the strange sensation lingering in his chest after she kissed him.

"You're makin' somebody nervous," Bob Ross said, his voice a bit garbled and distant in the earpiece. "Major Elliot received a telephone call this afternoon from a bigshot state senator in Austin by the name of Claude Atkins. He complained about how a Texas Ranger was makin' false accusations against some Longview citizens, and about illegal searches of somebody's property with no warrants."

Lee knew he would observe the code of silence to cover what Roy Woods had done. "None of it's true, Cap'n. We looked around at the Italian's warehouse, this Carlos Santini, but I wouldn't call it a search. One of Santini's hired guns kidnapped a girl who is a material witness in the William Dodd case. A county judge who has to be on the take let the guy go on a cheap bond before I got down to file official charges. It smells of corruption, and I believe the county sheriff and this judge are on the take. We found a load of moonshine in the warehouse, a building the Treasury boys feel can be traced to Santini and his boss in New York, Gino Tatangelo. I believe we'll be able to prove that gangsters have moved in on the oilfields here."

Ross said nothing for a moment. "That'd sure make Sterling happy, if you can prove it."

"I think we can. Treasury is working on the case now. They lost an agent in a shoot-out the other night."

"Don't trust the damn feds, Lee. They'll try to grab all the headlines for themselves. I'll keep Major Elliot informed. If it was left up to me, I'd tell this Senator Atkins to stuff his complaints up his ass. On the other hand, try an' get a warrant when you need one. Play by the rules whenever you can so I can keep the major satisfied. I'm gonna tell him he can whisper in the governor's ear we may have organized crime from back East in East Texas, an' that the Rangers are right on top of it, maybe fixin' to make some arrests. It'll help settle things down over in Austin."

"I'll call you as soon as I know anything new."

"G'night, Lee. Get some rest. This was supposed to be a vacation. You sure have one comin'." The phone went dead.

Lee asked the operator to connect him to Roy Woods' number at home in Tyler. After a long delay, a thick voice answered.

"I ran into a little trouble, Roy," he began. "That fat guy working for Santini grabbed the girl I talked to about the Dodd killing. I found her and arrested him, but a county judge by the name of Eldon Warren let him go before I could file charges. The fat boy is loose, and probably dangerous. I've got the girl hidden in Agent Whitaker's room. What I need is an arrest warrant for a Paulie Gambino from the district judge there in Tyler, so nobody can let him go again. Santini's feeling the squeeze. I expect him to try for the girl again because he thinks she knows something and he's worried over what she'll say."

"Damn," Woods exclaimed. "I'll get a warrant from Judge Baker tonight. Sure as hell hope he ain't already gone to bed. I'll drive over soon as I've got it an' help you find that potbellied son of a bitch. We'll drive out to Santini's house an' ask him some real pointed questions, the kind when he's got a gun pointed at his goddamn head. I'm tired of fuckin' around with these greaseball Italians. I'll be there in a couple of hours, if I can."

"I'm in room two-twelve at the Grand. Be careful driving up—they may be watching the place."

"I hope the hell they are," Woods snapped. "I'm gettin' sick an' tired of dodgin' their machine-gun bullets. It's high time we taught these sorry bastards a lesson, Lee, not to be fuckin' with the Texas Rangers. See you in a couple hours."

The phone clicked off. Lee resisted an urge to tell Woods about the lesson he'd given Paulie. He had the feeling he'd be meeting up with Paulie Gambino again . . . that the lesson hadn't been quite enough to be thoroughly convincing.

24

Roy drove his green Ford sedan into Longview shortly after ten o'clock with his shotgun lying across the back seat, racing past slower cars blocking the narrow streets to reach the city jail as quickly as he could. He was still fuming over being called out at night to handle some pissy-assed affair with a bunch of big-talking crooks from New York who thought they could come to his part of Texas and run things. Lee Garrett wasn't handling it right—you had to bust open a few heads and get their attention first, like handling mules the way his pa did. You got a mule's undivided attention by breaking a tree limb over its skull before you broke it to harness, and that's what Carlos Santini and his Italians needed—a skull busting. Garrett was being too soft on them.

He slid to a stop in front of City Hall and got out, slamming the car door, walking fast toward the basement steps to speak to the booking officer on duty. Then he'd call Chief Laster and get him out of bed to remind him who had the authority here. After that, he'd telephone Judge Eldon Warren and set him straight on a few things, like the warrant issued by District Judge Cleveland Baker calling for Paulie Gambino's arrest with bond denied unti there was a hearing in the district court at Tyler. He had half a mind to telephone Perry Bass too, to inform him that any local peace officer interfering with the Rangers' investigation into Santini's business dealings would be in boiling water up to his ass. Garrett may have been right to suspect that Sheriff Bass was looking the other way on some things. They sure as hell weren't getting any cooperation from city or county officials.

He almost ran across the jail booking room to a desk where an older cop sat staring at him from under a bare lightbulb on a wire hanging from the ceiling. A sign on the desk read SERGEANT TOLLIVER. Roy halted in front of the sergeant and took an envelope from his pocket, waving it angrily under Tolliver's nose.

"You see this?" he said, taking out the warrant, speaking in a voice filled with menace. "It's a warrant, a goddamn district court warrant for the arrest of one Paulie Gambino. When a Texas Ranger sends a goddamn prisoner to this jail, you leave the son of a bitch locked up 'til a Ranger comes to get him. It don't matter if Jesus Christ himself calls you an' tells you to let him go, you'd better not unlock that cell door unless you want to be charged yourself. You tell that to every other Longview cop who works behind this desk. Have I made myself real clear?"

Tolliver nodded once. "Judge Warren said to release him on bond. His lawyer showed me the bond signed by him. I do what the judge tells me to do."

"Not anymore, you don't," Roy warned, biting down when he said it. "I'll arrest you for obstruction of justice, an' I'll do the same thing to Eldon Warren if he ever lets an-other one of our prisoners go."

"I get off at eleven," Tolliver said quietly. "I'll tell Al what you said, havin' that warrant for Gambino."

Roy shoved the paper back in its envelope. "Grab that phone an' tell the operator to dial Judge Warren's number at home. It ain't too late for him to hear what I've got to say."

"He won't like it," Tolliver complained, although he reached for the telephone anyway.

Roy glared down at the sergeant. "I don't give a damn if he likes it or not. Just call him an' hand the phone to me. When I get done, I want you to call Chief Laster, so I can tell him the same fuckin' thing."

He saw the black car with two men seated in it as he rounded a street corner a block from the Grand. They weren't talking to each other, and that in itself seemed odd. His headlamps flashed over the car's license plate as he drove past—he couldn't read the numbers in the dim light.

"Yonder's trouble," he said to himself, glancing in the rearview mirror for a moment. "Just like Lee said. They're watchin' the hotel."

He drove in front by the curb and killed the motor, wait-ing a moment to watch the two men in his mirror. He could only see their outlines, heads and shoulders, through the dark windshield more than a block away.

I could slip up behind them, he thought, reaching over the seat back for his shotgun. "I'd better tell Lee they're out here so he'll know," he added aloud, opening the door care-fully so he could keep the shotgun beside his leg, out of sight until he got inside.

Roy entered the lobby. A silver-haired woman behind a desk noticed his gun immediately and her mouth fell open.

"It's okay, ma'am. I'm a Texas Ranger. I'm goin' upstairs to talk to Ranger Lee Garrett. I'm only cleanin' my gun."

"It seems several of our guests are cleaning their guns tonight," she said in a hushed voice as Roy took to the stairs.

He found room 212 without difficulty and knocked. "It's Roy Woods," he said. "I've got the warrant. Let me in."

Soft footsteps, then a lock turning before the door swung inward. Garrett had a pistol in his hand. His shotgun lay on the bed.

"Come in, Roy. Thanks for bringing it over. I've run into some local politics and I don't like the smell."

Roy handed Garrett the envelope and crossed to the window on the south side. "Turn out that light," he said. "We've got some company down the street, two gents in a black car. They're just sittin' there, watchin' the hotel from a couple of blocks away. You can bet your ass it's Santini's boys, waitin' for it to get late so nobody'll be on the street."

Garrett switched off the light.

"Can't see 'em from here," Roy said, pointing in the direction where he'd seen the car.

"I'll warn Agent Whitaker to get ready. He and the girl are down the hall."

"How bad is she hurt?" Roy asked, remembering it was some hooker Garrett had been questioning about the Dodd killing, and he only asked to be polite, having no use for women who sold pussy.

"Pretty bad. Cracked ribs, and her face looks like hell."

"It'll be a spell before she sells any more of herself with her face busted up. I can't work up much sympathy for a whore. Maybe she'll learn from it, workin' for an asshole like Santini."

Garrett didn't reply, walking softly into the hallway as if he had no opinion either way on the subject of whores.

Roy leaned against the window frame, studying the street and the alley behind the building. I can ease down that alley and get right behind them, he thought, if there aren't any dogs barking to alert them someone's moving around.

He recalled Howard Laster's reaction to his phone call half an hour ago, promising he'd find out which one of his officers had allowed Paulie to call a lawyer. But reaction from Eldon Warren had been much stronger, threatening to call Ranger headquarters over Roy's angry warnings not to interfere with a Ranger's arrest in the future. "He was scared," Roy said to himself, grinning a little, feeling satisfied. If a county judge was crooked, taking bribes for going soft on gangsters who paid him well, it would be a good notation in his record at headquarters if he could expose the judge and have him removed from the bench.

"This could be a big case," he muttered. "New York gangsters in Longview, sellin' everything from whiskey to pussy, an' runnin' gamblin' tables. Cap'n MacDonald would nearly shit if we rounded up a bunch of Italian hoodlums, an' a judge with dirt on his hands, maybe a crooked cop or two. Me an' Garrett will get all the credit. It'll be big news, bigger'n all this small-time shit 'round an oilfield." He thought about what his photograph would look like on the front page of the Dallas and Houston newspapers, standing beside Carlos Santini wearing handcuffs on the steps of the district court in Tyler. Of course Lee Garrett would be there beside him, and probably that four-eyed Treasury agent.

But Garrett's behavior continued to bother him. Lee had a solid reputation with the Rangers, and it was no small job to impress the top lawmen in the state, but when he'd encountered a tough situation with Carlos Santini, Garrett had behaved like a man afraid of his own shadow. When he'd shot that girl in the dark, he'd acted strange, as though he wished he hadn't fired back at anyone that night. Worst of all, he'd behaved like he didn't want Roy to fire that shot into the moonshiner's skull, a son of a bitch who had been trying to kill them. "He's too damn soft," Roy said with conviction, watching the street with his shotgun cradled in his left arm. To be a Texas Ranger, a man had to have fire in his belly and sand in his craw.

He thought about Santini. Their arrival at the Italian's house, wherever it was, would throw a scare into him tonight. Bust down the door and stick a gun in his face. Make him piss in his pants if he wouldn't tell where this Paulie Gambino was hiding. Tap him on the head a few times with the barrel of a gun to help him with his memory. But first they had to handle the two goons parked down the street watching the hotel. Santini probably sent them to get the whore. Garrett was so damn sure she could help him find the murderer he was after. . . . Footsteps in the hall took him away from the window frame, covering the door with his shotgun, hidden in darkness beside the dresser.

"It's me," Garrett said, walking in after Roy had time to recognize his voice. He closed the door. "Brad's got his guns ready. Let's go find out who those boys are in that car." He took his shotgun off the bed. "There's a back door. We can slip out the back and split up. You come around behind 'em and I'll take the front. An alley runs behind those houses. You oughta be able to make it in five minutes."

Roy was surprised that Garrett would walk right up the road to the car from in front. "They'll see you comin'," he warned, trying to decide if it was guts or stupidity on Garrett's part to be willing to show himself. "You'll be walkin' out in plain view the whole time."

"I'm gonna drive," Garrett replied. "Block 'em off with my Packard. They won't suspect a car until I swing

over in front of them. I'll jump out with my scattergun and
hide behind it. If they try to back up, blast their windows
and blow out one or two tires. If I'm right and they're
Santini's men, they'll be armed and they'll start shooting
right off. If it's just two guys who aren't guilty of anything, they'll get out with their hands up when I give the
order."

The plan sounded good to Roy. "You can bet your ass
they're watchin' this hotel, Lee. It ain't two guys havin' a
sarsaparilla in a car on a hot night like this. Let's go."

A white cur barked at Woods while he crept down the alley.
Were it not for giving himself away, he would have shot the
dog to shut it up. Guided by starlight, he reached the end
of the alley and headed for the street corner, readying his
shotgun, unfastening a leather strap holding his .45 automatic in its holster just in case he needed more firepower.
He paused when he came to the corner of a picket fence and
peered around it.

He saw the car, a dark Chevrolet sedan, and the silhou-
ettes of two men seated in front. All he had to do was wait
until Lee's car drove out of the Grand's parking lot.

He heard an engine. A pair of headlamps swung away
from the hotel. Garrett's big Packard drove slowly down
Commerce Street. Roy eased around the fence corner with
his shotgun to his shoulder, heading for an elm tree growing next to the sidewalk twenty or thirty yards behind the
Chevrolet.

Suddenly, before he made the relative safety of the
tree trunk, the Packard wheeled over to block the Chevy's
path. Woods heard a car door open and then a shout. "You
boys get out with your hands where I can see 'em! I'm a
Texas—" A booming explosion drowned out the rest of
what Garrett was saying.

Window glass shattered, popping almost musically,

shards tinkling to the roadway like a thousand tiny bells. Roy moved against the elm and aimed for the Chevy's rear window as another explosion, louder than the first, blasted from behind the front fender of the Packard.

More glass erupted in a shower of airborne bits, cracking loudly enough to be heard blocks away. Frightened dogs started barking all over the neighborhood while Woods was squeezing his trigger. The bellow of the twelve-gauge hurt his ears as he felt the stock slam into his shoulder. The Chevy's back glass flew into the car, pulverized by heavy buckshot.

"Jeez!" a howling voice cried. A dark figure tumbled out of the car's passenger door, falling on the pavement with a thump while pieces of windowpane swirled around it. The man made an attempt to get up. Woods aimed down and fired again, the power of his gun rocking him back on his heels, its explosion echoing off the houses lining Commerce Street.

Electric lights came on behind windows up and down the street as every dog within half a mile began barking— Roy saw the lights from a corner of his eye as the man he shot twisted in a curious way, rolling against the curb in a fetal ball.

Another figure dashed away from the driver's door in a low crouch. Garrett's shotgun roared, cutting the running man's legs out from under him instantly. He fell on his side as though he'd run into an invisible barrier, yelping with pain, thrashing back and forth on the pavement. Then he rolled over on his belly with a pistol aimed at Garrett's car, firing an automatic so rapidly the shots became a single sound as he cried, "Take this, you son of a bitch!" Slugs banged into the metal of the Packard until the shooter's gun was empty.

Woods was aiming for the second gunman when Garrett's Savage thundered three times, now from the rear of his car. A hail of speeding pellets lifted the fallen man off the ground in three successive jolts, driving him backward on his belly. The pistol flew from his hand, clattering on the pavement a few feet away. A singing noise began when buckshot ricocheted off the cement where the body lay. Then all was quiet, save for a chorus of barking dogs from every direction.

"You okay, Lee?" Woods shouted, leaning around the tree for a better look at things.

"I'm all right," Garrett answered in a softer voice, "only they shot the shit outa my car. My damn window's busted all to hell on the passenger side. My windshield's got a hole in it."

Woods relaxed his grip on his gun. "I'd say we shot the shit outa them, partner." From off in the distance, he could hear engines racing, probably local police on their way to the scene summoned by a citizen's telephone call. "The state'll buy you a new glass for that door, but there ain't nothin' anybody can do for these two bastards. Even money says they're both dead as fence posts. Serves 'em right. Maybe Santini will get the message now. We ain't here to fuck around."

Two police cars came speeding up Commerce Street. Woods got himself ready to give them all the necessary details.

25

Headlamps shining from both police cars showed the bodies in gruesome detail, pellet-riddled corpses sprawled across smears of crimson. Four uniformed officers stood at the scene; fractured glass lay scattered like glittering ice over everything inside the circles of light cast by the police vehicles parked behind the Chevrolet. Curious residents gathered near the automobiles, standing on sidewalks or in the road, watching from a distance, talking in hushed tones about the gun battle, while Roy Woods and Lee Garrett made a search of the dead men's pockets for identification.

Woods opened a billfold found on the man he shot, who was lying next to the curb. "This one's name is Billy Joe Walker," he said, paying no attention to the grisly sight where buckshot had torn most of the flesh off the man's cheeks and forehead. "His license shows an address over in Kilgore."

"I knew him," a young police officer said, unable to look at the corpse. "We arrested him a few times. He was a thug who got in fights pretty regular when he came to Longview. Somebody said he was workin' for Hunt now. Hadn't seen him lately. Word is he was livin' out at the Joiner roughneck camp, but I couldn't say for sure."

Woods glanced up. "Did he ever work for Carlos Santini?"

"Not that I recall. Billy Joe thought he was tough. He got a job with Hunt, keepin' an eye on things. I reckon you'd call him a security guard or somethin' like that. We hadn't seen him in jail for quite a spell, but that's the county's jurisdiction out yonder at the Joiner. You'd have to ask Sheriff Bass about Billy Joe."

Woods saw Garrett take something from the other body's pockets and hold it up to the light. "This one's name is David Matthews. It's a receipt dated today for a Colt .45 automatic bought from a gun shop called Honest Abe's on Third Street here in Longview. He paid thirty-five dollars for it."

"Everybody called him Davey," another policeman said after a cursory glance at the body. "He runs a pool hall a few blocks from here. Couldn't hardly recognize him be-

cause of the way his face is shot up so bad. The chief suspected him of runnin' a bit of shine now an' then, but we
never could prove nothin' on him."

Woods got to his feet. When he examined Garrett's
Packard, he saw a number of large bullet holes in the fenders and doors. "Davey wasn't much of a shot with his new
gun. Maybe he needed a little more practice. Did he ever
have any dealin's with Santini?"

The officer who spoke looked at the pavement. "He ran
this pool hall west of the square. That's nearly all I know
about him for absolute certain."

Woods wondered if the policemen were afraid to talk.
"I'll be sure an' ask Mr. Santini when we go out to his
house. One of you boys tell me where he lives . . . the address an' how to get there."

An older officer spoke up. "It's out by the sawmill, on
a road called Surrey Lane."

Woods grinned mirthlessly. "Why, that's the same street
where Judge Warren lives. Hell of a coincidence. A judge
who lets our prisoner go lives right close to Carlos Santini,
an' the prisoner works for Santini. Imagine that. Judge
Warren was bein' mighty neighborly, seems like. I'm gonna
ask both of 'em if there could be any connection between
settin' a cheap bond for Paulie Gambino and livin' in the
same neighborhood." His grin faded. "What's the exact address for Santini? I want the goddamn house number, so we
won't wake up the wrong man tonight."

An officer said, "It's the fourth house on the left. A big
two-story with an iron fence 'round the yard. You can't
miss it on account of that tall fence."

Woods looked over at Garrett. "We'll let these city boys
call for a meat wagon. Right now you an' me are gonna pay
Santini a visit, ask some questions, see what we can find."

Garrett protested. "We don't have a thing to prove that
these men worked for Santini, Roy. We don't have a search
warrant for his home address."

Woods gave Garrett a wink. "We ain't gonna conduct no kind of official search. All we're gonna do is look around . . ."

"I'll tell Brad Whitaker what we're gonna do," Garrett said, carrying his shotgun back to his car. Woods saw him dusting glass off the driver's seat before he got in and started the motor.

Woods motioned to the older cop. "Call the funeral parlor to pick up these bodies. Have somebody tow this car off, an' notify the next of kin. By the way, if any of you see that big fat gent who works for Santini, arrest him on the spot. His name is Paulie Gambino an' he got out on bond when he ain't supposed to be. If he gives any trouble, just shoot the son of a bitch. He's wanted for kidnappin', assault an' battery, an' resistin' arrest. He'll damn sure be dangerous, so watch your ass."

A policeman walked back to his car to make the phone calls, grinding gears when he backed away from the shooting scene. A few at a time, local residents started toward their homes. Woods handed an officer Billy Joe's wallet.

"What started all the shootin'?" the policeman asked, "and how come you asked if they worked for Santini Truckin' Company?"

Woods watched Garrett drive the windowless Packard into the parking lot beside the Grand, bullet holes pockmarked all over the car's right side. "We shot 'em because they started shootin' at us. Somebody paid 'em to keep an eye on that hotel where a Ranger is stayin'. We've got reason to believe Carlos Santini is behind this an' a hell of a lot of other things goin' on around Longview." He wondered if one or more of the cops could be on the take from Santini, like Garrett figured. "You can pass the word at police headquarters. Any man who's linked to Santini, or takes a fuckin' nickel from him to look the other way when he's doin' somethin' illegal, is gonna regret it. A Longview cop who took Paulie Gambino to jail allowed him to make a phone call to his lawyer before he was booked. When we find out who that cop was, we're gonna bring charges against him."

A silence told Woods that all three officers knew who he was talking about. On a small police force of about a dozen men, it was almost impossible to not know what the others were doing.

"Maybe it didn't happen that way," the older cop suggested. "Maybe somebody saw Gambino bein' arrested, somebody who knew who to call."

Woods examined the officer's face in light from the automobile's headlamps. "I suppose it could have happened that way, but me an' Ranger Garrett have it figured otherwise right now. Your county judge set bond before charges were filed. A lawyer shows up before the arrestin' officer arrives an' all of a sudden, Mr. Gambino is a free man. If that don't smell like horse shit, then you ain't got much of a nose."

Farther down Commerce Street, Woods saw a car speeding toward them. A Dodge sedan bearing an official insignia on its doors rocked and jolted over the uneven asphalt and patched potholes with its engine roaring.

A policeman said, "That's a sheriff department's car. They must have heard all the shootin' same as we did."

The Dodge slowed and braked to a halt in the middle of the roadway with its headlamps shining on Roy and the policemen and the bodies. Leaving the motor idling, Sheriff Perry Bass jumped out and strode purposefully toward Woods and the shooting scene. Woods didn't like the angry look on Bass's fleshy face.

"You're up kinda late ain't you, Perry?" he asked, adding as much sarcasm as he dared. "All that noise get you outa bed?"

When Bass saw Woods clearly, he stopped, resting a

palm on his holstered gun. "What happened here?" he asked, glancing around at the bodies, the windowless Chevrolet, and the street full of shattered glass.

Woods was glad to see Bass soften his expression. "A couple of local boys tried to kill me an' Ranger Lee Garrett. One's a feller named Billy Joe Walker. The other's Davey Matthews. They were watchin' the hotel where Lee is stayin'. We told 'em to get out of the car, an' that's when they started shootin'. Did you know either one personally?"

Bass seemed reluctant to answer at first. "We had Billy Joe in jail a few times. Davey runs the pool hall on Third. He had a few scrapes with the law. Nothin' serious."

"He don't run a pool hall no more," Woods said. "He bought himself a brand new gun today—the receipt's in his pocket. It makes me wonder why he needed to buy a gun so sudden, like maybe he was hired to do a special job requirin' a forty-five automatic."

Bass gave Woods a sideways look. "He don't need it now." He scratched his chin like something was troubling him. "Ever since you an' Mr. Garrett arrived in town, we've had more killin's than I ever remember."

Woods didn't like the implication. "There's sure liable to be a hell of a lot more, Perry, if Carlos Santini don't call off his dogs. I ain't gonna let some greaseball from New York set up a crooked operation in my district. I hear tell those Yankee hoods from back East think they're tough. They're fixin' to find out they ain't nearly as tough as they figured. If we have to shoot every goddamn one of 'em, we will, to put a stop to his bootleggin' an' whatever else he's involved in that's illegal."

Bass frowned. "As far as I know, Mr. Santini's a legitimate businessman haulin' crude oil to the railroad. Never heard of him bein' in bootleggin' or nothin' of the kind. He pays local taxes an' he's real generous to local charities. I'd call him a good citizen of Gregg County."

Woods stepped closer to Bass so he could look into his eyes. "That's bullshit an' you know it, Perry. You know about those twenty-six crates of shine we found in a warehouse a few doors down from Santini's. The feds are lookin' right now into who leased that warehouse. Some goddamn Italian goon with a Thompson submachine gun was with those moonshiners. An' just today, Lee Garrett arrested Santini's bodyguard when he found he'd kidnapped some whore from over at Maude's who may know somethin' about the murder of William Dodd. Then I find out a county judge has let Santini's boy go on a chickenshit bond before Lee can get down to the jail to file formal charges. It all smells bad to me, Perry, an' I intend to prove Santini's up to his fuckin' greasy neck in moonshine an' gamblin'. You can keep on believin' he's a legitimate business man all you want, but when we're done with him, I'd bet the price of a new hat we'll find out he's crooked as a dog's hind leg."

Bass appeared not to know exactly what to say. He gave the police officers standing close by a passing glance like he just remembered there were witnesses. "This is all news to me," he said quietly. "You can count on my cooperation any time. Don't see no reason for me to stay no longer, now that you men have the situation under control." He turned to leave.

"We're just gettin' started," Woods promised as Bass made his way to his car.

The sheriff drove off, leaving Woods with his thoughts as the Dodge rounded a street corner. "Seems kinda odd that Perry was up so late tonight. He sure as hell got here in a hurry. Maybe he was out on business . . . nighttime business," he wondered aloud.

The policeman holding Billy Joe's wallet said, "You sure got a suspicious nature, Mr. Woods. You make it sound like you think Sheriff Bass is up to somethin' wrong, maybe."

Woods saw Garrett walk out the front of the hotel, a shadow he recognized, broad shoulders and a Stetson pulled low in front, a gun belt buckled around his waist. "Havin' a suspicious nature is what makes me good at my job," he said. "I've got a good ear when it comes to hearin' bullshit. Perry Bass was tryin' to hand me bullshit when he said Santini was a legitimate businessman. I know better, an' Perry was tryin' too hard to convince me."

He watched Garrett's long strides, recalling how quickly the Ranger had blown Davey Matthews toward hell's gates. A more cautious man would have waited for a better opportunity, staying down behind his car until the shooting stopped. He had to hand it to Garrett. When the shit hit the fan, he was right there, pumping lead into a man who meant to kill him.

26

The road running past the sawmill was smooth and well-tended, with no potholes to jar their automobile. Lee sat on the passenger side looking out a window, feeling the cool night air caress his skin as they passed the mill under a clear sky filled with stars. He was dead set against what Woods meant to do tonight, fully expecting trouble when they knocked on Santini's door after midnight to ask him questions. Santini would call Senator Atkins again, complaining about their methods. But when Roy Woods was angry, there was no stopping him, or talking him into taking a softer position on things. He disregarded policy and state law whenever it suited him, and the code among Rangers would prevent Lee from telling the truth to his superiors or anyone else. It wasn't that Woods was not a good peace officer—he bent the rules the way Clarence Webb had, and usually got results.

"Santini may have somebody watching the house," Lee said as they slowed near a section of expensive houses clustered near the sawmill, homes surrounded by tall pines and painted fences, with manicured lawns and flower gardens he could see in the light from the stars and a waxing sliver of moon. "He's bound to know we're on his trail."

"I don't give a damn if he's got his house surrounded by the Texas National Guard. We're goin' in, an' any son of a bitch who tries to stop us is gonna get his skull bashed in. These fuckin' Italian crooks ain't gonna tell me when I can question a suspect in a case. I intend to make Mr. Santini's life miserable, until he cracks or packs up his shit an' leaves."

Lee wondered how long it would be before he got another call from Captain Ross. As long as Major Elliot believed the investigation in Longview might make big headlines, it was unlikely they would feel the tug of official reins. Governor Sterling needed a strong base of voter support in major cities like Houston and San Antonio and Dallas. A minor stir in the political winds way off in East Texas wouldn't concern a governor who had the formidable job of defeating a popular opponent like Miriam Ferguson, running for a second term on a platform designed to appeal to jobless men and women caught in the Depression.

Woods turned where a street sign read SURREY LANE. Lee began counting houses on the left until he saw a towering wrought-iron fence around a two-story home. The fence was at least six feet high, painted white, with pointed metal barbs along the top.

"There it is," Woods said, inclining his head. "Yonder's a gate. It'll be locked. I've got bolt cutters in my trunk so we can let ourselves in."

"I'm expecting an armed guard," Lee said, scanning the dark for any sign of activity. The windows in the house were black. A porch light shone brightly above the front door, casting odd bits of shadow across a recently mowed lawn set off by hedges trimmed evenly along a paved sidewalk. "This place cost money, Roy. I wonder if most of it was made trucking crude oil."

"Not likely. Whiskey an' gamblin'. Maybe profits from his whores."

Lee remembered the tears in Molly's eyes and the fear on her face when he'd gone to Whitaker's room after the shooting to recite his version of what had started all the commotion. He still pondered why he would feel anything for her. Was it sympathy? Or could it be something more? He couldn't think of a thing special about her beyond her youthful good looks. Perhaps it was only that she seemed so vulnerable, so frightened and alone.

Woods wheeled in at a gate blocking the driveway, allowing his headlamps to illuminate a pair of heavy iron gates joined at the middle by a massive deadbolt lock. As the car engine idled, a pair of German shepherds came bounding down the drive, barking savagely, the hair standing up on the back of their necks.

"We ain't gonna cut through that lock with no bolt cutters," Woods said. "About all I can do is ram it with the front of the car, only it's liable to bust the radiator an' it sure as hell is a long walk back to town." He frowned through the windshield for a moment. "We'll have to shoot those two dogs or they'll tear us to pieces soon as we get out."

Lee had been toying with another idea. "Remember what that policeman said about a roughneck camp on the Joiner lease? The girl showed me where the Joiner is. If Santini's running a big gambling operation or selling whiskey, maybe we could put some heat on him by showing up at the wrong time, busting up his game and arresting some of his men. He'll feel the squeeze if we put a dent in his gambling business. A roughneck told me down at the City Café the other day that the games are crooked . . . shaved cards and crooked dice, stuff like that. But we'd need a warrant to go on Hunt's property."

Woods took a final look at the lock and Santini's angry dogs before he put the Ford in reverse. "I keep tellin' you, a Ranger ain't gotta have a warrant just to look around." He backed out of the driveway and started back toward town, working the clutch like a man who was hopping mad. "You play by the book too much, Lee. A Ranger's gotta have the element of surprise on his side if he aims to catch crooks. In the old days we didn't have to have a damn thing but an inclination. You went where you needed to go an' did what you had to do, regardless. The most famous Rangers who ever lived, like Lone Wolf Gonzaullas or ol' Bad Ben McCullough, never fucked around gettin' warrants when they were after wanted men. They caught 'em first an' then got a warrant, which is the way it still oughta be. All this damn paperwork is a waste of time when we could be catchin' crooks instead."

"That was the way Clarence Webb did things," Lee said as Woods turned a corner. "He didn't pay much attention to regulations, but he got the job done. I started out with him on the Mexican border. He taught me to trust my instincts and a lot of other tricks. He'd go in single-handed against any size odds and face down the meanest sons of bitches they had in that part of the country, no matter how many of 'em there were. Cap'n Ross told me Clarence was one of the men who earned us that saying they keep putting in the newspapers: 'One riot, one Ranger.' "

Woods smiled, guiding his car down an empty street. "I knew Clarence Webb. Hell of a tough hombre. He was as mean with his fists as he was with a gun. He'd fight a mountain lion bare-handed an' never backed down from nobody. You had a good teacher if you learned from him."

Lee recalled what he'd done to Paulie, deciding he should tell Woods about it in case Gambino complained about how rough he was treated. "Some of what I learned from Clarence came out in me today," he said, gazing out the passenger window at nothing in particular. "I took the handcuffs off Paulie Gambino and took off my gun when I saw what he'd done to that girl. I gave him a dose of what he'd given her—knocked him down and stomped on his head a few times. Nobody saw it, 'cept for the woman. He was out cold when I put the cuffs back on him and called the police to pick him up. I lost my temper . . ."

Woods chuckled. "Say he fell down some stairs. Nobody's gonna take his word over a Ranger's. Hell, if we ever find him again, just shoot the son of a bitch an' swear he was tryin' to escape." He looked across the car at Lee. "I'm glad to hear you understand that sometimes we've gotta use our own ways of gettin' a job done. That's why nobody ever messes around with a Ranger. We've got a reputation to uphold for comin' down hard on lawbreakers. Fear can be a mighty powerful weapon. Take this guy Santini. He ain't afraid of us yet because he don't know how we handle things. After we give him a taste of Ranger justice, he won't be quite so high an' mighty. He'll pack up his shit an' head back to New York, decidin' any place has gotta be easier to run his crooked business than Texas."

Lee thought about it as they drove past the dark sawmill. "I'm not so sure, Roy. He strikes me as being tough all the way to the core. He doesn't get excited and I figure he won't scare easy."

Woods watched the roadway as they neared the business part of town. Downtown Longview was deserted. "They all crack if you put on enough pressure. He knows where Paulie is hidin', you can bet your ass. If we took Santini out in the country tomorrow mornin', he might be able to remember where Gambino is layin' low. Santini ain't no different than any other tough guy."

Lee paid little attention to the darkened storefronts as they approached City Hall. "If they make us a part of the Department of Public Safety, we'll have a new commander, Cap'n Ross says, and that'll change the way we operate. We'll be answering to a man who writes speeding tickets."

"I'll probably retire if that happens," Woods said icily. "I won't stay if they turn us into a bunch of sissies sittin' at a desk doin' paperwork. It won't be the same."

"Stop at the hotel so I can see if there's been any trouble while we were gone. I'll tell Brad Whitaker we're going out to have a look around at the Joiner camp. I expect Santini to try again to get his hands on Molly. He wants that lease document Bill Dodd got, and I wish I knew why. Santini knows there's some kind of evidence in it, or with it, that'll link him to Dodd's murder somehow. For the life of me, I can't figure what it could be."

Woods offered no opinion as he turned on Commerce Street, shifting into second gear. "They towed that Chevy away," he observed, "but there's still glass an' blood all over the place they didn't clean up. We both know damn good an' well it was Santini who hired those two local boys we shot. Smart. That way, they can't be tied directly to him if anything went wrong, which it damn sure did."

Lee surveyed the scene of the shooting as they drove past. "They sure shot the hell outa my Packard. That car wasn't hardly a year old. Cap'n Ross got me a Packard for surveillance I was doing on a car-theft ring in McLennan County—everybody there knows Rangers drive Fords. He's gonna be mad as hell when he sees so many bullet holes in it and pays for that window."

Woods stopped at the curb. "I'll wait," he said, switching off the headlamps and motor. "It's so fuckin' hot in that hellhole I can't hardly breathe."

Lee opened the door and got out. "Should I ask Whitaker to call the sheriff's office for a couple of deputies to take along with us?"

"Hell, no," Woods growled. "A Ranger don't need help from a hick deputy in the first place. Besides, I've got a feelin' that it'd be smart not to let Perry Bass know what we're doin' until it's already done."

Lee entered the hotel, noting that it was almost one in the morning. Cal was asleep on a lumpy sofa beside his shoeshine stand, a newspaper over his face. Lee wondered if it might already be too late to catch anyone running a gambling operation at the Joiner camp.

He climbed the stairs and knocked on Whitaker's door, saying in a quiet voice, "It's Lee Garrett. Let me in."

Whitaker peered out a moment later with his Smith & Wesson in his hand. "Come in, Mr. Garrett," he whispered. "The girl is finally asleep."

In the room, Molly lay sleeping on Whitaker's bed. A chair sat by an open window near the oscillating fan. Whitaker closed the door, looking expectantly at Lee.

"What happened at Santini's house?"

"Nothing. A big locked gate and a steel fence. Two guard dogs, leaving us no way in. Anybody showed up?"

"It's been quiet. Santini would be a fool to send anyone else tonight. A police car drives by every now and then. I was sorry to hear you had to kill those men. A lot of blood has been shed."

"Keep your eyes open anyway," Lee said, walking to a window overlooking Woods' car. "We're heading out to one of Hunt's big roughneck camps to see if there's any gambling going on. Roy is convinced we can put enough heat on Santini to break him down or send him back to New York. Me, I'm not so sure."

27

Brad Whitaker slumped uncomfortably in his straight-backed chair, idly watching the street, listening to the girl's quiet breathing and the hum of the electric fan. She had told him any number of things he might be able to use. Gino Tatangelo ran a string of whorehouses along the waterfront in parts of New York and farther south down the coastline, where sailors frequented an assortment of bars and cheap hotels. He trucked homemade liquor and beer at night, but the girl didn't know where it was being sent.

Tatangelo had shipped Molly off to Texas with a promise she could make more money here, where protection was better and competition was less. Carlos Santini, an old associate of Gino's from a rough section of Brooklyn, would see to it that she had few troubles with the law, she said. Molly had told Gino that almost any place sounded better than her neighborhood in New York and she'd accepted his offer. She knew about the wars being fought between rival gangsters over control of certain parts of New York City. Living a quieter life in a rural Texas town full of oil-field workers who made plenty of money seemed better than facing the difficult times people back home were experiencing during the Depression. She told Whitaker both her parents were dead and that she had felt she had no real choice. Prostitution had offered a way out of poverty and life on the streets of Brooklyn.

He gazed at her briefly in the starlight spilling through the open windows. She didn't look like a prostitute. Whitaker had two young daughters at home in Houston and he was silently thankful that a fate like Molly's could never befall them, as long as he kept his job with Treasury and stayed alive. But being a Treasury agent had become dangerous business lately. He could easily have become just another victim of the Thompson submachine gun over in Brownsboro had he not remained quiet until the right opportunity came to slip up on the Jeffreys from behind.

He noted how puffy Molly's face was and saw the dark bruises on her arms and cheeks. He shook his head, wondering how any man could give a woman such a terrible beating. Only a coward, or an animal that called itself a man, was capable of something like this. He was fast coming closer to the opinion that some men deserved to die, like Lee Garrett said.

Garrett was something of an enigma. He seemed to be a very conscientious peace officer, dedicated to his job, a thorough investigator with a calm, quiet reserve in most situations. But he had another side, a dangerous side, when provoked. He could kill remorselessly, hardened to it by years of police work, where violence was commonplace. He admitted there had been a scuffle, as he put it, with Paulie Gambino, which Whitaker felt certain was his way of saying he'd given Paulie a few lumps on the head. On the other hand, Garrett had shown a great deal of remorse after learning he had killed a young woman in the dark. And he showed tenderness when he was around Molly, a gentle nature belying a capacity for killing under fire whenever he thought it called for. Texas Rangers were widely known for violent tactics and he supposed Garrett fit the mold to an extent. But most dangerous and unpredictable of all was Roy Woods, a man Whitaker judged to be slightly out of kilter inside his brain, someone who should never have been allowed to wear a badge or represent the law in any state.

He heard an automobile coming down Commerce

Street and gave it a careful inspection from the window. A dark sedan, a Cadillac, drove slowly from the south over the uneven pavement toward the hotel.

"It sure is late to be out driving," he whispered, craning his neck to see over the sill. An hour had passed since Garrett and Woods took off for a campground on H. L. Hunt's lease to see if they could break up a gambling enterprise there. He watched the car slow down near the hotel entrance, and almost at once he sensed that something was about to go wrong.

The car stopped at the curb, its headlamps going out while the motor was still running. Two men in suits and wide-brimmed fedoras got out of the rear doors. One carried an umbrella—strange in dry, cloudless weather. They looked up and down the sidewalk. Then, one behind the other, they entered the hotel's front door.

Whitaker got out of his chair and hurried to a corner of the room to pick up his shotgun. The Fox held two loads, buckshot and a slug in the right-hand chamber. He crept soundlessly to the door and listened for footsteps on the stairs, feeling his palms begin to perspire heavily, his heart to beat faster, his mouth as dry as though it had suddenly filled with sand. Clutching the shotgun to his chest, he glanced down at the revolver in his shoulder holster to reassure himself. Someone had gotten word to Santini quickly that his first attempt to reach Molly Brown had failed. Little more than two hours had passed since the shootout farther down the block on Commerce, and it appeared that Santini was about to try again while Garrett and Woods were away.

"Damn the rotten luck," he whispered, straining to hear the slightest sound. The girl still slept. Whitaker eased across the wood floor and turned off the fan so he might hear better, then hurried back to the door and pressed his ear hard against it. The fan's blades clattered when the bearings wobbled on a worn shaft, and then there was absolute silence. He noticed that his breathing was faster now, his anticipation building, and that there was an unnatural ringing in his ears.

Soft footfalls came from the hallway suddenly, before he had time to think of a plan. He thought about his wife and daughters in Houston, wondering if he would ever see them again. He loved Mary and Elizabeth and Susan with all his heart. He tried to remember if he'd told Mary he loved her before he left to go to Henderson County with Tom Simmons. Surely he had.

The footsteps moved farther away, toward Garrett's room at the end of the hall. They don't know we moved her, he thought.

A splintering noise cracked so loudly he jumped when he heard it, followed by a series of earsplitting concussions that seemed to shake the walls. Bursts of machine-gun fire blasted endlessly, rattling like giant anchor chains dropped from the bows of the steamships Whitaker remembered from his childhood in Boston Harbor. Heavy gunfire, trapped inside the Grand's walls, was magnified, each banging report sounding louder than the other.

Molly sat up in bed and screamed. Whitaker was certain the men heard her voice, leaving him with few options: to wait for them to find the right room, or to go on the offensive. He'd never felt like a courageous man, preferring safety over risk, but now no time remained to debate his choices. He reached for the doorknob and pulled the door back, just far enough to get his shotgun into firing position.

A pair of inky figures stood in front of Garrett's room pumping tommy-gun lead through the door frame—flashes of light revealed small details of their faces as they fired. Whitaker aimed down the hall, clenching his teeth, and triggered one barrel of his gun.

A roar, muzzle belching flame, drove the Fox into his

upper arm and shoulder. A window at the end of the hallway ruptured, the glass flying outward to shower down on
Commerce Street as one of the figures spun around, staggering, dropping his machine gun to the floor. Molly
screamed again just as the second gunman made a half turn
toward Whitaker, bending over like he had a sudden attack of bellyache.

Whitaker fired his lead slug, recognizing the pounding sound it made leaving the firing chamber. In the same
split second, a burst of tommy-gun bullets banged from
the far end of the hall amid a lightning storm of muzzle
flashes. Lead whistled all around him, striking the pa-
pered wooden walls, and then he felt something pierce
his side, slamming him back against the door frame with
enough force to drive all the air from his lungs. A stabbing, white-hot pain exploded in his abdomen, spreading, robbing him of the strength to stay on his feet. He
knew he was falling, and his legs would not keep him upright, no matter how hard he tried to steady them. He
slid down to his rump and sat there, stunned, unable to
move either arm or his feet, his hands still grasping the
empty shotgun lying across his lap. Pain so intense it
threatened to render him unconscious racked his body.
He heard someone groaning in the darkness, and yet he
couldn't see a thing, his vision blurring, winking stars
flashing before his eyes.

I'm dying, he thought. I won't ever see Mary or the kids
again. Screw this lousy job. It isn't worth dying for.

A muted voice somewhere in front of him said, "Help
me. I can't see."

Whoever had spoken got no reply, only silence.
Whitaker rested his head against the door frame and closed
his eyes, thinking of Mary, wishing she could be here now
so he could tell her one last time how much he loved her
and the children. Increasing waves of pain invaded his

thighs, his legs, moving upward at the same time so that his chest burned.

A noise forced his eyelids open, the sound of feet coming toward him, although there was something about the way whoever was walking that seemed odd, irregular, slow, uncertain.

Through sheer determination, he willed his right hand to let go of the shotgun and reached for his pistol, even though it felt like his arm was mired in quicksand. His fingers were numb when they closed around the .38. He drew it out slowly, forcing his every movement, using all the concentration he could muster until he held the gun before him, aiming down the jet-black hall, curling a finger around the trigger. He waited, unable to see anything but darkness and a square where a windowpane had been at the end of the corridor.

The sounds stopped. A moment later, there was a moan, then a wheezing noise as if someone was having difficulty breathing. He tried to focus his eyes and saw nothing but black and the night sky where the window let in a pale glow from above. Now he noticed a wet sensation where his waistband encircled his belly and he did not need to look to know it was blood. He'd been shot, and in some remote corner of his brain, he remembered that a belly wound was serious, usually fatal.

Another footfall echoed close by, not far in front of him, but he could not see anyone approaching. His vision had become so clouded that now he had trouble seeing the window. Again he heard the wheeze of someone breathing heavily, when suddenly a voice came from his room.

"Are . . . you okay, Mr. Whitaker?" Molly asked softly. "You fell down . . . like you got shot."

Her voice would draw whoever was coming down the hall. Whitaker knew they'd been sent after the girl. "Shit," he whispered as he lifted the barrel of the Smith & Wesson, expecting to see someone charging the doorway any second now. He fought to stay conscious long enough to get off just one shot before his eyes closed again for what he believed would be the last time before he died.

A darker shadow stirred in front of him, beside the wall to his right. He aimed his pistol with a trembling hand and slowly squeezed the trigger.

The gun blast seemed distant, far away, too far to have been from his revolver. He smelled burnt gunpowder when he inhaled a ragged breath. Before the sound of his gunshot died, he heard Molly scream, followed by a heavy thud somewhere in the dark.

From off in the distance, he heard a car drive away with its motor racing. He couldn't be sure because his eyes would not focus, but an inner voice told him he'd shot whoever was coming toward them just now. With a bit of luck, he might have managed to save Molly before he bled to death.

"I think I got him," he told the girl quietly. "Turn on the light so you can see. Run downstairs and call an ambulance for me—but only if two guys are lying in this hall. I think I got them both."

A lightbulb flickered in his room.

"Gosh, Mr. Whitaker. You're bleeding real bad." Molly was quiet for a moment. "I see both of them and they aren't moving. I promise I'll get you an ambulance real quick."

He caught a glimpse of her when she dashed out of the room and after that, he closed his eyes and let his pistol fall to the floor. An ambulance would be too late to save him, even if the bullet had somehow missed his vital organs.

He thought about Mary, feeling himself slipping toward a fog, swirling through total darkness. How he wished he could hold her in his arms one last time. . . .

28

Nailed to a small guardhouse, a sign at the gate read HUNT OIL COMPANY, JOINER NUMBER 2. Electric lights burned behind dust-coated windows. Lee noted a telephone line on a pole beside the shack. A series of poles carried sagging wires alongside a gravel road running toward a distant group of lights, partially hidden by pine trees clustered between oil derricks.

"Those lights'll be the roughneck camp," Woods said, bringing the Ford to a hasty stop in front of a wooden barrier meant to halt traffic in or out. He glanced at the guardhouse. "We can't let 'em call ahead to warn anybody we're comin'. Let's go in an' cut that telephone cord before they recognize us."

Lee got out first and headed for a door in one side of the shack, passing an old flatbed truck parked behind a stack of oil drums. He pushed the door open and entered, Woods close on his heels.

A bearded man of thirty or so gave them a sullen expression as he was getting out of a padded rocking chair. A radio played tinny country music crackling with static from a shelf above a paper-strewn desk where a telephone sat. The desk and chair were arranged so a guard would have a view of the barrier from one window. The shack smelled dusty, and faintly of sweat. A gray cotton shirt the guard wore had SECURITY embroidered on each sleeve and above a pocket where sweat stains darkened his armpits.

"Texas Rangers," Lee said, striding over to the telephone. He saw a gun stuck in the waistband of the guard's pants. "We'll take that shooting iron until we get back. Wouldn't want that thing to go off accidental."

"Nobody goes in without identification papers from Hunt Oil Company," the man said, glancing down at Lee's badge, making a move like he meant to reach for the telephone.

Lee held up a hand, curling the other around his pistol grip. He spoke evenly so there would be no mistaking what he intended. "Take the gun out and put it on the desk. Don't touch the phone."

Woods strode over, snatching the guard's revolver from his pants with his .45 automatic drawn. "You oughta clean that wax outa your ears, son, because it's liable to get you arrested if you can't hear good. We don't need any goddamn identification papers or anything else. Sit back down in that chair an' don't say another fuckin' word."

"I'm supposed to call somebody if . . ." He fell silent when Lee wrapped the phone cord around his fist and jerked it out of the wall.

Woods aimed his gun at the guard's belly. "Sit down. You ain't callin' anybody now. I'm gonna give you some advice. If you wouldn't like spendin' a few weeks in jail for interferin' with the lawful duties of a peace officer, then you'll sit right here until we get back." He pointed to the chair and holstered his .45, tucking the guard's pistol in his gun belt.

The guard sat down, glancing from Woods to Lee. "The boss is gonna fire me when he hears 'bout this. I ain't supposed to let nobody in without papers."

Woods grunted. "Tell him we showed you some papers for the arrest of Paulie Gambino, a legal warrant signed by a district judge. That's all the paperwork we need to go any goddamn place we want. Remember to stay put 'til we get back. I'd sure hate to haul your ass to jail tonight."

Lee walked out with the telephone, tossing it into the

dark behind the building on his way to remove a pine pole blocking the roadway into Joiner Number 2. He wondered if Paulie might truly be hiding out in one of these oilfield camps as Woods had suggested. According to what he'd heard, there were too many of them for a search to be practical.

A small city of tents and trailers, converted to living quarters, filled a clearing in the pines, covering more than an acre. Bare lightbulbs burned, dangling from wires affixed to tree limbs or temporary poles. Near the center of the campground, an open-sided tent roofed a group of men gathered around several tables as Woods drove slowly, his headlamps extinguished, to a parking place behind a tall pine tree where he and Garrett could see what was going on.

"Gamblin'," he said, sounding pleased and switching off the engine. "We hit paydirt. Grab your shotgun. These boys ain't gonna be none too happy to see us."

Lee got out of the Ford with his Savage, removing the hammer thong on his pistol. Thirty or forty men were inside the tent and they were a rough breed: oilfield workers—swampers and riggers and drillers—who worked hard and drank hard when a day was done. He fully expected trouble. Off to one side of the tent, a makeshift bar, its planks resting on barrels, was doing a thriving business in glasses and tin cups of clear moonshine served by a chubby man with his shirtsleeves rolled up. The heat on this particular summer night seemed worse than ever, oppressive, heavy, and thick with moisture. Not a breath of wind stirred the treetops around him as he started forward beside Woods toward the tent.

"Seven come eleven!" someone shouted, tossing a cupful of dice onto a table with boxed sides.

"Snake eyes, you unlucky bastard!" another voice cried. A scattering of laughter began and died down.

Lee saw a tall, broad-shouldered man standing quietly at the edge of the tent, his face covered by shadow cast from his straw snap-brim hat. He wore dark slacks, unlike the others, who were dressed in khaki or denim work clothes, and a pale yellow short-sleeved shirt. A shoulder holster dangled below his left arm. He was watching the games intently from a spot behind the bar, failing to notice Lee and Woods as they walked quietly past a silent oil derrick to the edge of the tent village.

"The guy on the left has got a gun," Lee whispered, pulling the autoloader lever back on his shotgun.

"I see him," Woods replied. "There's sure to be more'n one who's armed. You go around an' cover him from the back. I'll be on your right. I'll yell for everybody to put up their hands. Shoot the first son of a bitch who pulls a gun or tries to run off. This'll be Santini's game as sure as stink comes with shit. We'll bust things up an' let the rest of 'em go, 'cept for the bartender an' the guy with the gun, or anybody else who looks like a fuckin' Italian."

Lee wondered if this were truly one of Santini's operations, or simply a small-time bootlegger running a few gaming tables as an added way of making money. The only real connection they had between Hunt Oil and Santini was a trucking contract for crude oil. There were camps like this all over the countryside around Longview, and it would be just a stroke of luck if this one happened to be provided its gambling and liquor by Santini.

He crept beneath the pine branches, passing two small tents and a trailer balanced on cement blocks and bricks, working his way closer to the man with the shoulder holster, coming up behind him. He was twenty feet away from the circles of light cast by the naked bulbs when a man in bib overalls turned from the bar and cried, "Look out boys, it's the law!" and pointed directly at Lee.

Lee was watching the man with the gun, raising the Savage to his shoulder. "Everybody hold it right there!" he bellowed. "If anybody moves, we'll shoot! Texas Rangers! If you're carrying a weapon, keep your hands away from it!"

"We've got you surrounded, boys!" Woods yelled from somewhere in the darkness. "Everybody stay real still!"

The man with the pistol wheeled, clawing for his gun. There was no time for any more words. Lee fired at his legs, blasting a load of buckshot aimed for his knees. The roar from his twelve-gauge thundered through the pine forest.

The man's feet were swept out from under him by a load of lead shot, dropping him to the ground so quickly he lost his hat and gun. Stray buckshot peppered the bar and bartender, evoking a shrill cry from the barkeep as he threw up his hands to cover his face, falling backward, knocking loose planks and jars of whiskey to the floor of the tent with a resounding crash. A man in khakis beyond the bar began to hop on one foot, howling in pain, gripping his pants leg where pellets had struck him.

Lee gave the crowd a sweeping glance before his attention returned to the downed figure, sprawled on a layer of old pine needles turned brown with age.

"Get those hands up, boys!" Woods demanded hoarsely. "I'm gonna shoot the next bastard who moves. Scratch your balls an' it'll get you killed tonight. I'd let 'em itch if I was you."

Hands started going up in the crowd inside the tent. Lee kept his gaze roaming back and forth, awaiting any movement that might be someone reaching for a gun. The bartender made a noise like that of a wounded animal, a squeaking sound, rolling this way and that with his palms covering his cheeks. Blood seeped between his fingers from the numerous pellet wounds—he'd been caught in a pattern of buckshot not meant for him, an unfortunate byproduct of a shotgun's tendency to spread its charge over a large area.

The man wearing a shoulder holster stirred, reaching for his pellet-torn knees and lower legs. Even in the half dark,

Lee could see blood oozing from holes in his shredded pants, glistening wetly in light from the bulbs strung across the tent roof. His pistol lay a few feet away, but it was apparent he had forgotten about it for the moment.

"Leave every fuckin' dime of your money on those tables an' walk outside the tent!" Woods commanded. "We're bustin' up this little game. If everybody goes home real nice an' quiet, we won't take any gamblers to jail. If you boys behave, nobody else will get shot. Walk out slow an' keep your hands where we can see 'em plain as day."

A few at a time, men began filing out of the tent, their hands held high. Whispered voices were hard to hear above the whine from the injured bartender. A man standing near one of the crap tables appeared to hesitate. "I won that roll," he said in a quivering voice, looking hopefully toward the spot where Woods covered the tent with his gun. "The money's mine. I won it fair an' square makin' a five—"

"Leave it!" Woods snapped.

Hearing this, the young roughneck backed away from the table and disappeared into the darkness without uttering another word.

Lee inched forward, still wary of a possible shooter hidden somewhere outside the tent; he aimed his Savage down at the man he'd shot but kept an eye on his surroundings. The wounded man grimaced in pain.

"Roll over on your belly so I can cuff you," Lee said after placing a foot on the man's pistol, a .45 automatic gleaming with a new coating of gun oil.

The face turned toward him. Coal-black eyes beheld him for a time.

"I won't tell you again," Lee promised, bringing his shotgun muzzle closer to the man's head. It was hard to be certain in the poor light, but he thought the gunman looked a bit like a foreigner, if he were any judge of these things, having dark skin, wavy black hair, and a nose that turned down sharply as though it had been broken. He could be

Italian, Lee supposed; he had the same skin coloring as Santini and Paulie and the machine gunner they'd shot at the warehouse.

With obvious reluctance, the gunman put his wrists behind his back, saying nothing, making no sound despite what had to be very painful leg wounds. Lee knelt and put handcuffs on him, picking up his pistol, glancing up when Woods edged closer to the tent's lights on the balls of his feet from the far side, sweeping his shotgun back and forth.

"Nice shootin'," Woods said, approaching the sobbing barman cautiously. "This one got a few marks on his face 'cause he was bendin' down to grab this here sawed-off shotgun." Woods leaned over a wooden crate behind a barrel at one end of the bar and took out a scattergun with barrels scarcely twenty inches long. "He didn't have to be much of a shot to hit anybody with this," Woods added, looking around quickly, making sure no one was out in the dark near the tent. "Maybe those little balls buried in his skin will teach him a lesson."

Lee looked down at his prisoner. "This one's shot up pretty bad, Roy. He'll need a doctor. It's just a guess, but he looks like an Italian to me. He was carryin' this big forty-five, which doesn't prove anything except he figured on doing some damage when he shot somebody . . ." Lee heard a door slam on one of the trailers close by, silencing him for a moment. He saw someone striding toward the tent like he had something on his mind.

A stocky man with an unruly shock of silver hair walked up, casting an angry stare at Lee and Woods. "What the hell's goin' on here?" he demanded, stopping where light from the tent fell on his face. He wore a nightshirt tucked into clean khaki pants and no shoes, looking like he'd been asleep.

It was the wrong thing to say to Roy Woods and it came at a bad time. "Who the hell are you?" Woods asked, turning his shotgun muzzle just enough to convey a clear warning.

Only then did the older man notice their badges. "You're the law," he said in a much softer voice. "I heard the shootin' an' got right out of bed."

Woods was still angry. "You didn't answer my question. Who the hell are you?"

He hesitated. "Ralph. Ralph Wiggins. I'm foreman over the crews here at Number Two."

Woods went closer to Wiggins. "Well, Mr. Wiggins, it's like this . . . you're allowin' an illegal gamblin' business to operate on this property, an' unless I'm wrong, that's moonshine in those jugs, makin' you an accessory to several crimes. I've got half a mind to haul you off to jail. We're Texas Rangers, an' unless you tell me some things I need to know, you're on your way to a jail cell."

"Like what?" Wiggins asked quietly, as though he already knew.

"Who runs this crap game an' whiskey business?"

"I ain't exactly sure."

"That isn't the answer I wanted to hear, Mr. Wiggins. Do you like the idea of goin' to jail?"

"Some guy in Longview. They don't ever give us any names. I was told to let 'em come so the men would have somethin' to do at night."

"Who told you to let 'em come?"

"My boss, Mr. Abernathy. Maxwell Abernathy is the manager for Hunt Oil."

"Where can we find him?" Woods asked.

"His office is downtown, in the bank buildin' on Main Street, up on the second floor. You'll see the sign on the door. I'd be obliged if you didn't tell him what I said or he'll fire me."

"Does Mr. Abernathy allow gamblin' an' whiskey into all his roughneck camps?"

Wiggins swallowed, sweat beading on his forehead now. "I'm not rightly sure. I suppose he does."

When Woods appeared to be thinking of more questions, Lee asked, "This guy who runs the games . . . what does he look like?"

Wiggins glanced down at Lee's manacled prisoner. "He's one of them. There's three or four different ones. They ain't from around here."

"Are they Italians?" Lee continued, pressing him for some detail they could use.

Wiggins closed his eyes, like he was worried over what his answer might cause. Several seconds passed before he offered a reply. "I believe that's what somebody said. I can't remember just who said it."

"A few weeks in jail might help your memory," Woods growled.

"I heard somebody mention they were from New York, an' that they might be Italians or somethin' like that, only nobody ever gave me any names. That's God's honest truth."

Lee nudged his prisoner with the barrel of his Savage. "We can see if this gent is carrying anything with his name on it and then we'll ask this Mr. Maxwell Abernathy for some names first thing in the morning."

Woods rested both shotguns against a barrel and bent over. "I'm gonna cuff this chunky bastard an' then we'll gather up all the money an' bust up everything else so they can't use it again. We'll smash those shine jars an' haul our prisoners back to town. You can go back to bed now, Mr. Wiggins, but if I was you, I'd be spreadin' the word it ain't gonna be healthy to let any whiskey or crap games on Hunt property, because the Texas Rangers plan to make it real hard to operate from now on. 'Specially for a goddamn bunch of Italians from New York."

29

At Longview Municipal Hospital, a few minutes past 4:00 A.M., as they arrived with a pair of handcuffed prisoners needing medical attention, Lee and Woods were advised of Brad Whitaker's condition by Dr. Lawrence Collins.

"A bullet went through his ascending colon, narrowly missing his right kidney and his liver, although the umbilical vein was severed and there has been extensive internal bleeding. He can go either way. I sutured the colon and did what I could to mend his umbilical vein. His vital signs are weak. If I were forced to venture a guess, I'd have to say he won't make it. Infection may kill him if blood loss does not. He's resting quietly now, but I'm afraid his chances aren't good. A young woman rode with him in the ambulance. However, she left some time ago. The two other men involved in the shooting are in serious condition and one of them will certainly die from a wound in his neck. The other has extensive shotgun wounds and is blind in both eyes. We have not been able to determine who they are. They carried no identification."

A Longview police officer stood beside Dr. Collins with bloodstains covering most of his uniform. He spoke to Woods. Lee recognized him as one of the officers who'd come to the warehouse that night.

"We got the call an' went right over. The place was shot to hell. Agent Whitaker was unconscious. Two guys with machine guns were lyin' in the hallway." He turned to Lee. "Your room was blown to pieces. They kicked in the door and must've fired a hundred bullets into them walls an' the bed. It was lucky you weren't there, Mr. Garrett. By the look of things, Mr. Whitaker shot both of them from the door of his room, only there was one unlucky bullet that got him too. He looked nearly dead when we found him."

In a corner of the emergency room, nurses were attending to the two handcuffed prisoners, although right then Lee gave little thought to them. "What about the girl who was with Whitaker?" he asked.

"She rode with him in the ambulance an' waited out here for a while. Then she said somethin' about goin' to get her clothes an' catchin' the next bus out of town. We didn't have no reason to hold her. She told us what she saw an' it wasn't much, since she was in Whitaker's room while all the shootin' was goin' on. The first bus leavin' Longview will be at five-thirty, bound for Dallas, in case you're interested."

"I'll find her," Lee said softly. He spoke to Woods. "Let me have the keys to your car. I'll check the bus station and if she isn't there, I'll drive over to Maude's. That's where she has her clothes, and she'll need money for a bus ticket."

Woods nodded. "I'm gonna have a look at the two guys they found in the hall. One of 'em could be Paulie Gambino. I hope he's the one with the hole in his fuckin' neck. Come back for me when you've found the whore . . . the girl. I'll have this officer take those two assholes over yonder to jail as soon as they've been bandaged up. Too bad about Whitaker. For a fed, he showed he had guts. I'll call Cap'n MacDonald an' fill him in on what we found. Maybe the newspapers will pick this up an' that'll be all the worse for Santini, his boys makin' headlines."

Lee walked out of the hospital without saying anything about Whitaker or making headlines. It had taken courage on Whitaker's part to challenge two men with machine guns. Someone needed to notify his wife in Houston and his superiors in Washington about his grave condition. That unhappy chore would probably fall to him sometime later this morning.

He was worried about Molly. After hearing what the police officer said, it was apparent she'd decided to run. He had to stop her if he could, for several reasons. He believed she knew something that would lead him to Bill Dodd's killer. And there was a personal side, a cloudy mixture of feelings he had for her that didn't make any sense at all.

The bus station was poorly lit at five o'clock in the morning, making it hard to see who was inside as Lee was parking the car. He got out and crossed the sidewalk to the front door. The station had been closed when he drove by the first time on his way to Maude's. A Negro woman told him Molly had left Maude's with her suitcase an hour earlier. Lee's watch told him he still had plenty of time.

In the narrow waiting room, lined with theater seats, he found Molly sitting in a corner chewing her fingernails. As soon as she saw him, she looked at the floor. The bus terminal was empty, a lone ticket clerk busying himself behind a counter. Lee walked across the room and stood in front of her.

"You can't leave just now," he said gently, seeing tears on her badly bruised cheeks. "Besides, you already told me you've got no place to go."

"I'm going to Dallas," she said. "I told those two cops everything I know, so how come I can't leave?"

He sat down beside her, thumbing his hat back on his head, feeling weary after so many hours without sleep. "Because I think you know something you haven't told me about William Dodd's death. I can't let you go until I solve this case."

She was still unable to look at him. "I told you all I can remember about him. I wasn't lying to you. Carlos is gonna kill me if I stay. He thinks I've got that paper . . ."

"I promised you I wouldn't let him harm you."

A sob escaped her lips, then she composed herself. "You

left me with Mr. Whitaker and look what happened. They were after me, and now he's dead."

"He's still alive."

"Just barely. The doctor said he wasn't gonna make it. If I stay here, the same thing's gonna happen to me. Carlos is mean. He won't stop until he finds me. He'll send Paulie looking for me again."

Lee rubbed his eyes, wishing he had a cup of coffee to keep him awake. "I can protect you, Molly. You've got to trust me on that. I'll find a better place to hide you. It was a mistake to stay at the hotel. I made it too easy for 'em. Roy Woods and I are gonna come down hard now on Santini. We busted up one of his games tonight. Collected over a thousand dollars in whiskey and gambling money and arrested a couple of his men. I know Santini had something to do with Dodd's murder, but I can't prove it until I find some evidence. Santini wants that lease document so bad he'll risk anything to get his hands on it. I aim to find it before he does, if I can. Whatever's on that lease, or something that's with it, has to be worrying him."

"I never saw it," Molly protested, crying again. "Nobody believes me. Bill told me about it, that it came in the mail. I swear I'm telling the truth."

"I believe you," he said, noticing dried blood on his boots from loading his injured prisoner into the car. "Let's get a bite to eat and some coffee. We'll talk some more. I'll find a place to hide you where Santini will never find you, and I promise to keep you safe."

"I already bought a bus ticket to Dallas."

"I'll get the agent to give you your money back." He picked up her battered cardboard suitcase and stood up. "C'mon, Molly. Don't be afraid. I won't let them get near you."

She got up slowly, drying her eyes. She wore a different dress, a white-and-pink summer dress with puffy short sleeves. "I don't want to stay, Mr. Garrett. You don't really know Carlos or Gino. They're bad men. When Gino hears about two more of his guys getting shot by Mr. Whitaker, he'll send somebody else down here. He won't stop. Nothing can make him stop until he gets what he's after, but I can't make anybody believe I don't have it. I never even saw that piece of paper."

Lee glanced out a terminal window at the street, thinking about what the girl had said. "Dodd hid it somewhere. Even his wife doesn't know where it is. He was being real careful, probably for good reason. He knew it was worth a lot of money if he got that lease recorded, so he hid it someplace that afternoon, waiting for the next day to take it down to the courthouse. It could be hidden at his house, or out at the Hawkins property where he was killed. Maybe in his car."

"How would I know? He didn't tell me where he put it."

He gazed down at her. Some of the swelling in her cheeks was gone. "Come on, let's get something to eat."

She bowed her head and followed him to the ticket counter for a refund on her one-way ticket to Dallas.

He held her arm as he escorted her outside to Woods' green Ford, feeling her trembling. He meant to avoid the City Café for breakfast this morning; too many oilfield workers who knew who he was, and who Molly was, ate there. A truck stop out on the road to Tyler was a better place to avoid being recognized.

It was a fishing cabin a few miles south of town at the end of a dirt road where Grace Creek joined the Sabine River. Hidden in a pine, elm, and dogwood forest, it had but a single room, containing a bunk bed, a sofa and chair, and a butane stove. Electricity gave it lights and power to run a fan and a radio. An outhouse sat in back, but there was a bathtub in a corner of the cabin, hidden by a dressing screen. Water came from the river by means of a hand pump on a tiny back porch. Cal had told him about the place, rented out by an old Negro woman who lived farther up the river road. It cost seven dollars a week. He parked the Packard in front. He'd changed cars with Woods earlier in the morning, and cleaned up bits of shattered glass from the car seat and floorboards before he left with Molly to rent the cabin.

"It isn't bad," Lee said, walking inside with the key in his hand. "A little sweeping and it'll be clean enough."

"I'll be scared out here at night if you leave me," she told him, giving the room a passing glance.

"You'll be safe. And I bought you a present, so you'll be able to take care of yourself. It's a thirty-two automatic with a seven-shot clip. After I teach you how to use it, you won't be so worried."

As he put her suitcase down, she said, "I never shot a gun before, Mr. Garrett. I'm not sure I can."

"I'll teach you. And why don't you call me Lee. Mr. Garrett sounds too formal. We'll drive back to town and get some groceries and ice for the icebox. And anything else you need."

She stared at him. "How come you're doing this?"

"I suppose I'm helping you out right now because I feel sorry for you. You didn't do anything wrong, but Santini doesn't believe you. You're hardly more'n a girl and you can't defend yourself from hired muscle like those goons Santini sent to get you. I'll get that pistol out of the car and show you how to use it."

She put her hand on the front of his shirt, stopping him at the door. "I wish things could be different," she said, a noticeable change in her voice.

"How's that?"

Molly looked into his eyes. "I wish I wasn't in all this trouble with Carlos, and I wish I'd never gone to work as . . . as a whore. There might be a chance we'd like each other, if you know what I mean, if it wasn't for me being ruined by working at a place like Maude's. Nearly every man I ever met wanted me for the same reason, and some were downright mean unless I gave them what they wanted. But you're different. You're nice, and you're real handsome too. You treat me gentle, even after my face got all busted up so I'm not pretty anymore. Too bad things can't be different. I think I'd like you a whole lot . . ."

He felt that same fluttering in his chest as before, like a butterfly beating its wings, and he found he couldn't take his gaze from her face. "I like you, Molly. It doesn't matter all that much what you did for a living, and you're still pretty. All those bruises and lumps will go away."

"I don't believe you," she said quietly, looking down for a moment, "about the part where you say it doesn't matter all that much what I did. Men don't forget something like that. I used to hear what men said about girls like me back in Brooklyn. I know you're only saying it to be nice."

Lee touched the tip of her chin with his fingertips to lift her face toward his. "That isn't true. I said it because I mean it. You're a pretty girl and I like you, maybe more'n I should."

"Why's that?" she whispered, coming a little closer to his chest, her deep green eyes narrowing with doubt, or curiosity.

He grinned self-consciously. "I reckon I never was much at being with a woman in a tied-down way. My job keeps me moving all the time and most women don't like that. To tell the truth, I've never found a woman I wanted to be with more'n once or twice."

"I don't see how you can say you still like me after knowing I worked at Maude's. Most men would say I was ruined."

"It didn't ruin you, Molly. You're still the same girl you were, but you've had some rough times. I suppose it's up to you what you do with the rest of your life."

Tears formed in her eyes. "You've got to be the nicest man in the whole world, Lee Garrett." She stood on her tiptoes and kissed him gently on the lips, closing her eyes, the tears running down her cheeks.

He returned her kiss lightly, placing a hand in the small of her back to draw her closer, allowing his lips to linger against hers longer than he intended.

30

When he got out of his car at the courthouse, he saw a man with a camera walking hurriedly toward him. A newspaper reporter, he thought. He waited by the Packard, accustomed to handling a newsman's questions, yet determined not to say much of anything now about certain aspects of the case.

"Mr. Garrett? I'm Mike Malloy of the *Tyler Tribune*. I've been to the hospital and the city jail, gettin' the story about what happened out at the Joiner lease. Give me your version of how events took place, and what you know about the triple shooting at the Grand Hotel." Malloy's gaze fell to the bullet holes in the side of Lee's car. "Holy cow! Those are bullet holes! I'd like to get a picture of those, with you standin' beside the car."

"I haven't got time to stand here, but you can print a story saying that the Texas Rangers intend to break up a big illegal gambling ring operating around Longview, and that we suspect it's being run by a bunch of Italian gangsters from New York and New Jersey. We don't intend to let organized crime get a foothold in Texas."

"What about the Treasury agent who was shot last night?" Malloy asked, placing his camera on the fender of Lee's car to jot down notes. "We know Agent Whitaker was investigatin' moonshining in Henderson County, and a police captain told us they raided some warehouse here filled with crates of moonshine. Are the two in any way connected to this alleged gambling ring? The Treasury Department in Washington refuses to comment, and the FBI claims it has no knowledge of organized crime in East Texas."

Lee phrased his reply carefully. "We have reason to believe these same gangsters are hauling moonshine whiskey to some of the oilfield camps. Our investigation continues."

"Can you name any suspects, Mr. Garrett? Are they local men?"

Even more caution was necessary for this answer, he knew. "We have local suspects. However, I can't give you any names at this time. We're closing in on the men behind it. I will tell you that our suspects came from New York and New Jersey a short while back, setting up what look like legitimate businesses in this area. They may be a front for illegal activities, but we haven't clearly established that yet."

"Wow!" Malloy exclaimed, writing furiously on a notepad.

"We expect to have more information soon," Lee went on as he caught a glimpse of Sheriff Bass watching him from the courthouse steps.

Malloy looked up, holding his fountain pen above his scribbled notations. "I was informed there have been six killings thus far, and three more men, including Agent Brad Whitaker, are not expected to live. Is that correct?"

"I haven't been keeping track, but it sounds about right."

Malloy wrote something down. "A policeman said some of the men involved carried machine guns. Was it a machine gun that was used on this automobile?"

"A forty-five automatic, but there have been tommy guns in a few instances. These criminals come heavily armed."

"Are more Texas Rangers coming to Longview, or are you going to stick with the credo: 'One riot, one Ranger'?"

"Two Rangers are involved at the present time—myself and Roy Woods from Tyler. We've been able to handle things."

"Are the local police providing assistance?"

"Some of the time," Lee muttered. "That's all I can say about the case right now." He walked away from the car for a look at the courthouse records. He hadn't been careful enough when he saw them the first time to note important dates, not knowing how critical they might be in solving the murder of Bill Dodd.

When he went up the steps, Sheriff Bass spoke to him. "I hope you was careful talkin' to that Malloy feller. He's a nosy little bastard an' he'll print damn near anything, even if it ain't the truth."

"I told him the truth," Lee replied, continuing his climb to the county clerk's office.

He went into the hospital room, his hat in his hands, after a nurse showed him the right doorway. Brad Whitaker lay on white sheets in a metal-frame hospital bed with his eyes closed. Lee had called the Treasury Department from the hotel as he collected his suitcase and promised to pay damages to his room with a state voucher. A man's voice on the line had said he would call Mrs. Whitaker with the grim news promptly.

Roy Woods was headed back to Tyler for badly needed sleep, and to deposit the money they'd seized at Hunt Oil. Woods said he would return early tomorrow morning to help Lee question Maxwell Abernathy at Hunt's offices, and then Lee hoped to continue the search for Paulie Gambino—he'd forgotten to ask if Gambino was one of the wounded men at the hospital.

Lee pulled a chair over to the bed and sat down.

Whitaker looked small, his cheeks sunken, as pale as the sheets on the bed, and when he took a shallow breath, his chest barely moved.

"Sorry, Brad," Lee said. "You took that bullet for me and I owe you. They tell me you're gonna die because of it, an' that sticks in my craw. I don't figure you can hear me, but I'm real sorry this happened. It wasn't your job to keep an eye on that girl for me. She had nothing to do with bootlegging. I know it doesn't matter to you now, but I'm gonna make those bastards pay for what they did to you. Santini and every last one of them are gonna be real sorry they crossed paths with me after it's over. I wanted you to know how bad I feel that this happened to you."

A silence hung heavy in the room. An open window let in the sounds of automobiles moving up and down the street. Lee put his hat on a bent knee and shut his eyes for a moment. "You showed courage," he went on, knowing he was talking to himself. "I aim to write a letter to your boss in Washington about it. When it came down to the nut-cutting, you had more balls than any of the rest of us, taking on two men with tommy guns. The girl is alive and safe because of you, but I don't 'spect that matters to you now. You told me about your wife and kids. You were a lucky man to have 'em, even for a short while . . ." He felt his throat going tight and swallowed to rid his mouth of a cottony taste. "Like I said, I'm real sorry this came about. If I could change places with you, I would. I've got no wife or kids depending on me for a living. I don't have much money saved, but I'll send a little down to Houston when I can. I and my brothers are having to be a help to our folks lately, on account of the damn Depression. If I'm able, I'll try and see to it that your family has enough to get by 'til things get better."

He realized then that a tear had formed in each eye. He dabbed at them with a callused fingertip and gazed out the window at a clear blue sky, trying to remember the last time he'd cried. He took a deep breath and said quietly, "I'm gonna get those rotten bastards, every last one of 'em, and when I do, I'll be thinking about you. You can count on it . . ."

He got up after a bit and walked downstairs to the nurses' desk at the emergency-room entrance. "Afternoon, ma'am. I'm Ranger Lee Garrett and I need to inquire as to the condition of two badly wounded men brought in last night. Doctor Collins said they carried no identification, so I don't know their names."

The nurse, a woman well into her sixties with gray hair worn in a bun behind her white cap, replied, "They are both deceased. If you need any more information, you may talk to Doctor Sanderson, down in the basement. He's preparing the bodies for burial right now, I believe."

Lee followed the woman's directions to a set of stairs leading down to a pair of swinging doors. Pushing through, he found a frail man dressed in a white smock peering into the chest cavity of a body resting on a metal table under the harsh glare of a lightbulb.

"Doctor Sanderson?" he asked.

The doctor nodded, peering at him over wire-rimmed spectacles.

"I'm Lee Garrett, with the Texas Rangers. I need to get a look at two men who died from bullet wounds sometime early this morning to see if I can identify either one."

"I'm working on one of them now, Mr. Garrett. Have as close a look as you wish. The other man is over there under the sheet. He had a serious wound in his neck, severing his windpipe."

Lee looked at the gray face of the corpse lying in front of Dr. Sanderson. It wasn't Pauli Gambino, although it did look vaguely like the Italian they'd arrested at Hunt Oil. He crossed the dark tile floor to lift a sheet off the second corpse. "I don't know either one of 'em," he said, noting a dark, round hole in the neck of this body. "Doctor Collins said one guy had been blinded by buckshot."

"That was this fellow. An odd case indeed. Although all fluid had drained from his eyes and his mandible was broken, his wounds were not that serious. He apparently suffocated when a pillow inadvertently fell across his face while he was unconscious."

"A pillow?"

"One of our nurses found a pillow on the floor beside his bed with bloodstains on it. She remembered that the man was conscious when she left the room to allow a peace officer to question him privately concerning a shooting incident." Sanderson lifted two handfuls of glistening intestines from the body cavity and dropped them unceremoniously into a bucket near his feet, paying no more attention to Lee or his questions.

"Thank you, Doctor," Lee said, shouldering back through the swinging doors with a sick feeling in the pit of his stomach. He knew with absolute certainty what had happened. When Roy Woods didn't get the right answers to his questions, he squared things for Brad Whitaker, using a pillow instead of a gun.

He stopped by Bill Dodd's house on his way out to the cabin, playing a hunch. Charley Waller had said something about seeing a black Cadillac parked in front of the house on Baker Street while Bill was out of town on business, and that Sara Dodd was no "white dove herself," having been a prostitute in Beaumont before she and Bill got married. If Sara had a questionable past, and if she knew someone who could afford a Cadillac, perhaps Waller's suggestion that Sara had a boyfriend on the side was worth asking about. Sam Dunlap had told Lee about black Cadillacs coming at night to Santini's warehouse. Could the same person be visiting Sara after dark? he wondered. It still didn't add up. If Sara was in partnership with whoever killed her husband for his lease, then why was she asking the Texas Rangers to investigate further? If she'd played a role in his murder for a share in the profits, then she would keep quiet and wait for her money.

"Maybe that's it," Lee murmured, climbing out of his car in front of the house. Maybe somebody double-crossed her and now she wants to get even, he thought. It sure as hell doesn't look like she got a dime, living in this cracker-box shack.

He knocked on the screen door, hearing the same radio music he'd heard coming from the house the first time. He was thankful that this time there was no cabbage smell.

Sara came to the door in a dressing gown and slippers, her face cherry red from too much corn whiskey.

"I remember you," she said thickly. "You're a Texas Ranger. Been readin' in the paper where you shot a bunch of moonshiners the other night. How come you ain't been lookin' for the guy who murdered Bill?" The woman's breath reeked of strong liquor. She made no move to invite him in.

"I have been looking, Mrs. Dodd. I need to ask you about a black Cadillac car that was seen parked in front of this house on several occasions when your late husband was out of town. Who owns that car?"

Her eyes flickered away from his face. "You're mistaken. I don't know nobody who drives a Cadillac. Who said that? It's a lie."

He didn't intend to tell her it was Waller. "Are you sure, Mrs. Dodd? The car was reportedly seen here a number of times."

"Whoever said that's a damn liar!" she snapped, backing away from the screen.

"I'll check into it further, ma'am. One more thing. Did

you or your late husband know ahead of time approximately what day the lease would come in the mail?"

Sara collected herself, pushing dull brown hair away from her eyes. "Some lawyer in Houston Bill knew was handlin' it for him, gettin' signatures. He called the week before it came to tell Bill he'd gotten the last signature in some place called San Saba an' that it should arrive in a week. He called again the same day it came to warn Bill somebody else was after that piece of property, callin' some of the heirs, offerin' more money to sign with them."

"Did you or Bill tell anybody about that lawyer's phone calls, or when the lease would arrive?"

"Bill prob'ly told Charlie Waller. I wouldn't have nobody to tell."

"And you say you don't know anybody who drives a Cadillac?"

"Nobody. It's all a damn lie, whoever said it."

"That's all for now, ma'am. Thanks for your time."

"You ever check to see who leased that land after Bill got shot?"

"A man by the name of Buster Davis. He subleased it to the Hunt Oil Company."

"Then Buster Davis is the one shot my husband. How come you don't arrest him?"

"I can't prove he did it, but I'm still checking on him and a number of other leads. I'll get back to you."

"Whoever Buster Davis is, he's a murderer!" she cried as he stepped off the front porch.

He didn't answer her, recalling her reaction when he asked about a black Cadillac. She knew something more — he was sure of it; however, there was still no logical reason why she would ask the Texas Rangers to investigate her husband's murder if she were even remotely involved.

Frustrated, too tired to think clearly, he drove toward the river road and the cabin, making sure he was not followed. He'd left Molly alone longer than he wanted, after her terrible ordeal at the hotel. He smiled pleasantly, remembering her kiss as he steered the Packard onto a deserted dirt lane, heading south.

31

Molly met him at the cabin door. Sunset turned skies over the river bright shades of pink and purple and orange, and in this light, she looked more beautiful than ever. Her hair was brushed, and she wore a simple white gown that modestly reached to her ankles and was buttoned high on her neck so none of her chest showed. She smiled as he came up the steps, and for some odd reason, he noticed that she was barefoot. She had tried to cover the bruises on her cheeks with face powder, and the swelling around her eyes was almost gone.

"You look mighty pretty," he said, carrying his bedroll in one hand, his shotgun in the other. He kept camping gear in the trunk of his car in case a wanted man's trail took him away from rented rooms.

"Thank you," she said, her smile broadening some, stepping back to let him through the doorway.

"Something smells good," he said, tossing his bedroll and shotgun on the bunk bed, casting a glance at the stove, where a steaming pot gave off wonderful scents, like soup or beef stew.

"I made beef soup with those bones we bought, some carrots, and a couple of potatoes." She closed the door and peered out a front window. "That river sure is pretty here, and those trees are nearly touching the sky. I've dreamed about owning a place like this someday. You can hear the fish jumping. Otherwise, it's so quiet outside you can almost hear your own heart beating."

He chuckled, watching her stare out the window; a quiet hum came from the electric fan.

"It's cooler down here because of the trees," she said in a little girl's way, excitement in her voice. "Texas can be the hottest place on earth, but it's cool beside this river. I wish I could stay right here the rest of my life." She turned from the window then and her expression changed suddenly to one of fear. "Did you find out about Paulie?"

"He wasn't one of the men Whitaker shot."

"It was too dark to see. They hauled them off in different ambulances while I was holding onto Mr. Whitaker's hand. He's gonna die, isn't he?"

Lee closed his eyes briefly, remembering the way Whitaker had looked in the hospital bed. "He isn't supposed to make it. He was still alive when I went there this afternoon. He's unconscious, so I hope he isn't feeling any pain."

Molly crossed the room, standing before Lee with a sad look on her face. "He was a brave little man. Gentle, like you."

"I've never been accused of being gentle. My ma tells me I've got the same bad temper my pa has. I can't control it every now and then. Something snaps inside my head." He grinned. "If supper's ready, I'd sure like some. Haven't eaten a bite since we had breakfast."

"I'll fix you a bowl and something cool to drink. After supper I've got a little surprise, only it's against the law. With you being a cop, I might get arrested for giving some of it to you." She smiled when she said it and there was a sparkle behind her eyes.

"I'd better ask what it is," he said, "so I'll know what to write down for the charges against you when I haul you off to jail."

"Peach brandy. Hattie Mae, the Negro lady who cleans up at Maude's, gave me a little jar of it before I left. It's in my suitcase. There isn't much, but it'll taste good after we eat. Hattie Mae was always real nice to me. She said I might need it if I got a bad case of nerves. She made it herself."

He grinned again. "Let's eat out on the porch steps so we can watch the sun go down across the river. It'll be cooler."

"I made iced tea, only there isn't much ice left over after filling that icebox. There's crackers, too."

"Sounds good to me, Molly." He noticed the gun he'd bought her lying on a small table between the worn sofa and chair, and said nothing about it. When he'd shown her how to fire it, she'd closed her eyes every time the gun went off. Her aim was terrible, even for a beginner. It would help her defend herself only if her target was at close range.

She went to the stove and began filling a tin bowl. He hung his hat on a nail near the door and walked out to sit on the porch as twilight came to the river bottom. Winking fireflies lit up the forest around him and somewhere close by, crickets began to chirp. The Sabine flowed sluggishly between its grassy banks on its way to the Gulf of Mexico. He thought about what the girl said, that she'd always wanted a place of her own like this. He allowed himself a moment to consider what it would be like to share it with her, discarding the notion promptly. He was too set in his ways to have a wife. He'd been a loner for so long that he couldn't imagine living any other kind of life.

Molly came out a few minutes later with a bowl of soup, a waxed-paper package of crackers, and a fruit jar of tea with ice chips floating at the top. She put them on the steps beside him and sat down, tucking her knees under her chin with her gown carefully pulled down over her legs.

"I put some sugar in your tea. I didn't know if you liked

it that way and there wasn't much ice. That block nearly melted before we got it here."

"It's the heat," he said, taking the bowl. "How come you don't eat some of this too?"

"I've been tasting it all afternoon, making sure it was just right, the way my grandmother made it. I'm not really hungry at all anyway. I was worried about you, and worried that Paulie or another one of Carlos's men might show up. I watched that road real close, but nobody came until you did. I'm scared. I feel safe when I'm with you, but when I'm all alone, I get scared real bad that somebody'll come, somebody like Paulie, or Carlos."

"They don't know where you are. They'll never be able to find this place, not in a million years."

"You don't know them like I do. They'll find me, sooner or later. I just hope you're here when they come . . ."

He tasted a spoonful of soup and found it delicious. "Roy Woods and I are gonna put so much heat on Santini he won't be looking for you. He won't have time. But if he does show up, I promise you I'll take care of him . . . or anybody else who comes."

She watched him eat. "You're like those cowboys I see in the movies, a quiet guy who's as tough as they come when some bad guy wants to fight. Nobody ever beat Paulie with his fists. You broke his nose and knocked him down like it wasn't nothing at all."

He drank a swallow of tea and took a cracker. "Big guys are usually too slow. He wasn't all that tough. I've met a few who were a hell of a lot tougher to knock off their feet. Size doesn't have all that much to do with it."

Molly gazed toward the river. "It's so peaceful out here that I don't want to think about Paulie or Carlos or any of them right now, only I can't stop thinking about poor Mr. Whitaker and that he's gonna die on account of Carlos, and me."

"He has a wife and two kids. They're the ones who'll suffer if he dies. These are mighty hard times, and for a widow with a couple of young'ns, it'll be twice as hard to make it. The Depression is making it hard on nearly everybody."

She had tears in her eyes when she said, "I know all about hard times. If you're all alone, with nobody to help look after you . . ."

He set down his soup bowl and put his arm around her gently. "I'll make sure nothing happens to you, Molly. You can count on that for sure."

She looked up at him in the fading light from the west and gave him a trace of a smile. "This is like a dream, a good dream. I never had anybody to look out for me after my mom died. When she passed away, I was so awful scared I couldn't sleep at night. I never wanted to be a whore. I hate what I did, what I'm doing at Maude's. I suppose I coulda quit as soon as I made some money, only I got to feeling so bad about it, about what I'd done, that I decided there wasn't anything else for me to do. Nobody'd want me because I was a whore."

He listened to what she said, wondering if her profession made any real difference to him. "Maybe that isn't true, Molly. Some men don't care about a woman's past, same as some women are able to overlook things a man has done in his lifetime. Nobody's avoided mistakes entirely. You don't have to go back to work at a place like Maude's."

She looked at him, then watched the river flow past. "If I could help it, I wouldn't go back, only I don't know what I'd do. I've been thinking that I could start all over someplace else where nobody'd know what I was. I could get a job as a waitress, or in a laundry. I can iron shirts and I can cook. My grandmother showed me how when I was real small."

Lee pulled her closer, ignoring his supper for now. She

smiled and rested her head on his shoulder. He caught the fragrance of scented soap in her hair.

"See those fireflies?" she said, pointing to the forest. "I wish we could just fly away from here like a firefly and go where we wanted, away from Carlos and Paulie and everybody."

He felt her snuggle against him and when she did, something stirred inside him. "It'll be over soon. We'll get the goods on Santini and toss him and all his friends in jail or send 'em back to New York. Then you won't have to worry anymore."

Molly turned her face to him and spoke in a quiet whisper. "If you want me to sleep with you tonight, I will. It won't be for money . . . it'll be because I like you and I'm real grateful for everything you've done for me."

"There's no need for you to do that. You don't owe me for a thing I've done."

"It wouldn't be because I owed you. It'd be because you're the nicest man I ever met, and because I wanted to."

He considered it, and decided against it for now. "There's no hurry. We've got plenty of time."

She frowned. "You don't want me because you know I was a whore. Am I right?"

"That's not it. I just think we should give ourselves time to get to know each other. If things work out, who knows what'll happen?"

She looked down at his bowl. "You didn't eat the soup. Is it too salty?"

He smiled. "I'd rather have my arm around you. The soup is just fine."

Molly tilted her face and kissed him on the lips, then drew back. "I'll understand if you don't want me because of what I am. You don't have to explain."

He bent down and kissed her, harder than he meant to as some powerful emotion took control of his actions.

32

Sometime during the night, Lee heard a sound. His eyes flew open. He reached for his pistol sleepily, trying to clear his head so he might identify the soft noise he heard above the whir of the fan. When he found his .38, he sat up cautiously, listening, watching for movement beyond the window screens, where dim starlight showed few details of the dark forest. Sitting on the floor where he'd spread his bedroll, he glanced over to the bunk bed when he thought he heard the sound again. The cabin was dark and he couldn't see Molly. Slowly, his eyes adjusted. She wasn't in her bed.

He came quickly to his feet, gripping his gun. He found the front door slightly ajar. Had she run away while he slept? he wondered, inching forward, covering the doorway with his pistol. Or had someone slipped inside and taken her? He knew himself too well for that. He'd always been a light sleeper and he was sure no one could have entered without awakening him.

Pulling the door back, he saw her sitting on the cabin steps in her nightgown. And now he could hear her soft crying.

"What's wrong?" he asked gently, pushing the screen door open, walking outside in bare feet and without his shirt, lowering the gun to his side. "I heard something and saw your bed was empty."

She wouldn't look at him. "It's nothing. I'm sorry I woke you up. I couldn't sleep, so I came out here. I can't seem to stop crying tonight."

He sat down beside her, placing the gun out of sight behind him. "It's understandable, I suppose. You've had a rough couple of days, what with that beating Paulie gave you and what happened at the hotel. You're awful young to have so many troubles all at once. It'll pass and maybe after a while, you'll forget about most of it."

She dried her eyes on the sleeve of her gown, staring off at the river. "You don't know how honest-to-goodness mean they are. It's just you and that other Ranger, the older guy. The cops in Longview aren't gonna help you, not one bit, because they're scared of Carlos, most of them are. Carlos says a cop is just another guy with a gun. He hates cops, and so does Gino. Paulie hates nearly everybody and he'll do whatever Carlos tells him. He won't forget about that whipping you gave him, either. He'll come after you when you don't expect it. I heard him tell Carlos he liked the idea of killing cops."

Lee listened to the bullfrogs croaking downriver and wondered how to reassure her. He didn't want to tell her that Roy Woods was not all that different from Paulie or Carlos, that he seemed to enjoy killing criminals who tried to use violence against him or any other peace officer, nor did it matter that a man was wounded or dying anyway when Woods practiced his own brand of justice, as a handful of early day Rangers did, before times changed.

"Some guys figure they're tough because they've never run into anybody who was tougher," he began, chosing his words carefully. "And being tough isn't nearly as good as being smart when it comes down to a fight, usually. Roy and I have had lots of experience with bad men. I know you've got Carlos and Paulie and the rest figured for dangerous types. Maybe they are. But they've never tangled with me or Roy Woods before. I know their kind . . . I know how they think, how they'll act. Santini is already starting to make mistakes because he feels pressure from us. If we have to, we can call in a few more Texas Rangers, or federal marshals and the FBI to back us up. There's no way

Santini or Tatangelo can win, Molly. They're breaking the law and they'll wind up in jail, or in six-foot-deep graves if that's what it takes."

She watched the river absently for a moment longer. "I never knew a man who could be tough and gentle at the same time, until I met you. How is it you can be both?"

He chuckled softly. "I'm not all that tough. There's a lot of men tougher'n me, I reckon. I've got an older brother who can whip me with one hand tied behind him. As to the gentle part, I can't rightly say I'm that way. My ma taught me proper manners, the way a man oughta act around a lady, and to always take my hat off inside a house . . . things like that."

She looked at him for the first time now. "It isn't that I think you've got proper manners. It's how you can be so gentle, like when you put your arm around me while you were eating supper, and that time you held my shoulders so soft. You didn't have to do any of that, only you did, and it made me feel special and safe and I wasn't scared anymore. When I kissed you, it made me feel warm all over because you kissed me back. You don't treat me like I'm . . . a whore. You didn't even want me to sleep with you tonight, and I would have, if you'd wanted. I've been thinking it's because of what I am that you don't want what most men want from me. But you did kiss me back, and that was real nice even if it was just a little kiss or two."

He was glad for the darkness, feeling his cheeks flush. "It isn't that I didn't want to sleep with you, Molly. I don't hold it against you that you worked in a place like Maude's. I suppose I've got some old-fashioned notions about a man and a woman sharing a bed. I never was much of a hand with the ladies or at saying the right things to a girl. You've had a rough life for somebody so young and I guess I don't want you to think I'm the same as Gino or Carlos, trying to use you the way they did."

She touched his forearm lightly. "I'd never think anything like that about you." She moved a little closer to him on the step. "But if you wouldn't mind it, I'd like you to put your arm around me the way you did before."

He smiled and placed his arm around her shoulders. "I don't mind a bit," he whispered. "Truth is, I wanted to anyway. Like I told you, I never could come up with the right words or do the right things when I needed to. Some of my buddies back in high school used to tell me I was too bashful, that I'd never have a girlfriend because I was too shy to talk to a pretty girl."

Molly rested her head against his bare shoulder, looking up at the stars. "Maybe you were just too nice to ask a girl to do something unless you knew she wanted you to . . ."

He couldn't explain it, why talking to a woman about personal feelings was so difficult. He'd never been any good at it, and neither the passage of time nor his limited experience with women made it seem any easier. He sat beside her on the steps in silence, listening to the bullfrogs calling for their mates. A frog could make its feelings known. He wondered why he couldn't.

Lee followed a speeding police car and an ambulance when he saw them turn onto Baker Lane, partly out of simple curiosity, partly out of a vague sense that somehow they were leading him to the scene of an event he should know about. When he saw both vehicles stop in front of Sara Dodd's house, he knew his instincts had been correct. Another police car was parked out front. Groups of people from the neighborhood stood in the yard and across the street, watching what was going on as two men got out of the ambulance. Police Chief Howard Laster swung his legs over the running board of a Dodge police sedan and stood up with shafts of early morning sunlight causing him to squint as he closed the car door.

Lee braked to a halt behind the ambulance, glancing

toward Sara's house before he climbed out of the Packard, noting that a policeman stood on the front porch. Something had happened to Sara—a sixth sense told him she was dead.

"No need to rush," he heard the officer say to both ambulance attendants as they crossed the yard. " 'Pears she's been dead for hours. Her body's done got stiff."

Learning that Sara Dodd was dead brought a tidal wave of questions churning through Lee's brain all at once. How had she died? Accidentally? Or had she been killed? He nodded to the police chief as they arrived at the porch steps together.

"What happened to her?" he asked, addressing the officer while he made his way to the door.

"Go look for yourself, Mr. Garrett. Looks like suicide to me. I found her hangin' just like she is now. Didn't touch a thing 'til somebody got here. 'Pears she kicked a chair out from under her with a rope 'round her neck. A neighbor called when he seen her through a window while he was walkin' down to the bakery about an hour ago . . ."

Lee walked past the officer into the living room with a frown on his face, wondering why Sara Dodd would kill herself. It didn't make sense. He stopped when he saw her body in the hallway. A rope had been tied to a roof beam through an opening into the attic. A chair, lying on its side, was beneath her. The end of the rope was knotted around her neck. She wore the same faded housedress he remembered. A slipper remained on one foot, the other foot rested on the floor. Her face was frozen in a grotesque mask of intense pain, her tongue distended unnaturally and was a dark shade of purple-gray, matching the color of her skin. A drying puddle of urine darkened the floorboards where her bladder had emptied the moment she died.

Chief Laster stopped beside Lee to study the scene, tilting his head for a better view of the attic opening. "She stood on that chair an' pushed it over with her foot. Must've happened sometime last night. I suppose she never got over grievin' for her late husband, to do somethin' like this."

Lee wasn't buying it. "She didn't act like a woman who was grieving over her dead husband when I talked to her. She wanted us to catch her husband's killer, but she damn sure wasn't in any kind of grief that I could tell. I smelled whiskey on her breath a couple of times. Someone I questioned said he'd known her from Beaumont, before she married Bill. She was a prostitute, the guy told me. I got the impression she was hard as nails, not the kind who'd commit suicide. She was mad. She wanted the murderer caught. I can't make myself believe she'd kill herself while our investigation was still going on. I talked to her yesterday, and she seemed okay to me."

Laster was watching him closely. "You think somebody killed her an' made it look like a suicide?"

"I'd come closer to believing that than anything else right now." Lee's gaze wandered around the living room. "There's a strong possibility her husband's killer got worried that I'm getting close to discovering his identity."

Laster scowled. "Why go to all this trouble? He could just blow her brains out like he done her husband's an' that'd be the end of it. Somebody had to climb up in that attic an' fix this rope so it'd look natural. An' then there's the chair, too. Seems a hell of a lot of trouble."

"Neighbors would hear a gunshot. Have your men ask those folks standing outside if they saw or heard anything last night while I have a look around."

"Sure thing, Mr. Garrett. We'll help any way we can, but if you ask me, I think you're grabbin' for straws."

"I've got it figured otherwise," Lee replied, taking another careful look at the living room and hallway.

Laster started for the door. "You want the ambulance boys to take her down?"

He shook his head. "I've seen enough, but I'm gonna examine her body for a minute before they haul her away."

"Mind if I ask why?"

Lee entered the hall and circled the dangling corpse, taking a long look at the back of Sara's head. "Just a hunch, but if I'm right, we'll find a bump on the back of her skull someplace. If somebody killed her, he had to knock her out before he climbed up there to tie the rope, to keep her from screaming loud enough to wake her neighbors. Maybe one of those folks out there heard or saw something that'll help."

The chief walked outside, allowing the screen door to slam behind him. Lee heard him speaking to the ambulance attendants.

He went to the kitchen and found nothing amiss. In the bedroom, a telephone sat on a small table beside the bed. Footsteps in the hall almost caused him to overlook a notepad and pencil next to the telephone.

Scribbled across the pad were the initials c.w. and a number: 387. Lee tore off the top sheet and stuck it in his shirt pocket, wondering if C.W. and the number would lead him to Sara's killer. Both were meaningless now.

"Mr. Garrett?" a voice inquired. "We cut the woman down like Chief Laster said. He told us you wanted to look at the body before we loaded it."

Lee turned on a light switch in the hallway and knelt down beside the corpse, running the tips of his fingers through its hair. As he expected, he found a lump the size of a large bird's egg above the right ear. "She was hit in the head," he muttered softly. "You can take her away now. I found what I was looking for."

An attendant asked, "Who would hit her on the head? Chief Laster said she committed suicide . . ."

Lee stood up, glancing past the attendants and through the screen door to where the police were questioning the neighbors. He was running late for his appointment with Roy Woods downtown, where they were to talk to Maxwell Abernathy about gambling and liquor at the Hunt

Oil Company drilling camps. But now with Sara Dodd's murder to solve, he needed time to find out every detail of what went on here last night.

"She didn't hang herself," he replied offhandedly, wondering where to begin. The initials and the number looked like the best starting place.

Crossing the grassless yard, Chief Laster motioned him over to a house across the road, where an elderly woman stood on her front porch holding a watering can. Rosebushes in full bloom lined a narrow strip of garden around the porch. Before Lee got there, he heard the woman say, "My husband said it was a Cadillac, a big black one. He couldn't sleep on account of it was so hot, so he came out on the porch fer a spell. He told me he seen it take off 'round midnight, an' how it was kinda strange fer a fancy car like that to be in a poor neighborhood like this'n. That Dodd woman was a heavy drinker, you know. She hardly ever went out at all, an' when she did, she smelled to high heaven of whiskey. My husband told me 'bout that car afore he went to work this mornin' at daylight. He'll be home 'round seven."

Chief Laster gave Lee a questioning look. "Did you find a knot on her skull like you thought you would?"

"Behind her right ear. The Cadillac may be very important. I'll come back after seven."

33

Roy Woods was growing increasingly impatient standing in front of the bank, tapping a finger on the butt of his pistol, watching the street for Garrett's car. He had news, plenty of it, and most was bad. Checking his pocket watch, he saw it was after nine and Lee was late. Woods didn't know where he'd taken the girl and now, as minutes ticked away, he began to worry that a mishap might have occurred, possibly another gun duel with some of Santini's men where Garrett was outnumbered, or ambushed, or caught unawares. But the more he thought about it, the less likely it seemed. Garrett was cautious. Woods' money was on Garrett if more of Santini's gunmen went after him.

Watching cars pass along the street, Woods thought about how he'd smothered that arrogant greaseball bastard at the hospital yesterday morning. "The sumbitch shoulda answered my questions," he muttered, his fingertip tapping faster, his frustration growing. He needed to fill Lee in on what Captain MacDonald had told him, and about the icy message from the Deputy United States Marshal in Tyler, Tilden McNamara, before they questioned Abernathy at Hunt's offices. A few bigwigs were putting a hell of a lot of pressure on the Rangers to back off, and Captain MacDonald was beginning to feel the squeeze.

He saw Garrett's bullet-scarred Packard cross an intersection and wheel over to the curb. "It's high time," Woods said to himself, resisting an urge to look at his watch so Lee would know he'd kept him waiting. Lee got out and banged the door shut—Woods noted with disgust that he wasn't wearing his gun. A Ranger wasn't a Ranger without his gun.

"Mornin', Roy," Lee said, coming down the sidewalk. "I was delayed. Bill Dodd's wife was killed sometime last night and they wanted it to look like a suicide. A neighbor saw a black car in front of the house around midnight, a black Cadillac."

"One of Santini's assholes," Woods surmised quickly. "They'll be after that little whore again . . . what's her name?"

Lee seemed a bit annoyed. "Molly Brown. I've got her hidden out in a fishing cabin down on the Sabine. I gave her a gun, but she isn't much at shooting it."

"I got some bad news yesterday. Plenty of it. A congressman from Washington is raisin' all kinds of hell with headquarters over what we're doin' here, an' the Treasury Department is blamin' us for what happened to Brad Whitaker, sayin' he wasn't supposed to be watchin' a suspect for us who had nothin' to do with the department's moonshine investigation. Cap'n MacDonald got calls from Washington all day, claimin' we were abusin' our authority and bustin' heads without good reason. H. L. Hunt has got powerful friends, too. The Deputy U.S. Marshal at Tyler gave me a good talkin'-to last night. Hell, I've known Tilden for years an' it ain't like him to warn me off a case. Tilly said we'd better be careful pushin' Hunt around, 'cause he can bring the roof down on our heads with all his money. He's been makin' phone calls to big shots all over the place. Tilly said Hunt gives lots of money to certain political candidates an' that he can put our asses in deep shit if we mess with him. We'd best have the goods on him, Tilly said, before we go much farther.

"I told Tilly 'bout that gamblin' tent an' the moonshine, an' how we know damn good an' well it's Italian gangsters from New York behind it, only he acted like he didn't believe any of it. He got a call from his regional office sayin' to tell us this is a case for the FBI an' the Treasury Department, not the Texas Rangers, an' that if we had good sense, we'd leave it completely alone."

Lee's face registered the same disbelief Roy's did when he heard what was going on.

"What did Cap'n MacDonald say?" he asked.

"He sounded real strange. He said he wasn't gonna tell us to back off, but that we'd better wrap things up as quick as we could an' not to make too much noise while we're at it. He says Major Elliot talked to the FBI an' they think we're crazy, that there's no organized crime from New York operatin' in Texas. If there was, they'd know about it. Cap'n MacDonald was gonna call your company commander, Cap'n Ross, to see why you're spendin' so much time on one murder investigation an' why you got sidetracked into this gangster business. He told me to go easy from now on."

"The two are connected," Lee replied, muscles working in his cheeks like he was getting mad. "I'll call Cap'n Ross and bring him up to date. I sure as hell hope he doesn't pull me off this case before it's finished. The major has always backed us up. I wonder what made him change so sudden this time."

"Politics," Woods declared unhappily, feeling his own anger rise, idly watching cars drive past the bank. "He's worried that they'll put us under the Department of Public Safety, which only means more goddamn paperwork an' a different chain of command. I swear, I'm gonna retire if they send me one more form to fill out on a case. I already feel like a goddamn file clerk. It damn sure pisses me off that Cap'n MacDonald ain't behind us on this. The Rangers have changed, an' it's all for the worse. They've tried to have us pussyfootin' around like a bunch of goddamn sissies in pink tights, goin' before a judge to get a piece of paper before we can go after a crook. I'm sick of it. In the old days, we were lawmen, not paper-shufflers. The fuckin' crooks are gonna be runnin' this state if things don't go back like it used to be."

"I'm worried about what that marshal told you," Lee said quietly, rubbing his chin, "telling us not to push Hunt, that this is a federal matter. I've worked real close with the U.S. Marshal's office over the years. Never had any conflict. It's making me wonder how somebody like Hunt, or Santini and Tatangelo, could have so much influence over the way a peace officer conducts an investigation. We've already got a crooked county judge to deal with, and a local sheriff who looks the other way, and at least one city cop who lets a prisoner make telephone calls to his lawyer before he gets locked up. Somebody sure as hell is trying to stack the deck against us."

"Somebody powerful, like Hunt. Or maybe this Tatangelo back East. I'll retire, Lee, before I let 'em take me off this case. I swear I will . . ."

Lee shrugged. "I don't have enough years in to retire. I reckon I'll know where I stand after I talk to Cap'n Ross. If he pulls me off, I won't have any choice but to obey orders and go back to Waco."

Woods flexed his fingers, making fists. "It's all this modern bullshit we have to take now. All the paperwork. The only son of a bitch makin' any money in this Depression is the guy who has a paper mill. Let's go upstairs an' talk to Abernathy. See what he has to say about allowin' gamblin' an' moonshine on a Hunt lease. We'll see if he sweats."

"Your cap'n said to go easy, Roy. I suppose we'd better do like he wants."

Lee's suggestion made Woods mad. "I've never gone easy on a fuckin' crook in my entire career an' I sure as hell ain't gonna change now." He wheeled for the bank and strode toward the doors with his teeth clenched, wondering if he should give it up and retire anyway. He didn't feel the same pride he once felt wearing his badge. If the Rangers wanted a file clerk, they'd have to hire somebody else.

Maxwell Abernathy was keenly aware of his financial power and it showed. He puffed on a fat Cuban cigar, blowing smoke at a spot on the ceiling of his expansive office where a fan circled lazily above his huge mahogany desk. Two candlestick phones sat on either side of an ink blotter before him. He watched Roy and Garrett impassively. He was small, round-shouldered, with a bald pate and pale skin. He wore a silk suit coat in spite of the heat coming through his office windows.

"Gambling and liquor are illegal, gentlemen," he said in a feathery, almost feminine voice. "Someone was mistaken. Mr. Hunt would never permit such enterprises to operate on a company site, and neither would I. However, I am aware of the . . . disturbance at Number Two the other night. I can assure you we were totally unaware of its existence on our property, and to suggest that we approved of it or allowed it is ridiculous."

Woods disliked Abernathy the moment they shook hands, for in his experience, a man with a weak handshake was weak-willed and couldn't be trusted. "One of your bosses out there said he was told to let 'em in every night. He said those orders came from you to let 'em on the property."

"He was mistaken. Seriously mistaken. The matter has been taken care of."

"Meanin' you fired the poor bastard who told us that," Woods said.

Abernathy did not flinch. "Those responsible have been sent home, Mr. Woods. Liquor and gambling are banned on all Hunt Oil Company properties. It was unfortunate that a misunderstanding of this nature caused the incident at Number Two. Some of our men were misinformed, or misled. The situation has been rectified. Now, if you have no further questions, I have work to do."

Woods glanced over to Lee, who had been silent during the entire meeting. "I reckon that'll do for now," Woods said as he came to his feet, "but I'm warnin' you, we intend to check on more of your leases from time to time, just makin' sure there's no more misunderstandings."

Abernathy's ice-blue eyes fixed Woods with a stare.

"Make certain you have a properly executed search warrant, Mr. Woods. Mr. Hunt has influential friends who can see to it that you are brought to task if you violate a citizen's rights against unlawful search or seizure. You violated Mr. Hunt's rights when you came on Number Two without a valid warrant. Make sure it does not happen again."

Roy's tolerance for Abernathy's disdainful attitude had reached its limits. He leaned forward, resting his palms on Abernathy's desk. "You tell Mr. Hunt I'm not the least bit worried about his influential friends," he said, keeping his voice low, even, controlled. "I'll take my chances that I can prove Hunt an' you have cut a side deal with these bootleggers an' gamblers. You don't scare me, Mr. Abernathy, an' neither does Mr. Hunt. I know how the law works. I've been a peace officer for twenty-seven years."

Abernathy smiled, although it was easy to see there was no real humor behind it. "I'm an attorney, Mr. Woods, and I assure you I know the law quite well. If you violate it as you did the other night, I can promise you I'll do my best to have your badge taken away." He stood up, appearing bent in the middle of his spine, so he had difficulty looking Roy in the eye. "Excuse me, gentlemen, but I really must get back to work."

Woods bit his tongue and walked out without a word, stalking past a secretary's desk to an outer door and a set of granite stairs leading to the bank lobby. He was so mad he was afraid to speak to Garrett until they got outside, fearing he might be overheard by bank employees if he started yelling and cursing.

"I hate lawyers," he snapped, stopping at the edge of the sidewalk. "In particular, a smart-assed hunchback like Abernathy, who sounds so goddamn high an' mighty. I'd like to take that little son of a bitch out back an' bash his fuckin' skull a few licks."

Lee paused at the curb. "No need to let him get you so

riled up, Roy. We can make him eat those words if we can find another crap game or bootlegger on Hunt's property. If we could locate that silver-haired gent who talked to us the other night, maybe he'd testify in court that Abernathy gave orders to let the games and booze on the place after dark. We'd have a case if there was a witness who'd testify."

Woods was still fuming, not really listening. "Let's go over to the jail. We can ask those two men we arrested who it is they work for, an' how they got on Hunt's lease at night, who gave the order."

"They won't talk," Garrett promised. "If they do work for Santini, they know he'll get them out sooner or later an' they'll be afraid to give us anything."

"Like hell they will," Woods growled. "You just let me have 'em in private for a few minutes, Lee. Your problem is, you don't know how to ask questions."

34

The prisoner's legs were wrapped in bloodstained gauze and his hands were cuffed behind his back. He watched Woods close the door to a small, windowless room in the back of the basement at City Hall. He'd given the booking officer a name, Leonardo Cusi, and an address in Fort Worth on the north side near the old stockyards. Cusi sat in a straight-backed wooden chair wearing only his undershorts. His olive-complected face revealed nothing and his obsidian eyes appeared almost closed behind heavy lids.

"I'll bet they call you Lennie," Woods began, going over to the chair. Lee was in another room questioning the overfed bartender, who had half a dozen swollen pellet wounds on his face and neck.

Cusi remained silent.

"Cat got your tongue?" Woods asked, standing over his prisoner with his palm on his holstered .45.

Cusi did not reply.

"Let me explain how this works," Woods continued, feeling a prickling sensation in his arms and legs like he always did when he was about to lose his temper. "I'm gonna ask you questions. You're gonna answer 'em. If you don't, I'm gonna help persuade you with a Colt forty-five automatic. I can use it several ways to help make you talk. I can bang on your head with it, an' let me tell you, it's one heavy son of a bitch an' I swing it just as hard as I can. If that don't work, I'm gonna shoot you with it an' tell the judge you were tryin' to escape, that you made a grab for my gun an' it went off accidental several times, bein' it's an automatic. I'll shoot you in the balls first, like we was havin' this terrible struggle while the muzzle was aimed down. Then I'm liable to fire a bullet up your ass, so you'll know what it feels like to have your hemorrhoids come flyin' up your neck. You'll even taste 'em if they wind up in your mouth. But then I'm gonna shoot you one more time, Lennie, an' I promise you won't feel a goddamn thing after that. You might hear this little crackin' noise when the slug goes through your skullbone. Then all the lights go out an' you've got nothin' else to worry about."

Cusi's stare did not waver and he said nothing.

Woods drew his pistol, moving to one side of the chair so he couldn't be kicked by his prisoner. "Who do you work for?" he asked. "I want a name . . ."

Cusi turned his head slightly, looking Woods in the eye, but he still held his silence.

Roy swung his .45 across Cusi's left cheek, the muzzle banging into soft flesh and then teeth. Cusi was spun out of his chair with enough force that he tumbled into the cement wall behind him, landing on his chest—with his arms man-acled, he could not break his fall using his hands.

"Now," Roy said softly, watching Cusi spit blood and tiny fragments of teeth onto the floor beneath him. "Tell me who you work for."

Cusi looked up, glaring at him. "You're wasting your time, Tex," he croaked, strangling on blood. "I ain't going to tell you nothing."

"We'll see," Woods replied, crossing over to the wall. "I say that depends on how much pain you can take. If you're tougher'n most, it's gonna take a little longer. But I promise you, Lennie, you're gonna tell me what I want to know or you're gonna die here in this room. You ain't leavin' this place alive unless you tell me everything. I swear it on my pappy's grave."

"You're supposed to be a cop . . ."

Woods knelt down. "I am, Lennie, an' I'm a good one. I don't take any shit from assholes like you who break the law an' wait for some red-mouth lawyer to bail you out of jail. I'm a good cop because I get rid of assholes like you when they don't tell me what I need to know in order to stop crooks from makin' Texas a bad place to live. Just a couple of days ago I smothered one of your greaseball friends at the hospital because he wouldn't answer my ques-tions. Smothered him with his own fuckin' pillow, only no-body can ever prove I done it. Just like nobody will be able to prove you didn't slip one of those cuffs off an' make a grab for my gun. I'm real good at this, Lennie. Had plenty of practice killin' shitballs in the line of duty. An' so help me God, I'm gonna give you a dose of the same medicine if you don't start talkin' to me right now."

A piece of chipped molar rolled off the end of Cusi's tongue to the floor, landing in a spreading puddle of red forming beneath his chin.

"Talk to me, Lennie," Woods whispered, "so I don't have to do what I promised I'd do. Don't force me to kill

you. It's messy, blood an' brains an' shit all over the place.
Did you know that a man shits an' pisses in his pants when
he dies? All of those muscles holdin' your shit inside relax.
Your underwear's gonna fill up with shit, an' you'll piss
like a racehorse until your bladder is empty. Somebody'll
have to come in an' clean up the mess while I'm upstairs
tellin' the police chief how you tried to escape, how I didn't
put one of those cuffs around your wrist tight enough an'
you slipped it off, grabbin' for my gun. He'll believe me,
Lennie. Me an' Chief Laster are old friends. There won't be
no witnesses. Just the word of a twenty-seven-year Texas
Ranger with a good record that it happened the way I said
it did."

"You're nuts," Cusi stammered, staring into the muzzle
of Woods' gun, struggling to keep his face off the floor,
crimson spittle dribbling from his lips when he spoke.

"Maybe I am," Woods replied, enjoying himself now.
Cusi was about to talk, the way he'd known he would all
along. Even the toughest men feared death when they were
made to believe it was imminent. "I'm also real serious
'bout killin' you if you don't tell me who you work for."

Cusi swallowed, searching Roy's face for a sign he might
not go through with it. "They'll kill me if I talk. The minute
I walk out of this jail, I'll be dead."

"An' I'm gonna kill you if you don't talk," Woods
promised. "I see it this way . . . you tell me what I need to
know an' you've got a chance of gettin' away, maybe down
to Mexico. But if you don't cooperate with me right now,
I'm gonna kill you as sure as the next sunrise. Only, you
won't be alive to see it. No more sunrises for you unless you
start givin' me names."

Cusi closed his eyes for a moment, moving the tip of his
tongue over his broken teeth and bleeding gums. "I work for
Gino Tatangelo. He sent me down to Texas, to a company
he owns in Fort Worth. I was helping set things up when my
boss up there said to come over to Longview, because there

was trouble. Somebody put the feds on Gino's operation in the oilfields. I was supposed to keep an eye on the games so we could clear out in time if the law showed up."

At last, Woods thought, we'll have something to give to Major Elliot, a witness who would name names. "Who runs Gino's show in Longview?" he asked, already certain of the answer.

"Carlos. Carlos Santini. He's the one who'll kill me when he finds out I talked. Gino will give the order. Carlos will do the shooting. I'm as good as dead right now. Carlos is one of the best. Then there's Paulie. These guys don't miss . . ."

"Who's your boss in Fort Worth an' what's the name of this company?"

Cusi seemed to hesitate. He closed his eyes again. "What the fuck's the use? I already spilled my guts. I take orders from Rudy Langella. The company is called Texas Supply, over on West Long Street. That's all I know, mister."

"What sorta supplies do they sell?"

Cusi grimaced, like his answer caused him considerable pain. "Whiskey."

Woods could see the headlines in the making, a Fort Worth warehouse full of whiskey seized by the Texas Rangers, and dozens of arrests—New York gangsters operating in Texas now, halted by a pair of Rangers who did good detective work. "Where does Santini keep his whiskey now that we raided his warehouse?"

"He moved it somewhere out in the country. It's a big barn north of town on this deserted road. I've only been there twice and it was dark. We drove north and turned off the pavement to the left. No houses. I swear, that's all I remember."

"He keeps it guarded, don't he?"

"Three or four guys."

"An' they've got machine guns?"

"Yeah. Gino sent some of his best shooters down when all this trouble started."

"Is that where they keep the gamblin' equipment, the tables an' all that other shit?"

"I saw some roulette wheels. Some of the trucks carry poker tables. They leave everything in the trucks so they can roll at night. Jesus, you broke out half my fucking teeth. Ain't I told you enough already?"

Woods stood up, his mind racing. He and Garrett could be on the front page of every newspaper in Texas with a seizure like this: gambling equipment, whiskey, arresting Italian gangsters from New York. "You can get up now, Lennie. You showed a lot of good sense, talkin' to me. You're still alive."

Cusi worked his way to his knees. "Not for long," he said, blood dripping from his chin. "They'll get me sooner or later when they find out I squealed."

"Look at it this way," Woods explained, holstering his pistol. "You're breathin' right now, which you goddamn sure wouldn't have been if you hadn't answered my questions."

Cusi looked up at him from the floor. "I've gotta know if you really would have killed me . . ."

Hearing this, Woods chuckled. "As sure as shit stinks, Lennie. You're a waste of space. Somebody decent could be takin' up the space you're using now. You're eating food an' breathin' air a good man could be usin'. Killin' you woulda been doin' the rest of us a favor. You can bet your ass I'd have killed you. Now, get up so I can take you back to your cell."

Cusi got to his feet with some difficulty on wounded legs and started for the door. A swelling and a dark bruise covered his left cheek.

"One more thing, Lennie," he said, catching Cusi by the arm. "I'm gonna say you tripped over that chair an' fell down. That's how you busted your teeth. Nobody's gonna believe you if you say anything else. But if you tell anybody I swatted you with this gun, I'll come back tonight after everybody's gone home. I know you don't want that, 'cause you know what I'll do."

Cusi nodded.

"I'm gonna have you sign a statement in front of a court reporter," he went on, "namin' those same names you gave me. I hope nothin' happens to your memory between now an' then. I'd advise against changin' your story. It wouldn't be a healthy thing to do."

"I never said I was gonna sign anything. Jeez!" He spat another bloody chip of tooth enamel on the floor. "If Gino finds out, there won't be anyplace in the world where I'll be safe."

"You'll sign it," Woods said. He opened the door and pushed Cusi out into a dimly lit hallway.

They passed rows of cells to a jailer's desk. Cusi limped badly on one leg. Woods spoke to a young jailer seated in front of a rattling electric fan, noticing that Garrett waited for him at the bottom of the stairs. "Lock this guy up again. He had a little accident. Fell over a chair. He ain't hurt bad enough to need a doctor. Chipped a few teeth, is all. I'll be back with a court reporter soon as I can find one. Mr. Cusi is gonna give a sworn statement. Don't let anybody near his cell until I get back, an' don't unlock the door for any reason."

The jailer stood up, keys in hand. Garrett appeared to be surprised by what he heard Woods say.

"Did he give you anything?" Garrett asked, watching as Cusi was escorted back to his cell.

"Everything. He named Tatangelo an' Santini an' an outfit in Fort Worth where Tatangelo stores whiskey. This is gonna be big news, Lee. We've got just about everything we need to bust this bunch. I'll call Cap'n MacDonald so he can call the major. You can tell Cap'n Ross we broke this gangster case wide open. I found out where Santini is keepin' his whiskey an' gambling stuff, so we can grab it right away. It's in a barn outside of town. We'll ask Chief Laster for some cops to back us up. Perry Bass is liable to tip 'em off if we ask him for deputies."

They started up the steps side by side. Woods felt pleased. Near the top of the stairway, Garrett paused.

"I heard you say the guy fell down."

"The floor back there was slippery. Somebody must have just mopped it before we went in."

35

Howard Laster was worried — Lee could see it in his eyes as Woods told him about Leonardo Cusi's confession and the location of Carlos Santini's gambling equipment, along with a barn full of whiskey. The chief's office was quiet for a moment as Laster chewed his bottom lip.

"You say there'll be three or four men armed with machine guns?" he asked. "That's a hell of a lot of firepower. My men have pistols and shotguns, a few rifles. I've got six men on day shift. We should ask Sheriff Bass for some deputies. It's out of city jurisdiction anyway. The county sheriff's office oughta be involved."

Woods shook his head. "I don't trust Bass. He's in cahoots with 'em, if you ask me. He could tip Santini off that we're on our way out to that barn, wherever it is."

"I think I know the place you're talkin' about," Laster said as he tented his fingers on his desktop. "It's the old Miller farm on the highway to Gilmer. There's a dirt road dead-ends off that pavement a few miles out of town. Miller's house burned in the twenties. It's just an old barn an' some sheds. Most of it's fallin' down, best I recall. Haven't been out there in years."

Lee was thinking about what Laster said. "I agree with Roy that we shouldn't mention a raid to Sheriff Bass. The fewer who know about it, the better. We could call in some federal help and the highway patrol, I reckon, but that'll take time. It's a mistake to give Carlos Santini too much time to move his operations someplace else."

"Perry won't like it," Laster warned, "and I could get some repercussions from the mayor's office and the City Council. We have a clear-cut system dividing city and county affairs; however, I suppose the Rangers have jurisdiction."

"Call in your men an' get 'em armed," Woods said. "If you let me borrow a telephone, I'll call my company commander to let him know what's goin' on. Lee needs to call his commander over in Waco, too. This is gonna be big news, Howard, an' we'll be sure to mention how you an' the Longview police cooperated with us on it."

Laster pointed to an outer office where three empty desks had telephones. "Make all the calls you want. I'll send my sergeant out to round up as many of my officers as he can find on routine patrols. We should be ready within an hour."

Sitting down at a desk to call Captain Ross, Lee decided it was enough for now to finally have a break in the Santini investigation. There was no doubt in his mind about how Woods got a confession out of Leonardo Cusi. The story about a slippery floor was laughable. He remembered Clarence Webb and how successfully he'd used the same tactics years ago. Perhaps there was something to be said for old-fashioned Rangering after all. It'd worked again this time.

Lifting the earpiece, he reached an operator and gave her instructions for calling the Ranger office in Waco. From over on the far side of the room, he could hear Woods barking into a phone with his request to be connected to Captain MacDonald. He gazed out a window at the street below, watching the citizens of Longview climb up and down City Hall steps.

After several minutes of waiting, Bob Ross came on the line.

"Mornin', Cap'n. We got a confession in this New York gang investigation and we're about to raid a barn where they store all their gambling apparatus and moonshine. The guy gave us names of his bosses in New York and Fort Worth. It's big, bigger than we figured. Gino Tatangelo sent several of his associates to Fort Worth and to Longview. They've been operating in Texas for more than a year now. They haul booze and gambling equipment out to the oilfields at night. We raided one on an H. L. Hunt lease and seized better'n a thousand dollars. Gallons of whiskey, too. We arrested two men. One of 'em talked to Roy Woods, giving him everything we need to take a case to the district attorney."

Ross sounded a little different when he said, "That's good to hear, Lee. You had me worried. I got a report you've been keepin' company with a young prostitute out there, makin' it too public, bein' seen together. It's a bad reflection on the Rangers when one of our men lets his personal life interfere with his job, gettin' involved with a prostitute. I understand she's pretty, Lee, but you've got to remember we have a public image to think about. A Texas Ranger has got no business bein' in the public eye with a hooker . . . not on a personal basis, keepin' her in his hotel room."

Lee was shocked to hear Captain Ross accuse him of a thing like that. "It wasn't personal, Cap'n. I believe she knows a few things about the Dodd murder, and I was trying to protect her from Santini. He had her kidnapped, and one of his boys gave her a bad beating. I put her in my hotel room for her own protection and it was never anything else. Whoever told you I was seeing her for personal reasons is full of shit . . ."

"I got a call from the county judge, Eldon Warren. He said you were consortin' with her—that was the term he used."

"He's a liar, and I also believe he takes bribes from Carlos Santini to let Santini's boys off easy. He ordered the release of one of my prisoners before I could sign a formal complaint. Judge Warren is in this crooked business up to his ass."

"You kept her in your hotel room, Lee, an' that don't look good. Major Elliot got a call from some guy at the Treasury Department in Washington sayin' you got one of their agents shot because of the hooker. The major wanted me to drive to Longview today to find out what the hell's goin' on between you an' this whore. He said that was all we needed, what with the legislature about to put us under the control of the Department of Public Safety. Elliot sounded madder'n hell about it. He got a call from some state senator about what you're doin'."

"It's bullshit, Cap'n. You oughta knew me well enough to know I wouldn't let something personal interfere with me doing my job. The girl's an important link to whoever killed Bill Dodd. I believe Santini's involved, maybe Hunt and a few others. That lease is worth millions of dollars to Hunt. Santini may have promised to deliver it by getting rid of Dodd. Dodd's wife was killed last night, and I think it was to keep her quiet. She may have sold out her own husband for a price, then somebody decided to double-cross her, to cut her out of the profits. It's looking real complicated now but I can get to the bottom of it, and the girl may be the only key. I need her alive, and I' sure Santini wants her dead." Lee's fingers tightened around the telephone in anger.

"You've got to keep in mind that we have a reputation

to protect in this matter," Ross said. "If you're wrong, it looks bad for us."

Lee was beginning to understand Roy Woods' frustrations a little better now. The Texas Rangers seemed to be more concerned with their public image than with solving a crime. "There's nothing one bit personal between me and the girl, Cap'n. I've got her hidden out in this rented fishing cabin. Nobody knows where she is."

After a pause, Ross asked, "Are you stayin' there with her at night?"

Lee took a deep breath. "Only for her protection. It isn't what you're thinking at all."

Another lengthy pause. "You've got a spotless record, Lee. I'd hate to see anything ruin it. Call me right after you pull that raid, so I can call the major an' tell him what you found. But I'm advisin' you to stay away from that whore. Send her to Tyler an' have her put in protective custody. The Rangers can't afford any kind of scandal before the elections."

The phone clicked in his ear before Lee could say anything more. He hung up the receiver and turned to the window again, doing his best to control his temper.

His gaze fell on a uniformed city policeman standing on the steps talking to a deputy sheriff. He recognized the deputy at once. Tim Carter, Sheriff Bass's chief deputy, was listening to what the police officer had to say, but with his mind on other things, Lee paid little attention to them right then. Why had his commander assumed there was something between him and Molly? It was all based on a telephone call from Judge Warren, a man up to his neck in dishonest dealings with Carlos Santini.

He heard Woods slam his fist on a desk across the room and looked up. "What's wrong, Roy?"

Woods got up slowly from a creaking swivel chair, his face the color of blood. He sauntered over to the desk where Lee sat, his thumbs hooked in his gun belt. "It's that damn whore," he said, giving Lee a hard stare. "Somebody called Major Elliot to complain about you, how you're shacked up with a girl sellin' pussy instead of tendin' to official business. The major wants you taken off the case. Cap'n MacDonald told me to haul her to county jail over in Tyler. You're gonna get a black mark on your record over her, Lee. Your shit's in the fan on account of her."

Lee nodded, taking another look out the window. Tim Carter and the policeman were gone. "I just heard about it from Ross. He said Judge Eldon Warren called him, claiming I was personally involved with Molly. It isn't true. We both know Judge Warren is taking money from Santini. Santini wants me out of his hair. It's all bullshit, Roy. Molly Brown may be the link to Santini in Dodd's murder. All I'm doing is protecting her from Santini's boys long enough to find out what she knows."

"If she knows anything, how come you didn't ask her an' then lock her up?"

"It isn't that simple. She wasn't involved directly. I'm hoping she overheard something, or saw something, that ties Bill Dodd to Santini. She's scared, Roy. And she has good reason to be. Santini sent Paulie Gambino to beat it out of her — where the lease document is. She doesn't know, but she may know something else just as important, only she doesn't know what it is because she wasn't a part of the deal. Dodd's wife was murdered to keep her quiet. It's gotten complicated as hell . . ."

"Cap'n MacDonald told me to put her in jail. You've gotta tell me where she is. It's orders."

Lee let out a heavy sigh. Perhaps Molly would be safer in protective custody. "After we raid that barn, I'll take you down to the cabin. It isn't far . . . a few miles out of town."

Woods nodded. "Sorry, Lee. In the old days, a Ranger could do pretty much what he wanted. The way things are

now, we can't take a shit without fillin' out a form or answerin' to some high an' mighty politician. I've been
thinkin' that after this is all over, I'm gonna go fishin'. Take
my wife to California just to see what it looks like there.
Maybe take my grandkids along. This job ain't what it used
to be. I was proud to wear this star an' call myself a Texas
Ranger. But those days are gone forever an' it's time for me
to quit. I stay pissed off half the time, an' my wife says I
ain't hardly fit company anymore. I can't get to sleep at
night, worryin' that I didn't get all my goddamn paperwork
done. It isn't worth it." He gazed out the window at a
cloudless sky. "Let the fuckin' crooks have Texas, for all I
care. I'll move to Arizona . . ."

An overgrown two-rut lane wound through wooded hills,
leading westward. Five automobiles left a cloud of dust in
their wake. Chief Laster rode beside Lee in the Packard, leading the procession over bumps and grass-bound tree roots
through a deep pine forest, then across open meadows and
into denser trees on gently rolling hills. A merciless noonday
sun beat down on the string of sputtering cars. Laster peered
through the dust-coated windshield at the hills.

"It ain't much farther," he said. "The Miller place
oughta be just over the top of that next rise yonder."

Lee leaned out the driver's window. "Plenty of fresh tire
tracks. Somebody's been using this road recently."

"Maybe it was crude-oil tank trucks," Laster said, although he didn't sound like he believed it himself. He held
the stock of an automatic shotgun lying across his knees.
"We asked the council for a bigger budget so we'd have
enough officers to get control of things. They approved
higher salaries for themselves an' turned my request down
flat. All this oil money makes everybody greedy."

As they topped a low hill, Lee saw a distant structure in
a meadow grown thick with native grass.

"That's it," Laster said. "We'll be better off if we go the rest of the way on foot. That way, they won't see us comin' or hear our cars."

Lee swung off the lane, parking under a lofty pine tree with plenty of shade. He cut off the engine, hearing the radiator as it hissed steam.

Laster got out as the other automobiles came to a halt in spots of shade on either side of the road. Lee pulled the lever back on his Savage when his feet touched the ground, giving the weathered barn a careful examination. Men were climbing out of the cars behind him, loading shotguns and rifles. The clatter of so many guns being readied for action echoed through pine thickets around them in an ominous cacophony of metal against metal. He was sure the next sounds they'd hear would be igniting gunpowder and the whine of bullets. Facing machine guns, the air would be full of flying lead by the time they circled the barn. He could feel it coming.

36

Shoes and boots whispered through the dry grass. The call of a bluejay warned forest creatures of their approach. Silent, grim-faced men fanned out in a wavering line, making their way through trees and undergrowth, carrying guns. A half mile away, in a small field gone to seed from lack of use, a weathered barn with holes in its rusted tin roof sat quietly in the brilliant sunlight. A three-sided shed lay west of the barn, aged boards curling away from the posts and roof beams. Behind the barn and shed, two rows of bobtail trucks were parked, some of the beds covered with iron bows and canvas tarps, others with metal cargo boxes. Lee counted the trucks as he walked along the lane beside Roy Woods and Howard Laster.

"Nine of 'em," he said, squinting despite the shade from his hat brim.

"That's a hell of a lot of whiskey an' dice tables," Woods said quietly. "Somebody must haul the drivers out after dark." He cradled his shotgun in the crook of an arm, tilting his hat to keep out the sun. "We got that fuckin' Italian cold this time."

"The tip-off you got was mighty accurate," Laster remarked, balancing an automatic shotgun in his left palm, sleeving sweat from underneath the bill of his policeman's cap before more of it ran into his eyes.

"It wasn't a tip-off," Woods reminded him. "We got a confession from one of Santini's boys."

Laster gave Woods a quick sideways glance. "That's the guy who fell over a chair downstairs. Mrs. Allen said she had some difficulty understandin' him when she recorded his statement, on account of some broken teeth."

"He fell real hard," Woods replied. "The floor was slippery an' his hands were cuffed behind him."

Lee tried not to think about what had really happened, or to wonder how many times Woods had hit his prisoner before he talked. He told himself it had been necessary to crack Santini's code of silence. Molly said Santini's men were afraid of the consequences if they said a word to anyone—his drivers came from New York, and they understood what happened to those who squealed on Gino Tatangelo.

"I don't see anybody movin' around," Laster said in a soft voice. "They'll have somebody guardin' this road, a lookout or two. Maybe we oughta get out of sight. They could be watchin' us right now with a pair of binoculars . . ."

"Let's move into these trees," Woods suggested. "Have your men spread out in a circle so none of the sons of bitches can get away."

Chief Laster waved his officers deeper into the woods and ordered, "Form a circle 'round the barn. Keep your heads down. We expect 'em to have machine guns, so don't show yourselves unless you have to."

"Kill the first bastard who fires a shot," Woods added in a flat monotone, as though he was discussing a matter of no real importance. "Blow 'em outa their goddamn socks if anybody shoots at you."

Lee looked for a spot on the road where a lookout seemed the most likely. "Those guards will be camped around here someplace or another. Down yonder maybe, where the ruts make a bend behind those trees." For some reason, he wondered about Molly then, and if she were safe at the cabin. She couldn't use the gun he'd bought her — it had been a waste of money. He refused to think about how she would feel being locked up in a cell in Tyler — "for her own protection," the higher-ups had said. It was crap, what Captain Ross and Major Elliot accused him of, although he had to admit to having feelings for Molly. Was it because she seemed so fragile, so vulnerable? Or was there more to it than sympathy? Nothing improper had occurred between them, unless you counted putting an arm around her, or a kiss every now and then.

From the corner of his eye he saw the policemen moving deeper into the forest, hunkering down with shotguns and rifles clutched to their chests. Two of the officers were hardly more than boys. He hoped they would survive a shootout with more experienced gunmen. He thought about Brad Whitaker as he moved quietly through clumps of summer-yellowed grass. Whitaker was no match for professional killers like those he'd battled in the hallway of the hotel, yet he'd won, in a manner of speaking, although it appeared it would cost him his life in the end. He'd leave a wife and two children fatherless because he'd faced hired guns with far superior weapons. Weighing this against some of the things Roy Woods had done, smothering one of Santini's henchmen with a pillow, beating a confession out of another, shooting a wounded gunman on the warehouse platform, Lee decided that a case might be made for Woods's methods after all. Maybe ruthless men on the wrong side of the law needed a taste of their own medicine once in a while. He pondered the possibility that he was becoming too much like Woods and Clarence Webb, thinking this way. Or had he simply seen too much violence over the years as a Texas Ranger?

The scent of pine needles filled his nostrils as they crept beneath drooping limbs. The sweet smell did nothing to allay his apprehension over what was sure to be a deadly encounter with tommy guns in the hands of men who knew how to use them. The quiet scene before them was about to erupt into a battlefield, and he could only guess at the outcome. More blood, more deaths seemed certain. Lee couldn't remember another assignment where so many shots had been fired, so many lives lost, beginning with the men who'd died over in Henderson County, a Treasury agent and a deputy sheriff among them. He hadn't kept a tally since then, or cared to.

The crunch of fallen pine needles under his boots reminded him to proceed more carefully now. Moving to the left, he stayed in the shade beneath the pine trees as much as he could, advancing from one thick tree trunk to the next in order to have cover when the shooting started. The air was hot and still even in the shadows. His shirt clung to his back. Sweat ran down from his hatband into his eyes—he fingered it away quickly and continued forward, more slowly now. On either side of him, uniformed men advanced toward the barn, widening their approach to close a circle. Lee could feel his heart beating faster.

Where the lane made a turn, he saw an open-sided tent

erected in a grove of pines. Folding cots and several chairs occupied the shady ground beneath it. He turned toward Woods and waved a hand in the air, then pointed to the spot. Two automobiles were parked near the shelter, dark sedans difficult to see in the mottled shade.

Woods nodded that he'd seen it, inching ahead with his gun leveled.

Someone in a white shirt with the sleeves rolled up, suspenders and a straw hat, sat in one of the chairs dozing, his chin on his chest.

They don't know we're coming, Lee thought. He'd looked very carefully for electric and telephone lines after they turned onto the lane, finding neither, relieved that no one could call ahead to warn Santini's men about the raid. The element of surprise might prove critical in a war against men with submachine guns.

Closer still, and he could see two men resting on cots in the center of the tent. He wondered how they were able to endure this oppressive heat, let alone find it possible to sleep.

Woods said three or four men were guarding the trucks. Lee could count three. Was there a fourth man out in these trees somewhere, watching them across the sights of a tommy gun, waiting until they were within range to sound the alarm and start shooting?

He got an answer before he expected one — a blast of automatic weapons fire coming from the rear of one of the automobiles, its sharp reports chattering behind the back fender in a five-second stream before it stopped.

"It's the cops!" a deep voice bellowed.

The men asleep on the cots jumped to the ground, scrambling out of sight on hands and knees. The man in the chair was slower to move, his head jerking upright, eyes peering vacantly a moment too long. A rifle cracked in the forest. He was driven backward, arms windmilling, feet kicking as his chair overturned. He fell, and in the following moment of silence, Lee heard him wail, saw him rocking back and forth while holding his chest.

Another thundering series of machine-gun bullets rattled from the rear of the car, chewing bark from the tree trunk where a few seconds earlier, the rifle shot had been fired. The singsong of lead whistled among the pines.

A second machine gun opened up, sending a hail of speeding bullets from the front of the other sedan. Then a third tommy gun began spitting from the shadow of a nearby pine, the muzzle winking in concert with every explosion. Now the forest reverberated with noise.

A lone shotgun shell popped somewhere to the west, hard to hear amid the endless blasts from the machine guns. East of the tent, as Lee raced to a thick pine trunk for protection, a rifle roared, shattering the rear window of one car into so many tiny bits they looked like millions of sapphires sparkling in sunlight as they fell.

Laster's men can't shoot, Lee thought, waiting for a clear view of someone firing a machine gun, an unlikely prospect with gunfire coming from so many directions. He was too far out of range for his Savage, and a pistol shot would have to be perfect at this distance.

To Lee's right, Woods began triggering his .45 automatic at both automobiles from a spot behind a tree. Heavy lead projectiles ripped through the thin metal doors and fenders, puckering a small crater around every bullet hole, rocking each car gently on its springs with the force of impact, until seven shots had been fired.

From another direction, even as the submachine guns pounded in unison, a policeman fired his rifle, tearing to bits the windshield on the car nearest the tent. Glass fragments went airborne, showering over the car's hood and front fenders.

"These cops must be half blind," Lee muttered, frozen where he stood without wasting a shot, unlike too many others who were surrounding Santini's men. "We should have waited for more backup from the Rangers or the feds." But he knew it would have taken too long for enough seasoned lawmen to get to Longview.

One machine gun stopped. A second fell silent, while the third continued to fire in sporadic bursts.

They're reloading, Lee thought. A Thompson's drum held more than thirty .45-caliber rounds, he remembered vaguely.

The gunman wounded in the chair began to crawl on his belly toward one of the cars, dragging a leg as if the bullet had damaged his spine. He was close to the sedan's running board when Woods began shooting again with a fresh clip. Two shots missed when a few dead pine needles flew off the ground around him, but the third bullet struck the man between his shoulder blades, slamming him facedown in the dirt, a dark hole in his white shirt.

Lee rested his shotgun against the tree and drew his .38, placing the barrel on his left forearm to steady it. His aim had to be dead-center if he hoped to hit anything with a pistol from this distance.

All three tommy guns resumed firing, withering blasts coming from three directions, spraying trees and bushes around them. Slugs tore off pine limbs, shredded small brush. In a single brief moment of quiet between bursts, someone in the forest shrieked in agony. One of Chief Laster's officers had made a fatal mistake with his choice of hiding places.

Woods's automatic exploded four times in quick succession, making Lee wonder what he could be shooting at. When a front tire on the closest sedan collapsed on its rim, Lee understood. It made sense to disable the automobiles to prevent any attempt at an escape.

After a short pause to inject another loaded clip, Woods began blasting away at one of the second car's rear tires. The tire ruptured instantly, settling the sedan lower on one corner, and now neither car could be driven.

Two machine guns took aim at the tree where Woods was hiding and let loose a hailstorm of lead. Bark chips flew as slugs thudded into timber. When Lee looked over at him, Woods stood calm behind the pine as though nothing could harm him, putting a handful of cartridges into an empty clip.

He doesn't get rattled easy, Lee thought, wondering how any man could be so unruffled by machine-gun fire meant for him.

A rifle cracked from the north. One of Laster's officers had managed to get behind Santini's gunmen without being noticed in the melee. A tommy gun returned the rifle shot, blasting into the thickets of tall pines at the edge of the field where the trucks were parked.

"We've got 'em in a cross fire now," Lee said, aiming his .38 at the rear of one of the bullet-scarred sedans, waiting patiently for a clear target. He intended to make every bullet count if he could, and that required discipline.

The machine guns fell silent. For a time, an eerie quiet lingered at the battle scene. From off in the trees, he could hear a wounded policeman sobbing. Lee knew it was only a lull before the fight resumed in earnest.

37

Woods' hands were shaking and he didn't like it. He rammed a loaded clip into his Colt and took a few deep breaths to calm his nerves. He was furious over the fact that Lee wasn't shooting—he hadn't fired a single shot.

"What the fuck you waitin' for?" he asked aloud.

Off to the northeast, Howard Laster was crouched

down behind a pine like a man wishing he were someplace else, unwilling to so much as peer around the tree trunk while the shooting was going on.

"Local cops," Woods muttered, growing angrier by the minute as he risked a cautious look at the tent, allowing just one eye and a part of his right shoulder to show while the machine guns were stilled.

He felt satisfaction, having killed the gunman blown out of his chair by a Longview policeman; he had shot the guy before he could crawl under a car. The officer who shot him first was a kid with a typically slow East Texas drawl who had told Woods he'd learned to shoot by hunting squirrels.

"The rest of 'em can't hit a goddamn thing but glass," Woods muttered, raising his .45, staying as far back behind the tree as he could. He looked at the flat tires. "Leastways the sorry sons of bitches won't be drivin' out of here . . ."

A large pine closer to the tent offered him a much better firing position, although he'd have to run hard and stay low to get there without being shot to bits by the Thompsons. It would take nerve to try it, but if there was one thing his nerves weren't built for, it was a stalemate like this. "We could be here all fuckin' day," he mumbled, reaching for his shotgun.

As the silence lengthened to a point where his hands grew wet around his guns, he bent down, eyeing the tree, twenty yards in front of him. It was as good a time as any to try for it.

Woods took off in a lumbering run, crouching as low as possible while still managing a reasonably fast gait across uncertain footing. His breath came in short, difficult bursts after the first few steps, and still no one was shooting at him. He was ten yards from the pine when he heard a noise, the rhythmic thud of automatic weapons fire coming from near a fender of one of the automobiles.

Spits of earth and pine needles flew from the soil around his boots, so close he could feel tiny dirt particles spray against his pants legs. Dodging back and forth, he made a dive for the ground near the base of the tree and landed behind it, gasping, wheezing, sucking air into his heaving lungs.

Suddenly the gunfire ended. He spit out a mouthful of pine needles and dust, crawling forward until he was able to sit up with his back against the pine, protected by the massive trunk of bark-clad timber.

"I made it, assholes," he hissed angrily, collecting himself before he stood up. He could hear someone moaning in a thicket to his right. Otherwise, all was quiet again.

He leaned around the tree with his Colt gripped in a damp fist, taking a hurried look at what he could see from this new vantage point before pulling back to safety.

He was within shotgun range now, not quite as close as he would have liked, but close enough to do plenty of damage, given the opportunity. He stood there for a moment, wondering why Garrett refused to fire or try to get any closer. Had Lee run out of nerve facing three Thompsons? The tree where Lee was hiding stood too far away to give him decent range. Woods decided after a bit that like so many times before in his career, he would have to go it alone to get results.

A lone gunshot abruptly ended the stillness, echoing from a spot far to the west. A slug whacked into the rear of one car and all was quiet once more.

"A waste of lead," Roy sighed, eyeing his hat where it had fallen to the ground as he dove for cover. He could get killed reaching for it, out in the open like it was, and he left it there for now, despite feeling only half dressed without it. Rangers were required to wear Stetsons, gray felt in winter and straw in summer. The hats were part of a Texas Ranger's identity.

A shout startled him. "We've got you surrounded, boys! If you come out with your hands in the—" A staccato of machine-gun fire drowned out the rest of what Chief Laster was saying as bullets sprayed the tree where he hid.

Woods knew these guys were never going to give up peacefully. "We'll have to blast 'em out," he said to himself as a movement in the trees caught his eye—Lee was coming forward now. It was high time, in Roy's opinion. Lee dodged and darted unnoticed to the base of another sturdy pine and knelt down in deep shadows, almost invisible to all but an experienced eye. A few seconds later, the machine guns stopped. Lee had wisely used the shooting as a diversion while making his run.

The tree trunk in front of Chief Laster was torn to shreds, with pieces of bark dangling by threads and bullet scars slicing through the pulpy wood on both sides. From three or four different positions, the pop and crack of police rifles gave a weak response to so much firepower as had been aimed at the chief.

"We're damn sure outgunned," Woods whispered, wishing for his self-loading Winchester .351 rifle now. He'd left it in the back of his car. Until a few years ago, when his vision had started changing—like most people's nearing fifty—he could knock the eye out of a crow in flight with it. He might have remedied the situation with spectacles, but he knew he would never wear them—glasses made men look sissified. Using a shotgun or an automatic .45, a man's aim didn't have to be all that good and he didn't have to look like some pantywaist.

He glanced over to Garrett again, finding him reloading his shotgun. For a time, it puzzled him, seeing as Lee had not fired a shot.

Then Woods nodded. "He's loadin' slugs. I wish I'd done it myself before we got here." He watched Lee lie down on his belly and raise the shotgun to his shoulder. A twelve-gauge slug would penetrate an automobile's thin metal if the range was close enough. Lee looked to be near enough now.

For half a minute or more, Lee waited, lying perfectly

still, sighting down the gun barrel. The silence grew heavier when no one fired a shot. Woods peered around the tree with the utmost care to watch what was going on near the tent. His gaze flickered across the body of the gunman wearing suspenders. The back of his white shirt had turned a dark shade of red and swarms of black flies surrounded the bullet hole in the corpse, feeding on blood.

A booming report from Lee's shotgun thundered through the trees. An automobile swayed, and in the same instant, someone cried, "Holy shit!"

Woods saw a man in dark trousers and white undershirt stagger away from the rear of the car holding his thigh, dropping a tommy gun to the dirt as he clutched his wound with both hands. Before Woods could get off a shot with his Colt, Lee's shotgun blasted for a second time.

The man was lifted off the ground, bent double at the waist, flying backward as though he'd jumped in that direction himself. He appeared to be suspended in midair before he twisted and fell in a patch of grass, his feet twitching with death throes.

Two machine guns beat out a merciless rhythm of .45-caliber explosions, aimed at Garrett's tree. Bullets whined and cracked into the green wood. Pine cones fell from trembling limbs above as the tree shook with the impact.

Lee had pulled back to safety, fingering more loads into his shotgun, completely out of harm's way behind the base of the pine.

The shooting stopped.

"There's just two of you now," Woods said under his breath, noticing a huge hole in the lower left rear fender of one of the cars. Now he understood why Lee had waited so long to fire—he'd seen a man's legs standing behind the automobile. For several minutes, nothing stirred and no guns went off. Roy imagined he could hear the buzzing of flies circling both corpses. Santini's remaining gunmen had to know the net was tightening around them. They had no way out, with two crippled cars and a circle of policemen blocking off any hope of escape.

More minutes passed in total silence. Woods decided it was too hot to wait here all day. "Toss out those guns!" he shouted. "It's over! You boys ain't got a chance of leavin' here! Make it easy on everybody! Toss 'em out an' come out with your hands in the air! We've got you surrounded!"

This time, there was no shooting. Seconds ticked away while everyone waited for a reply to his demand. The wounded policeman stopped groaning. Absolute quiet continued for several more minutes.

"We're coming out!" a muted voice cried from somewhere close to the vehicles. "Don't shoot!"

Woods leaned around the tree with his automatic pointed at the tent and cars. "Keep your fuckin' hands where we can see 'em!" he yelled.

Two men in sleeveless undershirts stood up with their palms in the air. Woods let out the breath he was holding. "Walk this way! Keep your hands real high!"

The first gunman to come into view was covered with tattoos on his arms. He came from between the automobiles and walked toward Roy with his hands in the air. The second man limped away from a tree close to the tent, his pants leg torn away below one knee, showing where a bullet had nicked him in the calf.

Woods was sure they were Italians by the olive tint to their skin and their heads of dark, curly hair. He felt a little bit of disappointment that Paulie Gambino was not one of them—he'd been looking forward to a confrontation with Paulie, wanting it, to prove the hulking giant was no match for him in any situation.

Both men stood in the bright sunlight with palms turned toward the sky. Policemen came from all directions, guns aimed.

Woods called over to Lee, "We'll handcuff 'em an' start

haulin' in these trucks while somebody takes the goons to jail. Then you an' me are gonna head for Santini's office. We'll arrest the bastard an' I'll take him to Tyler before Judge Baker, so there won't be no bail."

Lee ambled over to Woods' pine tree as police handcuffed both prisoners. He seemed distracted. "I need to question Santini about Dodd's death beforehand. I've got this feeling there's something I've overlooked. I don't think Santini killed Dodd, but I figure he knows who did. Probably the same guy who killed Mrs. Dodd last night."

Woods frowned. "This is bigger than one lousy murder, Lee. We've got New York gangsters caught red-handed in gamblin' and booze here in Texas. How come you can't let go of that killin' long enough to give the major an' the governor what they want? Dodd was just some oilfield speculator who pissed somebody off, or got his hands on the wrong piece of property."

Lee shrugged. "Cap'n Ross sent me here to find out who killed Bill Dodd. I intend to do that. I'm pretty sure Santini knows who I'm lookin' for. Maybe he'd cut a deal with whoever it was—a guy like Hunt, who stood to gain big money with Dodd out of the way. I want the trigger man, and I want the man behind him."

Woods holstered his .45. "If you ask me, you're chasin' too many butterflies. This is bigger stuff—major crime. We need to call for a raid on that warehouse in Fort Worth, too. Arrest this Rudy Langella an' everybody else who's there. It's headlines."

Lee rested his shotgun across his shoulder. "Let's have a look at what's in those trucks."

Chief Laster walked up just then. "That was some real fancy shootin', to kill a guy hidin' behind a car, Mr. Garrett."

Lee tipped his hat back, sounding tired when he said, "I used a slug. Not much to it, really. I saw his feet beside one of the tires and did a little guessing."

Woods made a half turn for the automobiles. Then he spoke to Laster. "We're gonna have a look inside the trucks. After you get those assholes cuffed, have some of your men drive 'em back to town. Call the newspaper over in Tyler an' tell 'em to bring cameras. We've got big news here."

Laster cast a glance over his shoulder. "I have somebody wounded back there. I need to get him to the hospital first. We'll get there as soon as we can with the trucks."

Woods hefted his shotgun and began the short walk down the lane to the barn. Lee walked beside him, strangely silent.

"What's eatin' on you, Lee?" Woods asked when they were out of earshot from the others.

Lee's face was aimed at the ground. He seemed reluctant to talk. "Nothing much. Just thinking."

Woods figured he knew what it was. "It's got to do with that girl, ain't it? You've got your mind on her."

"Maybe a little."

"Bein' associated with her could end your career with the Rangers. The major won't stand for it, one of his men gettin' involved with a hooker in a personal way."

"It isn't really personal. I reckon I just feel sorry for her."

"That could be dangerous, if you don't let it go. What the hell's so special about her anyway?"

"Nothing in particular. Maybe it's because she's so young."

"Bein' young ain't the tricky part," Woods continued, wondering why Garrett didn't seem to care about the consequences. "You could wind up without a job, because she sold pussy for a livin'."

Lee glanced up at the sky. "I may just take that chance, Roy. She's different. It's kinda hard to explain."

Woods let it drop for now. It was hard to reason with any man who let his pecker do his thinking.

They came to a Ford flatbed covered with canvas. Roy stopped and pulled back a corner of the tarp. Inside, a table with a roulette wheel sat alongside a crap table marked with painted pass lines and bet squares.

"Gotcha, Santini," he said, filled with keen satisfaction. "Your Italian ass is headed for jail . . ." He noticed that Lee had gone ahead and was entering the barn through a pair of sagging wooden doors. He dropped the tarp and headed over, the sunlight on his head reminding him he'd forgotten his Stetson.

"Paydirt," Lee said, standing before stacks of crates packed with newspaper protecting glass jars and clay jugs from jolting rides in a truck. Off to one side, kegs of whiskey and beer gave off distinctive smells of their own. "There must be several hundred gallons of this stuff."

Woods nodded. "Let's see how cool Carlos Santini is now when we have his picture taken beside all his goodies while he's wearing handcuffs."

38

The purr of the Packard's engine on the Gilmer highway did little to settle Lee's nerves after the shootout; the sound of gunfire was still ringing in his ears. There was something different about the thud of tommy guns, beyond the obvious fact that they weighed odds so heavily in their owner's favor. It was like battling a machine instead of a lawbreaker. The gun became the enemy, rather than the man who used it. In an odd sort of way, it made things detached, almost mechanical, trying to stop a killing machine from taking others' lives. He'd felt nothing when he shot the man behind the car; it was as though he'd stepped on a cockroach or chopped the head off a poisonous snake. Men who came home from the World War described the same lack of feeling about having killed Germans over in France. Lee wondered if he'd become so callous that taking a human life meant nothing now. Was this what had happened to Roy Woods after too many years as a Texas Ranger? Was the same thing happening to him? He remembered a doctor had told him once that a physician could soon became distanced from death, be hardened to it after a few years.

He glanced in the rearview mirror. Woods' Ford was very close to his bumper, pushing him to drive faster toward Longview so they could arrest Santini. It was newspaper headlines Woods was after, not just breaking up a gangster operation for the sake of upholding the law.

"I'm never gonna be like him," Lee muttered, guiding his car between the center stripes on the highway. "I won't let it happen to me."

At the outskirts of Longview, he slowed, watching for a turn beside the railroad tracks leading to Santini's warehouse. He saw a railroad crossing and a sign that read DOGWOOD STREET. He turned off and gravel on the street popped and cracked under the Packard's tires as he sped down the row of warehouses. He shifted to third gear and held on to the steering wheel, bouncing over bumps and deep chugholes, sending a cloud of white dust across the windshield and hood of Woods' car. He took his foot off the accelerator when he noticed that the parking lot beside Santini's warehouse was empty—no cars, no trucks; only empty space.

He braked to a halt in a cloud of dust in front of Santini's office and turned off the engine. "He's cleared out," he said to himself, climbing out of his car. "Somebody warned him."

When Woods ground the Ford to a stop beside Lee's Packard, he knew by the dark look on Lee's face what had happened here before they arrived. "Some asshole told 'em we were comin'!" Woods snapped. "Let's have a look inside." He stalked up to the office to try the doorknob and when it wouldn't yield, he drew his automatic and fired four shots into the lock.

The lock shattered. Woods kicked the door with his boot and sent it flying inward. Lee knew there was no need for a gun and he left his .38 holstered—the office would be empty, just like the parking lot.

File cabinets were overturned, others gaping with open drawers. A chair lay on its side behind Santini's desk. It was evident that all incriminating documents contained in the files had been removed quickly.

"They cleaned everything out," Lee said, giving the furnace-like room a final examination. "We might catch up to him at his house if we hurry, but I figure he's long gone by now. Somebody tipped him off, someone who overheard what we meant to do."

Woods glanced at the telephone on Santini's desk. "You take off for Santini's house. I'll call Cap'n MacDonald. That place in Fort Worth has to be raided real quick or the stuff'll be gone, just like everything here. When you get there, block that front gate an' don't let nobody in or out. I'll be right behind you. It may already be too late if Santini called Texas Supply to tell 'em we were onto their operation. I'll have the cap'n alert Highway Patrol to watch for Santini's black Dodge. He'll be on his way to the state line if he's runnin'."

Lee wheeled for the door. "I remember seeing a cop talking to a sheriff's deputy at City Hall. Didn't think much of it at the time, but I know that deputy's name. We'll question him as soon as we get back from Santini's. He's probably our leak . . ."

He took off at a run for his car, wondering if Deputy Tim Carter had been the one to send Santini a warning.

The gates were locked. Santini's dogs came down the driveway barking savagely as soon as Lee drove up. He got out with his shotgun in hand and studied the house. It looked deserted. On the drive over, the Packard had overheated and now it sat with curls of steam rising from the radiator cap and front grille. He'd driven as fast as he dared across Longview without stopping for stop signs or street lights.

He didn't want to think about the possibility that Santini had slipped through their fingers and was headed back to New York. It wasn't only that justice wouldn't be served in the bootlegging and gambling case; the Dodd murders remained to be solved, and without Carlos Santini, Lee didn't think he could ever get the information he needed to track down the killer.

He checked his watch. It was past four in the afternoon, and he figured the temperature had to be a hundred degrees. Waiting for Woods out in this heat was making him irritable, although he understood that most of his frustration came from missing a chance to capture Santini.

He watched the snarling shepherds as they snapped their jaws at him beyond the iron fence; then he took a second look at the house. "To hell with this," he muttered, walking up to the gate to examine its lock.

After a moment, he stood back, aiming a shotgun slug for the lock mechanism. When he pulled the trigger, it sounded like a bomb had gone off in Surrey Lane's quiet neighborhood, despite the noise from the nearby sawmill.

The lock burst on impact, sending metal fragments spinning across Santini's driveway. The explosion silenced the dogs. Lee climbed in the Packard and started it, pushing both gates open with the car's bumper.

One silver-and-black shepherd, barking angrily, trotted alongside the car as he drove toward the house. The other dog crept away to a row of hedges after hearing the gunshot. Lee didn't want to kill the aggressive dog and hoped it wouldn't come for him when he opened the car door. It wasn't the animal's fault it was owned by a wanted criminal.

He stopped in front of the house, where a circular driveway turned at Santini's front door. He killed the motor and got out cautiously, one eye on the dog, the other on the house. No cars were parked in the open two-car garage.

"He's gone," Lee said quietly, keeping the shepherd at bay momentarily with the muzzle of his shotgun. The dog snapped at the barrel but didn't charge him and for that, he was thankful. All the windows in the house were closed and curtained. No one could have withstood the heat inside behind closed windows.

He heard the roar of an automobile on Surrey Lane and gave it a glance. Roy Woods came speeding down the street at full tilt, a trace of blue smoke coming from the Ford's tailpipe, the accelerator pressed to the floor.

Woods's car slid sideways coming into the driveway, shifting to a lower gear. He stopped and jumped out, giving the barking dog an angry stare. "Why don't you shoot this son of a bitch?" he asked, drawing his .45.

Lee shook his head. "It's just doing its job, Roy. Can't see no reason to kill it." He aimed a thumb at the house. "You can see Santini's already gone. No cars in the garage."

"We'll look anyway," Woods replied, "an' if that fuckin' dog makes a pass at me, I'm gonna shoot it."

Lee kept the shepherd occupied while Woods went to the front door. He found it open and motioned Lee inside, covering every footstep with his Colt.

As Lee predicted, the two-story house was empty. Clothes lay scattered all over the bedroom floors and it was evident that someone had left in a hurry. Expensive furniture and imported rugs covered wooden floors polished to a brilliant shine. Signs of big money were everywhere — paintings hanging on the walls, glazed pottery and fine china in glass-fronted cabinets.

"He got away," Woods said at the bottom of the stairway after a search of the upstairs rooms. His voice was thick, disgusted with the result. "The rotten son of a bitch is probably in Arkansas or Oklahoma by now."

Lee walked over to a side door. "He left a bunch of stuff we can seize. Maybe his tank-truck drivers don't know he left yet. We can impound all the tanks, too. We got his whiskey trucks and most of his gambling equipment. I'd say we got in his pockets pretty deep."

"I wanted *him*," Woods declared, red-faced. "It ain't enough we got his gamblin' shit or his goddamn trucks. I'll have Cap'n MacDonald send a warrant for his arrest to New York. If the son of a bitch shows up there—"

"Let it go, Roy. We busted up his operation here. We got the governor and Major Elliot what they wanted, big news about a New York crime organization in East Texas that was stopped by the Texas Rangers. It isn't perfect, but it's enough."

Woods holstered his .45 and sighed. "I reckon I'll go down to the jail an' make sure those buzzards get booked in right, so Judge Warren can't let 'em loose. I'll tell Chief Laster to park all those fuckin' whiskey trucks in front of City Hall, so the newspapers can get pictures of what's in 'em. While I'm at it, I aim to talk to Sheriff Bass. Have him send out deputies to every Hunt Oil lease to impound Santini's tank trucks. I told Cap'n MacDonald about Texas Supply in Fort Worth a while ago, an' what we found out at that farm. Maybe we'll get there in time at the supply company. Like you said, this is still big news."

Lee walked outside, keeping watch for the dog. "I've got a favor to ask, Roy. Don't take the girl to jail in Tyler just yet, if you don't mind. I'm gonna stop by Municipal Hospital to see how Whitaker is doing, then I'm gonna check on Molly. If I can, I'm gonna keep trying to find out who killed Bill Dodd. With the girl in jail, I may not be able to get any answers."

Woods came out on the stoop. He gave Lee a passing glance and said, "It's your career goin' up in smoke if you piss off Major Elliot over her. I'll say I was too busy roundin' up Santini's men an' equipment to take her to Tyler right now. As to seein' about Whitaker, you're wastin' your time. He's gonna die, if he ain't already dead. He was a gutsy little guy, I suppose. He didn't look it, but he had big balls." He started for his car and spoke over his shoulder. "If I was you, I'd come down to City Hall after a bit, so you can get your picture in the papers." He headed for the Ford and climbed in as Lee got in the Packard for the drive to the hospital.

"Infection," Dr. Collins said gravely. "It has spread and we can't stop it. His internal bleeding has slowed, but it won't be enough to save his life. His wife and daughters are here. I understand they arrived on the bus this morning. Mr. Whitaker is still unconscious. A representative of the Treasury Department will be here tomorrow, I'm told. I'm sorry to be the bearer of sad tidings, but I do not expect Mr. Whitaker to live. We have done everything we can for him."

"Thanks," Lee said softly, looking into Whitaker's room. A blonde woman and two small girls sat in metal chairs close to his bed. He could hear one of them crying.

He walked in with his Stetson in his hands. "Sorry to be an interruption, ma'am," he said to Whitaker's wife. "Just dropped by to see how Brad is."

"He's dying," the woman said, tears rimming her eyes. "The doctors haven't given us any hope."

A little towheaded girl of five or six, her hair tied in pigtails, sobbed louder now, covering her face with her hands.

"Sorry, Mrs. Whitaker," Lee said. "I wish there was something I could do. He's a brave man. Real good at his job, too."

"What does it matter now?" she asked, her voice breaking as she looked at Lee. "His daughters won't have a father and I will have lost my husband. I don't know what we'll do without him."

It was the wrong time to offer financial help, as limited as it would be coming from him. "Nothing else I can say, ma'am, but to say I'm sorry about what happened. I'll stop by tomorrow to see how he is."

He left the room and walked out of the hospital in a black mood, remembering Brad Whitaker and how he'd put his life on the line to protect Molly. Lee supposed he was partly responsible.

As he was driving through the south side of town, he happened to glance in his rearview mirror. A dark blue sedan seemed to be following him from a distance, although he couldn't be sure with rays from the setting sun almost blinding him. He turned at a street corner and drove around the block at low speed, watching his mirror, turning back for a better look when glare from the sun made it hard to see. But when he looked closely, he saw nothing, no one following him.

"It's my imagination," he said, shifting into second gear at an intersection that would take him to the river.

39

He saw two of his shirts and a pair of pants hung out to dry on a line between the trees when he drove up to the cabin under a pink evening sky. He grinned and turned off the engine. Where had she gotten laundry soap? he wondered. Molly was sitting on the front steps wearing a white sleeveless blouse and a print skirt, her hair freshly brushed and tied in a ponytail hanging down the middle of her back. She smiled and waved when she saw him.

He got out and shut the Packard's door with his shotgun in his hand, feeling exhausted and hungry, remembering he had not eaten since she'd made him breakfast early this morning—fried eggs and bacon and coffee. He was dreading giving her the news—that for her own safety, until Santini and Paulie were caught or had left the state, she would be locked away in the Tyler jail. He told himself it wouldn't be for long, since it appeared that Santini and his men were on the run. Maybe she wouldn't have to go at all if he talked to Captain Ross about it tomorrow. He'd tried to reach Ross from a telephone at the hospital and was told there was a problem with the phone lines at Waco, which an operator said should be repaired by morning. Lee decided against telling her about it until he talked to Ross.

"Hi there," he said as she left the steps with the same smile on her face. "I see you've been doing a bit of washing. I'm obliged."

She came up to him and kissed him lightly on the cheek—he hadn't expected it.

"You look tired," Molly said, furrowing her brow, no longer smiling. "Is something wrong?"

He led her to the porch steps and sat down heavily, resting his shotgun against a roof support, placing his hat beside him to run fingers through his tangled hair. "Nothing's wrong, really. We found Santini's whiskey and gambling equipment at this vacant farm north of town. There was a little shooting, but we got his trucks and arrested two men. Santini skipped town before we could find him . . . cleaned out his office files and some personal things at his house. Somebody tipped him off that we were coming and he escaped. You won't have to worry that he'll come after you any longer. He's running for the state line most likely, to keep from being arrested. Roy Woods notified the Highway

Patrol, only it's probably too late to apprehend him by now."

Molly's eyes betrayed fear, and doubt. "He isn't afraid of anybody, not even the law," she said in a distant voice, turning her gaze toward the river. Reflection on the water from the red ball of setting sun turned the surface of the Sabine a blaze of mixed colors. "Was Paulie one of the men you arrested?"

"He got away too. I s'pect he knew he was facing a kidnapping charge, so he left the state. Paulie's not crazy enough to want to go to jail if he thinks he can hide from it."

"You don't know Paulie," she said.

He couldn't think of a way to reassure her and kept silent, watching the river.

"I fixed you something to eat. Cornbread and beans, the way Hattie Mae showed me, and some boiled turnip greens with bacon in it. She was a wonderful cook. She made good peach brandy, too." She smiled again. "There's still plenty of brandy left, if you want some."

"Sounds mighty nice, the food and all. You didn't have to go to so much trouble, 'specially washing my clothes. As to that peach brandy, I think I'll have some right now. It's been a long day. One more thing I didn't tell you. Somebody killed Dodd's wife last night. Tried to make it look like a suicide, like she hung herself. Now I'm really stumped, trying to solve his murder without her. I think she told somebody about his lease coming in the mail that day, maybe even told the killer. She could have been in on it, some kind of scheme to kill her husband so she'd get more of the profits from that oil. I found out she came from some pretty rough beginnings before she married Dodd. A guy told me he knew her from before, down in Beaumont . . ." For Molly's sake, he left out the part about how Sara used to make her living.

"She was a whore, wasn't she?" Molly asked without looking at him, staring off at the sky.

He waited for a moment. "That's what Charley Waller told me."

"You've got a real low opinion of whores, don't you?"

She caught him off guard with the question. "I'm not dead set against it, if that's what you mean. I don't see much wrong with it. Nobody gets hurt. I wouldn't say I had a low opinion on the subject, of women who do it for a living."

"Most men do. They like to pay for having their fun, but in daylight, when I see them on the street someplace, they turn the other way like they don't know me. It's too bad about Mrs. Dodd. Bill used to talk about her some, like he loved her a whole lot and hoped she'd come to Longview."

Lee took the piece of crumpled paper from his shirt pocket. With his sweating all day, it was limp and badly wrinkled, still damp from being against his chest in the heat. "I found this on a table beside her telephone—the initials C.W. and this number, written in pencil. It may be nothing. I'm pretty sure it's a telephone number, and the initials could stand for Charley Waller. But when I asked the operator while I was at the hospital seeing Brad Whitaker, she said that wasn't his number. I'll check telephone-company records tomorrow to see whose number it is. It's likely another dead end, maybe a friend she gossiped with, or a grocery store. The operator told me Longview doesn't publish a directory every year. It could be a new number. By the way, Brad Whitaker won't make it, the doctor said, but he's still alive."

"I feel bad about what happened to him because of me. Let's not talk about it. You think Mrs. Dodd was killed to keep her quiet?"

"That's about the only thing I can come up with that makes any sense. I talked to her the day before and she pushed me to find out who killed her husband. She didn't act like a woman who planned to commit suicide. Besides, she had this big knot on the back of her head. Somebody knocked her out cold, then tied a rope around her neck. She was murdered all right, probably by the guy who killed her husband. There simply isn't another angle I can make myself believe."

A fish jumped on the placid waters drifting past the cabin. A spreading circle of ripples marked the spot for several seconds, until the river's sluggish currents slowly erased it.

"You think I know something I'm not telling you," Molly said later. "I swear I don't. Bill was a nice guy. He came to see me about once a week before his wife got here. He was kinda shy at first. He wouldn't undress with the lamp on. He'd have come more often if he'd had the money, he told me. He was spending all he had trying to get that paper fixed up so the oil was his. He told me he could get the rest of the money as soon as he had that paper recorded."

"What did he mean by the rest of the money?"

"He didn't say. I don't know anything about stuff like that and he never explained it to me."

Even as tired as he was, Lee's mind would not rest. "Did he ever ask you about borrowing some money? Not from you, but from anybody else?"

Molly frowned. "He never came right out and asked. I did tell him Gino used to loan money back in Brooklyn. Everybody in the neighborhood borrowed money from him once in a while, only the interest was real high. And if you didn't pay him back when you were supposed to, something awful happened to you. Gino sent Carlos or Paulie to see you, and everybody was scared of them. I remember my mom borrowed twenty dollars from Gino one time and she worried something fierce she might not be able to pay it back on Friday."

"That's it," Lee said, cupping his chin in one hand. "Dodd went to Santini to borrow money against his lease.

Santini knew the lease was worth millions, so he agreed to loan Dodd the money when it was recorded in his name. Somehow, Santini found out when the lease came in the mail, and he had Dodd killed so his partner in this deal could get all of it and split with him, cutting Dodd out entirely. It doesn't tell me who killed Dodd, but it gives me a motive for Santini. Now all I've got to do is find out who was in it with him. It had to be someone who would know about the day the lease arrived. That only leaves Sara Dodd and Charley Waller as suspects, and Sara was murdered to keep her quiet. Waller had to be the one who killed her, or he had her killed, unless Santini ordered it as soon as I started getting too close to him."

Molly seemed preoccupied. "One other person knew about it. Bill told *me* on the day his paper came. He was all excited, too. I guess that makes me a suspect, doesn't it? I could have told somebody he had it. Only I didn't."

Lee grinned. "You have never been one of my suspects. But I did wonder if you'd told Dodd where he could borrow the money he needed to pay those heirs. You mentioned Tatangelo to him, and Dodd must have known about Tatangelo's connection to Santini. I think it explains how the killer knew there was big oil money at stake. Millions of dollars. All I've got to do is find out who was in on it . . . who told the killer that the lease had come. If Sara was alive, I think she could have told me. She's dead, so that leaves Charley Waller. Some way or another, Buster Davis must have been in on it too. He wound up with the oil. Someone else could have gotten a slice of the action, somebody who tipped off Davis, and whoever it was is also a murderer, or an accomplice to murder. But at the bottom of all this was Sara Dodd. I believe she meant to have her husband killed to get her hands on the oil for herself. She told someone the day that lease came."

"It wasn't me. I hope you believe me."

"I do," he told her sincerely.

"I'll get the brandy and your supper. Let's eat out here again where it's cooler. That fan only moves hot air around in the cabin, and it's so pretty watching the river." She smiled.

Just before she got up, he caught her hand lightly and drew her mouth to his, a bold move he didn't really think about before he did it. When he kissed her, her lips parted. One of her arms snaked around the back of his neck. He squeezed her palm and put his free hand behind her back, pulling her closer. His pulse began to race, and that same light sensation as before awakened in his chest when he held her.

A moment later, he drew away, staring into her eyes. "That was nice," he whispered.

"Yes it was," she replied just as softly. "Maybe you'll do it again after supper."

"I'd nearly guarantee it," he said as the sun dropped below the horizon beyond the river. "Please bring me that brandy and sit with me for a spell. Supper can wait."

Bullfrogs sang a chorus of throaty songs up and down both sides of the riverbank. Stars shone down on the water. Crickets chirped. Fireflies danced through the forest shadows. A quiet, gurgling sound came from the Sabine as it flowed past. Somewhere in the trees, an owl hooted. Pine scent mingled pleasantly with the smell of soap from Molly's hair as he sat beside her with his arm around her shoulders. The brandy relaxed him, making it far easier to say what was on his mind, easier to kiss her several times after they'd eaten. A slice of moon hung above the treetops on the far side of the river, silvering the forests around them.

"I've always had a hard time talking to women," he said as a nighthawk circled overhead, screeching its lonely cry while it searched for food. "I can't explain it. Somehow, the words don't come out right. They get tangled up on the end of my tongue."

"You're doing just fine tonight," Molly told him, her head against his shoulder. "You make me feel special, like I never did before."

"I'm probably talking too much now."

"You're saying just the right things. I really do like to hear them, coming from you."

"It must be the brandy. Usually I've got a bad case of lockjaw."

"It isn't so much what you say . . . it's the way you act when you're around me."

"I'm not good at this. Not much experience, I reckon."

She turned to him. "Do you think you could ever have real feelings for somebody like me?"

"The feelings I have are real. If I knew what to call 'em, I'd give 'em a name."

She waited for a moment. "Do you think you could ever . . . love me like you would a regular woman? Could you ever forget about what I did at Maude's?"

"I'm not rightly sure what love is, Molly. I've never been in love. Not that I know of."

"Never?"

"Never. There was this girl back in high school I talked to a lot. We went down by the creek and held hands. That was right at first. Later on, she showed me how to do a few other things."

"You haven't slept with very many women, have you?"

"Not many. A few."

"Maybe it isn't that you're bashful. Maybe you want a woman who means something to you."

"I wouldn't know. I'm no authority on the subject."

"You didn't answer my question."

"What question was that?"

"If you could ever learn to love me, to forget about what I did in the past."

"I suppose I could try. Never tried it before."

She kissed him on the lips. "That's all I'd ever ask, if you decided to try loving me. I couldn't ask you for anything more."

40

Newspapermen were gathered around him, reporters from Tyler and Marshall and Shreveport and Texarkana and, most important of all, a representative from the *Dallas Times* who had made a flying trip by automobile to get pictures for the front page tonight so they could make the morning edition. Woods stood behind one of Santini's trucks with its tarp flap open, revealing crap tables and crates of whiskey and a carefully placed keg of beer near the back, arranged so it would photograph well when flashbulbs went off.

The scene was only partially illuminated by a streetlight at a nearby intersection. Erected beside the truck was Woods' showpiece: a roulette wheel, mounted on a wooden table, that was the object of considerable attention by the photographers. Flashbulbs lit up the parking lot next to City Hall, where all nine trucks were parked in a row. Curious citizens mingled with reporters, all inspecting the cargo; however, most were clustered around Woods and Chief Laster, listening to an account of the big raid in Gregg County that afternoon. Sheriff Perry Bass was noticeably absent. Judge Eldon Warren had gone home early, Woods was told.

"They resisted arrest with submachine guns," Woods continued as a hush spread over the crowd. "Unfortunately, a local police officer was seriously wounded, a brave young man who risked his life to uphold the law an' protect the citizens of Longview from hardened criminals. Gangsters. These men were professional killers from New York City, part of an Italian crime organization recently moved into Texas. Thanks to the help of Chief Howard Laster an' his courageous policemen, this bunch of crooks has been stopped from makin' inroads into our state. A number of them were killed over the past few days. A brave agent from the Treasury Department in Washington is at Municipal Hospital now, probably dying from wounds he suffered battling these East Coast gangsters . . ." A flashbulb popped, halting his story for a moment.

"Can you give our readers some names? Who's behind all of this?" asked a reporter who'd introduced himself earlier as being from Shreveport.

Woods directed his answer to everyone. "A man by the name of Carlos Santini ran the operation here in Longview, posing as a legitimate businessman runnin' a crude-oil truckin' firm. But he made his big money at night, settin' up gamblin' tables an' his whiskey peddlers in a number of oilfield camps around Longview. We raided one the other night an' seized crap tables like the ones you see in this truck, besides a lot of white whiskey. An' we know just where to look for more storehouses full of booze an' equipment."

"Do you have proof this Mr. Santini worked for gangsters in New York?" the reporter from Dallas asked. A quiet murmur spread through the spectators upon hearing the question.

"We do. A signed confession namin' a criminal in New York as the big boss. His name is Gino Tatangelo, an' the Texas Rangers found out he has a long criminal history as head of one of the most dangerous gangster organizations on the East Coast."

Reporters wrote furiously on their notepads. Another flashbulb went off, blinding Woods for a moment, and it would have irritated him had he not been so keenly aware of the importance of these pictures.

"How many gangsters were killed or wounded? We've heard a few reports that the toll in human lives is quite high."

"I can't give you an exact count yet. These are extremely violent men. Some local moonshiners were killed in gun battles with peace officers when they refused to surrender to us. Over in Henderson County, we broke up a large still that was sellin' liquor to Santini. Another bunch from Gregg County met the same fate at a local warehouse when they refused to give up peacefully."

"There was a bloody shooting at the Grand Hotel. What can you tell us about that?" the reporter from Marshall asked.

"These gangsters were actually tryin' to kill a Texas Ranger that night, my partner in this investigation, Ranger Lee Garrett out of our Waco office. Santini's hoodlums believed they could scare everybody off the case if they killed a Ranger. They found out what it's like to go up against Texas Rangers. To the best of my recollection, four gunmen were killed that night. Unfortunately, that was also when Treasury Agent Brad Whitaker got shot. His doctors tell us he isn't expected to live. I want it stated for the record that he showed tremendous courage under fire. His bravery should be recognized."

"How many gangsters were killed today, Mr. Woods?"

"Two. We arrested two more. They were all armed with tommy guns. Chief Laster's men, along with Ranger Garrett and myself, faced them with shotguns an' pistols. Your local police chief gave us his full cooperation. He an' his men should be commended for doin' a hell of a fine job."

The reporter from Dallas was grinning. "I guess it's almost true, what they say about having one riot, one Texas Ranger. You said there were two of you, but that's close enough in my book."

"Like I said, we had plenty of support from Chief Laster an' his officers."

"How about the county sheriff?" someone at the back of the crowd asked.

Woods directed his attention elsewhere. "I'll take another question from somebody else. Texas Ranger Headquarters in Austin will issue a full statement regardin' this investigation as soon as it's available. Mr. Santini an' some of his associates are still fugitives. Another raid is goin' on right now over in Fort Worth involvin' these same criminals. The Texas Rangers won't allow any such criminal activity in this state, not now, not ever. We come down hard on lawbreakers, gentlemen. It's our tradition an' we intend to uphold it, so long as the legislature continues to give us a free hand. A Ranger can't get bogged down in paperwork. We have to stay on the move to keep track of criminals like Carlos Santini, an' any other hoodlum who thinks he can break the law in this state."

The Dallas reporter halted his fountain pen. "I take it you are not in favor of pending legislation making the Rangers a part of the Department of Public Safety."

"I'm dead set against it, an' so are most Rangers. We've always been an independent law-enforcement agency, an' I think that's the way it oughta stay."

"What about this raid in Fort Worth? Can you tell us about it?"

Woods stroked his chin to appear thoughtful. "All I can say is that an informant told me it's part of the same criminal organization we broke up here. Captain James MacDonald, in charge of our Dallas office, can give you the details tomorrow mornin'. Are there any more questions, boys?"

"Where's the closest telephone?" the Shreveport reporter asked. Others laughed.

Chief Laster spoke. "The telephone company office is over yonder. They have public telephones in the lobby." He pointed to a white stucco building across the street.

Almost in unison, the reporters took off at a run to call in an account of the story. Malloy, the reporter from Tyler, was the last to ask a question.

"Where is Ranger Lee Garrett tonight, Mr. Woods? I got a picture of his car all shot full of holes the other day and I'd like to hear his version of events."

Woods scowled. "His version'll be the same as mine. Garrett is investigatin' another matter right now."

Malloy raced across the dark street to the telephone company office with his notes under his arm. Woods turned to Chief Laster as the crowd started to dwindle.

"I'd like to use the phone in your office, Howard. I hope I can reach Cap'n MacDonald this late, to find out what they got at that warehouse in Fort Worth an' give him a complete inventory of what we got here today."

"Help yourself," Laster replied, leading him toward the steps to City Hall.

After a frustrating series of bad connections and busy signals, Woods finally got through to Captain MacDonald at home. "Evenin', Cap'n. Sorry to call so late, but I wondered what you found at the Texas Supply Company."

"An empty warehouse. Nothing. Someone tipped them off we were coming."

"You're kidding."

"I'm completely serious. We had Fort Worth police surround the building. It was empty when Dick Peterson went in, just some junk furniture and a telephone. Not a scrap of paper with a name or anything on it."

Woods knew Dick Peterson was a good Ranger, a thorough man who wouldn't miss something important. "Damn," he said softly into the mouthpiece. "I know my prisoner gave me good information. I was sure he was tellin' me the truth."

"He may have been, but somebody called to warn them

before we got there. We looked like fools, surrounding an empty office like that. It won't look good in the press."

"We've got plenty here to take care of that, Cap'n. Nine bobtail trucks full of whiskey an' gambling apparatus. A roulette wheel an' a dozen crap tables, some loaded dice an' shaved cards, along with cases of white corn whiskey, twenty-three kegs of beer, an' two prisoners who'll talk. We already got a confession from that guy who told us about the warehouse in Fort Worth."

There was a pause. "Did you help him with his memory on it, Roy? We've talked about this before. You can't go around beating confessions out of prisoners. Complaints have reached Major Elliot about your official conduct. You can't use force to get a confession. These aren't horse-and-buggy days any longer."

Woods wondered who might have suggested such a thing to his commander. "The guy slipped on a wet floor. Anybody who says different is a liar. He broke off a few teeth. It was a pure an' simple accident. Besides, we got what we needed to make a raid that proves those gangsters were running' shine an' gamblin' tables. The newspapers are all over it here tonight. Some guy from the *Dallas Times* took all sorts of pictures. Shreveport sent a reporter, an' so did a bunch more places. It'll give the major what he wants, a big story about New York gangsters here in East Texas. The governor's gonna be real happy too. Headlines all over the state, Cap'n. This is big news."

"I hope the guy who . . . slipped and fell don't change his story."

"He gave us a sworn statement, a deposition."

"Just lately some judges aren't taking too well to a sworn statement made under duress. The district attorney here has been complaining. We have to be real careful, Roy. Too many eyes are watchin' us now and it'll only get worse if we go under DPS."

"I'll retire. I've got in enough years."

"Maybe that'd be best, Roy. You've been a good Ranger, but things are changing. Send me a full report tomorrow on what you found, who you arrested, and on what charges. And remember, it's important to list the number and names of men who were killed or wounded. I need a complete list. Don't forget that list."

"Sure thing, Cap'n. Good night." He hung up the phone and clenched his teeth. His old and dear friend, James Mac-Donald, hadn't even made an effort to talk him out of retiring. In fact, he'd said it might be for the best.

Woods looked out a window at the lights of Longview. Perhaps he would retire at the end of the month. Rangering wasn't what it used to be and he was sick of it now.

He got up a moment later and waved to Chief Laster on his way out of the office, feeling tired and disgusted, his pride more than a little wounded.

Outside, he turned and walked slowly down a dimly lit sidewalk toward the street corner where he'd parked his car, passing store windows full of dresses and cowboy boots and Stetson hats and signs advertising items on sale, but he didn't really notice them. He made up his mind to retire and take his wife to California in the fall. Bernice would like the weather in California. Someone said it was cooler there.

He didn't see the source of the sudden noise as he was about to climb in the car. Something passed through his throat, and an instant later, he couldn't breathe. Choking, clasping a fiery pain in his neck, he sank to his knees on the pavement. When he tried to swallow, he couldn't. His Ford became a dark blur in front of him as he knelt beside the driver's door, reaching for the handle as if he meant to open it, his fingers curling around the piece of chrome. Then he fell slowly on his right side, thankful that now his pain was less. He experienced an odd floating sensation before his eyelids closed.

41

He lay beside her on the cabin floor, completely spent after almost an hour of frenzied lovemaking. The fan hummed on a table above them, aiming currents of warm air across their sweating skin and damp hair. He held her in his arms as long as he could, with perspiration covering him from head to foot. His bedroll was wet where their moist bodies had been locked together, consumed by passion.

"I've got an idea. Let's go for a swim in the river."

She shuddered in spite of the heat. "It's full of snakes and turtles and really big fish that might bite off our toes or something."

He laughed, lying on his back watching the ceiling shadows in the dark. "You're a city girl. There's nothing in a river that'll hurt you. It'll be nice and cool. The stars and moon will be pretty to look at."

She rolled over and kissed him. "I'll feel safe if I'm with you."

He sat up, admiring the sight of her milky skin as she lay beside him. She had small, firm breasts with light, rose-colored nipples that grew hard at his touch. Her waist was so tiny he was sure he could encircle it with both his palms. Everywhere he touched her, her skin was like velvet. With her hair spread out in a fan on his pillow, framing her face the way it was now, he had never seen her look more beautiful.

A moment or two before he'd taken off his clothes to lie down with her, he'd experienced traces of doubt and feelings of guilt. Talking to Captain Ross earlier, he had denied

any personal involvement with Molly, even though he'd
known he was developing feelings for her. Tonight he'd
made a liar of himself to his captain. Yet he had no regrets.
None at all. Their fevered lovemaking had been so different from his previous experiences with women. In the past,
his couplings with other partners had seemed mechanical,
more a purely physical thing. When making love to Molly,
he somehow felt a closeness he'd never known before, a
joining of minds as well as bodies, even though it didn't
make sense to think of it that way.

"Let's get in the water," he said, reaching for her hand
to help her to her feet.

She stood against him with her palms pressed to his
chest. Her eyes were locked on his. "Tonight you made me
feel so very special, Lee Garrett," she whispered. "Like a
real lady. I've never felt like this with a man before. You
never made me feel used. It was like you really wanted me
because of who I am. I guess I' the one having trouble with
words right now, but you need to know I wasn't doing this
because I felt I owed you for saving my life or anything like
that. I wanted to make love to you. I hope I didn't disap-
point you."

He kissed her damp forehead. "I wasn't disappointed at
all. You're a beautiful girl. You made me feel special too. I
guess I wanted to see if it happened sorta natural, not because you thought you owed me anything, or you figured I
expected you to do it. I wanted it to happen like it did
tonight, because we both wanted each other and not for
any other reason."

Molly stood on her tiptoes and kissed his lips, pressing
her bare body against his. She let her mouth linger there,
breathing softly through her nose.

When she pulled away, she was smiling. "Let's walk
down to the river now, if you're ready."

He took her hand and led her out on the porch, watching the silver surface of the Sabine. Tonight is like a dream, he told himself. He couldn't ever remember feeling so lucky.

They stood in waist-deep water with the river-bottom mud oozing between their toes, feeling the current tug gently on their legs. Stands of bulrushes and cattails in the shallower water near the bank swayed gently in the light night breezes. He held her in his arms and for seemingly endless minutes, they said nothing as the river swept by. Staring into each other's face, now and then they shared a brief kiss or a stronger caress. Lee was a bit surprised that he felt no embarrassment about being naked around Molly. All his life he'd been careful to avoid showing his genitals to women he slept with, as foolish as he knew it was to prefer keeping himself covered while sharing intimacy. But with Molly, he felt no need to hide his nakedness, and while this seemed strange to him, it felt natural tonight. He couldn't blame it on peach brandy; its calming effect had worn off hours ago.

Molly tilted her head in an impish way. "I'm only day-dreaming, you know, but wouldn't it be nice if we could stay right here forever? A place like this is all I've ever wanted as far back as I can remember, 'specially after Mom died. I wanted to be away from the city . . . it didn't matter where. A little cabin like this is enough. It's surrounded by pretty trees, and this river is about the prettiest thing I ever saw in the evening, or in the morning early. And if I could have my wishes, I'd wish that you could be here with me. I'd do my very best to make you happy."

He held her close, gazing past her to the cabin and the forests of pine around it. "It's a real nice place. Quiet, away from everybody. A little small, maybe. There'd be room for a garden out back if some brush was cleared off. We could raise our own vegetables like we did when I was a kid back on the farm. The cabin could use a coat of paint and some work on the roof, but I know how to do all that. My pa taught me."

"I could have a puppy. I always wanted my own puppy. As long as I'm wishing, I might as well wish for a puppy too." She giggled as soon as she said it. "Dreams are fun. Too bad it's only a daydream."

"Some dreams come true, Molly. I used to dream of meeting a woman like you, only I never figured I would."

She nestled her face against his chest. "This is nearly the happiest time in my whole life, Lee. I wish it never had to end, but I know it does. Life never works out like we want. There's always something ugly that comes along to spoil it."

It was like listening to a little girl, he thought, although Molly was a woman in every other way. She was a girl who'd been forced to become a woman much too soon. She reminded him of his niece, the second child of his brother Carl, when she'd told her father what she wanted from Santa Claus at Christmastime.

"I could get you a coon-dog puppy," Lee said. "Coon hounds make good pets. They've got floppy ears and they watch a house better'n most any other breed. Got the loudest bark you ever heard."

Her embrace tightened around him. "No reason to talk about it anymore," she said. "Dreaming just makes you want things so bad you can almost taste 'em. Thinking about how you want things to be doesn't change what's real. But tonight this is real, and I'm so happy I could nearly cry."

He held her, not knowing what to say. How could he promise her anything? Even if he could learn to love her, which was a subject he knew nothing about, he could never marry her and live a normal life as a Texas Ranger. Captain Ross had made it plain he wouldn't tolerate one of his men becoming involved with a prostitute. Taking up with Molly would most certainly cost him his job with the Rangers. He supposed he could find another job, if his record wasn't tarnished by a vengeful commanding officer.

Cupping water in one hand, he let it trickle down her back and shoulders. "Sure hope you won't cry," he said. "I never did know what to do for a crying woman."

The river's sounds—the noise of bullfrogs and crickets and the whisper of moving water passing by the banks—lulled him into a calm state of mind. But it was the woman he held in his arms that truly gave him a sense of peace tonight. The river was only an added touch. He closed his eyes.

The distant sound of an automobile's engine awakened him with a start. He bolted upright from the grassy bank where they had been lying in each other's arms. A mosquito buzzed near his left ear—he brushed it away and shook his head to clear it. He listened closely to the noise. Deep in the forest where the lane came down to the river, a pair of lights winked, passing between tree trunks, and a motor roared.

"Wake up, Molly. Somebody's coming."

She raised her head sleepily. "Who would it be?"

Lee rose to a crouch, watching the headlamps intently. "It won't be smart to take a chance. Get in the river. Hide behind those cattails and stay there, no matter what happens or what you hear. Don't make a sound. I'll get my guns, just in case."

He took off in a run for the front porch, reminded he was naked when he glanced down at himself. His shotgun was leaning against a porch post and his clothes were inside the cabin. A box of shotgun shells was in the trunk of the Packard—there was precious little time to get everything he needed if the automobile spelled trouble.

Dashing up the porch steps, he grabbed his Savage on

his way inside. Taking only his trousers, he ran out again and raced for the car, reaching it just as the oncoming headlamps turned so they gave a view of the cabin, illuminating the trees and his Packard parked in front of the outhouse.

He found the box of ammunition in the trunk, grabbed it and hurried into a clump of brush. Hopping on one foot and then the other, he got his pants on. A dark sedan drove slowly toward the cabin and Lee knew he'd been correct to get ready for unwanted company. He ran deeper into the stand of pines in back of the outhouse and crouched down, gasping for breath, hoping Molly would remember to stay hidden in the reeds and keep quiet.

The automobile stopped fifty yards from the cabin and its headlamps went out. For a moment, nothing changed. Then two of the car's doors opened, a pair of hinges creaking.

"That's his car," a voice said, making no effort not to be heard.

"They'll be inside," another remarked. "Blow the fucking place to pieces."

The stutter of machine-gun fire blasted throughout the quiet river bottom. Explosions in rapid succession preceded the sound of splintering wood as bullets struck the cabin's thin walls. Glass shattered in windows while the tommy gun sprayed back and forth from one end of the building to the other.

A dark silhouette ran forward as the Thompson continued to fire. Seconds later, another machine gun opened up, banging away at walls already riddled with bullet holes. More glass ruptured in windows on the far side of the house. The noise of the pair of Thompsons emptying into the cabin was deafening—Lee knew that if he and Molly had been inside, they would be dead by now, shredded by .45-caliber slugs fired at deadly close range through the clapboard planks.

He heard bullets ricocheting off the stove and cast-iron

bathtub inside, and a series of thuds when slugs became embedded in wood. The cabin's painted white exterior quickly filled with black holes as the guns pounded in a steady stream. A bullet hit the electric fan beside the bed, making a clattering noise.

Suddenly the first machine gun stopped, empty. Lee caught a glimpse of a bulky figure quickly reloading the drum, digging handfuls of cartridges from his pockets. Then the second tommy gun fell silent. The other shooter hurried to reload. But Lee's attention was on the larger man—he recognized his shape even in the dark.

"Paulie Gambino," he whispered, sliding the autoloader back on his Savage. "You haven't got near as much sense as I figured."

He crept forward on the balls of his bare feet, moving from tree to tree, focusing all his attention on Paulie. Anger turned to rage inside him.

Lee heard a voice.

"Nobody can be alive in there, but take a look anyway. That fucking cowboy cop has been hard to kill, according to Carlos."

Paulie grunted, readying his Thompson for automatic fire as he started for the cabin. "He owed me," Paulie said. "He had it coming, the sorry fucker. I'm gonna see how he looks with an ass full of lead."

"Make sure the whore's dead too. If either one of them is breathing, shoot them in the head." The one who spoke held his machine gun beside his leg now, watching Paulie's slow approach toward the cabin door.

Lee raised the shotgun to his shoulder. Paulie was out of range—the other man had his back turned to Lee, standing less than thirty feet away. A twelve-gauge slug placed in the right spot would kill him almost instantly. But even as angry as Lee was, he wouldn't shoot a man in the back. He'd give him one chance to drop his gun and turn around when Paulie went inside.

Paulie started up the steps. He opened the screen door, aiming his tommy gun through the door frame. He stood there for several seconds. "Can't see a fucking thing in here. It's too dark," he said, keeping his voice low.

"They're dead, like I told you. Nobody could survive that many bullets. Turn on a fucking light. There's an electric wire running to the corner of this dump. Look for a light switch someplace. Hurry up. We ain't got all night. Somebody had to hear these guns."

Paulie went in. "I can't find a goddamn light switch," he yelled. "Don't see any bodies either . . ."

Lee fixed his sights on the gunman's back, curling his right forefinger around the trigger. With Paulie inside looking for a light switch, there would be just enough time to warn the other to drop his weapon.

"Keep looking for the fucking light switch, Paulie. C'mon, so we can get the hell outa here!"

Lee leaned away from the pine tree and spoke in even tones, just loud enough to be heard by the man in front of him. "Put the gun down and turn around real slow . . ."

42

Time seemed frozen. The gunman stiffened. His head turned slowly to see who was behind him.

"Drop the gun," Lee hissed. "I won't say it again." He didn't recognize the shooter's face in the silver moonlight.

"It's empty," the man replied, letting the tommy gun fall to the ground. He turned at the waist so his left hand was hidden momentarily. "The boss was right—you're hard to kill."

A lightbulb came on in the cabin, and it was just enough diversion to keep Lee from seeing a sudden motion by the man in front of him until a pistol came up in his fist.

Without hesitation, Lee pulled the trigger. His Savage gave off a mighty roar, driving into his right shoulder, muzzle rising upward while it belched flame. A thumping noise accompanied the blast, a thumbtip-sized lead slug entering human flesh, striking bone.

The gunman was jarred off his feet, twirling like a ballet dancer on his toes, arms swinging outward, his pistol flung into the darkness. His mouth fell open and the sound he made reminded Lee of the chicken's squawk when his ma used to twist a bird's head off in the barnyard to fry a hen for supper. Dark fluid squirted from the back of his shirt as he whirled in the air on his tiptoes. Then he slumped to the grass, moaning while he rocked back and forth in pain.

Paulie raced out on the porch as Lee ducked behind the pine tree again.

"What the fuck was that?" Paulie cried, waving his machine gun back and forth, unable to see in the dark after being under a lightbulb in the cabin's ceiling.

It was a long shot for a slug, but Lee took it, his sights on Paulie's chest. He squeezed the trigger, and immediately knew he'd missed. A porch beam split into kindling near Paulie's head, followed by a blast of machine-gun fire, sending Lee scrambling for cover.

Bullets flew all around him, peppering trees and limbs and underbrush while the rattle of the Thompson continued until its drum was empty. Paulie jumped off the porch and disappeared in the darkness behind the cabin.

Lee took a fistful of shells from the box and stuffed them into his pocket—he knew what he had to do. More than anything else, he had to lead Paulie away from the river, from the girl. Drawing Paulie deeper into the pines, it would become a game of cat and mouse between a New

York City killer and a country boy who grew up in the woods. Despite facing a man with a machine gun, the advantage would be Lee's.

He ran hard to another group of pines and fired a shell at the cabin to bait Paulie, moving higher, up a gentle hill thick with trees. He triggered a round from the hilltop and took off at a trot, balancing the Savage in the palm of one hand.

Pausing at the rim of a shallow ravine, he took time to load a full magazine with buckshot, wishing he'd remembered to take a few slugs from the trunk, but there hadn't been sufficient opportunity before the sedan drove up.

He was off again at an easy jog, dodging between trees, now and then halting long enough to listen for the sound of heavy footsteps coming from the forest. Once he heard Paulie crashing through limbs in a thicket farther down the ravine. He aimed a harmless shot in the direction of the sounds and took off running, the roar of the shotgun ringing in his ears.

Paulie fired a short burst of cartridges in Lee's direction, as far off the mark as Lee's shot had been. Lee was satisfied for the moment. His plan to lead Paulie away from Molly appeared to be working.

Locating the source of noises in the night was tricky. When he turned his head, sounds seemed to come from a different place. He lay on a shelf of rock overlooking a range of forested hills. In the distance he could see a silvery ribbon of water winding its way southeast half a mile away. He had continued to bait his adversary with occasional shotgun charges, but for the last few minutes, there had been no answering fire and that began to worry him. Had Paulie turned back?

Lee rested on the rocks a while longer, then crawled off

to one side and stood up behind a tree. His bare feet bled where rocks and sticks had cut through his flesh, and his arms and chest bore similar scratches. Dashing blindly through the dark forest, there hadn't been time to dodge obstacles or to take care where he placed his feet.

"Where the hell are you?" he whispered to himself, watching the forest shadows for movement, listening for any noise, no matter how slight. Paulie's tremendous weight might have forced him to turn back as the climb steepened.

Would he go back to search for Molly? Lee wondered.

When the silence lasted too long, he started back down to the river, swinging wide of the route he'd taken to reach the ridge. If Paulie meant to ambush him, he would need good night vision and keen senses to hear a barefooted woodsman moving through a black forest. Trees grew so close together here that they blocked out light from the moon and stars completely. Lee made his way carefully, for the same darkness cloaking his descent would also hide every detail of the landscape before him. A bushwhacker with a gun needed only to have patience, and enough luck to be in the right place at the right time.

He sensed another's presence before his eyes or ears gave a warning. Halting in a clump of waist-high brush, he knelt there for a time scanning the dark, listening, wondering what it was he felt that made him hesitate. Tiny hairs prickled on the back of his neck. Goose bumps appeared on his arms. He thought he could almost smell human sweat somewhere close by, although there was no breeze to carry a scent to where he knelt, surrounded by tall pines. Yet he knew to trust his senses, something so subtle alerting him that he couldn't define what it was. He waited in the bushes, listening to his heartbeat and the chirp of crickets. It would be a fool's move to continue downslope until he knew what awaited him there.

Off to his right he heard a dry twig snap, then the rustle of shuffling feet. Straining to see any shadow, a swaying branch or a stirring of any kind, he tensed and brought his shotgun to his shoulder.

The forest was too dense, hiding everything. The sounds continued downhill at a regular pace.

He's heading for the river, Lee thought. He'll be looking for Molly now.

He crept through the brush in a crouch, keeping the noises within earshot — he guessed at the distance, maybe thirty or forty yards of almost impenetrable pines and bushes, broken only by tiny clearings carpeted with clumps of dry grass. Paulie's shoes and his bulk made it impossible for him to walk without announcing his direction, and his lack of experience in the woods made him unaware of how clearly he gave his position away.

Lee could hear bullfrogs croaking along the river now, and he hoped Molly hadn't come out of the water too soon. If Paulie saw her, he would kill her with one deadly blast of machine-gun fire before Lee could stop him.

He saw a light through the needled tree limbs down below. The cabin's windows glowed yellow when he caught glimpses of them as he descended the slope. Paulie was just ahead of him, still hidden by deep forest, his feet crunching softly over dead pine needles and twigs.

I'll kill him when he walks into that clearing behind the cabin, Lee thought. He'll be outlined by light from those two windows on the west side.

Pain in Lee's bleeding feet forced him to be more careful in the dark, cautious where he placed each foot, slowing him down. Neither could he afford to let Paulie hear him slipping up from the rear. Padding quietly around pine cones or dry sticks that might give him away, Lee continued toward the cabin's lights with his shotgun clamped against his shoulder, listening to Paulie's heavy footsteps somewhere in front of him.

He could see the river now through openings in the forest. Suddenly the sounds Paulie made stopped.

He's being careful, Lee thought. He won't cross open ground until he's sure it's safe.

For half a minute or more, there was absolute silence. Lee crouched down, sighting toward the cabin, hoping for a glimpse of Paulie when he entered the clearing. Light from the cabin's open windows formed golden squares on the grass below each opening. There was no sign of Molly anywhere. Lee prayed she was still hidden in tall reeds growing along the riverbank. She had surely been frightened by all the shooting, and that alone might keep her out of harm's way if she stayed in the water.

A black silhouette inched forward from a line of trees near the outhouse, farther away than Lee expected Paulie to be, out of range of his shotgun.

"Damn," he whispered. He needed to be forty or fifty yards closer for a load of buckshot to have any effect.

Moving as quickly as he dared, staying behind tree trunks to keep from showing himself, he started toward the silhouette of a man with a gun in his hands creeping up on the rear of the cabin.

Paulie Gambino was out of breath, almost out of bullets, and entirely out of patience with the night's events. Gino would have him fed to the fishes unless he finished the other Texas Ranger. Carlos had called Gino to tell him what had happened and that was when Gino had started to yell, demanding to know why Paulie and the others couldn't take care of two lousy hick Texas cops.

There had been no opportunity to explain why one Ranger was particularly hard to erase because he was lucky, and because he appeared to have nine lives, like a fucking alley cat. And he could fight. Paulie had never been

punched so hard in his life as he had that day. The cowboy
cop was tough as nails, a sneaky son of a bitch who hit
from the blind side if you gave him half a chance. His fists
had been like iron when they'd struck Paulie's head. He'd
told Carlos the Ranger had used a set of brass knuckles. It
was the only way to explain what had happened without
pissing Carlos off, which it had anyway. The other Ranger
had simply been careless, walking to his car like he was out
for a Sunday stroll after everyone went home. He died quietly. He'd been easy to rub out.

Paulie hated Texas, and he hated Texas Rangers and the
heat and everything about this place. Watching the shack,
he wished for a big piece of cheesecake and the sounds of
the elevated trains instead of this muggy Longview swamp
full of mosquitoes and crickets and overridden with cowboy
policemen who were difficult to kill. They wore stupid hats,
and boots with pointed toes, and sounded ignorant when
they spoke. There were no movie theaters here that didn't
show a bunch of cowboy shit, like Tom Mix and Hoot
Gibson jumping on the backs of stupid horses in a phony
gunfight. Movies were Paulie's favorite form of entertainment, the popcorn and hotdogs and soda and candy they
sold, but not if you had to watch a dumb western movie
about horses and cows, and women who looked like shit in
a pair of men's pants. The movie theaters in Longview were
always showing some stupid cowboy feature. He'd quit
going to movies here some time ago, when they didn't show
anything worth the nickel admission.

Making matters worse, there was no good Italian food in
this shithole. He longed for a big pan of his sister's lasagna
dripping with cheese, or a hero roll full of sausage and pep-
pers and sweet onions. These fucking Texans didn't know a
damn thing about good food. They ate fried shit, even pieces
of steak, which always gave him indigestion. Here, you
couldn't even buy a decent jar of olives in a grocery store.

He saw Pelligrini's body sprawled in front of the car and

his fists tightened around the Thompson. Anthony was his cousin. He would have to explain his death to his family back home. His aunt, Maricella, would cry for a whole week and blame him for what had happened to Anthony. How could he explain it so they would understand? "Anthony got in the way of a bullet in Texas"—it sounded bad just thinking about it. He had promised to look out for his cousin.

Paulie stared at the cabin. The fucking cowboy lawman had not been inside when they started shooting or he would be dead. The skinny bitch wasn't there either. How had they known to be outside? No one could have heard the car coming in time to run. Carlos wanted the little whore killed too, in case she had some piece of paper, or knew where it was. He'd tried to convince Carlos the girl didn't know anything—if she had, she'd have spilled her guts while he was kicking her. All she'd done was try to scream with a gag over her mouth, and when he took the gag off so she could talk, she'd cried and begged and swore she didn't know anything about a piece of paper.

He stayed wide of the lighted windows when he started around the shack a few steps at a time, his eyes darting back and forth looking for the cowboy. The yellow bastard had run too fast up the side of those hills and Paulie couldn't catch up. In the end, he was like every other fucking cop, a coward with a gun and a badge who thought everybody should be afraid of him. But when things were equal, he had run like a frightened rabbit, hiding in the woods to save his ass.

Paulie came to Anthony's body and felt like weeping, until another emotion turned his attention back toward the hills. "I'd like to pull your fucking head off," he growled. Carlos and Gino would never understand how the Ranger had gotten away. Paulie knew there was a good chance he'd be fish bait unless he got the cop, and the girl. Carlos had been so sure the whore was with him. But where was she now? She damn sure wasn't in the shack like Carlos said.

His gaze wandered to the river. Could she be hiding there? Maybe they'd been swimming, or fucking in the water, when he and Anthony drove up. Cops liked pussy too, and the little bitch was a whore.

He started for the riverbank, keeping his machine gun on a patch of tall grass growing in the river's shallows. The bitch could be hiding there after the cop had fucked her, afraid of the guns.

43

Lee noticed that with every few steps Paulie took, he would hesitate and look carefully at his surroundings. But when he saw reeds growing along the water's edge, he abandoned his earlier caution and aimed his Thompson at them, walking directly toward Molly's hiding place as though he knew she was there.

Can't wait any longer, Lee thought, rushing from the trees behind the cabin, running alongside the Packard on silent, bare feet until he slid to a stop beside its rear bumper, bringing his shotgun up, steadying it. "Hey, Paulie!" he yelled. "Over here!"

Paulie whirled, triggering off a burst of machine-gun fire. Bullets sprayed the front of the cabin, blasting out the last of its undamaged windowpanes, moving to Lee's Packard in a sweeping hail of lead as Lee dove to the ground. The rear window of the car shattered. Bullets pierced the back fenders and trunk, puckering the metal with .45-caliber holes. All at once the gun clicked empty, the opportunity Lee was waiting for.

He pumped four loads of buckshot in Paulie's direction and heard a grunt. In the dark, Lee couldn't see him clearly, but he was sure he had not missed. It was the range that was wrong and he recognized it now. Paulie swayed momentarily and then threw his Thompson into the grass, reaching into his waistband for his Remington 380 automatic pistol.

A single load remained in the tubular magazine of Lee's Savage, and if he wasted it, he would be unarmed. Even at this distance, he found it impossible to believe Paulie was still standing, staggering forward with his shirtfront torn to shreds by buckshot, a pistol in his hand. Paulie had to be bleeding from any number of buckshot wounds, and yet he advanced toward Lee as though he only suffered from minor bee stings.

Paulie raised his automatic before Lee rolled behind a rear tire of the Packard. A shot rang out. A flying slug whistled past the car, wide of its mark by a considerable distance, landing with a crack against the outhouse wall.

Lee fit the shotgun to his shoulder, forcing himself to wait a few moments longer so his final shell would count.

Paulie fired again. The tire beside Lee's head made a loud popping noise. Air hissed from a hole in the tread while the car settled down on its wheel rim.

There wasn't time to reach into his pocket for more shells, or to load the magazine. Paulie kept marching toward him, rocking when he placed a foot down, tilted forward at a curious angle as if he were bending into a gust of wind.

"Fucking cop!" Paulie cried, his knees wobbling more than ever as he approached the automobile. "You can't stop me with that fucking bird gun!"

Lee aimed for Paulie's face, hoping to blind him with his last load of buckshot. As he was about to nudge the trigger, Paulie took a hurried shot. A banging noise was instantaneously accompanied by a blow to Lee's right shoulder. He flinched as the power of the bullet's impact scooted him backward on his belly across the grass, while a knifelike pain blossomed down his back and side, flaming with growing intensity.

His jaw clamped shut to keep a sharp cry from exploding deep within his chest—he knew immediately he'd been hit. Tears flooded his eyes. He blinked and shook his head. He saw a watery blur moving closer, and when he willed his finger to pull the trigger on the Savage, there was no sensation in his right arm, no feeling at all.

The blurred object grew larger, a wavering outline, the shape of a man. Using his left hand, doing his best to aim accurately, he found the trigger guard and then the trigger. It required every bit of concentration he possessed and all the strength he could summon to pull the trigger, but as he did, his shotgun barrel fell to the ground.

The explosion signaled the end of his effort to stop Paulie from killing him. Buckshot shredded dry grass as his last charge blew harmlessly into the earth near Paulie's shoes.

"You missed me, cowboy!" Paulie shouted. "You can kiss your ass good-bye."

Lee saw Paulie taking careful aim at his head. Rivulets of blood trickled from wounds on Paulie's pockmarked face. Pellet holes across the front of his shirt leaked red in light spilling from the cabin windows.

"You got lucky," Lee groaned, feeling consciousness begin to slip away. He couldn't move now, weakened by raw agony pulsing through his right side.

"You wasn't good enough," Paulie said, his breath coming in short, labored gasps. "You fucking Rangers think you're so damn tough . . ." His head turned when he heard something close by.

From the corner of his eye, Lee saw Molly standing on the cabin porch completely naked, her feet spread apart. Then he noticed an object in her hands. She held the .32 automatic he'd bought her, steadying the gun, using both arms the way he'd taught her that first day here at the river.

"You rotten little whore!" Paulie cried, turning, bringing his pistol up.

Five shots cracked in succession, sounding small compared to a tommy gun's bark and the thunder of a twelve-gauge. Paulie's giant body jerked five times in concert with noises from Molly's .32.

Paulie dropped his gun, reaching for a jagged hole in his right cheek with a hamlike palm. His eyes bulged. He took a half step backward. His lips moved, but no words came. A twist of dark hair dangled from the rear of his scalp, dribbling blood down the back of his shirt, marking the exit hole in his skull of a .32-caliber slug.

Molly whimpered and let the gun fall to the floorboards of the porch, a hollow thud. She threw her hands over her face and stepped back, stifling sobs.

Paulie staggered toward her and now she screamed, her shrill voice filling the river bottom with a cry of fear. Lee tried to rise up on one elbow but fell back from exhaustion after a feeble effort as Paulie stumbled to the edge of the porch, grabbing for Molly's ankle.

A garbled sound came from Paulie's throat. He fell forward, landing with his chest on the steps, one huge palm closing in an empty fist. His arms and legs trembled.

Molly screamed again, and that was the last thing Lee heard before he slumped unconscious beside the flattened tire.

A face hovered over him, indistinct, no one he recognized. A voice spoke to him, and the words made no sense.

"Where am I?" he asked.

More undecipherable words, another face, then nothing.

He knew he must be dreaming. His brother Carl was only nine or ten, and Andy was there, watching him with a smirk on his face.

"You're chicken, Lee. You're a gosh-darned chicken or you'd fight me."

"You're bigger," he heard himself say, remembering that day at the creek. "Older, too. How come I gotta fight you again?"

" 'Cause everybody says you're a chicken, little brother. I get tired of hearin' it all the time, so I'm gonna teach you how to fight or bust your danged jaw. You're gonna fight this time. If you cover up like you done the last time, I'm gonna kick your gosh-danged head plumb off your skinny little neck."

"Ain't fair," he protested. "I can't whip you and you know it."

"You're danged sure gonna try or I'll knock out all of your teeth. We don't raise no sissies in the Garrett family. Me an' Andy are tired of hearin' how our little brother is nothin' but a danged sissy."

"Ma's gonna raise Cain if you tear my shirt again. This is the best shirt I got."

"Take it off."

"Can't make me, Carl. You aren't nothing but a bully to make me fight you again when you know I can't whip you."

"You'll learn. Take that shirt off."

He felt tears threaten. "I hate you, Carl. Same goes for you, Andy." He began unbuttoning his sackcloth shirt, the one his mother had made this spring out of blue-and-white flour-sack material. Other kids teased him because he wore homemade shirts and hand-me-down britches. His shoes had holes in the soles from where Andrew wore them ahead of him, and there wasn't any money to have them fixed.

He hung his shirt on a cottonwood limb and doubled up his fists, squaring off against his older brother. "Don't call me no more names, Carl. You aren't all that tough yourself. That boy from Eagle Springs whupped you good . . ."

Carl swung a right hook. Lee ducked it and aimed a punch for his brother's jaw. He missed badly, making Andy and Carl laugh.

"Don't laugh at me no more!" he cried.

Carl punched him in the nose. He could feel blood running from it and it hurt like the dickens, stinging and burning. Drops of red fell on his bare chest. He dug his toes into the sand and took a roundhouse swing at Carl's nose to pay him back.

His knuckles struck bone, landing harder than he dreamed a fist could land. Carl stumbled backward and fell in the creek with a splash.

"See there!" Lee shouted. "I'm not a gosh-danged sissy!"

Carl sputtered to the surface, holding his nose. Blood made his fingertips pink. "You little bastard," he bellowed, climbing to his feet in shallow water. "I'm gonna teach you never to hit me like that again."

Carl came toward him, windmilling punches left and right, and when one struck Lee in the temple, he sank to his knees, too dizzy to stand any longer.

"You said I was supposed to hit you," he protested as a shadow fell over his face when Carl, looming over him, blocked out the sun.

"Not so damned hard as that," Carl said, wiping his bloody nose on his forearm. He kicked Lee in the ribs, doubling him over in pain.

"That's enough, Carl," Andy said. "Maybe he learned a thing or two. If you ain't careful, he'll tell Pa what you done an' you know what that razor strop feels like."

"I'm not a tattletale," Lee groaned, looking up at his big brother. "You can kick me 'til the sun goes down and I won't say a gosh-danged word to Pa."

Carl adopted a smug expression. "You ain't never gonna be as tough as me an' Andy."

"Maybe," Lee said, holding his throbbing ribs as blood from his nose fell on creek-bottom sand beneath his knees.

"I'll grow some, and when I'm big as you, I'm liable to whip your ass every time I take the notion."

"Ain't likely you'll get that big. An' if you tell on me, I swear I'll tell Pa you was cussin' down at the creek today."

"Wasn't cussin'. I just said I'd whip your ass when I got big enough."

Carl laughed. "Wash that blood off'n your face, Lee, so you'll look presentable at the supper table. You won't never be tough enough to whip me an' that's a fact. Not if you growed to be ten feet tall."

Carl and Andy left him alone on his knees at the creek with aching ribs and a bloody nose. After a bit, he got up and washed off his face in the water, wishing for all the world that if he could grow big enough, he'd have one chance to show Carl just how wrong he was.

He put on his shirt and climbed the creek bank with a heavy heart. It was a curse, being so small, the youngest of three in the family.

44

She entered his hospital room carrying a bouquet of pink and red carnations. Molly wore a pale yellow dress with a yellow bow of silky ribbon in her hair. She smiled and went over to the bed to give him the flowers.

"These are for you," she said. "I bought them for you, hoping they'd cheer you up."

He took them with his left hand; his right arm was in a sling and tightly bandaged against his chest. "Thanks for the flowers. Tell me what happened after I blacked out. I remember you . . . shot him. I didn't think you could." Lee noticed the dark circles under her eyes, as if she'd been without sleep. He tried to smile, still feeling woozy. A dull ache in his right shoulder throbbed with every heartbeat.

Molly looked out the window and it appeared she was about to cry. Traffic noises rose from the street below. "I put on some clothes and ran all the way to that Negro lady's house. She didn't have a telephone, but she sent her nephew for help in their old car. I never learned how to drive, so I couldn't put you in your car to get you to the hospital. I ran back to the cabin and tried to stop the blood from running out of your arm, only I couldn't help much. I waited there until the ambulance came. A couple of cops took me to the police station. I told them how it happened. One was real nice. The other said I might have to go to jail because I shot somebody and only a judge could decide if I could go free. Early this morning, the police chief came and he said to let me go, that he knew all about Paulie and what he'd done to me." A tear ran down her cheek and then she looked at Lee, sniffling once. "What Paulie did to you last night wasn't all of it. They killed that other Ranger, your partner, Mr. Woods. They shot him in the neck when he was getting into his car. He was already dead when somebody found him."

Lee closed his eyes, thinking about Roy. He had a wife in Tyler and had mentioned some grandkids when he'd talked about retiring early because of the paperwork. He wouldn't be bothered with paperwork now. "Damn. I can't believe they got Roy. He was always so careful."

"Paulie liked killing cops. I told you that."

"Yeah, I remember. I suppose I'm lucky he didn't kill me. If it hadn't been for you, I'd be dead. He got me with a lucky shot. I couldn't use my right arm. Have the doctors said how bad it is?"

She touched his left forearm lightly. "Doctor Collins said it missed everything important because of a bone, or something like that. He said you'll be okay in a week or two, if it doesn't get infected."

He gazed up at the ceiling. "I can't lie here for a week or two. It'll have to be sooner than that. And I owe it to Roy's widow to attend his funeral. One way or another, I've got to get out of this bed." From off in the distance, he could hear a train whistle. He looked up at Molly. "Thanks for what you did. I owe you my life."

She was crying more openly now. "I couldn't let him shoot you. I tried to remember what you said about using two hands and pulling the trigger. It all happened so fast. Before I knew it, bullets were coming out. I was so scared I didn't know what else to do."

"You did the only thing you could. Don't cry over it. He would have killed you after he got rid of me. I'm sure Santini sent him to kill both of us. What you did was self-defense."

She nodded, but without much conviction. "I couldn't look at him or the other guy. As scared of Paulie as I was, and as much as I hated him, I couldn't look at what I did to his face."

Lee remembered the bullet hole in Paulie's cheek and the one at the back of his skull. "I'm just glad your aim was better'n I thought it was." He grinned. "When I was trying to teach you to use the gun, you didn't show a lot of talent for that sort of thing."

"I hope I don't ever have to shoot a gun again," she told him softly.

He rested the flowers on his chest and took her hand. "It's over now. Paulie's dead and Santini is on the run. You won't need a gun."

She shook her head. "As long as Carlos and Gino are alive, it won't be over. Carlos still thinks I have Bill Dodd's paper, and nothing's going to change his mind."

"They have bigger things to worry about than Dodd's lease agreement. Santini faces murder charges, among sev-

eral other things. A warrant for his arrest will be sent to
New York when my shoulder is well enough to let me out
of bed to file it. In the meantime, don't worry. You'll be
safe."

"I can't stay at that cabin again. I'd always be reminded
of what happened there last night. You never saw so many
bullet holes, or so much blood. It was so nice being with
you there, but I could never go back. I'd be remembering
Paulie and how I shot him dead, how he looked. I wish I
didn't ever have to think about it again, but I know I will.
I'll never be able to forget it."

"There must be a good boardinghouse here where you
can stay until I get released. I'll ask one of the doctors if he
knows of a place, maybe a sleeping room near the hospital
you can rent by the week."

"I don't hardly have any money. A couple of dollars,
maybe."

"There's money in my pants. Open that closet and take
out as much as you think you'll need."

"I can't take your money. It wouldn't be right."

"Take it," he said, perhaps a bit too sternly. "I can't get
healed up right if I'm worried about you. We'll call it a
loan, if that makes you feel better."

"I'll put the carnations in some water," she said, taking
the bouquet to a table near the window where a pitcher and
two glasses sat. She poured water into a glass and put the
flowers in it. "If you don't mind, I'd like to wait here a
while," she added, with her back turned.

"Don't mind at all," he told her.

She smiled and went over to a chair with a view out the
open window, drying her tears with a fingertip while watching the cars go back and forth below. "Mr. Whitaker is still
alive. I asked a nurse about him, but she said I couldn't go
in his room because his family is there."

Lee thought about Roy Woods for a moment, wondering why he had been so careless last night. One of the last

of the active old-time Rangers was dead. And if the doctors were right, Brad Whitaker would soon join him. A hell of a high price had been paid to rid East Texas of gangsters.

Later, Dr. Collins looked in on him. "How's the shoulder, son?" he asked, glancing over at Molly.

"Sore as hell. Hurts when I try to move it."

"You were extremely lucky, Mr. Garrett. The bullet came at just the right angle, glancing off your scapula, or shoulder blade. There is significant damage to the rhomboid and levator muscles and the axillary nerve trunk. You may always have some impairment in your right arm."

"I suppose I'll have to learn to shoot with my left hand," he said, intending dark humor.

Collins saw nothing funny in the remark. "Quite frankly, we have had enough shooting in this small town to last us for the next hundred years. I hope no one else gets shot or killed. We have a basement full of bodies, and wounded men in too many rooms. I suppose it would be too much to ask if law-enforcement officials stopped killing people for a while."

He left the room before Lee could offer an explanation, could tell him that sometimes killing was necessary to enforce the law. He told Molly to take some money and ask one of the nurses about finding a rented room. Dr. Collins wasn't in a cooperative mood right then.

It was dark, past eight o'clock, when another visitor arrived at his door. Bob Ross stuck his head in first. When he saw Lee's bandaged arm, he frowned. "They told me downstairs it wasn't too bad, Lee." He came in and strode over to the bed. He was perspiring heavily after the long drive through the heat from Waco to Longview. Ross had thinning gray hair and a paunch from too many years behind a desk, although he ran his company like he always had, tough-minded and showing no quarter with his men or anyone who broke the law. He'd policed the wilds of West Texas and the Permian Basin in his younger days, back when cow thieves and Mexican bandits rode horses and carried six-shooters. "They told you about Roy?" he asked gravely.

"I was told. We think we got the guys who shot him. I had a little help from the girl, Molly, the one I've been questioning in the Dodd case. She killed the guy who shot me."

"The prostitute," Ross said. "We need to talk about that a bit later. Meantime, get well. Jim MacDonald is jumpin' up an' down to get his hands on this Carlos Santini. He's asked the FBI for everything they have on Santini and his cohorts back East. The major asked the attorney general for extradition, if anybody can find him. By the way, Major Elliot is mighty well pleased with what was in the newspapers. He wants your full report as soon as you can get it to him, so he can give the governor all the details. Ma Ferguson may have a tough time beatin' Sterling at the polls this year. Dick Peterson an' Dan Kitchens just broke up a big Klan meetin' in Dallas the other night. Arrested some jerk they call the Grand Dragon, or somethin' like that, an' a whole bunch of idiots wearin' bedsheets. Headlines in all the mornin' papers about it. With this seizure of gamblin' equipment an' proof it was run by New York mobsters, that ol' bitch Ferguson couldn't get elected dogcatcher." Ross lowered his voice. "Roy's gonna get a posthumous citation from the governor, too. There'll be a big ceremony at the capitol next month, honorin' Roy for what he did here an' for all his years of service to the Rangers. Hope you can be there."

"I'll make it. This shoulder's not that bad. I've still got a lot of digging to do in this Dodd murder. Plenty of good leads, but they don't take me anywhere just yet."

Ross looked thoughtful. "Why don't you just let it go? I can use you in a dozen other places. It's just one murder,

Lee, an' we can't solve 'em all. That business of you bein' seen with a prostitute don't look good."

He couldn't deny it now, couldn't say that he hadn't become involved with her in a personal way. "Those reports got exaggerated, Cap'n. She's probably the only link I've got to whoever killed Dodd. I think I can prove Santini was a party to the murder. I need a little more time."

Ross seemed somewhat annoyed. "Just so you don't go paradin' around with a hooker while you're at it. Major Elliot gets real concerned about our public image, with that goddamn legislation to put us with DPS hangin' over our heads. Be real careful to conduct yourself properly around her. Wouldn't want anything to spoil a good man's record. I'm headed down to the police station to talk to their chief, a guy named Howard Laster. He's the one who called me early this mornin' an' told me about what happened to you, an' to Roy. Hell, I drove sixty miles an hour damn near all the way just to get here. Hotter'n blazes out in that sun today. I'll drop by tomorrow. By the way, in case I forgot to say it, nice work on this gangster investigation. Too bad Roy didn't live to see how it all turned out."

As Ross was walking down the hall, Lee's jaw muscles grew tight, thinking about what his captain said in regard to Molly. What right did he or anyone else have to tell him who he could or couldn't see privately?

I suppose I could quit, he thought. That way, he could see whoever he wanted. But he wouldn't have a job and in these hard times, finding work was no easy task.

He wondered if any other Texas Ranger had quit because of a woman—in some commanding officer's view, the wrong kind of woman. Did he love Molly that much? Did he even know what love was? How *could* he know, never having been in love. Was he truly in love with her, or merely lonely enough to put aside the knowledge that she'd been a prostitute?

Beyond his window, the sounds made by automobiles passing by came less frequently, yet he scarcely noticed, thinking about the girl and pondering what love was all about.

Half an hour later, a nurse brought him two tablets, painkillers prescribed by Dr. Collins. He took them and watched the young woman turn off the light in his room. In just a few short minutes, he drifted off to sleep.

"It's called Selman's Boardinghouse," she said, looking rested and happier than she did the day before. "The lady who runs it is so nice. I've got a downstairs room, with a view of her big rose garden. She cooked pancakes for breakfast and they were delicious, as good as Hattie Mae's. Maybe better. It's just half a block from here, so I can come see you as often as you want me to." She sat in the chair near the window, watching him.

He admired the way she looked today, in a white short-sleeved blouse and a green skirt that matched her eyes. All morning he'd been thinking about what Captain Ross had said. "You look pretty as a picture," he told her, rubbing his chin where a nurse had shaved him at daylight, a nick where the razor got too close.

"Thank you," she said, and it appeared that she almost blushed. "It's an old dress. The kind I wore at Maude's isn't proper to wear in daytime. I left them there. I knew I was never going back to . . . that again, not there or anyplace else."

"You can find other work."

"I know. I don't ever want to go back to what I did before, and that's the honest truth. I didn't want to do it in the first place, but I already told you why I did."

"Moving someplace else, nobody'll ever have to know."

She looked at the floor, at her shoes. "I wish I could go

someplace with you, Lee, but I don't think you could ever stop remembering what I did. Men don't forgive a woman for something like that."

He wasn't quite sure what to say. "Maybe forgiving isn't the right way to look at it. You did what you thought you had to do. Forgetting it sounds simpler to me."

"Could you ever forget it?"

How could he tell her that Captain Ross and Major Elliot weren't likely to forget about her former profession? "I'd be willing to try, I suppose. I've sure made plenty of my own mistakes."

"You wouldn't actually have to love me. I decided that last night, out in the rose garden. If you could just be nice to me like you are now, I'd be happier than I've ever been in my whole life."

He motioned her over to the bed. She got up slowly and went to him, the flush in her cheeks unmistakable in the daylight from the window.

"Maybe I already do love you, Molly . . ."

45

With a trace of amusement on his leathery face, Captain Ross watched him ease off the edge of the bed. "I hate a damn hospital gown," he said. "A man's ass is always hangin' out, makin' him look like a fool."

Lee looked down at himself. His arm was still bandaged to his chest and the hospital gown made him look like an amputee missing a right limb. "I can't see my ass from here, but I sure can feel a breeze when I stand up."

He straightened up slowly, feeling dizzy until he steadied

his legs. "I've been seeing how far I can walk today. I've got to get out of this room by tomorrow, so I won't miss Roy's funeral."

"You may not be strong enough yet, Lee, an' I don't see how you'll drive with one arm. I had your car windows fixed, but it don't hardly seem worth it. I never saw so many bullet holes in a car. The glass they put in this mornin' is only temporary. I know we'll have to junk that Packard after you get back to Waco next week. I had 'em put a new tire on it, too."

"I may need more time, Cap'n. It's Friday. I can't say for sure I can wrap up the Dodd case so quick."

"You're comin' back, either way. I can't justify spendin' any more time on it. We've got file cabinets full of un-solved murders, an' this'll have to be another one if you can't finish by Monday. And if you can't drive all the way back, I'll send you on the train and junk the Packard here. Too bad, 'cause it's a pretty car if it wasn't for all those holes."

"I can drive," Lee said. He wondered why Ross was in such a hurry to get him out of Longview. Molly had to be the reason.

Ross walked to the window. "The radio's predictin' rain for tomorrow. It's already gettin' cloudy. Too bad. I don't reckon Roy cares if it's rainin' on his casket. By the way, one guy's name was Anthony Pelligrini. He had identifica-tion in the car they were drivin'. The other guy was Paulie Gambino. He's on a half dozen warrants in New York for extortion an' murder, I found out today. The FBI was lookin' for him. No word yet on Santini. Appears he slipped right through our fingers. Maybe a highway pa-trolman somewhere will get lucky."

"He was involved in Bill Dodd's murder, Cap'n. And there may be somebody else running loose who played a part in having him killed. That lease is worth millions. When I first started out as a Ranger, Clarence Webb told me to follow the money if I wanted to solve a crime. An oil speculator named Buster Davis got Dodd's lease a few weeks after Dodd was killed. I know Davis is in it up to his neck, only I can't prove it. Another guy by the name of Charley Waller knew Dodd got his lease in the mail the day he got shot. They both had a possible motive with Dodd out of the way."

"Where does Santini fit in? I don't see the connection."

"That's where the girl may be important. She knew Santini and knew his boss in New York, Gino Tatangelo. Dodd didn't have enough money to pay the heirs to that land for signing the rights over to him, so he needed to borrow. Molly told Dodd that Tatangelo was a loan shark. I believe Dodd went to Santini to arrange for a loan against his lease, which was damn sure enough collateral, with so much oil at stake. Greed got to Santini and he made up his mind to double-cross Dodd, but he needed someone with inside information to know when to kill him. If Dodd was killed before the lease arrived, the rights would go to Dodd's widow as soon as the documents came. And there had to be somebody else involved, someone who would record a new lease and cut the profits up with Santini.

"So there could have been two more people in on the conspiracy besides Sara Dodd. She could have killed him herself, but she didn't have the nerve, and then suspicion would fall on her when she put the oil rights in her name at the courthouse. It sounds complicated, but I think there were two double-crosses. In exchange for a piece of the action, Sara agreed to tell the killer when the lease came. But when she did, the killer double-crossed her, figuring she couldn't afford to say a word or she'd be charged as an accessory to murdering her husband."

"But why did she ask us to investigate it?" Ross asked.

"Simple. She didn't get any money, so she wanted revenge. When the county sheriff wouldn't listen to her, probably because he knew Santini was involved somehow and because he was taking bribes from Santini so he could run his gambling tents, she had no choice but to come to us. She wanted to get even with whoever had double-crossed her and this was the only way without revealing the part she'd played in it. She said when I first talked to her that whoever recorded a lease on that land was the man who killed her husband. She wanted me to think she didn't know it was Buster Davis, and I think she was hoping I'd follow that trail all the way to Carlos Santini. I also think she was getting ready to talk and that's why they killed her, trying to make it look like suicide, a grieving widow who couldn't stand to live without her husband."

"Sounds mighty far-fetched, Lee. And mighty hard to prove."

"I think I can do it, if you'll give me enough time."

Ross shook his head, turning away from the window. "I'd be more inclined to agree if you hadn't gotten on intimate terms with the hooker. It causes a stir when a peace officer with an organization like the Texas Rangers is seen with a prostitute in public places. It reflects badly on every man who wears this badge. You've never disappointed me before, but this time you forgot who you are, what you represent in this state. We have a proud tradition for honesty an' integrity, an' I won't let you tarnish it."

"She's just a girl, Cap'n, a girl from New York who made a bad choice. Her folks died and she was broke, with no place to live. She took the only work she was offered back then, and she doesn't do it anymore. She quit, and I say she deserves a second chance."

"Not with a Ranger, she doesn't. I won't argue this with you, Lee. Get rid of the girl, or you can turn in your badge. It isn't up to me. This comes from headquarters, from the major himself. He won't stand for one of his men associatin' with a prostitute."

Lee sat back down on the bed, staring at the floor. "I'll let you know what I decide as soon as I get back to Waco, Cap'n. I reckon I've got some thinking to do."

Ross cleared his throat. "I don't see how any decent, God-fearin' man in his right mind can believe there's a choice. You mean you'd throw away your career over this . . . this scarlet woman you hardly know?"

Lee felt his anger begin to rise. "I might. I say it's my own affair who I see when I'm not on duty."

"A Texas Ranger is always on duty, twenty-four hours a day."

"That isn't it. I've done my job the best I knew how every time. When I'm at home, I can't see how anyone can tell me whose company I can keep."

"What's gotten into you, Lee? You've never talked like this before."

He thought about it. "I guess I want something more than a badge and a law-enforcement career after all. I'd like to see if I can be happy with someone else. You've got a wife, Cap'n. It looks like you'd know what I'm talking about."

"But this woman's an admitted prostitute. Can't you see it makes a difference? How it looks?"

"I don't suppose it matters to me how it looks to anybody else, not right now anyway."

Ross went to the door. "It's up to you," he said, his voice changed, no longer sympathetic. "You can turn in your badge an' keep her, or be in Waco by Tuesday morning, ready for desk duty until that shoulder heals up. Think it over, Lee. Don't throw a good career away. You haven't given me any choice."

Ross walked out of the room. Lee listened to the captain's footsteps going down the hall, then a stairway. He wondered if anything could change Ross's mind, or the major's. Knowing the code of ethics imposed upon every Ranger, he doubted it.

Later, he walked down to Brad Whitaker's room, expecting the worst. Whitaker's wife and daughters were gone. Whitaker lay on the bed with his eyes closed, an oxygen mask over his face. Lee didn't know much about the practice of medicine, but he assumed the oxygen mask meant that Whitaker couldn't breathe on his own now.

He walked into the room, being careful to keep the opening in the back of his gown from showing. He stood over the bed for a moment, examining Whitaker's pale face and sunken cheeks.

"You weren't supposed to die for her, Brad," he said in a sorrowful voice. "You were brave as hell to do what you did and I can't tell you how much I appreciate it, 'cause you can't hear me. Sorry 'bout what's gonna happen to your wife and kids. I promise I'll do what I can for 'em, but I may not have a job after this Tuesday anyway."

Whitaker's chest rose and fell slowly, shallowly. Lee saw his thick eyeglasses resting on a table beside the bed. "For a man who can't see all that much, you did some real fine shooting that night. Thanks again. I wish the hell I could shake your hand . . . so you'd know how grateful I am."

A gray rain fell on Greenwood Cemetery at Tyler. Raindrops pattered on a mound of freshly dug earth beside a grave where a coffin containing Roy Woods' body rested on straps that would lower it into the ground. A small group of mourners stood around the grave holding rain-slick umbrellas while an elderly pastor recited a funeral service from memory, holding his Bible under his raincoat to keep it dry.

Lee stood beside Captain Ross. Flanking Ross were Captain James MacDonald and Ranger Dick Peterson. Roy's wife wept as the service went on. A son and a daughter, along with several small children, gathered around her, offering soft words of comfort now and then. Chief Laster and another police officer had driven to the funeral to pay their respects.

Lee tried not to listen to the preacher's words, listening to the rain instead, remembering Roy in his own way. It would have been inappropriate to say what was on his mind, that with the help of Molly, he'd gotten the men who killed Roy that night and he felt no remorse, no regret. It occurred to him that he was becoming too hard, too thick-skinned. Death had taken on less meaning lately. He should be feeling something now, and yet he didn't. Or couldn't. Had too many years as a peace officer robbed him of the capacity to feel sorrow? He reminded himself that he did feel deep sorrow for what had happened to Brad Whitaker.

The service ended. Mrs. Woods cried bitterly, clamping a wet handkerchief to her face as her children led her away from Roy's grave.

"He was a good Ranger," Captain MacDonald said, putting his Stetson back on his head. "We can't afford to lose good men like Roy. The organization won't be the same without him."

Lee buttoned the top button of his raincoat and headed for his car, wondering how sincere MacDonald had been when he said the Rangers couldn't afford to lose good men. Walking beside Captain Ross past rows of headstones, he thought about what Ross had said to him at the hospital. Good Rangers were only good if they kept proper company, as well as enforcing the laws of the state. No matter how well a Ranger did his job, he had to please his commanding officers by virtue of his associations with others, and by how willing he was to give up everything else to maintain something called "proud tradition."

"I'll see you Tuesday morning," Captain Ross said when they reached their cars, parked outside the cemetery fence.

Lee did not reply, offering his left palm for a handshake. He'd had great difficulty shifting gears with his left hand and also found he couldn't write anything legible. Dr. Collins told him his sling could come off tomorrow, that the stitches would be healed sufficiently to keep his wound from opening.

"Drive carefully," Ross added, glancing up at the rain. "I hope you'll come to your senses, Lee. That woman can't possibly be worth givin' up everything for."

Lee climbed in the Packard and closed the door, biting his tongue. The way he felt now, being with Molly was worth far more than having empty words spoken over his grave. There had to be a better way to make a living.

He touched the starter with his boot toe and managed to get the Packard in gear without too much trouble. He drove off down a puddling gravel road, past where Captain Ross and Captain MacDonald stood having words with each other between their automobiles. Turning on the windshield wipers, Lee stared into a drizzling rain with his mind elsewhere, listening to the rhythm of the wipers beating back and forth across the glass in front of him.

I'll resign, he thought. I won't give her up.

Turning on the highway to Longview, he made up his mind to devote everything he had to finding Bill Dodd's killer before he gave up his job.

That note with those initials and the number on it is the place to start, he mused.

Using his knees to steady the steering wheel, he shifted gears again and pressed the accelerator. Two men in Longview were the only suspects he had left. Charley Waller seemed a less likely murderer than Buster Davis, although the initials "C.W." pointed to Waller.

The telephone company is where to begin, he thought.

The rain came down harder as he drove out of Tyler, the sound of water splashing under his fenders becoming a drone in his ears. He had one last case to solve before submitting his resignation and he meant to solve it, come hell or high water. Both hell and high water seemed more likely between now and Tuesday morning.

46

He couldn't tell Molly what he meant to do. Parking at the curb in front of Selman's Boardinghouse, he got out and hurried up the sidewalk with his raincoat collar turned up. He wanted to tell her why he'd be out of touch for a while, first with a visit to the telephone company office, then looking for Charley Waller and Buster Davis. On the drive back from Tyler, he'd decided that bank records might provide some sort of clue. If big amounts of money had entered either man's account in July, he might have something to go on. But no matter where the investigation took him, he wouldn't tell Molly he intended to resign. Not until the time came for him to make his choice.

He knocked on the screen door, standing under a porch running the length of the house, which had a gabled roof, railings, and intricate carvings. A smiling woman wearing an apron answered his knock, wiping her hands on a dishcloth.

"May I speak to Molly Brown?" he asked.

The woman noticed his empty sleeve. "She went out not too long ago. I loaned her my umbrella. She said she'd be back before dinner."

"Thank you, ma'am. Will you please tell her that Lee, Lee Garrett, stopped by."

"Of course. You're the Texas Ranger. We saw your picture in the newspaper and Molly told us about you. It's plumb scary to think we had Italian gangsters right here in Longview. It was such a quiet town until they discovered all this oil."

"It should be quieter now," he told her, tipping his hat on his way down the steps, wondering where Molly could have gone on a rainy day like this.

The telephone company office was closed, leaving him frustrated, undecided what to do next. He was running out of time. Playing a hunch, he drove out to Buster Davis's office, the car slipping and sliding in mud when the tires sank in deep puddles. Then, surging through the ruts on Judson Street upon leaving the pavement, he decided this road was poorly named, calling it a street when in fact it was little more than a cow trail running between hastily built offices at the edge of town.

He got out and found Davis's office locked. It began to look like Saturday was going to be a bad day for investigative work in Longview. Looking up and down the muddy road, something snapped in his memory when he remembered a sign above the office door. He turned, and suddenly things began to fall into place when he read the words painted in small letters above Davis's door.

"C.W. Davis Investment Company," he said aloud. Now he was quick to recall seeing those same initials on the courthouse records for the Hawkins mineral-rights notation. If Buster Davis was the owner of telephone number 387, the slip of paper at Sara Dodd's house pointed straight to Davis as someone she knew, perhaps the man who killed her, or ordered her execution.

I've been thinking it was Charley Waller all along, he thought, his mind racing. He'd overlooked Davis's initials, believing they were meaningless. He remembered that Davis told him he was at home with his wife the night

Dodd was killed. It was time to ask Mrs. Davis a few questions.

Navigating through the puddles, he walked to the car and got in, knocking mud off his boots on the running board. He took note of the fact that the rear window was leaking rain where it was poorly sealed. Ross had said it was only temporary glass.

He drove off with tires spinning, slinging mud when he made a half circle in the middle of Judson. Locating Davis's house might not be easy on Saturday with the telephone company closed for the weekend. He'd ask somebody, maybe at the police station or the City Café.

He arrived at City Hall in time to see Captain Mac-Donald and Dick Peterson escorting Leonardo Cusi and the bartender to a Ford parked at the curb. Lee got out and walked over just as both men, wearing handcuffs and leg irons, were being loaded into the car.

"Howdy, Cap'n," Lee said, also nodding to Peterson.

MacDonald, a wiry man in his early fifties with reddish-gray hair and mustache, spoke to Lee as soon as the prisoners had been secured. "Wish things could have ended differently," he said, a note of dissatisfaction in it. "We're takin' these two an' the two you an' Roy arrested with the whiskey trucks over to jail in Tyler."

"You mean you wish Roy hadn't gotten shot?"

"That's exactly what I mean, Lee. And maybe he wouldn't be dead if you'd been where you belonged."

"I don't understand . . ."

"You know damn good an' well what I mean," Mac-Donald spat as he glanced at Lee's empty right sleeve. "If you hadn't been with that whore instead of doin' your job, Roy might still be alive an' you wouldn't have that bullet hole in you. Chief Laster told me you weren't here that night answerin' questions about the raid for the papers. He said you were at some shack over by the river, bedded down with the whore while Roy was doin' his duty."

Lee was speechless for a moment, unable to believe that he'd been accused of neglecting his duty, or that Captain MacDonald could think his absence from the picture-taking by news reporters played any role whatsoever in Roy's death. "I felt I needed to guard a possible informant in the murder of Bill Dodd, the case Cap'n Ross sent me here to investigate. Threats had been made on her life. She'd been kidnapped once, and I believed they would try again. I thought I was doing my job. Nobody knew those two gunmen would be going after Roy."

"That's bullshit an' you know it," Macdonald said evenly. "Bob Ross told me you're liable to quit the Rangers on account of this whore. You were bedded down with her that night, so don't try to deny it."

"I was protecting her," Lee stammered, clenching his good fist, fighting back a rush of sudden anger. He wheeled, stalking off before he said something he might regret later, climbing into his car, slamming the door so hard it rocked the Packard on its springs.

He backed away from the curb and drove off seething mad, a grip on the steering wheel so tight his knuckles turned white as he rounded a street corner.

"Fuck this job," he said, grinding gears. The slap of the windshield wipers seemed louder, worsening already badly rattled nerves.

A filling station attendant told him where to find Buster Davis's house. Davis lived in a modest neighborhood of quiet streets and tall shade trees. Lee found the house number despite a steady downpour and parked in front. A dark blue Cadillac sedan sat in the driveway, appearing almost black with water coating its metal surfaces, triggering another memory of a lone remark Sara Dodd's neighbor made after Sara was found hanged. The woman's husband had said he'd seen a black Cadillac parked at her house, leaving around midnight. Was Buster Davis her killer? Had he decided to make sure Sara wouldn't talk to the law?

Lee got out, sensing that he was very close to something important. Crossing the sidewalk, he climbed the slippery porch steps and knocked on the door.

A slender, frail-looking woman in her thirties came to the screen. She wore a summer dress, navy blue with a floral print, and blue slippers. Her blonde hair was bobbed, done up in tight curls. "May I help you?" she asked.

"I'm Texas Ranger Lee Garrett, ma'am. I need to ask you a few questions."

"Regarding what?" she asked quickly, worry lines appearing suddenly across her brow.

"Several things. Your husband's whereabouts on the night of June twenty-third, and if he ever knew anyone by the name of Sara or William Dodd."

"Who is it, dear?" a voice called from somewhere in the rear of the house.

"A Texas Ranger," she replied, and Lee was sure her answer betrayed a slight tremor.

When the woman did not open the door, he asked, "May I come in?"

"I suppose so. Buster will be here in a minute." She gave the door a gentle push to admit him. "Can you tell me what this is all about?"

He walked into a dark living room full of expensive chairs and an upholstered sofa. An oscillating fan whirred on a floor stand near an open window.

"Take a chair, Mr. Garrett. My husband wasn't dressed when you knocked."

Lee took off his hat and slipped awkwardly from his raincoat, using one hand. She took the garments and hung them on a coat tree near the door. "My name is Thelma," she said, glancing to a hallway leading into the back of the house. "Why are you wanting to know where Buster was that night? He hasn't done anything wrong, has he?"

He sat down, appraising Thelma, her nervousness over his arrival. "I don't know, Mrs. Davis. Perhaps you can help me clear up some matters."

"I never heard of those names," she said too quickly, with a second look down the hall. "Are they in the oil business? You know Buster is in the oil business."

"They're both dead," Lee replied. "But I suppose that in a way, they were in the oil business, until someone killed them."

"For goodness sake," Thelma whispered, covering her mouth with a trembling hand. "You don't think my husband had anything to do with it, do you?"

"Right now I'm only asking questions. By the way, what is Buster's telephone number at the office?"

"Why, it's three six two. Why do you ask?"

"What's the number here?" Lee continued.

Thelma's eyes were growing damp, not quite tearing when she said, "It's three eight seven. Oh, I do wish Buster would hurry so he could answer your questions himself."

Now Lee had something concrete to go on. The number beside Sara Dodd's telephone was 387. "I can wait, Mrs. Davis. I've got questions for Buster, too. Try to remember where he was on the night of June twenty-third. It could be important to my investigation."

Thelma went to the sofa and sat down, folding her hands in her lap like she needed to steady them. Her bottom lip had begun to quiver slightly. "I'm quite sure he was at home. On a few occasions, he goes out of town on business. I don't recall that he was away in the latter part of June."

Heavy footsteps in the hall announced Buster's approach, and they were quick strides. When he came into the living room and saw Lee, he stopped. "You again," he said. "What is it this time, Mr. Garrett?" He looked at Lee's bandaged arm briefly.

"It's about a dead woman this time, Mr. Davis. Sit down."

"I don't have to answer no more of your damn questions. I talked to my lawyer. You ain't charged me with nothin'. Until you do, I don't have to answer questions, an' I damn sure don't know nothin' about any dead woman. Get out of my house or I'll call my lawyer."

"You're wrong, Buster," Lee said calmly. "You do have to answer my questions if I take you downtown on suspicion you may have committed murder. I've got circumstantial evidence to back up the charge. Your telephone number and initials were found on a notepad at the dead woman's house. I can have you locked up and hold you for questioning, and that's what I'm about to do if you can't come up with straight answers."

"Oh, Buster!" Thelma cried. "Tell him what he wants to know so you won't have to go to jail!" Tears streamed down her cheeks and she ignored them for now.

Davis scowled. "Just because some dead woman had my number on a piece of paper don't make me a murderer. A judge will turn me loose before sundown, if that's all you've got."

"I have a great deal more," Lee said. "Someone identified your automobile in front of the dead woman's house around midnight on the night she was killed. I've got a strong case and I believe the district attorney will bind you over for trial. If he needs more, there's the fact that you leased property that was previously leased to a man who was murdered. That's two murders you'll have to answer for, your whereabouts both nights, and how you wound up making a handsome profit from Bill Dodd's death. A jury could easily believe you had a motive for killing him, and I think a jury will also believe you were in a partnership with the dead man's wife to have him killed, so she'd get a bigger share of the money. I believe you're also connected to Carlos Santini in a scheme to loan Dodd money, only somebody decided to double-cross him. Maybe it was you."

"You can't prove a damn thing," Davis said, glancing

quickly at his wife. "Neither one of us is sayin' another word until we talk to my attorney. I'm callin' Mr. Abernathy now."

"That's another interesting connection," Lee remarked. "It might sound strange to a judge and jury that Abernathy works for H. L. Hunt, the man you sold that lease to. They've been allowing Santini's crooked dice tables and whiskey peddlers on Hunt leases and we already have proof of that. You tell Mr. Abernathy I'm headed down to the district attorney's office right now, and he can meet us there. You'll be going with me."

"You can't do that!" Davis snapped.

"Yes I can. Ask your lawyer. You can call him as soon as we get to jail."

"You're gonna put me in jail?"

"I'm holding you for questioning. It's the law. I have all the evidence I need, a witness who saw your car, and a note with your initials and telephone number on it found at the scene of a murder."

Davis looked at his wife again. "Don't say a damn word 'til Mr. Abernathy talks to you, Thelma. You don't have to answer any more of this fool's questions. Don't let anybody trick you. It's me they want, an' they can't prove a damn thing against me."

47

District Attorney Kenneth Cook wasn't too happy to be called down to the County Courthouse on a Saturday, and a rainy Saturday at that. He unlocked his office after a perfunctory handshake with Lee and a quizzical look at Buster

Davis. Cook was a pear-shaped man in his middle forties, dressed in baggy slacks and a sports shirt open at the neck rather than his usual attire during office hours. He switched on a light and then a ceiling fan as he entered an outer office.

"You said this couldn't wait, Mr. Garrett," Cook muttered unhappily. "Please explain why."

"I'm here to file charges against this man, C. W. Davis, on suspicion of murder."

Cook's frustration surfaced quickly. "Why not just lock him up until Monday morning? I'll look at your evidence then. I do presume you have sufficient evidence to bring charges . . ."

"He's got nothin'," Davis growled. "My attorney's on the way down here. I'll be out on bond in an hour. When you hear what he's got on me, you'll laugh. I ain't sayin' no more until Mr. Abernathy gets here."

"Indeed," Cook said, still standing in the middle of the small waiting room lined with chairs. "You say Maxwell Abernathy is your attorney?"

"That's right. I called him while we were waitin' out in the hall," Davis replied.

"Have a seat, Mr. Davis, while I talk to Mr. Garrett in my office. I see you're not wearing handcuffs, so I presume Mr. Garrett does not believe you will attempt to leave."

"I ain't goin' no place. As soon as my lawyer gets here, I guarantee you I'll be goin' back home." Davis sat down heavily in one of the chairs, glowering at Lee.

"Come in, Mr. Garrett," Cook said, leading the way to a door at the back of the waiting room. "Frankly, if you believe you have sufficient evidence against this man, I don't see why you didn't merely put him in jail until Monday."

They entered a cramped office lined with bookshelves. Cook closed the door, giving Lee a closer examination. "I've been reading about you in the newspapers, Mr. Garrett. You understand that I'm only an assistant district attorney handling cases here in Longview. If this is truly a murder case, it will be tried in Tyler in the district court. All these killings lately, including the death of a Texas Ranger and the probable demise of a U.S. Treasury Agent, as well as the uncovering of an organized crime ring where no one suspected it, has focused a great deal of attention on our community. Now you tell me you have a murder case?"

"I know it's one murder case, quite possibly two," Lee told him. "I don't have much physical evidence yet."

"Sit down," Cook said, taking a chair behind his cluttered desk. "I sincerely hope you're not wasting my time here. What do you have in the way of evidence? And what's the rush?"

"It can't wait," Lee replied without explaining. "I have reason to believe these murders may also be tied to the crime ring, as you call it. I think I can prove that Carlos Santini was behind them. However, I lack one critical piece of evidence to make that connection. As to the evidence I have, a witness can put Davis's car at the murder scene of Sara Louise Dodd on the night she was killed, around midnight."

"Did your witness actually see Mr. Davis there?"

"No, just his car."

"He'll claim he loaned it to someone perhaps, or that he left the keys in the ignition that night."

"There's more. A piece of paper at the murder scene had a note with his initials and his home telephone number on it."

Cook frowned. "That's a bit stronger, but not enough to convict. It's circumstantial. I believe the paper said this woman was hanged. It may be hard to prove it wasn't suicide."

"She had a knot on the back of her skull. I saw it myself after they took her down. She was knocked unconscious to keep her from screaming, then the killer made it look like a suicide with a rope and a chair."

"Your testimony regarding the lump on her head will be some help, but still not enough to convict Davis. What was his motive for committing the crime?"

"To keep her quiet. Her husband was killed before he could record a mineral lease he'd secured on property adjoining the Dad Joiner lease. Those rights are worth millions. Just a few weeks after Bill Dodd was murdered, Davis recorded his own lease on that same property. Then Davis sold his rights to H. L. Hunt. I think Sara Dodd was in on a scheme to murder her husband so she'd get a larger share of the oil. I believe Davis was in on it, as was Carlos Santini. Santini probably ordered the actual killing. I reckon you know by now that Santini had plenty of hired guns to get that done, since you read the papers."

Cook's frown deepened. "But you can't prove any of this, can you?"

"I'm missing one important document I believe is with that lease, which has never turned up. But I think Davis will crack under pressure if he believes he'll go to jail. I'm hoping he'll name names, if we ask him the right questions."

"His attorney will advise him not to answer. Mr. Abernathy is a good lawyer. He'll know right away we have nothing solid to charge his client with, not unless you can come up with evidence he can't refute."

Lee was growing impatient. "Are you saying you won't accept my charges against him?"

"I can present what evidence you have to a grand jury. But until they indict him, or decide to no-bill him, there isn't a judge in the world who'll leave him in jail based on nothing but circumstantial evidence. He'll be free on a minimal bond in a matter of hours. Abernathy will present Judge Baker with a writ of habeas corpus demanding that

Davis be charged or let go. I don't see enough in what you have for Judge Baker to hold him."

"He's guilty," Lee complained bitterly.

"Then you must prove it beyond reasonable doubt. With the authority granted by your badge, Mr. Garrett, you can arrest him and have him thrown in jail. However, I assure you that Mr. Abernathy will have him out before the ink is dry on your official complaint.

"I still say he'll crack if he feels heat. He won't take a fall for this by himself. I'm convinced he'll name Santini as an accomplice, or tell us Santini was behind the whole thing from the beginning, but he'll have to be made to talk. He'll have to believe he's headed for prison. If you'll pressure him . . ."

Cook held up a hand. "Let me stop you right there. I won't be pushed into using the district attorney's office as a tool to pry or frighten a confession out of a suspect. It is widely known that some Texas Rangers employ questionable tactics to get confessions. The late Mr. Roy Woods allegedly beat a significant number of his prisoners to make them talk. I won't be a party to what you're suggesting, Mr. Garrett. Bring me hard evidence and I will prosecute Mr. Davis to the full extent of the law. What you have now is insufficient and purely circumstantial. Now if you'll excuse me, it's Saturday and I'm going home. Arrest Mr. Davis if you wish, although I warn you he'll be out on a writ in short order unless you have something more."

Lee got up, sighing. "That's all I have now. You'll be the first to know when I have anything more."

He went out of Cook's office and came face-to-face with Maxwell Abernathy. He paused long enough to glance down at Davis. "You can go home, Buster. I could arrest you if I wanted, but I won't just now. One thing I promise you can count on . . . we'll be seeing each other again real soon. If you're smart, you'll tell me who was behind you in all of this. It'd be a shame for you to take the fall by your-self if you had partners."

"My client has nothing to say," Abernathy remarked, holding an umbrella still damp from the rain. "Either charge him or let him go."

Lee gave Abernathy a withering stare. "I fully intend to charge him with murder, Mr. Abernathy. Somebody else will talk and then I'll have your client by the balls. It won't be long now. Tell your client he can count on it. I warned you we'd bust up the gambling and entertainment business on Hunt's property. I'm giving Buster the same message . . . cooperate with me or I'll see to it he gets a taste of how the law works."

Lee walked out of the district attorney's office before his temper got the best of him. He heard voices coming from Cook's office but not anything distinct. Going downstairs, he made a promise to himself. He wasn't letting Davis off the hook, even if it cost him his job.

Molly sounded excited. "I think I know where that piece of paper is!" She'd been waiting for him on the porch at Sel-man's when he drove up. Her dress was soaking wet despite the umbrella she'd borrowed from Mrs. Selman.

"Where?" he asked, still in a bad mood over his meet-ing with the district attorney, though his thoughts suddenly improved somewhat when he heard what Molly said.

"I'll show you. I remembered something Bill did that day, and that he said he hid it from everybody. He looked at his old car while he was saying it. He hid it in his car someplace, and I think I even know the right place to look."

He wanted to share her enthusiasm, yet there were ob-stacles. "I'd have to find out what was done with his auto-mobile. I don't recall seeing it in his driveway."

"I already found it!" Molly exclaimed. "I walked over

to a neighbor's house on Baker Lane, where Bill said he lived. A real nice lady told me a wrecker picked up the car after a sheriff's deputy drove it home the morning after Bill was killed. She told me what was painted on the wrecker's doors — JOE'S SALVAGE. So I walked all the way down there. I nearly drowned because it was raining so hard. But I found Bill's old car. It's parked out in front with a 'For Sale' sign on a window. I told the guy I knew somebody who'd be real interested in that car. I said I'd bring you back, only I didn't say who you were or why you'd be interested."

Lee examined her soaked clothing. "Go put on something dry and we'll drive over there. You really think it's hidden in his car?"

"I told you, he *looked* at the car when he told me about how he'd been real careful to hide that paper. That time we drove out to the Hawkins farm, he even showed me this special place where he hid his money. C'mon. I'll show you where his car is." She was smiling and her smile was infectious.

He grinned. "Hurry up and change clothes. It's worth a try anyway."

"I don't need to change. Let's go before the guy closes up. It's Saturday, remember?"

How could he tell her how painfully aware he was of the day, and the number of days he had left to find out who murdered Bill Dodd?

It was a badly rusted Model A Ford with dents in its fenders and doors. Joe Carver looked on with disappointment on his face while Lee and Molly walked to the car in the pouring rain, as he now knew there was no possibility of making a car sale today.

Molly opened the passenger door. "It's right under here," she said, pointing to a spot beneath the worn seat. She reached

under, feeling her way. Then she bent down and peered up at
the seat's innersprings. For a moment, she frowned. Then her
face lit up. "Here's an envelope!" she cried, giving Lee the
handle of her umbrella so she could use both hands.

Straightening up, she handed him a thick manila envelope addressed to William P. Dodd.

"This is it," he whispered. "This is what everybody has
been looking for all this time." He tucked it inside his raincoat
to keep it dry. "I'll tell Joe we appreciate his time. Then we'll
go someplace where we can read it very carefully. If I'm right,
this envelope will convict a murderer. Maybe more'n one."

He closed the Ford's door and hurried over to thank
Joe. Molly was climbing in the Packard when he got back.

"Aren't you gonna read it now?" she asked.

He touched the starter with his boot toe. "I aim to read
it slow under a good light. These clouds are making it hard
to see and it's almost sundown, if there was any sun today."

The motor sputtered to life. With Molly's help, he shifted
into low gear and drove away from Joe's Salvage Yard, his
mind so full of questions about what was in the envelope
that he had some difficulty keeping his attention on the road.

"I was right, wasn't I?" she asked.

"You did some great detective work. I hope I won't be
in for a big dose of disappointment when I read this."

"You think there's something in there besides the lease
he got in the mail, don't you?"

"Dodd needed money to finish what he started. I'm
gambling there's something in this envelope that'll show he
meant to get the money from Carlos Santini, possibly
through Buster Davis."

"What if you're wrong?"

"Then I'm right back where I started, looking for a murderer with no solid clues to his identity."

Molly stared through the windshield as he drove
through the business district of Longview. The slap of wipers
on wet glass did not irritate him the way it had before.

48

Lee rented a room from a nervous desk clerk who recognized him the moment he walked into the lobby at Modern Tourist Courts.

"I saw your picture in the Tyler paper. I sure hope there won't be no shootin' here. I read where the Grand Hotel was shot all to pieces the night you were there. Four guys got killed, if my memory ain't failed me, an' I sure don't need no shootin' here at my place. We rent quiet cabins. Mostly travelers an' salesmen on their way somewheres else."

"The shooting's over," Lee assured the clerk, placing two dollars on the desk. "I'll only be staying a couple of nights." He signed the register and took a key to room number 6. He was in need of a place to stay until Monday anyway, and when he drove past this tourist court on his way back from Roy's funeral, he'd made up his mind to stay here.

"Is it true you killed those guys who shot the Texas Ranger from over at Tyler?"

Lee headed for the door and the driveway where his Packard was idling. "They're all dead," he replied, walking out in a heavy cloudburst, raindrops splattering on the roof and hood of the car as thunder rumbled overhead.

He drove to room number 6 and parked in front. The building was small, roughly twelve feet square, its roof shedding water in a torrent. Five more cabins were sitting in a row beside it, but tonight they were empty.

He and Molly got out of the car and hurried to the tiny front porch, where he fumbled with the key, using his left hand. His mind was on the envelope and what he hoped it would contain.

The room was stuffy, smelling of cleaning agents and dust. He opened a side window after turning on a light switch. Molly flipped on a small electric fan.

He shed his raincoat and Stetson, then sat on the bed to open the envelope. Molly sat beside him, helping him with the folded papers inside. On top was a printed document entitled, "An Agreement Conforming To Annotated Civil Statutes of The State of Texas, Title 134, Article 7853: Jurisdiction and Supervision of the Transfer of Mineral Rights, Oil and Gas."

"This is the lease," he told her quietly, thumbing past a few pages to a second sheaf of papers. He frowned in the harsh glare of the bare lightbulb, reading at the top of a page: "Promissory Note."

"Here it is," he said. "I knew it had to be here. This is what Santini wanted." A few typewritten paragraphs contained wording regarding a loan of seven thousand dollars made by the party of the first part to the party of the second part. But at the top of the page, he found what he was looking for. "Right here it says the party of the first part is the Santini Trucking Company. The party of the second part is William Porter Dodd."

He flipped to another page and continued reading aloud as Molly looked on. "The amount to be repaid is fourteen thousand dollars, payable on January first of next year. That's double what he meant to borrow! Mighty damn high interest in anybody's book." Glancing farther down the page, he found a line and a signature marked, "Agent for Santini Trucking Company."

He blinked when he read the name. "It's signed Charles D. Waller, Agent. Looks like I was wrong. Charley Waller arranged this loan for Dodd, but Dodd didn't live to borrow it. This means Waller was in on the double-cross. I had

Davis figured for the guy who sold Dodd out, but it was Waller instead. Maybe they both were cut in for a piece of the action."

Molly said, "Bill talked about Charley being his friend. He said they had coffee together nearly every morning."

"This proves Waller was in on it. Maybe I can get him to crack when I show him this. He struck me as the nervous type. I've got to find out tonight where he lives. I'm running out of time."

"What do you mean by that?" Molly asked.

He wasn't ready to tell her the truth. "My commander has a backlog of cases. He wants me back in Waco next week. He can't give me more time to investigate this. It's a matter of priorities."

"Then you'll be leaving soon," she said, on the verge of tears. "I don't know what I'll do . . ."

"We'll talk about it later. Right now, I'm taking you back to the boardinghouse so I can look for Waller. With a bit of bluff, I might be able to convince him to talk." He got off the bed and kissed her forehead. "Let's go," he whispered. "Don't worry so much about things."

He entered the movie theater and stood for a time while his eyes adjusted to the dark. The theater was almost empty and Lee guessed it was because of the rain. On the screen, a movie titled *Law And Order,* starring Harry Carey and Walter Huston, played to an obviously disinterested audience. Waller's neighbor had said Charley went to the movies every Saturday night.

He recognized Charley Waller's bulbous nose as he strolled down an aisle between seats. Waller was eating a bag of popcorn, his attention fixed on the screen. Lee entered the same row of seats and sat down beside him.

"Evening, Charley," he said.

When Waller saw him, he stopped chewing. His cheeks were stuffed full of popcorn and he had difficulty swallowing it all before he asked, "What are you doin' here?"

Lee watched the screen for a moment. A gunfight between four cowboys was taking place, gunshots ringing from theater speakers on side walls. "I'm here to give you a chance to save your ass, Charley. All you have to do is give me some straight answers."

"I'm watchin' this movie. Besides, why would I need to save my ass? From what?"

"From taking the blame and facing charges for murder all by yourself."

"You gotta be crazy. I never murdered nobody."

"You were an accomplice and I can prove it. You may even have pulled the trigger yourself. That's what the charges might say. You'll have to prove you're innocent in a courtroom before a judge and jury. You see, Charley, I found that promissory note to Bill Dodd. And your name's on it as agent for the Santini Trucking Company. Santini's running from the law right now, facing a number of charges, including murder. I've got you cold. When you signed your name to that note, you put your neck in a noose, so to speak. Unless you tell me who else was involved, you're going to prison all by your lonesome. Maybe looking at a death sentence."

Waller swallowed again, this time with nothing in his mouth. "You can't prove a thing, except that I arranged for an operatin' loan for Bill. He didn't have any money or collateral, besides that lease. All I did was set things up for him so he could pay the heirs an' hire a drillin' rig. I got a commission."

Their conversation had begun to irritate a few theater patrons sitting close by, attracting stares. Lee stood up and put his hand on Waller's shoulder. "Let's go, Charley. I'm taking you to jail on suspicion of committing murder . . . unless you can convince me somebody else did it. It's up to you."

Waller's eyes flickered. He got up slowly and put the half-eaten bag of popcorn in his vacant seat.

The little basement room behind rows of jail cells was hot, but not hot enough to produce the amount of sweat running down Charley Waller's face now. He looked down at his folded hands while Lee stood over his chair. Lee hadn't charged him yet for several reasons, and he didn't have anything to convince a jury that Waller had killed either Bill or Sara, or both. The desk sergeant on duty had only shrugged when Lee asked to use this interrogation room.

"I didn't kill nobody," Waller said again.

"Tell me who did. You'll get a lighter sentence if you can name the killers. I want to know who killed Dodd, and who killed his wife. You might even get a suspended sentence if you cooperate and if you didn't kill anybody."

"I swear I didn't."

"Then start giving me names."

Waller took a deep breath, sleeving sweat off his forehead. "There's a whole bunch of people involved," he said quietly as he stared at the floor. "They'll all be tryin' to kill me when they find out I talked. There was a lot of money in this deal, enough for everybody. Everybody was gettin' a piece until things started to go wrong. But I swear I didn't kill nobody. That was Santini's idea."

"Who killed Dodd?"

"The big gorilla, Paulie Gambino. A deputy sheriff took him out there to show him where the place was. Sheriff Bass has been takin' money from Santini, so he'd do nearly anything Santini said to do, 'cept kill somebody. Deputy Carter didn't know Paulie was gonna shoot Bill that night, but he had to keep his mouth shut on account of the bribes."

At last, Lee thought. The proof he needed was being

handed to him now by a seriously frightened accomplice to
two murders and fraud. He was reasonably sure Waller
hadn't killed anyone by himself, although he might have
been a witness to murder. "Who killed Sara?" he asked.

Waller shut his eyes. "That was Buster's doin'. He got so
scared she'd talk to the law that he couldn't stand it. He
said he knew how to do it so nobody'd know."

"She was in on the deal too?"

He nodded. "She sold Bill down the river. She was
nothin' but a whore in the first place. Bill took a fancy to
whores. He married one an' he liked that little Molly a lot,
he told me."

"Davis tried to make it look like a suicide."

"He bungled it. Santini didn't know he was gonna do it
or he'd have stopped him. You guys were gettin' too close
an' you was killin' off some of Santini's best people. He
couldn't ever understand how you done it, you an' that
other Ranger. Santini sent his top shooters. Some got sent
down from New York because they were supposed to be so
good at shootin', only you killed 'em all or locked 'em up.
He kept on sayin' how no cops in the world were all that
tough, but you kept right on provin' he was wrong."

"Judge Warren was taking bribes?"

"Nearly everybody important was gettin' money from
Santini. He said that's how things worked in New York. A
man takin' money won't squeal . . . he can't afford to. Santini was makin' the most off gamblin' an' whiskey, but
when he got a chance to get in on a big deal like Bill's, he
took it. Right at first he said he was only gonna loan him
operatin' money. Then he found out what that lease was
really worth . . ."

"So he had him killed."

"Yeah. Poor ol' Bill was unlucky even when he got
lucky."

Lee felt a flood of relief. He'd solved a murder case,

two in fact. "Sounds to me like Dodd had a little help with his bad luck this time. Was anybody else involved?"

Waller shook his head. "Just the four of us. This whole damn thing was Sara's idea right from the start. Rotten bitch wanted Bill dead so she could spend money any way she saw fit. Santini went by to talk to Bill one day, to see about makin' him that loan I set up, only Bill was out of town. She told Santini right up front that if Bill was out of the way, she'd take in a few partners on the drillin'. Make everybody rich, she said. I heard about it from Santini, what she said to him. Santini told her he could arrange it, only they'd need somebody else to front the deal so nobody got suspicious. That's where Buster came in, because Santini knew he could make Hunt pay big money for a lease right beside the Joiner. Buster told Santini that Hunt would be real generous. Right after that, the trouble started with Sara."

"What sort of trouble?"

"She didn't want to sell to Hunt. She wanted to keep it an' hire drillers, and she wanted the biggest share, half of every barrel of oil. That's when Santini decided to cut her out, when she got too greedy. All she had was a verbal agreement between her an' Santini. Santini knew if he double-crossed her, she had to keep quiet about it. I figured he was gonna have her killed too later on, some kind of accident maybe, but when the big dumb gorilla couldn't find that envelope the night he shot Bill, we all got scared it might turn up. Santini believed Sara kept it for an ace in the hole, but when Paulie searched her house an' slapped her around real good, she swore she never touched it. An' if she'd had it, she would have recorded the lease in her name as Bill's legal wife. When she didn't do that, Santini said it proved she didn't have it in the first place.

"Buster got all the heirs to sign with him an' paid 'em their money. But Sara got mad as hell when she found out

Santini was gonna have Buster sell the rights to Hunt anyway. Santini offered her twenty-five thousand dollars for her part, only she just got madder. She claimed half of everything ought be hers, but she couldn't say a word to the law because it was her idea to kill her husband from the beginnin'."

"Sheriff Bass wasn't likely to look too hard for the killer because he was taking money from Santini," Lee concluded.

"Bass knew all about it because his deputy was there when Paulie shot Bill. Everybody knew they had to keep their mouth shut."

X "But at some time or another, Mrs. Dodd decided to call in the Rangers. She must have known there was a chance we'd find out she was involved."

Waller made a face. "She was drunk an' mad all the time as soon as she found out what Santini really meant to do. She was as dumb as a rock. She thought callin' in the Rangers would work like a squeeze play. She believed that when you guys started lookin' around, askin' questions, Santini would give her a bigger share of the money Hunt paid us. It backfired on her when you started to get too close to the truth."

"How much did Hunt pay for the mineral rights?"

"Two hundred grand, an' it was cheap at that. We was to get fifty thousand apiece, only Sara didn't think it was near enough for her share. I kept thinkin' Santini was gonna have her killed just to shut her up, only you showed up too quick. He got real busy tryin' to hide his gamblin' stuff an' whiskey from you and that Ranger from Tyler, too busy to do anything about Sara since he already knew she wouldn't talk . . . she couldn't tell you the truth or she'd go to prison like the rest of us. The stupid bitch was the reason this whole thing caved in, when she asked the Rangers to find her husband's killer. Hell, she knew it was Paulie all along.

She was only tryin' to squeeze Santini, and he ain't the kind who'll squeeze."

"Who has the money now?" Lee asked.

Waller looked at the floor again. "Mine's in the bank. I only got twenty-five thousand. Buster an' Santini split the rest because they knew I could never talk. For a while, after all the shootin' started 'round here, I got scared Santini might have me blown away too."

Lee nodded. "That's enough for now. Let's go up front to the booking desk. I'll charge you as an accessory to fraud right now, until I check your story. After you're booked in, I'm gonna enjoy myself a little."

"How's that?" Waller asked, apparently puzzled. "Are you goin' back to watch the rest of that movie?"

Lee opened the door. "I'm gonna arrest Buster Davis. This time, he won't be going back home. I'm gonna enjoy the look on his face."

49

Federal District Judge Leon Baker looked down at the pair of defendants through wire-rimmed spectacles with a stern expression on his face. The courtroom was quiet, without spectators since the proceedings consisted of an arraignment. Assistant District Attorney Kenneth Cook stood for a moment after presenting a case for the people — charges of conspiracy to commit murder, murder in the first degree, and fraud under Title 134 of the oil- and gas-rights statutes — against Claude William Davis.

Previously, Cook had read a charge of conspiracy to

commit murder and Title 134 fraud against Charles Daniel Waller, recommending leniency for Mr. Waller's cooperation and sworn deposition in the case. Maxwell Abernathy had withdrawn as counsel for defendant C. W. Davis upon hearing a reading of Waller's sworn statement for the record. Abernathy left the courtroom after a private consultation with Judge Baker in his chambers.

"I'm binding both of you over for trial," Judge Baker said. "Bond for Charles Waller is set at five hundred dollars. Bond for Mr. Davis is hereby denied, pending a further examination of the possibility he might not appear. Trial is set for September the eleventh in Mr. Davis's case. Mr. Waller will be tried at a later date, after consultation with the district attorney." He motioned to a bailiff. "Escort these gentlemen to the county jail. This court is in recess while I meet with Mr. Cook regarding the people's case against Mr. Waller." He tapped his gavel, got up and walked through a door behind the bench.

Lee turned to FBI Agent Miles Kingsbury. "I don't believe Davis knows where Carlos Santini is. They weren't close friends. It was simply a business deal."

"We're looking for him in New York. Criminals of his kind generally go back to familiar territory when they need a place to lay low," Kingsbury said. "We'll find him. He'll turn up sooner or later."

Lee flexed the fingers of his right hand. It was good to be out of a sling, although his shoulder still ached and pain tablets made him sleepy. "How about Gino Tatangelo?"

"He's also gone into hiding, I was told. He'll surface someplace and we'll be waiting for him. Treasury agents found one of his liquor-storage depots Friday night. They confiscated hundreds of cases of whiskey."

"That'll put a dent in his operations for a while," Lee said as Buster Davis gave him an icy stare while handcuffs were being locked around his wrists by the bailiff.

"Mr. Hoover isn't happy about what happened here in Texas," Kingsbury said quietly, rocking back on his heels for a moment when he said it.

"Why's that?" Lee asked.

Kingsbury pursed his lips. "We should have been the ones to know when a crime organization like Tatangelo's sets up in a new location. We're supposed to be keeping track of them. Honestly, neither the Dallas nor our Houston office had any idea what was going on here. Mr. Hoover has summoned a few people to Washington because of it, and believe me, heads will roll. He was most unhappy when he was informed the Texas Rangers broke the story to the press last week about the seizures and arrests you made. We looked like blithering idiots, he said. Mr. Hoover has a very low tolerance for public embarrassment."

"We got lucky, I reckon. That and we tracked down even the smallest lead. It helped that Santini believed he could outsmart us. If he'd closed down and gone back to New York for a spell, we might not have been able to expose what was going on."

"It sounds like a bloody business. A lot of people died on both sides."

"Yeah. A good Treasury agent passed away this morning, Brad Whitaker. Ranger Roy Woods was gunned down beside his car. Two officers died over in Henderson County, another Treasury guy and a deputy sheriff. Those of us who survived it will need to clean our guns."

"You took a nasty wound in your shoulder, didn't you?"

Lee flexed his fingers again. "It wasn't all that bad. I feel lucky to be alive."

Kingsbury turned. "I should find a telephone. My chief wanted me to call him with a full report after the arraignment was over. Good luck, Mr. Garrett, although it would appear you have plenty of it already." He nodded and walked hurriedly out of the courtroom.

Gregg County Attorney Ronald Hall had been listening in. He spoke to Lee when Kingsbury departed. "Before I drove over this mornin', Judge Warren gave me a letter of resignation. However, it won't stop me from having him called before the judicial review board of the state bar. Sheriff Bass and Tim Carter resigned at the same time. I appointed Sam Dunlap acting sheriff until the county commissioners meet next week. It'll be hard to prove in court they took bribes. I understand your witness said they were always paid in cash. We've got a lot of housecleaning to do, as you know."

Lee wasn't really listening. He was thinking about Molly and what he would face when he took her with him to Waco. "Dunlap's a good man for the job. He told me things were going on when all he had to do was keep his mouth shut. But he'll have his hands full since they keep finding more oil around Longview. That much money's always gonna attract undesirables. I'd better be on my way, Mr. Hall. It's an all-day drive to Waco. Tell Sam Dunlap I appreciate what he did to help me."

Lee found Molly waiting for him on a bench beneath a shade tree near the courthouse steps. The skies had cleared early Monday morning and under the noon sun, humidity from the previous rains was so thick he felt he could cut it with a spoon.

"How did it go?" she asked, holding up a copy of a newspaper featuring a front-page story about Lee and the murders in Longview.

"They've been bound over for trial. It's finished. The FBI still can't find Santini or Tatangelo—they've gone into hiding—but Agent Kingsbury feels sure they will. If you're all set, let's head for Waco. It'll be dark before we make it."

"Are you sure you want me to go with you?"

He aimed a thumb toward the Packard. "Get in," was all he said.

His little house on Orchard Lane was dark when they got to town, and his shoulder was throbbing. He'd driven straight through, arriving after midnight. They'd done some talking, though he couldn't bring himself to tell her about the choice he had to make the next morning, a grim choice between a woman he loved and a job he liked. Captain Ross made it plain he could not keep both.

And as he entered company offices on Tuesday morning to tell the captain of his decision, it seemed no easier, despite knowing it was the right choice at this point in his life. He'd grown tired of a solitary existence, and it didn't matter what Molly had done before. He stopped at the top of the granite steps.

Don't let him change your mind, he thought, opening a glass-fronted door on the County Court House, facing Columbus Avenue, across from the county jail.

He found Bob Ross in his office early, sipping coffee from a stained china cup. "Mornin' Cap'n. I need a minute of your time if you can spare it."

Ross smiled. "I'm glad you made the right decision, Lee. I need good men like you."

Lee took a chair opposite the captain's desk. "I don't think you're gonna like what I have to say. I brought Molly back with me, and I know that means I lose my job, according to what Major Elliot told you. Sorry. I found out I love her. Can't really explain how it happened. It doesn't matter to me what she did for a living before I met her. She deserves a fresh start. I don't know exactly what I'll do, but you can have my resignation any time you want."

Ross's smile faded quickly. "You can't be serious. It means givin' up your career. Hundreds of peace officers across the state would give nearly anything for an appointment to this job, an' you're ready to walk off an' leave it because of a . . ." He didn't finish what he was saying, toying with his cup.

"I was always proud to be a Ranger, Cap'n. Still am. But I found something more important to me than this badge. It's real hard to explain how I feel."

"Damn," Ross said under his breath, his eyes darting to an open window. "I never would have guessed it." He stared thoughtfully at the skyline of Waco for a moment. "You an' Roy Woods broke one of the biggest cases in recent history, Lee, exposing a bunch of New York gangsters operatin' out of East Texas like you did. It sure as hell ain't gonna look good if you resign like this. What are people gonna think?"

"I hadn't given it much thought, Cap'n."

Ross looked at him. "Until today, I've always believed you were the smartest man in my command. But this is a dumb move on your part. You're not the dedicated Ranger I thought you were or you'd come to your senses. No tellin' what the major's gonna say when I call him. Step outside for a minute while I give him the bad news. This conversation's gotta be private."

"I understand," Lee said, climbing out of the chair without using his aching right arm—the drive to Waco had only made it worse.

He walked out into the corridor, nodding to a young secretary he knew at the public works office passing in the hallway.

"Good morning, Mr. Garrett," she said, pausing in front of him, smiling. "We read all about the excitement in Longview and how brave you were, catching those awful Italian gangsters. Makes a body wonder what things are coming to in Texas, when we can't live here without gangs of Eastern hoodlums running all over the place. It's good to see you again." She hurried off, snapping a piece of chewing gum between her teeth before he could say a word.

He went downstairs and strolled outside to watch the

traffic on Columbus, wondering if this would be the last time he stood here as a Texas Ranger. He could sell his small house, he supposed, and move elsewhere. But where? And what would he do to make a living? There were plenty of other law-enforcement jobs, but not for a former Ranger who had a tainted service record. Anyone would wonder why he'd left his appointment and make inquiries with headquarters before they hired him. He told himself there were other lines of work.

He recalled his first day here under Captain Ross, how glad he was to be away from the Mexican border for a while. Rookie Rangers drew the roughest duty assignments, and the Mexican border was the worst. Coming to Waco had seemed like a trip to paradise back then, a place where it actually rained and things were green instead of desert-brown. He'd grown up in green country like this at Lockhart. Waco was more like home.

He stood for a while at the top of the steps remembering all manner of things, mostly good, and a few that had seemed bad at the time. All in all, Rangering had been satisfying. Now he was giving it up for Molly, and in his heart, it was the only choice.

A few minutes later, Captain Ross came outside, motioning him over to one side.

"The major wants to see you right away. He said to get down there today if you could."

"I won't let him talk me out of it, Cap'n. I've made up my mind."

"Talk to Major Elliot. It's out of my hands now. You get goin'." Ross wagged his head from side to side and offered his hand. "I wish I wasn't losin' you, Lee. You're one hell of a fine investigative officer, an' you're as thorough as any man I ever had in this company. Good luck, son." He took Lee's right hand gently, then turned on his heel to go back in the building, walking with a stiff spine like a man on parade.

50

The three-room adobe house at the edge of Carrizo Springs looked empty and forlorn. A blistering South Texas sun made its dried mud walls seem whitewashed, reflecting tiny particles of glittering sand in the slanted light. A few live oak trees provided a bit of meager shade over a grassless yard, packed hardpan that would grow few crops in the garden Molly planned. The Rio Grande was less than fifty miles away, and temperatures in summer would be above a hundred every day, lasting well into October in good years, longer during a drought.

"It isn't much to look at," Lee said, putting his arm around Molly's waist as soon as they got out of the Ford. "This can be the hottest place on earth." He noticed a few red tiles cracked on the roof, but they wouldn't matter un-less it rained, if it rained at all.

"I love it!" Molly exclaimed, clasping her hands. "It's a place of our own and it isn't right in the middle of town like I thought it would be."

"Carrizo isn't much of a town," he admitted. "Things can be mighty primitive down here. The electricity won't work half the time and our well may run dry every now and then, so we'll have to haul our water."

"I don't care. We'll have a garden, and it's our very own house. I can plant flowers—"

"They likely won't grow," he told her. "It's too hot down here for flowers most of the time, I think."

"I'll fix them some shade, an awning. Let's go inside and take a look."

He grinned over her enthusiasm, although he supposed it was better than the alternative if she hadn't liked the place. "You can have that puppy now, but I'll have to build a doghouse."

Molly ran to the front door with the key. He watched her for a moment before he walked toward the house. She was tougher than he'd imagined when it came to making do with what they had, with what they'd been given. He'd been given an assignment with the Ranger Company out of Corpus Christi under Captain Allen, and he still had a job. He knew it was punishment for refusing to give up Molly and he didn't care. Major Elliot hadn't wanted to answer questions about Lee's resignation, or explain his ultimatum to Lee during an election year. Therefore the assignment to Carrizo and South Texas. Out of sight, out of mind, and no embarrassing questions to answer.

A poorly made concrete slab provided all the adobe had in the way of flooring. A potbelly stove offered the only heat they would have in winter, although winters were short and usually mild. Water would be a bigger problem, depending upon a well in back for what they needed. Wells in this part of Texas often ran dry when there was no rain.

"We can hang pictures on the wall," Molly said, her voice still full of excitement. "It needs a good cleaning, and that window glass and screen will have to be fixed." She opened the back door and looked out at their yard. Surrounded by a sagging wire fence, the house came with two acres of dry caliche ground. "We can have goats," she went on, caught up in her fantasy about what the house would look like when it was fixed up the way she wanted it.

"They'll eat everything you plant in your garden," he said, chuckling. "You can't have both unless we build a better fence."

She turned to him and threw her arms around his neck,

and the smile on her face was worth everything to him. "Just as long as I have you, I'll be happy, Mr. Garrett. It doesn't matter if we can't have goats."

He bent down and kissed her, while a voice inside his head promised he'd be enjoying her kisses far more than he'd miss a cooler climate or greenery. "I'm happy, Mrs. Garrett," he told her, "with or without any goats. You'll get tired of the heat, but I hope you won't get tired of me."

"Never," she whispered, looking deeply into his eyes, and he knew with even more certainty that he'd made the right choice. Molly was someone he needed; she filled an empty space within him. If he stayed in South Texas for the rest of his life, it would seem all right, just as long as he had her by his side.

Author's Notes

This is a work of fiction, although for more than 170 years, a legendary state police force in Texas has faced down virtually every type of criminal imaginable, and until recently, it was the most revered organization of its kind in the world, and certainly the best known.

The Texas Rangers, founded in 1823 or 1876, depending upon which historian you can believe, policed Texas as the Washington County Volunteer Militia, known as "special state troops," under the command of "Captain" Leander McNelly between 1874 and 1877, even though Stephen F. Austin hired ten men to "protect settlers from Indians" in 1823, calling them Rangers, charged with ranging the frontier to end lawlessness with any weapons at their disposal. Meaning guns. Not much has changed in passing years, except the absence of Indians and a vanished frontier.

The Texas Rangers earned a reputation as a law-enforcement agency early on, employing men like Big Foot Wallace, John Hays, Rip Ford, Ben McCullough, Lone Wolf Gonzaullas, and later, Frank Hamer, who tracked down Bonnie Parker and Clyde Barrow in 1934. Tom Horn, who was hung for murder in 1903, was also briefly a Texas Ranger. Texans saw nothing wrong with fighting fire with fire. Desperate men from all over the country escaped to Texas, thinking it a haven from their previous crimes. The Texas Rangers usually proved them wrong.

A later period of lawlessness began with the oil boom, in places like Beaumont and Longview and West Texas. Poor men made millionaires of themselves literally overnight during and after the Depression. The lure of so much money attracted all manner of criminals to Texas during a period when money and jobs were in short supply elsewhere.

Texas was a right-to-work state, prohibiting the establishment of union shops. Historians believe this is one reason why organized crime, often associated with labor unions, did not fare well in Texas. But when so much oil money was being generated in what was called the Texas "Oil Patch," mobsters did make attempts to cash in. Perhaps the Mafia was also wary of the Rangers, whose most lasting legend involved a Dallas mayor who had asked for help to stop an illegal prizefight near the turn of the century. When the nervous mayor met the train to pick up the Rangers, only one man stepped off. The mayor asked why there weren't more men, and Ranger Bill McDonald replied, "Hell, ain't I enough? There's only one prizefight." McDonald took care of the problem, resulting in the motto, "One riot, one Ranger." Frank Hamer was assigned by Governor Miriam Ferguson to singlehandedly track down

Bonnie and Clyde. After three months, he trapped and killed the pair, earning a special citation from the U.S. Congress.

Historian Walter Prescott Webb wrote: "The real Ranger has been a very quiet, deliberate, gentle person who could gaze calmly into the eye of a murderer, divine his thoughts, and anticipate his action, a man who could ride straight up to death and stare it in the face." Frank Hamer, who had been wounded seventeen times, some so seriously his doctors thought he would die, was described by a biographer as "a giant man, moonfaced, always in boots, and as talkative as an oyster." Hamer killed more than fifty men in his lifetime, loved to whistle for birds and "talk to his feathered friends."

In support of Webb's more sympathetic view, "border boss" Captain John R. Hughes was a devout minister who "will not keep a man in his Ranger company who will swear or who drinks." Others, like Ranger Sergeant Bass Outlaw, described as a "murderer and drunk," and Ranger William Sterling, tried for murdering a South Texas rancher with a bullet to the back, claiming self-defense even though no weapon was found on the deceased, are written about less often. Captain W. J. McDonald is more frequently quoted: "No man in the wrong can stand up against a fellow that's in the right and keeps on a'coming."

In later years, men such as Colonel Homer Garrison, Jr., head of the DPS and the Rangers from 1938 until 1968, kept a'coming with men like Lewis Rigler, hired in 1947 to police the area around Gainesville, Walter Russell, Clint Peoples, Levi Duncan, Jim Nance, and the head of Company D in South Texas since 1947, Captain A.Y. Allee. Allee's methods were frequently called into question, and he was sued and investigated a number of times for his conduct; he said, "We use what force we deem necessary to make any kind of arrest." Later, the U.S. Supreme Court found Allee had violated farmworkers' rights to peaceful assembly in 1967 during a United Farm Workers strike in Starr County when he delivered a concussion to an organizer.

Ever since, it seems that misfortune and outmoded methods have haunted the Rangers' public image. There was the ugly Clarence Brandley case at Conroe in which Ranger Wesley Styles was ruled to have lied on the witness stand and suppressed crucial tape recordings of witness interviews. Classic Ranger tactics would not survive modern legal scrutiny. In the Henry Lee Lucas case, Ranger-in-Charge Bob Prince was accused of "leading" Lucas into confessing to more than six hundred murders, when in fact he was in jail or out of the state when many of the murders were committed. Lucas turned out to be a hoax. A Ranger memo confirmed that Rangers "helped refresh Lucas's memory" by giving him details of offenses he could not possibly have committed. A number of retired Rangers who were involved in questioning Lucas have said they knew they were dealing with a habitual liar, but the damage had already been done.

There have been other Ranger misfires such as the fiasco at Brownsville, where twenty-three indictments of city officials resulted in twenty-one being thrown out, one not-guilty verdict, and a lone conviction that was later reversed.

With the long-standing reputation of the Texas Rangers on the decline, it did not take much to prompt resignations from a battery of good Rangers who had grown tired of changes for the worse. In 1993, men like Glenn Elliot, Joaquin Jackson, Robert Steele, George Frasier, Clayton Smith, Jack Dean, and Joe Bailey Davis retired, prompted further by the hiring of two women to the Ranger force. An all-male era of law enforcement in Rangering had come to an end.

But to sentimental Texans, this does nothing to diminish the Ranger myth, nor should it detract from the Rangers' significant contribution to law enforcement in Texas history. Without Rangers, the practice of outlawry in such a large geographic area would have been unmanageable. Heavily armed Rangers roamed the state almost at will, meting out justice in a land where there was often very little to be had. Reckless lawbreakers were frequently dealt with in kind, and citizens were grateful, not overly inclined to worry about a criminal's civil and legal rights. In the opinion of a number of retired Rangers, an avalanche of laws and court rulings descended upon them. Miranda and the Civil Rights Act. It was no longer possible to have nothing but evidence against a known criminal—you had to remember his rights, and if you didn't follow them to the letter, he was set free on a technicality. If you didn't tell him he couldn't confess without a lawyer being present, he was let go. A sad state of affairs for lawmen who "had the goods" on someone who had broken the law.

Today the Texas Rangers face an uncertain future. Once a revered branch of state law enforcement, they are rarely called upon to investigate a case now. As a mere formality, they were invited to the crime scene of the Branch Davidian compound near Waco. They accepted the FBI's version of events and went away quietly with a similar report, avoiding critical questions as to who fired first, Davidians or agents from the Bureau of Alcohol, Tobacco, and Firearms. In the words of retired Alpine Ranger Joaquin Jackson, other law-enforcement agencies are "not as dependent on us as they used to be."